Hugh

A Hero without a Novel

David Lawrence

PREFACE

Two hundred and forty-two years is a long time to be in the closet.

Well, not a closet. An old, rusted trunk.

The trunk came from the attic of a family home in Yorkshire. Inside, a yellowing manuscript: the coming-of-age of a queer man written by my 6th great-grandfather Sir John Carleton, also known as John of Beeford.

Included with the manuscript was a portrait of John in all his finery – reclining in silk stockings, with powdered wig and a beauty mark pasted to his cheek. The first mention of his novel *Hugh* comes from his diary of 1779. He describes long days 'writing my Fancy *Tom Jones*.' Integral to John's process was composing in just a nightshirt. This he did to receive, what he called, 'the Stimulating Airs'.

Whenever he finished a passage which pleased him, John would drop his quill and run through the village, waving his manuscript, and celebrating his airy freedom. He was branded, somewhat sourly, 'John of Beeford' after a gusty day sent the notorious Yorkshire sprinter, and his airborne nightshirt, to the village lockup.

Yet he was not disconnected from reality or the times in

which he lived. Prominent figures, such as John Wilkes, and issues of the day are key to his novel. Hugh's chaotic growth toward adulthood is framed around relationships with three men, each of whom represent a concept taken from philosopher Edmund Burke: Beauty, Indifference, and The Sublime. Hugh at eighteen is planning a dazzling military career. But first he has a brush with Beauty (the rebellious son of a country parson), and his life takes a much different course.

What John ultimately wished for his novel I really cannot say. The settings of his story are far from Beeford so perhaps he wished some distance from it. However, the novel's Yorkshire boxer, his Sublime (awe and terror), leaves some room for doubt. Whatever the case publishing the novel was, of course, out of the question.

Still, I can say this: John's old, rusted trunk had no lock.

And perhaps I am being fanciful (I am, after all, his descendant) but I think this was intentional. Because even an eccentric like John of Beeford understood it was not a lock but the times in which he lived which would ultimately keep his manuscript from the eyes of the public.

And when the time was right, some unsuspecting soul would stumble upon it and simply lift the lid.

David Lawrence

EVERY CHARACTER IS TOLD TRUE

BOOK ONE

CHAPTER 1

Some miles downriver, past Kennet Mouth and the bend to Newbury, lived Entwistle, a man of appetite. By the time he was eleven he strove to take tea – and curry favour – in the best homes in Berkshire. The best homes housed the best people, men of leverage, of influence, and so of what use boys his own age? Frederick Entwistle had ambition and was pleased to be deemed precocious; he cut out the middlemen and befriended their fathers.

But such vanity, *Dear Reader*, is not without a measure of virtue, any more than virtue survives without some vanity. For one day his father had told him of the South Sea Company. The South Sea Company had lured investors, rich and poor, promising fortune in a faraway land. Promoted by the government, and so assured of a tidy profit, the public clamoured to fund this dazzling ship. The ship rose on a wave towards South America, swelled by speculation and the promise of trade. When the ship foundered, the fortunes of many sank too. This was the great financial fright of the age.

"But for lack of ready cash," said his father, "which the Good Lord kept from my hands, you had been ruined Frederick!"

The chill this produced in his son was strangely gratifying; Sir Joshua supposed it must be a feeling of piety. Wishing to enhance the sensation, next day he told of a new investment – a tragic, ill-advised investment now failing. Stepping into a shaft of sunlight, his head tilted heavenward, he declared they must accept this misfortune as God's will. Then his gaze returned to earth, and upon observing the child's look of alarm, he felt another, still more delicious, tingle of pleasure.

"Sir," returned Frederick, "what is the sum lost?"

His father retired to his study to consider. He needn't imply they might lose their home, Deerhurst Hall, which had been in the family for generations. But a loss of, say, ten percent of their total estate might bring his tingle of pleasure to a prickle. When he returned to the drawing room he had settled upon twelve percent. This produced from Frederick a wail of concern, a dropping to his knees to pray the tragedy would cease; Sir Joshua shivered with a sting of satisfaction. In the weeks which followed, the stories of imagined losses grew worse, and the man was driven to nothing short of a religious ecstasy. "Thirty percent lost!" he cried, "And what shall become of you, Frederick, when it is forty? You will be received nowhere but as a stable boy – only the Good Lord will save you from poverty and certain death!"

Frederick fled to his bedchamber in a transport of horror, vowing to never lose his place in Society. To never invest in the South Sea Company, or in whatever had lost them thirty percent. He would conserve his money and invest his time in people – those of influence who might adopt him and keep him afloat.

Soon he had learnt passion for any passion of a country squire, be it tinkering with clocks, or the foxhunt of an ageing libertine of the Dolman clothing empire. Both in his village of Deerhurst and in neighbouring Newbury, he disparaged the hunting for robins' eggs, the prized diversion of most boys his age. Then he declared a Gentleman's opinion of their Prime

Minister, Robert Walpole, whatever it might be, identical to that of his father. For this he received advice on stimulating wealth, tips on women, drink, and the game of Hazard.

In a similar way, he performed for any ladies of Quality who wished amusement. Drawing aside his small frockcoat in a deep bow, he appeared in silk stockings, white as snow, velvet knee breeches and heeled slippers glinting with hefty buckles. Still safely within the realm of childhood, he extended his head for caresses, flattering all the ladies at lunch who must otherwise have rehashed stale gossip. Loudly did he disdain all the boys he knew as cruel and undeserving of their wonderful sisters, and saintly mothers. And Oh! how his audience fought to hold him, admire him, and instruct him how not to do a lady wrong, how not to gamble and drink and flirt freely, before predicting how tall and handsome he would become if he took heed.

Frederick Entwistle's path to success was assured. Every Gentleman in the county admired him. Every Lady adored him and wished him for her daughters. Whatever would be his father's financial losses, Frederick knew two things for certain. He would be knighted at twenty-one, as was the God-given right of any future baronet. And he could make shift for himself in the world.

Later that month Sir Joshua announced Frederick was to board at Rugby School. Fully confident in his abilities, the boy packed his trunks and counted the days. Rugby, he understood, was a fine school, administered by intelligent adults keen to promote him. Upon arrival, however, he discovered it was not the instructors, but the other boys he must strive to please. Must pacify and fag for – not for praise and future preferment, but merely for survival.

For Frederick was each night falling victim to some good-natured pranks: hauled from bed at midnight, dunked in a freezing pond, tossed in a blanket with orders to 'kiss the ceiling' and bowled down a flight of stairs. In desperation, he pleaded assistance from the fifth form scholars, and was always first to arrive when the service bell rang. When ordered to shine shoes, a boy's ego also received a polish until, at last, he secured a full-time protector.

At Queen's College, he envisioned the day he would be called 'Sir Frederick'. The pride of inheriting the baronetcy was tempered knowing there were Dukes and Lords and Earls to shine still brighter. Nevertheless, Frederick's rank, though modest, meant leverage, and so a duty to climb.

Lord Walter George, fourth Baron George, was a fellow student at Oxford. Headstrong, indulged, and obscenely wealthy, he was revolting even to the most hardened of young climbers. Frederick suffered six months of indignities in good humour, and gradually benefited of Walter's confidences for, Philistine though he was, Walter George believed he was entitled to friendship. "Laughter and companionship are enjoyed by others," he complained, sucking a cherry pipe, "why the Devil are these blockheads afraid of me?" Frederick had but to merit this confidence, to understand he had him firmly in hand.

To bring himself fully into favour, he let emerge what must be termed his more effeminate charms. Effeminate, *Dear Reader*, must be the word, though he was hardly different from other men of the age. Submissive obedience became passive cultivation. Frederick began to show glimpses of his wit and charm. And slowly this subtle voicing of himself produced a modicum of respect in his Lordship, who paid the expense of every meal, every excursion into town, every prostitute, and those elements of his wardrobe which were thought to need replacing.

Upon his son's graduation Sir Joshua, now mostly blind but with an ever-strengthening vision of Heaven, informed him he was to be married in four weeks' time. Frederick's bride would be Ellen Higbee Reynolds, a Yorkshire cousin in possession of a fat dowry. Though promised since childhood, the suddenness of the proposal prompted Frederick to voice concerns. He did not know her, he might not like her, to which his father praised her for having 'by way of needlework and the raising of paste plenty to recommend her.'

"And shall I like her more on account of her pastimes?" asked Frederick.

"Pastimes occupy a young lady when one does not wish to see her. Else she is forever underfoot."

In truth, Miss Reynolds was a great devotee to the Protestant faith and Sir Joshua wished a young lady in the house to bring him the light of God.

"Sir, I understood her dowry to be my primary incentive. As that is assured with a promise of marriage, might I not keep her laid up in Yorkshire?"

"Laid up?"

"Rather like India bonds?"

"Blasphemy!" shouted Sir Joshua. He came forward and took a swing at Frederick, but, not well able to see him, achieved no more than to slip from beneath his wig. "Fall on your knees tonight and ask the Lord's forgiveness!" he told the footman, who was of a similar height to his son.

The union of Ellen with Frederick soon took place but was not, alas, a happy one. The first child arrived after ten months. Anne was colicky and though quickly dispatched to wet nurses in a neighbouring parish, her father felt no fondness and, if truth be told, never would. It may be that, benefiting from alterations which would have made of Anne an Andrew, this bad temper might have been dismissed as vigour and lusty health. As it was, Frederick rather hoped for another.

About this time Lord George returned from his Grand Tour of the Continent and met Frederick in London, at an alehouse near St. John's Gate. They were joined by four schoolfellows from Oxford who had been unable to avoid the invitation. To nobody's surprise, Frederick alone merited a trinket from Naples.

Now brasher, worldlier, and two stone heavier, George dominated every soul in the tavern, soon driving his former schoolfellows to take refuge down the bar.

"A fine welcome," he grumbled, "I cannot think why I summoned them. And do you know, I had only one reason to meet you today, Entwistle?"

"To thank an old friend for his loyal correspondence?"

"The deuce! For your name, swab, why else continue the friendship?"

Frederick took this to mean the recording of his name in the baronetage, for his father had at last died and so relinquished his title. "Very well. Address me as 'Sir Frederick' and give a bow of courtesy."

"I shall address that with an oaken cudgel, my boy," the man said. "I speak of surnames, not titles."

"You continue our friendship because of the name Entwistle?"

"As a keeper of curiosities, yes I do. I collected many while travelling, but this one I maintained at home. I have only an ordinary name myself, and while I was away, I grew fond of recalling yours. *Entwistle.*"

"The name *George*, Sir, you will not deny, is the name of our king."

"George Augustus is a German king who barely speaks English. Georges may be found in every parish in the country – but what else can an *Entwistle* be but a Freddy from university? That is why I like it." And he held his pint of ale suspended.

This was too much of a piece with his Lordship's other oddities to rate much comment. Sir Frederick said, "Then I trust you will not complain should another of that name be soon of this world?"

Walter dropped a hand to his beefy thigh and threw the other onto his friend's shoulder. "You dog! Another child so soon then? I doubted you could generate more than one. I own it freely."

"Perhaps many more than one, in time. My wife has accompanied me to London. I shall see to business tonight once I have my Lord's blessing for a favourable outcome."

After a minute, in which nothing but the purest flattery could be felt, George whispered, "He will be a boy, and an heir, depend upon it. And I'll warrant the *homunculus*, at this moment, takes his shape now there's been a good word for him." The belief in a fully formed, miniature human living in sperm was somewhat antiquated and not Frederick's own. Still, he smiled and thanked the man for his blessing.

"A boy and an heir. Nine months shall prove it out."

Success announced itself on an August day in the year of our Lord 1749. A child born of speculation and flattery, who secured his father an heir, and a godfather for that heir. And from the moment the man-midwife brought him forth, Hugh Entwistle held favour.

Still, Frederick would not spoil or indulge him until, by sound reasoning, the boy was capable of petitioning. Years passed in frustration, for the babe was unable to plead his way out of all that troubles young hearts: the swaddling which suffocates, or the stays, though essential for good posture, which cuts and bruises. By the time of his breeching, however, he could argue his case, for he did detest the strange new constriction of breeches and wished a return to the free-flowing gowns of infancy.

One day the boy came forward to present his case. Now a fair-skinned boy of seven, Hugh possessed a full head of sandy coloured hair and stood unusually tall. And though promising to be rather plain, he possessed a strong chin and large, blue eyes which appeared formed for nothing so much as petitioning and charming.

"Father, the weight of the buckles and fastenings is so dreadful that I cannot move."

Raising his eyebrows Sir Frederick set his newspaper aside. "Demonstrate this inconvenience," he said. Hugh tottered rapidly to a far wall, turning at the conclusion of this performance with silent, pleading eyes. "And back." The boy returned wearing a look of great martyrdom.

Said his father: "In the first place, you must suit the action to the word. You say you cannot move, but you move very well. Rather, say you are not fond of your breeches, for their design or fit. Else demonstrate by slow, laboured movements the difficulty."

"Yes, Sir."

"And though such small buckles may perhaps have weight, the buttons and other fastenings do not. Say instead it is the weight of the buckles, together with the constriction of the fastenings which troubles you."

"Yes, Sir."

"Lastly, and most importantly, is this – the wish to return to your gowns is like a wish to stand shorter than Nature instructs. It cannot be. You shall wear breeches, just as you shall grow taller, proceed to grammar school, marry, and sire children. This is the natural course."

"But Father, the misery which is my portion!"

This explosion of grief drew a look of disapproval, and Hugh placed fingertips to his mouth.

"Should you like to be a jester when you grow up?" said Frederick. "A man other men may laugh at – is that what you wish?"

"No, Sir."

"Do you intend to be a member of the mob and scream because you have not the vocabulary to persuade?"

"No Sir, not a member of the mob, nor any manner of trumpery."

"Your supposition that it must be either gowns, or tight breeches is a wrong one. That you may not return to gowns, does not mean the breeches you have cannot be altered or exchanged. I see they cut too tightly at the waist. Compromise, Hugh, is an altered pair of breeches, or a new pair altogether. It is that middle point between what you have and what you wish to have."

"And may I have my gown again until the new breeches are got?"

"No, you will wear these for the remainder of the day. And you will smile. If anyone asks how you go, you will say you go very well indeed, and love to be in breeches."

"Must I?" said the child, with a frown. "Who will ask me?"

"Your own father will ask you. Depend upon it. And you will convince him how much they are to your liking." He watched the boy closely. With contortions, the small face worked to understand and fight despair, then to wonder what he could say and, lastly, what he might be wished to say.

"I shall. And," the man nodded for him to continue, "if I say it very well indeed, that I like my clothes, Father will not decide that I wish to keep them too tight?"

This appeared to amuse the man, and he descended to one knee.

"If you can convince me at dinner tonight that you would not quit your breeches for all the gold in the world, I shall see you have two new, roomy pairs tomorrow. I may even send the footman into Newbury for a box of Mrs Thomas's sweetmeats."

The following morning Hugh tasted one of Mrs Thomas's famed sweetmeats. By the afternoon he had received two new pairs of breeches – the first a blend of cotton and silk, the other of fine velvet.

CHAPTER 2

With the last of the sweetmeats in hand, Hugh joined his mother at the parlour window, where she spent much of her time gazing outside with her copy of the King James Bible. Tugging at her sleeve he asked if she would take the treat. She instead took his head to her breast, which took shallow breaths in the weakening sun of the outside world.

This would be the first lasting memory of Hugh's life. In it he awoke to the sadness of Ellen Entwistle, which seemed somehow tied to her existence at Deerhurst Hall. Yet why should this be? The Hall was ten acres of park and forest with a winding stream and a granary. It dated from the reign of Elizabeth and had come into the family early the following century, when General Entwistle was made baronet. During the reign of Anne, the Hall had been remade into a square of ashlar stonework, and the grounds, which Ellen walked each day her health would allow, had been redesigned with French gardens.

Her walks in these gardens, however, had concluded before Hugh could well recall them. Four years after his birth, when she bore a third child, Ned, her health had begun to decline. Only the warmest, sunniest days could draw her outside, and after the birth of Alice, Lady Entwistle grew ill and never recovered. Three weeks after Alice's birth, she died.

For the two younger children the loss of a mother was like a question asked of an empty room, for Sir Frederick wished not to remind them of the loss and refused to speak of her. However, for Anne, who was nine when her mother died, Ellen was a presence who would never fade, whom she kept alive by strict adherence to the Protestant faith and in the performance of maternal tasks. Under Anne's direction, fruit was never served without it was twice baked – her mother's security against The Plague. And Hugh never entered the parish church without a brisk brush of his shoulders, long after he had left off invading their father's periwig powder.

Hugh himself was directed to education; his tears dismissed as want of employment for a restless mind. Not disinclined to the idea of improving himself he found many hours of distraction with his private tutor. When he looked up from his Latin primer to find his mother absent, his brow furrowed, and he displayed a whimsy that would only increase during childhood. If his mother *seemed* not to be there, it was not because she was dead. For as anyone could see she had only shrunk to a nine-year-old girl. His mother was, by every account and most probably, his sister. Anne – forever quoting the Protestant Manual, brushing his shoulders, and forcing at him bowls of mushed fruit.

Sir Frederick soon decided his son required more comprehensive instruction. Thus far, he had refrained from indulging too many of the boy's whims and follies, yet in his education, Hugh would be a little indulged. This moment of grief was chosen for removal from the country to a townhouse in London, where the Entwistles resided at least half of every year. Hugh would commence at Harrow School but, seeing his son's look of trepidation at the change, Frederick agreed to allow him a veto. Should the school prove intolerable, he might withdraw provided he could argue for another.

The veto was employed within the first month, for a shyness born of excessive indecision brought upon the young scholar all the pain of bullying. Rather than confess to this, Hugh complained of being persecuted for resisting the ways of *the mob*, as *the mob* received much of the blame whenever his father lamented society's ills. Hugh had also learnt of his father's unfortunate experience at Rugby School and, by the age of eight, was enough like him to employ what he knew to his own advantage.

"I only wish to please my instructors and excel. But the mob, *the mob!*, mistreat me cruelly for it! They are beastly to me!"

The boy departed Harrow and received a live-in tutor. This was one Mr Hastings, who gave stern instruction and liked to beat his pupil with a wiry piece of birch. Though sometimes harsh, this treatment was preferable to the thought of returning to the boys at Harrow. Hugh endured it even as his father, though not averse to the rod, knew other instructors who might do as well. After seven months with the Entwistles in London, Hastings attended his pupil to the country to continue the instruction.

"For shame child!" cried Lady Highborough, a new acquaintance of the family who had begun visiting Deerhurst Hall. "Can you prefer those beatings to a little teasing by your schoolfellows?"

Hugh did prefer it, just as he feared a new tutor potentially more vicious than Mr Hastings.

"For shame Frederick!" shouted her Ladyship in her own home in Newbury, for he had begun visiting her as well. "You cross your legs and recline on my settee – like a cat stretched in the sun after your son receives forty lashes! How can you remain so indifferent?"

"Four strokes, not forty, for being listless. Hugh may petition for another instructor."

Despite this dismissal, the man shifted somewhat uneasily

in his seat. After the loss of his wife, afternoon teas with Matilda Highborough had become his joy. She was the widow of a decorated General, made Baron after the Jacobite uprising of '45. Her beauty and accomplishments had been celebrated at Court. And she made him smile. He did not doubt her wish to remain a dignified widow – she proclaimed it loudly for she saw herself as little less than a regal dowager. Nevertheless, he believed he detected an interest.

After a long moment in which her eyes never relinquished those of her visitor she said, "You wish my company, but I say this: a Lady receives Gentlemen into her drawing-room. And a Gentleman looks after his own."

A minute passed as her guest waited for her to continue. When she did not, he ceased rotating the solitaire around his end finger. He believed they suited because of their differences, even in a common pursuit of control. She controlled by shouting and one was persuaded by her passion. He controlled by studied silences, using what he learned by listening and then provoking with a raised eyebrow. So, when her Ladyship spoke in a low voice, then fell silent, Frederick noticed. As the years progressed, Hugh enjoyed primary control of his veto, but the decision to dismiss Mr Hastings was Frederick's own. This was just as well as the instructor had broken his stick and was, at that moment, on the grounds of Deerhurst Hall searching out a stouter.

That summer it was retirement from study and play on the downs for Hugh. For his father, afternoon teas and courtship. Yet his new romance soon encouraged an early removal to London – a place with fewer interested eyes. In the country, the intimacy with her Ladyship was like a pineapple. Known to exist, rather enticing, but a thing from elsewhere and subject to suspicion.

In the country, marriage is twice-cooked fruit – rendered of impurities and safe for consumption. Overnight visits without the benefit of matrimony brings The Plague.

. . .

A week before the family returned to London, Hugh petitioned his father for a place at Westminster School. Westminster was, in fact, Frederick's own choice for his son, and he had already set about having him admitted. However, he believed Hugh had not valued his place at Harrow and was determined upon a better outcome at Westminster. After the departure of Mr Hastings, the school was mentioned often at Deerhurst Hall. These passing references allowed the boy to hear it praised yet still believe the wish to attend his own. When at last he asked to enrol, to his great surprise, Hugh met with resistance. Sir Frederick remained entirely unmoved when his son reminded him of the school's history, architecture, and the quality of its instructors. At last the boy understood he must do more than parrot what had been said previously, and so professed an overwhelming passion to master the Latin tongue.

"And can you devote the attention required to learn it?" said the man. "It was your inattention, Hugh, which so often animated that piece of birch."

"I shall work day and night to master the language of Cicero."

"But why Westminster? Latin may be learned at any school worth its salt."

"Because at Westminster I shall join true scholars of the language! Only recall the play, Sir, performed entirely in Latin in the boys' dormitory last Christmas. I wish to be one of the players!" He clapped his hands together: "Why, I wonder we shall not all live like Romans together! Perhaps even wear togas to dine!"

Though unusual, this impassioned petition met Frederick's requirements for a new and serious attitude toward the forthcoming school. Yet however starry the boy's wish, Hugh was quickly grounded upon installation in the new school.

Students perceived the newcomer as lurking, even suspicious. Hugh Entwistle studied and assessed them, was even a little conniving, taking individuals for secret interviews to ask what they knew of other students. For this and other indiscretions, he found himself cornered in the dormitory and roundly chastised.

But the bitterest pill was the discovery that Westminster School was not Ancient Rome. No Senators strolling the halls, eager to bring his Latin to fluency – and not a soul wore togas to dine! These were pert, rotten schoolboys like anywhere else. Hugh shouted at his persecutors and was quickly shouted down. Next day he attempted his father's motionless contemplation, coiled and cool as a grass snake. This tactic was interpreted as fear – the silent student had his ears boxed and was locked in a cupboard for hours.

The veto was employed at Westminster and, alas, often during the following years. Hugh argued his way in and out of a school on the basis of its blue uniforms, arguing first for the dignity of the blue, not unlike the cape worn by George III at his coronation. When he wished away, he argued against the blue, which was too like the blue coats of charity schools. Sir Frederick was not a stupid man; rather he wished to reward the boy's increasing skills in debate and so accommodated his wishes.

About this time a Member of Parliament rose from prominence to notoriety. John Wilkes, member for Aylesbury, criticised George III's speech endorsing the Paris Peace Treaty of 1763. Issue 45 of *The North Briton* trumpeted his vicious condemnation, and, for good measure, Wilkes also began a rumour accusing the king of sexual relations with his mother-in-law. Everywhere in England the question was asked: should an MP, should an Englishman, be allowed voice for such opinions? For there was a term for such disrespect, *seditious libel*, which was a criminal felony.

The continuing antics of Wilkes, always framed as the fight for Liberty, soon made him the most famous man in England. By the time Hugh was fourteen, "45, Wilkes, and the Fight for Liberty!" had become the anthem of much of the country. Like most young men Master Entwistle was swept up in the sensation, as the idea of 'liberty' appealed very much. 'Fight' without a doubt. By the time Wilkes fled to France to avoid his trial for seditious libel, Hugh was a vocal young man brewing for a fight as he made his entrance into a new school, Mr Harvey's Academy for Boys.

So perhaps Hugh's fate, like that of the disgraced MP, was inevitable. In '64 John Wilkes was officially declared an outlaw; Hugh, after being viciously thrashed in the yard at Mr Harvey's, was carried out of the school, utterly senseless. When questioned, Hugh told a story of boys from an unnamed school setting upon him without provocation. Some said Hugh's attackers were actually drunken soldiers from the nearby barracks who, upon wandering into the yard, had upset a game of nine-pins. Hugh, they claimed, had grown enraged and struck out. Neither story satisfied Sir Frederick, for he suspected his son was no innocent in the conflict. And having a black mark so early in his career at Mr Harvey's, he chose not to return him.

The troubled scholar recuperated in Beaufort Buildings, the family's townhouse in Westminster. This was a fine home situated in a quiet pocket between the river and the Strand, well-stocked with plenty of domestics. Nevertheless, Hugh was a sad sight – confined to bed, swollen, and scabbed almost beyond recognition, his large blue eyes staring up from the ruin pleading for sympathy.

"I was set upon, but fought valiantly," he said. Then after a dry swallow, continued, "For I wished only Peace, Freedom and Liberty."

This was no bad imitation of the celebrated David Garrick performing *Julius Caesar*, but not at all what would please his father. And for the first time in his young life, Hugh felt the disdain of Sir Frederick:

"You confuse Brutus for Mr Wilkes, Hugh. Well-reasoned in soliloquy, the doer of ill deeds, nonetheless. All of you losers in the end. As to your freedoms – none remain, certainly not the choice of your next school. That choice is mine."

Hugh's widening eyes, failing to charm or give a moment's pause, filled with tears as his father exited the bedchamber. The boy sank down in bed, where he was laid up for three days, black and blue for as many weeks only to discover, once he had recovered, all his freedoms had indeed been withdrawn.

In despair Frederick proceeded to Lord George's home on Fleet Street. Over brandy, he took his friend back to the night Hugh was conceived and reminded George of his blessing. Then he said in a lowered tone, "Our son needs your assistance." The men regarded each other. It was the closest either would come to declaring something both suspected – that Hugh had been twice conceived. Once with Ellen, and once, a few hours earlier, in an alehouse near St. John's Gate.

Evendown was an independent school on an estate twelve miles from London. Full board, rigidly religious, and attended by Walter's second son Horatio. Though it enjoyed a stellar reputation, Frederick had always resisted bringing their sons together at school, fearing any misstep in Hugh's behaviour toward Horatio might jeopardise the decades-long relationship with Walter. Evendown, however, was the man's recommendation.

After a month of anxiety, Frederick received a positive report of Hugh's performance and temper. The following report declared him well-disposed to leadership and admired by the other students. Lord George himself not only confirmed the good account but confirmed it at the expense of Horatio, for though two years older, his son worshiped Hugh as the ideal man. And though George was never slow to criticise his son for a simpering and childlike temper, Sir Frederick suspected that Hugh, at long last, had found his place.

One year passed at Evendown without incident or complaint. Hugh continued for a second. Then a third and a fourth. Latin, Greek, Mathematics, Debate, Sport and Temper – each report was of a model student, admired as much for peace-making as for leadership. Ushers and instructors proclaimed him a marvel – indeed, with no knowledge of his previous failures, they saw something approaching perfection. Hugh counselled, consoled, and gave guidance. By his final year, upon connecting himself to a scholar from a decorated military family, he had decided that, come autumn, he wished to proceed to London to seek a commission in the Guards. So, in May of '68, Hugh stepped from Evendown with his trunk for a summer at home – a young man of promise catching that first scent of freedom. Not merely freedom from school or as an abstract thought; Liberty – as a future in which to define and distinguish himself.

That year Liberty sang in the air of England, over the moors, across the towns, from the Midlands to the salty coasts. The month of March had seen the arrival of John Wilkes, for after five years in exile, the outlaw now sought a new election and a return to Parliament. Before departing for Berkshire, Hugh Entwistle looked south toward the city of London, which was now roiling at the return of the most hated and admired man of the age. Watermen, weavers, and coal workers rioted in support of the man who decried the corruption of governments. Reports of musket-fire were not only in the papers, but in the air. Smoke rose from burning vessels championing the cause of John Wilkes and Liberty!

Liberty: a dangerous thing.

CHAPTER 3

James Bramble — your father's greatest fear…
Rain, like fat gooseberries across the carriage…
Oh, how Bittersweet thy Homecoming…

Hugh started from his daydream as fresh horses woke the stagecoach. Six passengers braced for the mud-slicked highway and the rattling commenced. Hugh and a Clark up from London were serving as unhappy bookends to an unsmilingly matron in a wide, crimson hoop, the dimensions of which obliged the young men to wedge themselves into their respective corners of the carriage. Across from the trio, a man with a red nose sat quite at ease, flanked as he was by a petite woman in a modest green frock and a second Clark whose bony posteriors took almost no room at all upon the bench. Hugh shifted in his seat, willing his bones to bear this last stretch in the rocking carriage, willing himself to bright thoughts, as the ladies complained of damp sheets in coaching inns, and the Clarks launched into a series of dirty jokes.

By this, the second and final day of travel to Deerhurst, Hugh's optimism for the future had begun to wane. What were the cares and comedies of these baboons to the stories of

Edwards, the usher at Evendown? Intimate teas when he enchanted the boys with tales of his time at sea. The blaze in the common room lighting Hugh's way through forty lines of Virgil. That recessed window on drippy days, or days of snow; his fingertips touching the spine of *Roderick Random*. Afternoon rambles; the breeze on his skin when the sun was long…

But this would never do. With a sigh, Hugh withdrew a sheaf of papers tucked inside his copy of Edmund Burke's *Treatise upon the Sublime and Beautiful*. Here were the beginnings of Hugh's ode, 'Oh, how Bittersweet thy Home-coming!' A noble effort, but sentimental − fated to descend into vulgarity and so unworthy of additional labour. He set it aside and reread a letter from Anne, received earlier that week:

7th May 1768, Deerhurst Hall

Dearest Brother,

Though I miss you terribly, I must begin with a reprimand: what a strange letter was your last! What can you mean going on so long about Mr Jewett? No less than half your lines were devoted to our 'rich, well-travelled neighbour', or, as you call him, Stephen Jewett: the admirer of Anne Entwistle. I deny every accusation you make. So, pray, Hugh, no more about that man.

Lady Highborough wishes a lavish dinner party when you return and intends this to be at our home. You are harsh to say she makes herself the mistress of Deerhurst Hall that I should be. She is not so very often with us. Remember, we have known her longer than we knew our own mother. We must be grateful − she is a surrogate provided by Our Heavenly Father until we meet our own again.

I called this morning on Mrs Bramble. She and the parson have their eldest at home again. Can you believe it is four years since James left home to help on his uncle's farm? I daresay you will not recognise him; he is much changed. Time, alas, does so much. Oh Hugh, the thought of change does make me melancholy, even when they are happy alterations (remember her in your prayers, brother, who does occasionally suffer the Vapours).

Matilda made a curious comment the other day. We were speaking of the parson and his family and she said, almost like she was commenting on the weather, "James Bramble, you know, is a thing your father fears above everything else". I said that was a rather extraordinary thing to say and asked her to explain. "Well, he is first born of a family which lost, in its entirety, its station and independence. Frederick can conceive no greater hell upon earth." I wondered these were not her own senti-ments, and she acknowledged they were hers as well. (With such admissions, Hugh, can I wonder you are harsh upon her?)

You may ask what our mother would say. It is this: if the Lord reduced the Brambles from their former station in life, depend upon it he has a plan for him. Is James not rich in his stepsib-lings? Has not he a devout father who has brought him home to prepare him for the Cloth? Do seek a closer alliance with him when you return, Hugh. Mrs Bramble tells me he is not recon-ciled to a life serving the Lord and she would be grateful for a few encouraging words.

I count the days to your return and am, as ever, your most obliging and affectionate sister,

Anne Entwistle   Sister

23

Anne, thought Hugh, *you are wrong on so many counts. You, not her Ladyship, are that mother to me. Stephen Jewett not only admires you; he is cultivated by my father to be worthier of you. And as for the parson's son – I compassionate him, I do indeed, that heir to nothing but a book of sermons, and shall avoid him every chance!*

"Trouble at home?"

Hugh stirred from his reverie. The question had issued from the red-nosed man, squinting at him from the opposing bench. The woman beside him, after a sidelong glance, shushed him and addressed the lady in the crimson hoop: "That's my husband for you – friend to everyone. Where was his concern last night, when I bid him fetch me a glass to place between the bedsheets? Sure, it's the best way to prove the damp what's cost me my health this morning. But would he believe me? Would he take the smallest trouble to save me from catching cold overnight?"

The Clarks laughed at some muttered joke, and Hugh, ignoring the lot of them, tucked the letter from his sister under the treatise and looked out the carriage window.

What could Anne be thinking? James Bramble would be mad with jealousy when they met again. *Hugh Entwistle* was the incarnation of everything James might have had, for his family had been wealthy and in recent memory. And despite what she believed, there was no friendship to renew; Bramble had been but another face in church or on the High Street during Hugh's childhood, only occasionally visiting Deerhurst Hall with the parson. He was two years younger, said childish things, and, as Hugh recalled him, not so much shy as strange.

"Speak up, *chuff,* now," the parson commanded his son upon entering the Hall. "Your host welcomes you into a fine house."

But James, a tow-headed boy who refused to speak, collapsed to a heap, then polished the floor into a far corner. With the laugh he employed in presence of those well below him in station, Sir Frederick assured the parson he desired only that his guests be comfortable: "Be it with you and I in the drawing room or in a quiet corner of the vestibule, which, incidentally, houses a lovely Italian vase. Perhaps he has gone to admire it."

The vase, placed where its agate-coral surface might catch natural light, was ignored by child and sun on this cloudy day. Once he believed attention to be elsewhere, James began edging into adjoining rooms, lifting drapes, and peering behind sideboards. Hugh watched in horror at this complete incapacity to self-regulate; regardless he was inside or out, the visitor continued the hunt for Moor-hens' eggs or whatever he thought he would find. Proud to comprehend decorum, Hugh had stood a bit taller, stepped over James whenever he ventured too close, and preened before the men. And God forbid any female venture too close, for they took quite unkindly to the thought of a nosy child up their hoops.

But as it turned out, the floor of Deerhurst Hall had possessed its share of treasures: a missing key and the discovery of a tear in Lady Highborough's gown. This information was gathered like pearls for presentation, James's reticence to speak vanishing entirely when motivated to tell of his discoveries. Payment for these services, however, varied like the pounds, food commodities and wampum one might trade with in the colonies of America. For the lost key the boy received tuppence. But more often it was a shout, shove or kick bestowed.

As the journey home from Evendown proceeded, continued laughter from the Clarks lifted Hugh's eyes. During his daydream, his gaze had fallen to the green gown opposite him, for, as a result of the wet weather, it had received a hideous trimming of mud. Hugh frowned as he looked around the carriage, observing that the woman's husband was also enjoying a titter, catching his wife's eye, and tilting his head at Hugh. To this the man received a swat with a closed fan, after which he pinched his red nose and attempted to collect himself.

"Sir," said Hugh, "may I crave to know the source of this amusement?"

"Not at all young master," said the man. "Or should I say – young scholar! I had observed, you see, Burke's *Treatise upon the Sublime and Beautiful* sitting upon your lap. I recall it well. Do you reckon it of any merit?" This inspired great merriment from the Clarks and a huff of disgust from the man's wife.

"You saw as well, Sir," said Hugh, "with that perceptive eye, they were my own letters which occupied me, and not the treatise."

Laughing merrily: "But all the *smoothness* of the other! All those 'deceitful mazes through which the unsteady eye slides giddily, without knowing where to fix'. Come now, what man will take the trouble to obtain the work and not peruse it?"

"A scholar, such as you have termed me, who works methodically and may well leave it unread in preference to something else."

Like a comic upon Drury Stage, the man addressed his audience of four and spread his arms. "But Ladies and Gentlemen," he bellowed, "he must confess to knowledge, at least, of the First Part. For I saw its lines plain as day upon his face: *Curiosity* and *Novelty*! Burke holds these to be the *Elements* of man's path to know *Beauty*."

At last understanding how his stare at the woman's green gown had been interpreted, Hugh said, "Sir, I conjure you to recall the Second Part of Burke, which holds that *Pleasure*, *Pain* and *Indifference* comprise the entirety of man's experience."

"Well!" said his persecutor, "he is at last betrayed into the rudiments of knowledge."

"But you, Sir, are betrayed as what? For what you take as pleasure is, for Madam, who hides her face, as much pain. I then, who can be neither of these, am left to feel indifference, which you do inspire, for all your learned wit."

One Clark, who had been pleased to titter at the student, now extended a finger at Hugh's persecutor. "You're a pretty fellow for a scholar, Jack, subjecting your wife to such abuse. I believe the student's got the better of you there."

After a moment's consideration, the man sought bolstering from another self-inflicted tweak of the nose, which he employed as might another a bumper of brandy. When this failed, he descended a darker path. "Withdraw that claw, dog," he said to the Clark, then returned to Hugh, "And I'll thank you to keep your dirty gaze from my wife. You can thank Providence I saw fit to make merry with you rather than box your ears – or draw steel!"

But despite the bluster, this was said with such bad grace that Hugh was content to make a face, fold his hands, and digest his win. This was a welcome entrée for a mind hungry for distraction – a feast to delight his palate. For a bit of dessert, Hugh employed his lace cuffs and a great deal of noise to bring every eye in the carriage to himself. Then he took up the treatise and, with wide, expanding eyes, and audible gasps, commenced to discover what distinguishes *Beauty* from *The Sublime*. This elicited from the Clarks peals of laughter so shrill and insipid that, at the next stop, Hugh's persecutor exploded from the carriage and into the rain-soaked day.

"Delightful!" said Hugh, having a go at stage acting, "*Delight*, you know, as defined by Burke, is that extreme pleasure at the relief from *Pain*."

Clearing skies greeted him as he neared his destination. Pastures were soon traced by thick, fine timber. Thatched Greystones sprouted like mushrooms in shaded pockets before distant, verdant dales. After changing into the family carriage at Newbury, he came at last to the long drive of Deerhurst Hall. Here was Samuel the footman, stepping forward to shake his hand. Next Hugh's brother Ned, striding up from the paddock, followed by Alice, in a yellow dress running circles around everyone. Just then departing to the tavern for his pipe and can was the lanky, somewhat subdued figure of Jasper Sharp, his father's valet. He was followed by Sir Frederick, who merely nodded to his son and directed him to be embraced by the women.

Whatever their differences, Anne and Matilda were equal sources of warmth and tenderness. Anne's attentions were tearful and maternal. Then, upon his release from her arms, Hugh was pressed headfirst into the double-bumper of Lady Highborough's overflowing breasts. She was something over forty, with fine bones, a fine intellect, and a very fine belief in herself. Her wig was a honeyed flow around her bosom, her cheeks blossomed with all the sincerity of rouge, her eyebrows perfect grey arches culled from the backs of dead mice. Yet one was seldom sorry to be brought into orbit – she was a fount of wit and sensuality which only increased with years.

Anne played the harpsichord, Hugh's uncle arrived from Newbury, and Deerhurst Hall at last welcomed Hugh fully into its embrace – he was truly happy to be home.

As was the case in much of the country, the discourse at supper centred around not so much a topic as a number. Uncle Barlow, who managed a bank and enjoyed counts of things, wished to know how many 45's his nephew had encountered during his journey.

"Beastly practice," said Hugh, knowing his father's dislike of the topic, but when pressed said he supposed no less than one hundred 45's had been chalked and whitewashed upon carriages and public buildings.

"What is 45?" inquired Alice, pulling apart her loin of veal and looking around the table.

"45 is whatever one wishes it to be," said Sir Frederick. "It represents that most indistinct of concepts – liberty – a thing no one can sufficiently define, yet a thing one can never be allowed to be against."

"Number 45," said Uncle Barlow, with a twitch of his mustachios, "is the issue of *The North Briton* in which criticism of our sainted King was found to be intolerable. So intolerable that John Wilkes, duly elected this March to represent the county of Middlesex, has been refused his seat and arrested."

Said Hugh, "As outlaws must be, one supposes, regardless they choose to stand for knight of the shire or king of the world. Do, Alice, add to your definition of 45 *confinement*. Liberty and confinement – that is 45."

In the study after supper Samuel poured claret for Hugh and his younger brother Ned as Frederick settled behind his desk. Unlike Hugh and Alice, who spoke copiously and with ease, and Anne, whose words, though few, were timed to maximum effect, Ned had no gift for oration. At fourteen, he could produce words only after long consideration, and so was quite out of his depth during noisy dinner parties. The introduction of claret in the study, in the presence of his older brother, was meant to prompt him to begin seeing himself as a young man.

From an old mezzotint behind Sir Frederick's shoulder stared Robert Walpole, his sharp, but congenial, expression delivering to Hugh a flood of memories. Time was he had believed it to be a print of his grandfather, Joshua Entwistle. His father had reluctantly corrected him. "Walpole is grandfather of loyalists and true Whigs," Frederick had said, "which Entwistles are through and through. Walpole was a great man who knew how to unite a nation after the South Sea fiasco, and how to exile those of a dangerous political persuasion. Many of your friends, and their fathers too I daresay, have never met a Tory – at least one who will own it publicly. For that you may thank Robert Walpole."

Smiling at the memory, Hugh turned to his brother and said, "Looking at that portrait, Ned, I am reminded of those circumstances which led to my departure for Even-down. Come to think of it I was just about your age; funny, that…" He met his father's eyes and was, for a moment, genuinely startled by the passage of time. "Some-times good things require the complete collapse of what one holds dear, publicly and before the entire world. That is what was required of me. My world when I was your age centred around impressing my friends at Mr Harvey's Academy in London. You cannot imagine how well I was used to think of myself – how you would have hated to know me there."

"Would I?"

At his father's nod of encouragement, Hugh continued. "Picture a bruised and bloody monstrosity, pummelled out of whatever good looks he may have possessed (Lord bless me, Ned, I never have had your fine turn of feature!). There I was, sitting before my father and scarcely able to lift my swollen, blackened eyes for shame, my lip threatening to erupt at the first word. When I did speak, I chose of all things to compare myself to Mr John Wilkes!" Hugh glanced at the man behind the desk. "Do you recall that?"

"I recall it."

Hugh wet his palate with claret and continued in a boy's soprano: "'Sir,' said I. 'I have ruminated long upon the error of my ways. I was persuaded an ardent admiration of Mr Wilkes was the natural consequence of my admiration of the great Walpole!'" Then, in his best imitation of Sir Frederick's baritone, Hugh growled, "'And what the Devil persuaded you of that Hugh?!?'"

Ned covered his mouth and laughed, and Hugh cleared his throat, before reclaiming his soprano: "'Wilkes's being the arch-rival of the King's favourite, Lord Bute, is what convinced me. Everybody knows Bute is a Scotch Jacobite and a Tory. But now I understand disloyal factions and such, and how many radicals will call themselves Whigs in this degenerate age.'" Hugh coughed, then thought it best to set aside his play acting for what remained.

"And our father, Ned, tapped his porcelain pipe and, after a moment, let slip a smile. 'Becomes a bit of a mishmash, doesn't it? Do not be too hard on yourself,' he said, and I might have wept with gratitude. I looked up through eyes now more swollen with emotion and vowed, 'You have allowed me to prattle on about Wilkes and Liberty, Father, when I only wished an excuse to misbehave. I vow to be a success at Evendown, whatever is required.'"

Ned sat waiting for whatever came next, not appearing to have understood the little encouragements embedded throughout the performance from which he might take heart. He was, it seemed, of an ilk entirely unaware of his own shortcomings – he wished no improvement, would not request to go to Evendown himself, or desire to know how Hugh had gained confidence in speaking.

"Is that all?" he said at last. "Do the funny voices again!" Then his brow furrowed when he saw his father's displeasure.

"My brother does not believe my return merits your good claret, Sir," said Hugh. "He sees it only as a reward for a wayward spirit."

But Ned was lost here as well. Literal where Hugh might be whimsical, enlivened not at all at the fortune of an opened liquor cabinet. Sensing something more was expected from him, Ned said, "All very well," a phrase he added like salt to any dish which would admit of it. "But I should never complain of the school here at home."

Seeing little to encourage where Ned was concerned, Sir Frederick turned to his elder son and said: "We shall be in London in September to pursue the commission. Just a few months away – I trust you will maintain a correspondence with your schoolfellows until then."

"Yes," said Hugh, "even my weekly letters to Horatio. Such an ill-contented fellow. Two years now at Jesus College and still entirely dependent upon my advice in the most trivial matters."

"I wonder you should not simply correspond with his father," said his father dryly. "If Walter were not such a miserable correspondent, I would have you do it. That Horatio, at twenty, the son of Nobility, should lean so heavily upon a boy of eighteen, and his social inferior, is little short of a disgrace. I play the part of his Lordship, you understand," he added, somehow looking more towards himself than to the son he hoped to reassure. "We must thank Providence that birth dictates not every advantage. 'Hugh Entwistle is what every son should be.' Did you know that?"

Hugh could only stare, his goblet interrupted in its rotation towards his lips.

"Did my godfather say this?"

"Those were his words to me. His eldest, Allan, did modestly well at Pembroke and now makes shift for himself in London. Horatio, however, is a trying disappointment to him."

Ned looked from one to the other: "Isn't Hugh going to university then?"

"Not at present," said Hugh, keeping his eyes on their father. "I shall first petition for a commission in the Guards once summer is passed and the right people are returned to London. And should he succeed," he added, "will you drink a bumper to your brother's health?" For Hugh had grown restless observing the lively crimson legs inside Ned's neglected wine goblet.

"All very well," his brother exhaled, without a promise to drink or even look at his claret. "A commission in the Blues!"

"The Royal Horse Guards or the Foot Guards – the Blues as you call them."

"More of that in September," said Frederick. "At present, we do enough to cultivate those relationships which can too easily slip, despite the most solemn vows of friendship. All is for naught if the connections cannot be maintained. The onus is on you, Hugh, to habituate to the practice to letter-writing those you wish to benefit by."

After a few more minutes, Frederick dismissed the boys. As they departed, he took the full goblet from Ned, who could not manage it, and the empty from Hugh, who could very well.

CHAPTER 4

For five days Hugh fulfilled the demands of his friends and acquaintances. Each morning he mounted his steed to pay calls of courtesy. Afternoons he rode into the countryside in parties of pleasure, and in the evening indulged his tastes for brandy and piquet. He belonged to that class which assumes a general acquaintance with any of independent means – sons and daughters of those country squires who peppered the land of West Berkshire. Yet from this net he took pains to eject the coarser and more egregious – the sportsmen who minded nothing but foxhunting and the bucks who tarried about the George and Pelican, regaling themselves with ale, riling the stabled horses with pistols, and terrorizing the fair sex. In their place Hugh installed the cream of the middling sort – well-mannered and ambitious young men like Isaiah Dawson, son of Newbury's foremost physician. By this method he culti-vated a circle of acquaintance most suited to admire his genius and taste – those willing to accept a certain aloofness in his manner, who would not question him or ask about much beyond his hand at cards.

Sunday morning, steps trimmed with sweet violets led the Entwistles inside St. Timothy's, the stone church belonging to the parish of Deerhurst. In a well-maintained wool coat, James Bramble was standing beside his father as they greeted parishioners and the alteration in him was indeed startling. James now stood tall, four times his former height it seemed, neatly composed from head to toe and with eyes which fastened upon Hugh the moment he arrived. This inspired a moment of concern – this concentrated gaze was so intense one might mistake it for anger.

Then their fathers came together, and as the sons shook hands, Hugh saw in those green eyes less of anger and more of focused interest. And, somehow, a look of expectations fulfilled. Then, with the manners of a Gentleman, James welcomed him home, asking about the journey and his time away without a hint of jealousy. So deferential, so engaging – and he inquired into the health of the absent Lady Highborough without the trace of a smirk.

If his manner savoured of the rehearsed, which, after a minute Hugh understood it to be, one could only feel flattered. Praise for Deerhurst Hall, the 'castle of my youth' as James termed it, touched Hugh with a hitherto unknown feeling of pride. And what modesty of address! – quite uncommon in so pretty a fellow with his glowing cheeks and head of golden waves. And though somewhat stoic, no doubt the product of years on an isolated farm in the Cotswolds, his mouth betrayed a hint of former mischief. It twitched at secret amusements as his gaze travelled around St. Timothy's collecting information. A turn of the head as he scratched his neck purchased a moment to observe Hugh's shoes, which were of black leather, tied with blue bows sitting atop tongues of metal lace. Rather too fine for the country, but Hugh wore them defiantly whenever he could, and relished the looks they received. Yet Bramble's gaze gave him pause. He seemed to see a thing beyond the blue bow, a thing stepped in and stuck to the sole. Then upon lifting his eyes, he was the child of years ago presenting a pearl for payment. Only Hugh was unsure what the payment should be. Or, indeed, what had been discovered.

After church, during a carriage tour of the countryside, Sir Frederick spoke of the parson and his family. The Brambles had been landed Gentry with a good fortune on an estate in Wiltshire. James's grandfather had invested heavily in the South Sea Company and after the bubble burst took loans to maintain the family. Irregularities in an inheritance and an ill-advised sally into trade had obliged additional loans, and when James's father married for love, and love alone, the estate was sold to settle the debts. Shortly after giving birth, James's mother died of consumption and the destitute, grieving widow took solace in divinity. He won the living at the parsonage in Deerhurst, re-married and sired four more children. Everything of his former life, besides James, had been lost.

Hugh listened entranced. The family history was more heart-rending than he had ever understood – the valiant struggle to stay afloat, the defiant choice of love over money, only to lose that too! This was worthy of Euripides – this was a modern tragedy! As the carriage continued home, Hugh saw no verdant hills bathed in Spring light. Saw no Ash or Elm or anything beyond the palm of his hand. This he studied, tracing the lines where they had joined with those of Bramble on the threshold of St. Timothy's. Bramble – so altered, just as Anne had said. Bramble – so captivating and attentive. And if he were a little angry, which in the final assessment Hugh guessed he must be, it was directed not at himself, but at the world in general. And rightfully so.

That night Hugh surfaced many times from shallow pools of sleep, wandering the shores of wakefulness to consider and reconsider the source of this restlessness. Each attempt to re-submerge was halted by the sight of his reflection in a pool, and yet the image of the young man shifting on the surface was never quite his own. He appeared distorted, bent, assembled, then shattered. He knew he must submerge to reclaim the peace of sleep, but no matter how he approached the pool, he could not pass beyond its surface. Then, without knowing he had fallen in, he would surface again, disorientated, to the same dark and restless shore. Turning, he crawled once more to the edge of the pool.

This time he saw reflected James Bramble. It was James without a doubt, staring back, paled to white in the water of his memory.

Then he realised: Hugh Entwistle *was* James Bramble but for the grace of God...

Awaking with a start within the darkness of his bedcurtains, Hugh cried, "But however Fortune may have betrayed you, James, good breeding never shall! And yours, poor soul, was the handshake of a Gentleman!"

Next morning, he strode into the French gardens, feeling very much the master of the Deerhurst estate and acutely aware of all he possessed. The mania of the previous night had unsettled, and yet excited him. He yearned to make some display of power and wealth. How he should love to present Bramble with an estate ten times that of the Hall simply to bask in his admiration!

But that was a flight of fancy. The Hall as it stood more than sufficed and was acknowledged by everyone who mattered to be among the finest for some miles. Even Isaiah Dawson, on his visit a few days before, failed to conceal his family's desire — not just for such a place, but for the place itself.

"No doubt you are aware of the needed repairs," had been Isaiah's wily approach as they strolled the grounds. "Still, bearing this in mind, it would fetch a good price. Your father should consider selling."

Their evening saunter had, from this point in the conversation, revealed Hugh's eye teeth. "No need to look like that, Entwistle. Your father's a London man; no shame in admitting it. He might devote himself year-round to the pleasures of city life. I wish nothing so grand for myself. Only to expand my father's practice, which has been tireless service to the people of Newbury, and *environs*, for the past twenty years."

As they turned up the long avenue of elms bounding the drive, Hugh said, "Twenty-*one* years ago, nobody had heard of a Dawson in Newbury."

Eyes widening, Isaiah rounded on him and said, "And my mother, *Georgiana-Newcombe-that-was*? Had nobody heard of *her*?"

This was true enough, though, to Hugh's mind, rather an unusual line of defence. Dawson's mother had been a member of the Newbury Newcombes, of wealth and connections in the county unsurpassed. Her marriage to a physician's assistant from Gloucester had been the biggest scandal of its day and she was despised for marrying a struggling man of trade. Now that her husband was a success, she was despised for having the temerity to rise again, and so continued to be condemned behind her back as Georgiana-Newcombe-that-was.

"My dear Dawson," said Hugh, extending a hand to his visitor's shoulder, "you must admire, a little, a woman's willing descent from all respectability to pursue her one true love."

"From all respectability? Now see here—"

"Utterly and completely fallen, Isaiah – in the pursuit of becoming your mother. I confess I should never have the courage to follow my own heart to such depths."

"Such *depths*!"

"The very deepest! To the Devil with false modestly – you must admit she was, and still is, reckoned among the handsomest in the county. She might have married anyone she wished. Will you not allow her even this much praise?"

"Of course I will allow praise!" cried Isaiah, "I have – I

have *nothing* but praise and admiration for the woman who gave me life!"

"As it should be. So, I'm shocked you would stoop to slander in the defence of yourself. *Georgiana-Newcombe-that...* I daren't even say it. Give me your hand." When the hand was not immediately produced, Hugh blocked their progress down the drive. "Come, what have I said?"

"You seem to be implying... somewhere in all that... How long, must a name be *in* a place to be reckoned *of* a place?"

With a shake of the head Hugh said, "Well, Sir, why not accuse me outright? Tell me I accept as being of Newbury only those families established since the reign of James I, as mine have been. That is – honestly, Isaiah, that is a little hurtful."

"And is not *twenty-one years* hurtful?"

"Forgive me – I had believed we might speak freely. Give me your hand now, I insist." When the hand at last appeared, it was taken not for a shake but at an angle more suited to the slipping on of a ring. The wounded visitor looked on helplessly, his indignation melting as Hugh ran his thumb across the top of his hand then, joining them arm in arm, directed them farther down the drive toward the lane. Softening his tone Hugh continued, "When I engage you in conversation, I do so in the belief we are equals on the battlefield of discourse. With friends one should never concern oneself with the words one employs, only insist that the point be made as well, and as directly, as possible. *Twenty-one years* was said to demonstrate a common attitude."

"But—"

"Just as you employed shorthand when speaking of your lovely and accomplished mother. *Georgiana-Newcombe-that-was.* Perhaps you were a little harsh. In my opinion you were to speak of her like that. Yet your point was made, and I do not question your choice."

"But I only said—"

"Must I fear your reactions, Isaiah? Must I be cautious and treat you with polite reserve?"

"Certainly not!" said the young physician. "Do ever speak your mind to me! I value our friendship, our open and honest friendship, too much ever to wish polite reserve!"

"Very well," said Hugh, patting his friend's shoulder and smiling. "We are entirely in agreement. Upon my soul how came we to quarrel?"

"I… I don't know."

They were by this time at the end of the drive and Hugh, suddenly recalling another engagement, directed him down the lane. Dawson reached for his hand. "Till we meet again then. God bless you, my good man!" he said and continued on his way.

Hugh waited until Dawson was some distance away. Then he said, "I am *aware* some repairs are needed to the house? Good God – men have been called out for less."

Hugh's thoughts returned to Bramble and around ten o'clock he came into the house for honey cake and a cup of chocolate. Unwilling to speak of what was really occupying his mind, he regaled Anne with the tale of Dawson's ill-considered offer.

"I determined never to speak to the rascal again," he said, popping a piece of cake into his mouth. "But I never can stay angry at my friends. He is in love and thinks of his future – rumour has it Miss Benning's got him to propose but it's a famous secret. What, haven't you heard?"

Anne was looking at her brother in some confusion. In addition to adopting a very erratic manner of speaking, he had commenced pinching pieces from a second piece of cake while tapping the table with his other hand.

"Something on your mind, Hugh?"

"Something?"

"Tell me you are happy to be home at least." At her brother's furrowed brow, she continued, "You have been so occupied, every moment of every day since you returned, I don't know… I scarcely have had a moment with you."

After some hesitation he said, "I know I shall not return to Evendown. It is a queer feeling."

"I rather thought you would enjoy a summer in the country."

"So did I. But I realise now that the concealment of fourteen years of my missteps and tantrums, everything which had occurred in my previous school career, lent me the appearance of perfection at Evendown. Now I must begin again, somehow, as an adult. For a few years I possessed a glorious, shining crown. Now I understand not only what it was to have a kingdom, but what it is to be driven from it – I wouldn't wish the feeling on my worst enemy."

"How can you take such a pessimistic view? Think of the confidence you've gained."

"Tell me how success in such a confined, controlled place as Evendown translates to success in the world. Never again will ground be so well-prepared for me."

Her silence was confirmation he would have rather done without. At last she said, "You promised to show me your poems when you returned."

"Yes I did – I shall fetch them presently," he said and ran to retrieve the bundle. Upon returning he said, "I nearly tossed them in the fire. Every one. Read them only after I am gone—"

"Hugh!"

"Departed from the room, you goose. I cannot bear to see your disappointment."

"I see. And now that my expectations are depressed you expect I shall be pleasantly surprised. I shall give you my honest opinion either way, you know that."

"You accuse me of false modesty?"

"Yes. Were they as bad as you claim the poems would have long since gone into the fire."

Hugh bit his lip, met her eyes a moment, then looked away.

"Do you call often on Mrs Bramble? To help with the children?"

With a laugh and a shake of the head at yet another change of subject Anne said, "Yes, once or twice a week. Whenever she pays her visits around the neighbourhood. A good, selfless woman is Mrs Bramble – James is certainly no help to´her." Hugh raised his brows. "Don't misunderstand me. His being home is a help to the family, particularly to his father during planting and harvest. But he is a trial to then both, Hugh – his odd humours and moods drive them to distraction." She caught his eye. "You two must meet oftener now he is home."

"It was always our lot to lead different lives, Anne. It cannot be."

Expelling a huff of exasperation, she frowned, for he had resumed his tapping of the table. "Then why intentionally lead me to speak of that family? He needs encouragement to continue his studies – I had hoped from you. The parson has done all in his power to see he is educated for the clergy. Still James complains and grows obstinate whenever the subject of his future is raised." After meeting her eyes Hugh shook his head and leant back in his chair.

"Were I inclined to recommend anything, it would be the Law or Medicine – something to improve him. Convince him to be a clergyman? I'd hardly know where to begin."

"Have it your way," said his sister, straightening her dress. "Anyhow, I don't suppose you will see him before they depart for Salisbury."

"And how long in Salisbury?"

Hugh realised, too late, that he had said this too quickly and with far too much urgency.

"I understand about four weeks," she said with a smile, and reached for his hand. "I see in your eyes you wish to help

him so why must you fight your better nature? It's decided –
you will call on him before they leave. Today would be best."

"No Anne," said Hugh, taking her hand for a kiss then
setting it aside. "A visit from me would be seen as charity,
which I would not have in his place."

"*Charity?*"

But despite her protests, he changed the subject and would
say no more. He hated to disappoint her, but he simply could
not do as she asked. No, he mustn't…Yet an idea was coming
to him, and the more he considered it…Yes, he *would* snatch
Bramble and question him about his future – only by stealth.
He would offer encouragement, of sorts, only it should be
done secretly.

Yet he was to discover that stealth and secrecy came at the
cost of added time – nearly two hours elapsed guessing
James's whereabouts and following false leads. The glebe lands
behind the parsonage yielded no sight of him, and Hugh
refused to inquire within. The day was splendid with sunshine
– perhaps he had stolen off for a bit of angling at the chalk
stream. But there, too, he was not to be found. And when at
last Hugh tracked him to the common well drawing water, he
was met with quite a strange welcome: James observed him,
their eyes met most certainly, then the wretch turned his back
as though he had not seen him and threw a second bucket
down the well.

This outrage fired Hugh's determination, and a short time
later, as his prey advanced down the path toward the parsonage, Hugh intercepted him.

"Didn't like to call attention to myself," said the boy,
halting with buckets sloshing. "You looked to be on your way."

"Shall I lend a hand?"

Bramble looked at Hugh's clean shirt and breeches,
perhaps to excuse him from an offer both understood he had
not meant. "I've not far to go," said James, and began a wide
arc to circumvent him.

Said Hugh, "Archimedes never described a more a perfect parabola," then, determined not to let his annoyance get the better of him, came forward and blocked Bramble's advance. "I have a mind for a saunter. Walk with me to Ox-Bridge." Bramble's hesitation, though no more than a moment, was all the encouragement Hugh needed; he advanced and said in a softened tone, "After being so long from home I find myself grown sentimental. Is it the same for you?"

Though James showed no sign of having missed home, his eyes flickered to attention. Hugh softened his tone still further.

"Nine years ago, I extracted my first stickleback from the stream by Ox-Bridge – from that sweet bend that pools beyond the crossing. Just now it came to me that I must, this instant, see it again. May I show you the place?"

They agreed to meet by the bridge in forty-five minutes. It appeared Bramble felt unworthy of the attention, though a thing of more worth Hugh had not encountered since his return. The parson's son was like a precious metal nobody noticed or even thought to look for. Unknown, even, to himself. He was so very... so very...

Time slipped down the clear flow of the chalk stream, and when Hugh looked up the young man was standing on the bridge. His hands were pushed into the pockets of a fresh pair of breeches, his hair curled behind one ear where he had combed it neat. On a sunlit breeze the gold in his hair caught fire and, for a moment, Hugh lost the power of speech. When a group of children passed over the bridge, pushing and playing, Bramble came forward.

"That you recalled so much of my history recommends you very much to my thoughts and warm regard," Hugh said as they began their walk. "I was used to think you were a little mouse briffuting about for cheese, hardly aware of me or anyone else."

"There are not so many people to remember in this place," was the response, which Hugh found rather sly.

"I trust lost keys and marbles no longer hold the same charms for you – what are your passions today?"

"Are you come at my stepmother's bidding? To bring me to the Cloth?"

Hugh halted their progress. "What was that?"

Looking away Bramble muttered, "It's well for some folks to do a good deed."

"I am not *some folks*, James. And I am never directed by course subversion." Hugh stared at his companion until he at last met his eye.

"Tell me about your own passions, as an example of what you mean."

"Nothing could be simpler," said Hugh, "I wish to bring myself to public attention with a great ode like Johnson or Goldsmith."

"My passion as well."

This was not what Hugh expected, or even wished, to hear. "Do not say it because I did; I don't ask you to. You might say angling, or gaming, or star-gazing."

"Writing poetry," said Bramble. "Verses, odes, sonnets. All are my passion."

It seemed too good to be true. The ability to compose must prove breeding beyond doubt. And so unsure what else to do, he smiled and shook the young man's hand. "Very well. No doubt, but I must think this most fortunate."

"Would you recite something you have composed?"

Seeing this as an opening to another meeting, Hugh said he preferred to read one out rather than recite by memory. Perhaps tomorrow morning, under this tree?

"We depart in the morning for my uncle's in Salisbury." Then, like a child on to a shinier object, Bramble said, "But did you see any of the riots in London? Yesterday being the

Sabbath, you know, I didn't like to ask… but I wished to know the moment you arrived!"

Hugh groaned inwardly; riots in London? Was this the origin of those attentions which had so gratified him? He let pass a moment of silence as he stared into the distance. Then, stooping to pick up a stone, he hurled it into the stream. Once he resumed their walk, it was with a note of coolness. "You speak of the incident at St. George's Field. Do you know the place?"

"I've never been to London."

Hugh knew very well his companion had never been, and to punish Bramble's implied indifference to him, he spoke of the incident in St. George's Field with passing disdain. Implied he had been present when a citizen, no doubt drunk and deranged, protested the arrest of John Wilkes. Described in detail the cheap red coat worn by the protester who was chased by a soldier into a barn. And when, by accident, the soldier mistakenly killed another in a red coat, Hugh placed blame for the death and the subsequent riots squarely upon the protester.

Sensing his misstep, Bramble said, "I supposed you might have seen Wilkes or even met him – I hear they let the public into King's Bench Prison to visit him. Nobody can decide if he is a hero or a villain; I admire, and wonder, at that. Still, I like you very much on your own merit."

Oh, gratifying words were winds to sweep Hugh's vanity to the sky! He grabbed Bramble's hand and gave it another shake, liking very much that coarse, dry palm in his own. Never could he recall having met another who engaged him so immediately and whose manner so well pleased him.

Then he understood. James sought a benefactor, a person of more worldliness and leverage to improve him, as Hugh sought to do himself in September. It was the most natural thing. Such efforts demonstrated understanding of the ways of the world, and Hugh was a hypocrite to begrudge his first attempt. *Hugh: The Benefactor*. Was this, then, that strong feeling he could not place when he thought of James? Perhaps what every Gentleman experienced when he helped a worthy soul. It was a most singular feeling, and more pleasurable, by far, than one might suppose.

For nearly an hour, they ambled about to no destination but a greater knowledge of the other, engaging in some of the most pleasant discourse Hugh had ever enjoyed. He indulged Bramble's every inquiry into the city, detailed his experiences at school and bestowed advice on what a poet should strive to be. Bramble took each word as gospel, and even betrayed a little smugness at having drawn his notice.

At last Hugh said, "Now we must say *adieu*. I wish you a good journey and ask the pleasure of your correspondence."

"Without a doubt you will have it."

"Expect a note tonight. It will arrive under cover of nightfall – with a token of my affection. Look for it in the opening at the base of the large elm at Ox-Bridge."

Pleased as Hugh was at his previous success with the youth, he took particular pride in the unchecked thrill this hint produced. The promise of secret treasure was to James Bramble the greatest joy in life. His eyes lit in expectation, pleading silently to know what manner of gift he might expect. But Hugh reminded him that such precautions were an integral part of their working to improve him, which must be done without the knowledge of his parents, or of anyone else.

Then he grabbed James's hand for a final shake, bid him think of something else during the many, many hours he must wait for his gift, then ran off to leave the young man restless to the point of distraction.

May 28th, Salisbury

Dear Hugh,

My sincerest gratitude for the gift. It is the smartest I ever beheld. Nobody can guess how I have come to have it. We arrived at Salisbury yesterday and already I have been called a 'pretty fellow'. A Lady of Quality smiled at me a long time while I was walking on the High Street, and I set this down, entirely, to your stylish cocked hat. My brother Mose cries for one of his own, and Step cannot imagine where it came from and tells me I must have stolen it. What fun. I fancy you know me very well, Secret Friend and Benefactor.

We are four weeks more with my uncle and his family, whom I mentioned to you a little when we spoke at the bridge. That most fortunate encounter is often on my mind. However, your note and your generous gift, though gladly received, are wont to plague my mind. Despite your fair request, that I compose a poem for you, I can get no further than two lines…

I have a confession, Hugh. I said I desired to write as a Passion because you said it. I cannot do the thing myself and have no real desire for the Trade. Yet one must aim at being something, and a Poet sounds very well. Perhaps you will break our correspondence now you know. I hope you will not. We spoke of Real things, Worldly things, and always how I could benefit by your experiences. Nobody has yet desired to know what I desire. Father and Step wish me to seek ordination, but this heretic prays that our fortunes decline even further, and we cannot afford even the course in Divinity.

To race a horse every day, until there are no more days, is my heart's wish. You will think such an ambition unworthy of your friend, yet I can only shine in demonstrating what I am master of, which is horseflesh. Horses consist of a great deal of knowledge: their care and maintenance, and how they are best employed. Your father complained Sunday of the slowness of his carriage, and said he wishes to purchase another. Tell him he has only to latch his machine to a troupe of Cleveland Bays – none are better for speed and endurance.

I am very curious to know your ideas for me here, how to 'bring me to the attention' of my 'indifferent uncle', as you say. To answer your question: yes, he has a daughter. She is about my own age and her name is Sarah. To my knowledge she is not promised. I must guess your intentions, and she does like me in the hat. But, of course, one must do more than wear a hat to gain her money, for I have nothing beyond the family connection to recommend me. So, I beg your instant response, provided I continue to merit your correspondence, and pray you will advise me how to proceed for the remainder of my stay.

Ever, your humble servant,
J. Bramble

June 3rd, Salisbury, 10.45 a.m.

Dear Hugh,

The joy I feel at the letter just delivered cannot be surpassed! I put the feeling down on paper, as you urge, the moment I experience it! I shall retire to my bedchamber now to inspect your letter with additional Scrutiny.

June 3rd, 11.35 a.m.

How came I to merit such an acquaintance? Thank you, Sir, for appreciating my prose. My father saw I was educated in grammar, as well as mathematics and all the things to make a scholar. My tutor in the Cotswolds was a man of letters, and after my chores on the farm I had nothing to do but study Latin and the Bible. At least in terms of education, I have received what should have been mine had our family continued to be what it was. My face burned when you said you knew about the grandfather who lost so much for me. But as you say, 'our manner of Quality is in the blood, not the material representation thereof. Money may be lost and, perhaps, regained.' In the blood… I should not have thought of that, left to my own way of thinking. I was brought up to disdain Wealth, which I am told all the living day is a Sin to desire. Yet, as in many things, you set me right.

Your continued wish for a poem I shall oblige presently. But I must first thank you for finding 'much merit' in my passion for riding. And your comment hinting that I might somehow join passion and fortune: Hugh, I am WILD to know what you have in mind! I Tremble, absolutely Tremble, that some misunderstanding of your words has misled me. Though by the clear manner of your writing I know this is impossible. As you say: 'Diversification in all things. Why be one thing or another, when one might be all? A Racer, a Poet, a Parson, a _____. The lack of Diversification brought your grandfather to ruin, and you must learn from his error.' This is such sound advice I wonder I never received it before.

Need we continue secretly when I return? I will do as you instruct, for:

> *I do long to see you once more*
> *When I am once more at your door*
> *Just as you were, my secret friend*
> *That first fine day at stream's end*

That I may continue my education
The finest, say I, in all the nation
Be it wooing
Be it writing
Teach me Diversification!

Your affectionate, and grateful Servant,
J B

CHAPTER 5

Every three or four days, Bramble sent a letter equal parts
news of the Wards and longings to return home. These letters
he directed to a chocolate house in Newbury, subsequently
retrieved by a boy runner tutored in subterfuge. For the price
of a cup of chocolate little Arthur, the child of Anne's maid,
retrieved the correspondence, held under an assumed name,
and delivered it to Hugh's private apartments. The answers
Hugh delivered personally to an office for outgoing post in
Speenhamland, which duty became less and less frequent in
rather a short time.

For Hugh, assured of his hold over Bramble, had grown
bored with the Wards, who were a family of little ambition
and no connections. Their daughter Sarah would, upon
marriage, bring no more than five hundred a year, and the
constant mention of her name had become a source of irritation to him. Why it should, Hugh failed to understand. He
had commanded his friend to study her, then chastised his
fixation with her. When Bramble became confused, Hugh
counselled cool observation at a distance and further discussion only when he returned. Until then, he directed, no more

details of Sarah, or indeed of the Wards at all. This fired the boy's passion to return home, which Hugh, nearly forgetting his mania to attain him, also began to resent – and fear. His responses became abrupt at the unsettling thought of James's return. And so, after quickly assuring himself each new epistle contained the required level of worship, he threw it into a corner of his escritoire having hardly perused its contents.

Mornings he read – taking long draughts of Hume's *Human Nature*, interspersed with sips from French comedies from the home's well-stocked library. After lunch and a turn in the garden he composed the letters aimed at furthering his military ambition. He wrote to men young and old, from school or known through his father, who often perused the letters before sending them on. By three in the afternoon Hugh was free to stroll into Newbury, attend card parties or prepare for a country dance. And unless happening upon the parsonage or Ox-Bridge in his perambulations, it must be admitted he thought little of his possession in Salisbury and very nearly forgot him.

So it was a shock one bright summer day, when Alice appeared at his apartment to announce the arrival of the parson and his family.

"Downstairs," she said breathlessly, "We are to entertain the children before supper and my father wants you immediately."

"I did not announce my return," said Hugh. It was only a whim to begin *Joseph Andrews* which had brought him home before six.

"But I did," said Alice. "You never are quiet coming or going and so I told him, and he requires you."

With a sigh, Hugh allowed himself to be dragged downstairs, confounded to understand the tangles of seaweed around his ankles. Could this really be the day of their return? And why to Deerhurst Hall, and not the parsonage? At the bottom of the staircase Alice released her grip and skipped forward, but the air of his own reluctance no doubt attended him into the front parlour.

Seating Mrs Bramble on the large sofa, Anne was turned this way and that by the woman's roiling brood. The men were in the middle of the room talking, and James stood before a west-facing window, hat in hand. It was not the hat which first drew Hugh's eye, but rather the impression left by the hat. For there remained a clear, circular imprint atop the boy's head, the golden waves framing his face lending the appearance of a crown in diffused light.

Their eyes met; a hurried approach; a damp palm clasped to Hugh's. "Sir," said Bramble, his reddened eyes attesting to a night of wakefulness.

Directing his gaze past one shoulder Hugh said, "This is a surprise. I am myself only returned from tea with John Newcombe. Do you not proceed to the parsonage?"

A shadow fell over the visitor's face. "Your father was kind enough to send his carriage to the coaching inn in town. Your sister invited us to dine and rest before proceeding home."

Hugh, though feigning sudden recall and pleasure at the news, read his failure from the growing alarm in the boy's expression.

"Take our traveller to see the new mare Hugh," said Sir Frederick. "Nothing revives after a journey like air and exercise."

After a long moment Hugh gave Bramble a nod and led him from the room. In the afternoon sun they walked in silence to the stables; Hugh increasingly uneasy and increasingly aware of the terror beside him. When he recalled the stable hands were just then in the lower kitchen for supper, his anxiety eased considerably. And so, upon passing into the stable he turned to his friend and said: "I am glad you are come."

In an instant the visitor set the hat aside and threw himself against his friend. Pressed together with the violence of his emotion, Bramble breathed wordlessly into Hugh's ear, damp with travel and weeks of expectation, while his host remained rigid, unable to think or move, silent not from a hard nature but from mounting perplexity.

"I've dreamt I must awaken to nothing again," said Bramble, withdrawing to display a face flushed with emotion. "My every terror seemed realised. Just now you gave me to believe I had been cut."

Just words must always be felt; Hugh shook himself from his stupor and made a hasty apology. The new mare was quickly brought forth and, after receiving Hugh's assurance it was alright, the visitor mounted her and commenced a canter about the runs keen to display his skills in the saddle. Once the lively pair were dispatched and at a safe distance he closed his eyes and took a long, uncertain breath.

If the letters could be believed, Salisbury had been indifferent day trips and long, deep sleeps of boredom. Even James's seventeenth birthday had passed with a shrug. Nothing in the letters indicated this extraordinary evolution, for evolution it had been. Bramble had departed a handsome boy, and was returned the pattern of youthful, masculine beauty. His every movement grace, every feature perfection. Had he been lilting or swaggering or childlike it must have been affectation; rather he was all three, and with the refinement of a victorious youth from Antiquity. As he turned at the end of the run, saluting his host with a wildly waving hand, Hugh put his own to his heart, for he felt quite faint.

"Is this envy?" he said. For Hugh would never be such a picture of perfection. Yet he did not hate him; he wished to be near him, to admire and care for him, and never relinquish him.

"Is this sympathy?" he said. Yes, sympathy this must be. What Burke held to be the first of the Passions for Society in General: "We enter into the concerns of others; that we are moved as they are moved and are never suffered to be indifferent spectators of almost anything which men can do or suffer." And Bramble had suffered as much as anyone.

"Then you have my pity," said Hugh as the rider took a low fence, turning Hilda like a partner in a minuet. "Perhaps Nature has recompensed with Beauty that which Fortune stole." Jumping from the horse, Bramble brought Hilda forward to a run until they became a unified flame in the sun. At the end of the run he pulled a sugar cube from his pocket, stroked her mane, then commenced a counsel which, if the horse's expression were anything to judge by, was some of the best sense yet proposed to Equestrian ear.

When Hugh met the eyes of his visitor James nodded and began back; but did he want him back? He rode too well, his handling of the new horse too outstanding. So, when he returned, Hugh followed his first and most basic instinct: he criticised Bramble's riding technique, was, in fact, quite harsh. For some criticism there must be, of something, and Bramble must take it.

When a returning stable hand took charge of Hilda, Bramble relinquished her, curiously unmoved by Hugh's censure, and asked to bathe his face and arms in the stream which crossed the estate. Hugh should have denied him simply for having asked. Instead, without knowing what he did, he nodded and was led forward. As they advanced, they stepped into a copse of trees. Once they were concealed from view Bramble looked about then took Hugh into his arms. His head tilted to the shoulder of his host, naturally, like they had done this all their lives. And in that moment, Hugh's shoulder seemed meant for nothing but to support his friend. They remained in this curious attitude for some time, in silence.

"No, I cannot bear that!" said Hugh at last, drawing away. "Why will you torment me?" Bramble stepped away scratching his head, slack with the sugarplums of riding and happy reunion.

Taking elaborate trouble to straighten his suit, Hugh sneered, "Damn me if I ever saw the like of you! How can you be so happy?"

"Because you acknowledge me."

"Sir, you take liberties," said Hugh coming closer, "great liberties! Remember your place, else you will leave my house!"

It was an easy, decisive blow; his young visitor descended to one knee and dropped his head. "I only wished to repay your interest in me. Allow me to return your hat; it should never have been mine to cherish."

The apology, overwrought though it was, struck Hugh in many dangerous places. It sliced his heart, his lungs, his gut – this beautiful wretch who had nothing. Yet who had everything.

Hugh sniffed, "You might simply have asked pardon. Still, an excess of sentiment should not be faulted." He bid him rise and assured him the hat was his to keep.

"Thank you."

"And I expect next time we quarrel—"

"Never, we never shall."

"Should we cultivate the relationship I require, we must needs quarrel. Gentlemen who are not milk-sops quarrel; it need cause no injury or distress. However, I expect you to adhere to the rules of decorum as I do." After a moment's hesitation, Bramble nodded. Hugh softened his tone – God help him, but those waves terminating in blond curls nearly made him weep! – "You scuff your stockings, brother. Come back to the house and let us see what can be done."

That evening Hugh minded they were always in the presence of others and under no obligation to speak. To Sir Frederick, James praised Hilda in the highest language he knew, but was otherwise silent. As they supped, he grew sullen, then at long last the Brambles departed. Before Anne could step out for an evening walk, Hugh led her to the music room to hear his heated confession. Why had he never told her of their friendship? It was now five weeks of secrecy, five weeks which had driven him into a frenzy the more he worked to conceal it. So here, seated on the window seat, all was made known: the origin of the hat – and with it, a confession to the friendship.

Anne took his hands and offered what could only be called a look of condolence. "It may have been a great mystery to the Brambles, but as soon as you came into the drawing room, I saw you had been secret friends. It was in your manner. I recognised the hat and supposed you must have given it to him."

"There must be five hundred just like it!"

"A woman will always recognise a garment selected for a loved one, be it the most popular cut in England. I was with Matilda when she bought it for you; had she been here tonight I daresay she would have seen it as soon as I did."

Hugh had not himself recalled the origins of that hat, supposing it to have been his own purchase in a careless mood. But however it had come, he was now free to tell of his relationship, which he did now in a great torrent. What should he do now Bramble had returned? Could their friendship be generally known?

"He is the son of our parson and I, for one, am pleased you have befriended him. Why should anyone take issue with the friendship?"

But did it not seem prudent to treat with caution this connection given their differing stations?

"When no such ceremony is required of me with his mother."

"My dear Anne, everybody knows that is charity! She of too many children, who cannot otherwise pay her visits around the parish. James should – well, he should mind his reputation. But honestly, do you think our acquaintance may be known? It would ease things considerably."

"Provided you will exchange the amusement of a secret

for an ordinary friendship. If you believe him your equal as you say, you must own him in full daylight."

"Own him?"

"Yes, own him. Then alone may he bask in all the connection can provide!"

"Anne!" Hugh cried, "this is unforgivable sarcasm from the last place one might expect it!" He could only stare as she rose and walked to the harpsichord, a smile playing on her lips. "And so, I shall receive only ridicule after opening my heart?"

"Is it ridicule to be confused by confusing behaviour?" she said, setting a sheet of music before the instrument. "Unless you believe you can raise him only by lowering yourself, I cannot understand the secrecy."

"It would not debase me to own James Bramble!"

"Then by all means own him. There never was a need for caution."

Looking out the window, humiliated too many times in a day not to indulge a moment of self-pity, Hugh said nothing more. After a time, he realised his sister would refrain from playing until the air was cleared, and he said, "Though you will not, you would like to say more to condemn me. Perhaps I should be condemned and laughed at. I had determined not to rush in, despite the strong feelings of sympathy he awoke in me. I asked myself: how could the most good be accomplished, mindful of what I thought the potential harm, and this motivated everything which followed. I see now I should trust neither the passions of my heart, nor the process of my reason."

Anne turned from the instrument and rose, her eyes upon him as she resumed her place at the window.

"Charity or friendship, that you consider his improvement at all does you honour Hugh." She placed a kiss on his forehead and attended him until he produced a smile. "No genius, only a different perspective is wanted. Which, in a young man of eighteen, cannot be faulted."

His eyes stinging, Hugh nodded. His head had not been right for five weeks; without her words five more may have elapsed in equal torment. He recalled the knock at his door while at Evendown, the cool-headed counsel he had given to the younger students. But they had been, in the main, the problems of children, and his counsel not so very extraordinary. Come next term, that role would be fulfilled by someone else.

"Enough of your misguided brother then," he said. "Who will be the guests for the dinner on Thursday? Does Highborough have the final say?"

"My father chose the guests," said Anne, patting his hand. "He selected an evening when Ned and Alice will be away. We shall have a man from Uncle Barlow's bank, a Mr Willis, and his wife. Mr Jewett as well and his friend Mr Carlton. With her Ladyship we shall be eight."

Hugh waited, but no hint came to acknowledge Jewett as her potential suitor. The man was not handsome or a dazzling wit, but she might be settled just nine miles away on a beautiful estate. Only Anne would feign ignorance and, if pressed, would remind him even her father had criticisms of him. Stephen had been extravagant coming into his inheritance, had taken a trip to the Continent everyone for twenty square miles had heard quite enough of, and had against him perhaps his biggest strike: her Ladyship simply did not like him. How long, complained Matilda, would Frederick coddle the oaf into respectable behaviour? Nevertheless, the dinner on Thursday would be his first invitation to dine at Deerhurst Hall and everyone understood why. Even Anne.

"Stephen rates not even a pause when—?"

"Do ask James Bramble to make a ninth on Thursday," she interrupted, the look in her eyes saying she wished not one word more about suitors. Suitors meant being forced to leave home. Suitors meant change.

"Shall I?"

She nodded. "As her Ladyship is years outside a church, you may 'introduce' her to your friend. She is well-connected, and perhaps can help him on in life. Let this be your first service to him." A moment passed, then she added, "After the hat, of course."

CHAPTER 6

The night of the dinner, brother and sister stood before a mirror judging the effects of their costumes. For him: a coat of trim-cut blue velvet, embellished with gold braiding in the French fashion, his wig tied on the queue with a black silk ribbon to produce a jaunty tail. For her: a gown of pink satin, her dark hair powdered grey and swept back, which exposed a port-coloured birthmark below her left ear.

That Jenny Mapplethorpe, her maid, took no care to cover the mark was owing to Anne's own indifference. "If I am judged by a birthmark so be it – I should like to hear what it says about me." She was far more concerned with the lacing of her stays and preserving her ability to breathe while sitting in an elegant posture. Hugh praised the final effect until she was reconciled to the pain then led her to ground level in growing expectation of what the evening might hold in store.

But from the first the night promised little of enjoyment. This was to be Stephen's moment to distinguish himself, but there were fears an already outspoken man might become overbearing, particularly in his praise of the Continent. When he and his friend arrived, Hugh brought forth Mr Carlton and James Bramble for introduction to her Ladyship; she declared them charming creatures without really looking at them, more intent on whisking Anne aside to fix her hairdressing. Next to arrive was Mr Willis, an associate at the bank managed by Uncle Barlow who was keen only to secure a friendship with Sir Frederick. What his father meant by inviting this man, who was one of the most cantankerous in Newbury, Hugh could not imagine. Joining him was his wife, who was one of those women who makes no effort to converse should no other woman be present, supposing it a show of great decorum. Port was introduced rather early.

By the time they were seated at table, having endured half an hour of Jewett's praise of Spanish climate, Italian history, and French everything else, Mr Willis, a proud Englishman, had mellowed to an explosive, mute crimson. It was his belief that by venomous stares, he might silence the young man while his wife glanced nervously about and, like a housefly, sought to distract him. *This* was why Mrs Willis detested the male sex! If men would only eat and be quiet, a dinner table could be tolerated until the ladies retreated to the drawing-room to converse and trade recipes. Mrs Willis sought solace from continual looks at Anne, who could only look unhappily at Hugh, who could not help any of them.

The general irritation grew as Stephen Jewett, beginning to over-imbibe, condemned as insufficient the appreciation of everything he had seen during his travels, wondering aloud if he should not describe in greater detail the Chateau de Chantilly. Before he could begin, Matilda said:

"One discovers the charms of three remarkably different countries identical in one regard: their complete superiority to our own."

Stephen laughed as men of his temper are quick to do, and said, "You mistake me your Ladyship! I mean no disrespect to England, I assure you. But such is one's perspective after extensive travel. One cannot submit to the rains of

England, you see, with the glow of Spanish sun so lately upon one's skin."

This comment produced a low growl from Mr Willis, which fed Lady Highborough's smirk, on full display during the subsequent awkward silence. Then commenced a full minute in which Jewett worked to clear his throat, blaming the port, though so very fine, for a sudden insurgence of phlegm. At last he straightened in his seat and turned grandly to Anne. Bramble, who was looking steadily at his hands, received a kick in the shin from Hugh, that he might regard an entertainment not often enjoyed at table.

"I ask you Miss Anne," said Jewett, "does not this appear plausible?"

"I beg your pardon?"

"As regards the Spanish sun?"

Not quite meeting his gaze Anne said, "Pray excuse from such a question one who lacks the qualification to respond."

"In what manner," said Jewett, "can such a lovely, accomplished young woman ever lack qualification? Let not the lack of exposure to international wonders suppress an admission that they may indeed *be* wonders!"

"Sir, you mistake my meaning," she said, lifting her gaze. "By qualification, I mean only the place in a conversation in which I have no interest."

The tipsy man put a hand to his breast and heaved. "*Mon Dieu*, your answer affects me more than I can say. The complement of my esteem *must*, my nymph, supply the interest you lack – *enlighten* me, nay, take the part of her Ladyship and *contradict* me, so I may understand my error. Only leave not unsaid that which resides in your heart!"

"Sir," said Anne, becoming heated, "the interest I want cannot be supplied by supplication. Do excuse me."

Anne glanced at Lady Highborough, who shrugged. "The sun appears to have set in Spain," she said, and from this point controlled the table. Soon the din of many independent conversations rose like little pies, with her Ladyship's fingers in most of them. Jewett glared into his port while the eyes of the uneasy Mr Carlton darted like two tennis balls never at rest. The air of unease elevated as her Ladyship's continual references to the English court, the English countryside, and English gardening seemed fashioned to sting Jewett in each pointed instance. When at last she ventured across the channel to praise the gardens of Versailles, Stephen could bear it no longer.

"I, too, have had occasion to visit the grounds at Versailles," he said, "but believed I had best confine myself to praising Ranelagh or Vauxhall or some other domestic wonder."

"A similar caution might be given to Mr John Wilkes," said Highborough, "who would rather invade England from France than return a loyal subject."

By dessert and the arrival of more port, Mr Jewett's mutterings to Mr Carlton had increased in volume. After the ladies took their sweet wine into the drawing-room he declared his *regard for Anne could no longer remain a secret! Anne's like was to be met with nowhere else – not in Italy, France, or Spain, and he was well qualified to say it! Mr Jewett*, he declared of himself, *cared not at all for the earlier impertinence at table, with all due respect to an ageing lady, except in how it had affected sweet Anne!* This was said loudly to Mr Carlton so that the table might hear, and even James gaped at this spectacularly ill-advised swing at her Ladyship. Mr Carlton attempted to remove the port from the reach of his friend; but, seeing the manoeuvre, Jewett snatched the goblet to his breast and asked if Carlton was in his right mind. And through it all Sir Frederick looked placidly on, attempting no defence of Matilda, or intervening when Stephen bid the footman discreetly forward to request just a small measure more of that excellent port.

Then Hugh understood. Frederick's silence, the early availability of port, the insistence upon hostile presences like

Highborough and Mr Willis – the entire dinner had been a noose. His father had waited long enough for Jewett to make a better showing for himself; a trial by fire must decide the thing. And Stephen, though ridiculous, admired Anne, which must be of the first merit, and had money and a sprawling estate, which ran a close second. Hugh experienced a jolt of sympathy for him. Once it was clear Mr Willis too had cottoned on, made clear by a smile which showcased every one of his bad teeth, Hugh stood from the table, unable to take any more of this slow lynching. He asked pardon and hauled Bramble from the room as Stephen, with his port suspended, toasted the *divine red kiss placed by Cupid upon Anne's maiden neck!*

The young men proceeded into the drawing-room where Mrs Willis was just then praising the plum tart. Her words died as Hugh came forward to kiss his sister. Then he turned with great ceremony to Lady Highborough, who set aside a glass which had been refilled too many times to count and rose to her feet. Bowing deeply, his eyes locking with hers, Hugh brought her hand to his lips then said, "Should I ever merit such a hand, I must be the happiest man upon Earth."

"And pray what motivates this high praise? I declare your words rejuvenate a lady to a girl of eighteen."

"That you might be mistaken for one any sighted man could attest to," crooned Hugh. "My praise, however, comprehends not just beauty, but this wonderful mixture of wit and elegance Milton himself had been at pains to convey."

"Aye?" said her Ladyship to Mrs Willis, who looked away; "Aye?" with a meaningful stare at Anne, who appeared fatigued. "I foresee great things for our nation should Hugh be a fair representation of his generation. Let all vulgar men sink from profligacy as Mr Polo in there sank tonight." With a return to Anne: "Even your father must relinquish his pet tonight. And now," withdrawing her hand from Hugh's, "I crave introduction to your little friend. I declare he seems a pretty fellow, relegated to a corner with such a boar in the dining room and himself such a mouse." Bellowing: "And you saw, nameless young man, what becomes of rodents in this house, when feline passions are aroused? Come ye hither!"

Bramble advanced. "An honour milady."

With a finger, Lady Highborough tilted his head to the candlelight and turned to Hugh. "Whence came this individual?"

"Firstborn son of the parson at St. Timothy's, of his first marriage. James Bramble."

"Bramble? I know thee now, of course, Master Bramble, and thy parentage, though so altered from under tables and chairs I should never have known thee." Her hand rose, the glittering rings catching the candlelight as she tapped his mouth with her fingertips. "Upon my soul, what beauty is he? These full, red lips. This strong, yet delicately supple neck. Were they possessed of a girl, she must fall under lock and key until her wedding night. But on a youth…" She reached for another sip of wine and perused him top to toe. "I do tonight discover what impels man to ravish the fair maid."

Mrs Willis let out a wail of despair as Anne hurried forward to beg the release of the young man.

"He is a budding poet," said Hugh. "My particular *ingenue*. You will recall the day you knew him before he was known to the nation."

At last overcome by the absurdity of the evening, Bramble let out a laugh of confusion, though so twisted by discomfort it took on a quality of triumph.

"I shall relinquish thee James, now I have madest thou smile," said Matilda, "and am well pleased to find thee instantly beyond that hesitation which only ever savours of inferiority. Make use of the honour paid thee young man. Hugh does well to adopt thee. Obey him in all things. And now," tilting the last of her wine from view and turning to Hugh, "as I seem to have discovered latent masculinity within

67

myself, I shall proceed to the men for sherry. Take my arm, child, and lead me."

But this was not to be, for just then a scuffle sounded, and a moment later Jewett was being hurried past the drawing-room door. The passionate man began shouting to see *Miss Anne!* demanding to make himself understood only to *Miss Anne!* Then, howling, he was carried from the house as the object of affection rushed upstairs in a flood of tears, a hand-kerchief to her mouth. Hugh grabbed James and hurried them out of the house and past a group of domestics attempting to hoist Stephen into the Entwistle carriage.

In the dark of a crescent moon the two raced across the property to the stream. There they splashed and threw stones and retold tales of the wretched dinner party, happy to be outside, happy to be together, bound closer by a ridiculous evening. They remained at their riparian retreat until the dust appeared to have settled at the house. Then they proceeded up the stairs to Hugh's apartments.

Morning light. The scent of dew on summer grass arrived by an open window. And there, within the partially drawn bed curtain, Bramble lay in Hugh's arms. Blood pulsing into his neck, Hugh came fully awake, his heart beating like a fury inside his head. He had not a solitary memory of what had brought them to this close attitude – they had collapsed after their swim on either side of the bed and gone to sleep. That was all, he was certain of it. He attempted several times to extricate himself discreetly, soon discovering his arm was hopelessly trapped beneath the dead weight of his friend. At last he gave it up as fruitless and left his arm where it was.

Then the words of Highborough returned to him.

The lips.

The neck.

The supple skin.

Lovely by the light of a candle – but *this* was the unbearable light of morning! Hugh stroked the hair, which rolled in glorious soft waves. He kissed the forehead, sweet where it had rested during the night. He considered the lips; lips which had been ravished were they... And then, growing quite weak, he fell forward and allowed his mouth to press where it would – to his lips, his jaw, his cheek, and temple. He must not, indeed he must not. And yet he already had. And James, perhaps feigning sleep longer than was strictly honest, at last opened his eyes.

Rising up in panic, desperate to explain himself though his heart was pummelling the breath from him, Hugh said: "Christ, why do I tumble you?"

Bramble, however, appeared undisturbed. "It's well for some folks to act without asking why."

"Some folks will say 'yes' without knowing what I mean to do."

"But I do know and have done for some time."

Dare he believe his ears? His eyes felt to be filling with stars...

Continued Bramble: "Some folks will not take what has been ten times offered."

"Some folks do not wish it and offer only to oblige."

"Some folks *will* oblige if only they are *asked*." Bramble's voice had risen, and he jabbed his finger into Hugh's side. Then he said, more thoughtfully, "Some folks wish it as much as other folks."

Bramble slipped a hand behind his head and waited for whatever came next. Hugh, however, did not *know* what came next. So, after a moment considering, he buried his face into the warm, golden mound of James's armpit. *Here* lay the answer to all society's injustices! They were all right here – one need only search in naked bed! Here were no divisions, only unifications. Ten thousand old, strange images assaulted Hugh – idle wonderings, passing thoughts, a close encounter from years before. Only now he was presented with a young man willing to submit he could not act. How could he consider a mouth sentient and expecting? A cheek waiting to be caressed? Oh, for the quick relief of a well-delivered blow! But where fists dealt fluently, open palms lacked the most rudimentary vocabulary. And Bramble, fully expecting to be led, remained ungainly as a new-born foal. Some time passed in false beginnings and timid touches, and then a noise sounded from without the bedchamber door as footsteps neared.

The bedcurtain purchased a moment – James withdrew to face the wall smooth as a cat. Hugh, however, still seized in the grip of aching and indecision, met the valet's gaze in the character of a knotted-up root. Their eyes met for a long moment, then Jasper Sharp opened the room, stepping nimbly about two suits of clothing, wigs, small clothes, candle stubs, open books, and the other accoutrements of a young man's apartment. Polishing the buckle of a pair of shoes he came forward; pulling the bedclothes to his neck, Hugh announced that they were not ready and would rise later.

"And have me catch it from yer father so ye may be slothful?" said Jasper. "I'm not to leave ye lie about later than eight, that's the rule. Now rise, that I may get ye in morning dress and give ye a shave. Aye, and James too."

"I trust you to keep a confidence, Jasper," said Hugh, "So here it is: We broke into my father's port before it was put away last night and indulged. We are not well."

"Am I to believe," said the reedy man, knuckle twisting into his side like he was looking for the hilt of a sword, "yer father, the greatest miser of wine, for one moment lost track of his port while it was out? By all accounts, there were only two drunks last night, and they were not the two of you. So, forget tall tales – I saw the kitchen log myself before I come up, approved by his own hand."

"How came you to worry yourself over the kitchen logs?"

"That log is out in the servant's mess morning after a

dinner party. Samuel regales the staff with all the vulgar practices of his betters, describing in detail the distribution of food and drink what incited it. And very amusing his tales of last night – a love-struck spendthrift ejected from the house after insulting a stupefied lady. But never ye mind, for Sloth be the Devil's workshop. Rise up, and yer friend into the bargain for he wakes now, *I see it!*"

With this he took hold of the bedclothes and yanked. Depositing all into a heap, he placed Hugh's shoes beside the heap and laid two dressing gowns at the foot of the bed. Then, grabbing hold of Hugh's wrist, he brought him to his feet. Breathless, his eyes large, Hugh shrank back as Jasper, after a quick inspection, sighed in disgust.

"And if that's all prevents ye, have I not seen it a hundred times since before Master himself knew what it was for?"

CHAPTER 7

Save the turning pages of *The Briton*, breakfast was a silent affair. The younger children had returned from a night with friends and Alice, always a close observer, immediately perceived something amiss. Her eye knew not where to alight: On Anne, pale and listless, and showing all the disappointment of a failed dinner party. Or on a guest she had thought very pretty – only now, mumbling and staring at his plate, the parson's son appeared a little deranged. Her eldest brother, though pale, appeared her best bet, and so in a loud whisper she asked to know what had happened. Hugh directed her to the footman.

Shortly thereafter Bramble rose from the table, thanked Sir Frederick for his hospitality and bid Hugh farewell until Sunday. Their eyes met once, then he was upon the green running towards the lane. Hugh glanced at his father, who could be supernatural in his ability to know things he should not, but any glances from his newspaper were reserved for his sullen daughter. A few minutes later Hugh was outside walking towards the granary, pounding across the open field and chastising James to the open air.

"I believed you had matured and so trusted you! But there

was always something underhanded in you – looking under coaches and cabinets and pews, discovering everyone's secrets. Then this morning, contriving to get into my arms, tempting me to what might, with the force of a lion, have overtaken me entirely! Now I am wretched thinking of you – who would have me cherish you and make you my pet!"

Such were his wailings, twenty minutes at least, as Hugh wandered the open field to the east of the house. His indiscretions while at school were hardly comparable to the physical and emotional union he now desired with James Bramble. Hasty fumblings with a companion in a clothes cabinet were but exercises in manual dexterity – the cracking of knuckles.

How had he not known?

And yet... he *had* known. Known from his days at Mr Harvey's.

Dear Bramble,

As I was indisposed Sunday, it has been nearly a week since your note of thanks for the dinner in my home, which you understand did not itself require a response. I know I am remiss in communicating but trust it has caused no pain. As regards your postscript, yes, I recall our plans for your improvement. We will discuss it all. Call on me tomorrow morning about eleven or send a note to inform me of prior engagements and another time will be selected.

Yours, HE

PS: I found your pocket watch not far from the stream. You may collect it tomorrow.

Next day at half eleven James Bramble arrived red as a Spring strawberry. After following his host upstairs, he received the pocket watch with such distraction that, for the pacing about and passions which were to follow, he set it down and forgot it once more. Upon Hugh's bedchamber door being closed, the visitor was in his arms, shaking them with emotion so violent Hugh was thrust against the wall. Then Bramble dropped to his knees and took Hugh's hand, kissing it until the limb was tugged back and the visitor again brought to his feet.

Covering his face with his hands Bramble sobbed, "Tell me what I have done! Anything is better than not knowing!" then dissolved into such piteous groans he lost his way, stumbling over a pair of boots, which he kicked out of his way. When the guest turned to meet his gaze, eyes brimming, Hugh felt a great churning in his breast. But he quickly aligned his troops and retreated his roiling regiment into a far corner.

"I've brought you to a path you are too good to know," said Bramble, wiping his eyes, "you despise me as the Devil. I *am* the Devil. No wretch has yet been as confused as I am, who only wishes—"

"Speak no more of it!" Hugh hissed. "I feel more shame than you can possibly understand! I know what I have promised, and the pain I inflict by cold silence! I..." He broke off. Then he sprinted to the door and smashed his foot beside the crystal knob, yanking it forward as a girl in a yellow dress fell upon the floor. Pulling her into the room he slammed the door.

"I shall scream if you hold me in this horrible dungeon against my will!" shrieked Alice. "Is this what boys will be about? Speaking in riddles, wailing like beasts in the yard, and altogether more confounding that ever I thought they could be! What, pray, *can* you be speaking of?"

Bramble had gone deathly pale, but as Alice scrambled to her feet Hugh took a deep breath and caught his friend's eye.

"Well James, we are discovered. I told you my sister's

sharper than a foxhound. There is no choice but to plead for compassion. Now Alice," he continued with his tenderest fraternal tone, "what you heard cannot be helped, and I do not begrudge you your curiosity. I myself was always curious. But you must understand James is shy of his love attachment, as many men are. We speak in riddles to preserve honour."

"Love attachment?"

Hugh nodded. "The rules declare that I may not, lest I offend his honour, make clear reference to his love unless granted permission. If I slip and say her name, he will be obliged to *call me out.*" He paused, then lowered his voice, "Must I explain further?"

Alice straightened her dress and smiled. "Other young ladies may not understand, you cannot imagine how stupid they can be, but I understand quite well. You speak of a duel. If honour is offended, your friend could demand satisfaction of you, and this requires your both choosing Seconds to pass the pistols, and each dueller firing upon the other till he is dead!"

Hugh slapped his forehead: "I had not thought it possible! She understands our encoded vocabulary. No doubt through the keyhole she observed your hand signal to me, just this moment, communicating I might refer by name to the Secret Lady with no risk to my life. Oh, would it were not so – all the secrets of brotherhood discovered!"

Looking brighter than ever she appeared in a new bonnet, Alice said, "Indeed I observed the hand signal, and inferred the likely meaning."

"Damn me for a villain!" cried Hugh turning to his friend. "James, I beg pardon my carelessness in choosing a room so ill-equipped to your clandestine affairs. Have I your forgiveness?"

Without too much hesitation, Bramble said, "I hereby grant forgiveness, as thou art my particular friend. I shall demand no satisfaction."

"And now we must," said Hugh, spinning upon his heel, "sayeth the solemn rules, continue the conversation at a Point of Secondary Rendezvous, which may not be out of doors. Do, Alice, leave us to it. I can say no more."

The back parlour, a location particularly suited to eavesdroppers, was selected as the Point of Secondary Rendezvous. There the young men proceeded, and a performance was given. Then the players awaited their reviews.

Fifteen minutes later, upon finding her Ladyship alone in the drawing room, Alice announced, "I have a secret to confide." Continuing to the window she said wistfully, "A secret such as will distract your Ladyship from that dinner party I am never to ask about."

Seated on a sofa across the room, Matilda said, "Never mention that night to me, child. But what is this of secrets? Is it a very diverting secret?"

"To be sure it is. More diverting than anybody could conceive. A secret which pertains to the parson's son, though his own parents do not know it."

Around the corner in the darkened dining room, Hugh grinned and poked Bramble in the arm.

"Child, get away from that window and attend me. Now what do you mean?"

"A Secret Friendship, a Secret Hat, and a Secret Love in Salisbury. James Bramble is in love with his cousin Sarah Ward! And do you know, Sarah is not unlike myself? A compliment I took to mean quite a lot, as I was not strictly meant to hear it. Hugh told him girls admire a man of fashion, and James having no hat, Hugh lent him one of his own. And do you know, I noticed him hold that hat the day they returned, and supposed it to be Hugh's, even though Moses said nobody knew where it had come from and swore it had dropped like Manna from Heaven! Is this not diverting!?"

"Upon my soul girl, where was I during these intrigues?"

"Do not feel bad, for even I did not perceive it at first.

When Hugh saw how much his friend liked the hat, he bestowed it as a gift. I declare, Hugh is a fine fellow, though he would please nobody to discover it. Well, Miss Sarah simply adored the texture of the hat, which they call a cocked hat, the pretty ones with three corners. And so now, like an Irish Charm, it has succeeded only too well! She is *crazy* for James, and he wants to marry her! So, Hugh said he must ask permission to begin writing to the family. And I hear tell the Wards are vastly wealthy, and would not that help the Brambles, who have not a pot to peel a turnip in?"

Hugh turned to James, who was at pains to stifle a laugh, and his heart surged with tenderness for him. Wretched just an hour before, now aglow with merriment, Hugh pushed the hand from his mouth, and with only a small tremor in his stomach, kissed him as tenderly as he could. At that moment Alice shrieked that she should like to be adored by a such pretty young man! and Lady Highborough chided her, and Hugh, after withdrawing, raised his eyebrows. To which he was given to understand another attempt was required.

So again, Hugh pressed them together, taking the fevered scent of the other into his nostrils, and the salt from his lips. And in the darkened room, though Hugh could not well see him, he felt the smile spreading across his friend's lips.

Hugh closed his eyes. His knees weakened, yet with an inhale he stood taller than he ever had.

They had passed the point of return.

And so, he motioned them out a side entrance, and away.

CHAPTER 8

For some years, purchasing a controlling share of the burgage tenements of Deerhurst had been Sir Frederick's greatest ambition, as ownership of the key homes in the borough meant ownership of votes in local and Parliamentary elections. As every vote was a matter of public record, any vote contrary to the owner's wish might well herald eviction for the man who had cast it. After a decade of borrowing and manoeuvring, Frederick had secured these properties and furnished them with an agreeable block of voters. Then, in the general election of March 1768, he had seen elected Mr Hill, his candidate for the borough, and with it his position of importance, both within Deerhurst and nationally, rose considerably.

Yet the achievement was tempered when he relinquished an ambition almost as dear to him – the union of Anne to one of the wealthiest men in West Berkshire, Stephen Jewett. Three weeks had passed since the fateful dinner party, and he had begun to question his decision to dismiss the silly man. The matter remained on his mind on an overcast day in July when a messenger came into the vestibule and handed him a note.

Anne was preparing for a walk around the grounds with Margery Clarke, a close friend, who observed Sir Frederick's glance at his daughter before retiring to his study. Margery seized her friend's arm, certain this was a defiant letter from Stephen proclaiming undying affection. Once they were in the garden, she assured Anne many such notes had been covertly delivered in *Miss Betsy Thoughtless*, a novel which everyone knew to be the very mirror of life. No doubt Stephen's undying passion would be made known at the evening meal.

Unfortunately for Miss Clarke, the conversation at table was only familiar goings-on and gossip – the parish exciseman accused of stealing and plans for the August horseraces on Enbourne Heath. After Margery's departure the house received its only hint: a Gentleman would call before noon the following day and the two elder children were to dress and remain upstairs should their presence be required.

Next morning at eleven a man something over fifty, something over six feet and something over twenty stone stepped from a carriage into the Hall. This was all that could be discerned from a first-floor window crowded with faces which fogged the panes. Fifteen minutes later the footman arrived to fetch down the two eldest children. They descended arm in arm in complimentary silks and continued into the drawing-room, a room which tended to seriousness with its elaborate woollen tapestries and scheme of darkening browns.

The smile of the visitor, however, immediately warmed their reception, his oversized figure commensurate with a presence which filled any room in which he resided. Hugh realised they had met this man some six weeks before, and as recognition showed on their faces, the visitor's full cheeks ripened like Flowers of Kent as he came forward to greet them. As the group settled on sofas, their father said, "Our guest honours us with a visit while on business in the area. I understand you were introduced at Mrs Benning's assembly in May."

"Mr Charles Sallow, International Trader in Boston who now resides in London," said Hugh. "Our conversation was a high point in a memorable evening."

When Anne merely inclined her head, Mr Sallow said in a hearty bass, "A memorable evening with the good people of this country, Frederick, I'm sorry you couldn't be there. All is life and vivacity at a country dance. And the young ladies! They are wise men who understand partners of such calibre are not to be found at every gathering. Your son, as I recall, snatched any who were more than two minutes at rest. Even an old dog like me was entertained beyond every expectation in that revelry of uncommonly wholesome, and to my eye uncommonly lovely, young women. Each one a gem." This last he enunciated with a jeweller's precision.

From Frederick's decidedly formal nod Hugh understood a name had been dropped and this stranger had simply invited himself. Yet in his father's deferential manner and glances at Anne, Hugh saw hope so great he dared not acknowledge it, not with a sidelong look at his son, not even, it seemed, to himself. "I shall make it a point to attend Mrs Benning's next," he said. Then turning to his children, "But I should like very much to be introduced now and you are both qualified to do it. Anne?"

Her face betrayed a moment's discomfort, but once she had begun, she gained confidence. "Mr Sallow is a native of Wiltshire. Management of the family malt distillery was given to his brother when he became an agent in West India for an international trader. From there he proceeded to Merchants' Row in Boston, where he resided for twenty-six years. There he organised the importing of sea coal and Madera wine, and was praised by the Chancellor of the Exchequer for settling a trade dispute with Indian tribes which may well have turned violent. As the leader of an influential group of tradesmen he was a key negotiator in repealing the Stamp Act. He has two sons, Benjamin and Duncan, one of whom wishes to enter politics. Since his family's return to England, his proudest moment has been attending a dinner with Horace Walpole."

One correction to this history came in Charles's somewhat garbled French, and when he urged her to continue in that language, Hugh began to pale. However, Anne, put entirely at ease by the man's manner and by his request that Hugh join them, appeared to think of nothing beyond continuing the recital in French, in which language she was particularly adept. She described the man's impressions of England upon returning nine months before, his home in The City and his preference for Ranelagh as a pleasure garden. As she spoke her hands led the man's eyes as she flourished her descriptions and smoothed her gown. Frederick's eyes remained fixed on his visitor who, though presumably here on account of one of his sons, looked set to marry her himself.

"Miss Anne! You have given me more pleasure, more absolute pleasure, than you can imagine! That you should have French and dancing and music (I do expect you are a musician as well!) must delight, though these days cannot much surprise. What is not taught, by which I mean taught successfully, is this extraordinary ability to listen, which you practice quite by inclination." Continuing to her father: "The accuracy is astonishing! That your daughter should ever again meet a Mr Sallow from Wiltshire was highly in doubt. Her kindness in attending me, I see now truly attending, warms me to the tips of my extremities."

At this Anne did at last begin to pale, as one might upon discovering one has been auditioning without knowing it.

Said Charles: "I see from your countenance that my meaning in coming here is known. In trade, Miss Anne, to be truly great one must have that thing which cannot be taught: instinct. It is no witchcraft, no miracle, but a spontaneous decision made after extensive exposure. You may count yourself among those rare treasures which bring me particular joy to discover. My sons are, in a very real sense, my shareholders. Does my frankness distress you?"

"Pray continue Sir. I feel no distress."

"I am perhaps new money to some," he continued, with a nod at Sir Frederick, "I do not care if I am. My pedigree of hard-working, honest people is yours to inquire into. We Sallows are men of passion. Duncan's passion is service to his country; he was made Brigadier General fighting the French in Canada, and in his wish to continue into politics he will continue to serve. He is of my height, of a better figure and a handsomer aspect, though a vested interest," he chuckled, "must always be partial. Nevertheless, my own success, reputation and connections give a fair idea of his prospects."

Anne had now gone ashen, Hugh short of breath and Sir Frederick quite still. "You will sup with us, of course," he managed.

"I shall return to London this afternoon. I can spare an hour, Sir, no more."

"Let us speak in my study then," said his host, standing, his face a blend of disbelief, avarice, and impatience.

Anne started up from her seat.

"I ask you to meet my son – nothing more," said Charles. "But no matter my wishes, and no matter the wishes of your father, I request a note in *your* hand, informing me of your decision once you have had time to consider. Take ten days. Duncan resides in London; no doubt he leads a very different life to yours here in the country. You cannot make him happy if you are not happy yourself. If you come to the city to meet him, come because you believe you should; come at the behest of another and I shall know it immediately."

Anne said what was appropriate and gave a hesitant curtsy.

Then Charles Sallow turned to his host and asked to be led into the study.

CHAPTER 9

"A pipe!" exclaimed Matilda entering the back parlour, where Hugh sat rewriting a new poem. As he exhaled smoke, adjusting the porcelain pipe in his mouth, Highborough snatched his poem and read it through. The poem was meant for Bramble, whose family were arriving shortly for supper and, though only the work of an hour, Hugh felt vulnerable where his words were concerned.

"A trifle," he said. "We've a challenge, James and I, to compose a poem under a common theme – that of courage."

"Courage?" said her Ladyship, looking it over again. "Oh yes, yes I see that. Very pretty. But do, child, pull that pipe from your mouth. I wish to speak of Anne."

"I am permitted to smoke in the back parlour."

"Oh, why must you suck the horrid thing? When did this start?"

Hugh set the pipe aside and directed her back to his sister. The news of the proposal, said her Ladyship, was spreading quickly. What was she to tell people? Why would not Anne tell her what she meant to do?

"Anne does not tell you because she has not decided."

"Oh, she will agree to meet this Duncan Sallow – and his

83

father Mr Charles Sallow of Boston – be still my heart! I have initiated a correspondence with him. No doubt, once she accepts, he will bid her to an interview in his home, but no, I insist they come to us at your father's in Westminster. It will be no trouble to rouse the place early from its summer slumber, but I must know in time to notify the city servants."

"Do allow her time to decide – and let me finish my poem."

But soon enough it was not just Matilda, but Uncle Barlow who had entered the room, telling that the Brambles had just arrived and asking why he had not been invited to sup? And why must he hear news of a proposal made to his niece on the High Street, for now he was obliged to come personally to confirm it and stay to supper unannounced.

The Bramble children soon enlivened the house and were, at least, a welcome diversion for Anne, who appeared aggrieved under the weight of her decision. Lady Highborough shouted at Hugh again to stop his puffing – she seized the pipe, but not before Hugh exhaled a thick cloud of smoke before the guests. This produced a grin from James, who stood in a dark green frock coat and a new lace jabot recently purchased by his friend. They had been three days separated while he helped his father work the glebe lands, and their reunion tonight was highly anticipated.

"I must fetch a change of shoes," said Hugh, which James took as an invitation to follow him up. But he stopped him, saying he would not be a minute, then slipped the poem into his hand. The boy's cheeks blazed with excitement and Hugh, after a moment to enjoy the delicious sight of him, chewed his lip and turned up the stairs.

"I shall join you," said Barlow, and followed his nephew to his apartment. "What are those for?" he said, looking at the pair of shoes, rather the worse for wear, Hugh intended to take downstairs.

"James and I are visiting the stables after supper. He's not seen Green Pea in three days – what, didn't you know? He is riding her in the races on Enbourne Heath, 31st of August."

"No, I did not know! Neither had I heard of Anne's engagement. Your father is a total and complete lout."

"Mr Sallow's visit was just yesterday, and there is no engagement yet. Pray do not speak of it tonight, Anne wishes time to think it through."

When they returned downstairs Hugh searched out Bramble. His pulse quickened as his visitor touched the folded paper to his breast, flushing with pleasure. Hugh had been promising a poem for some time, and, while not exactly an ode to love, he hoped to convey something of his newfound understanding of passion...

Awake! 'pon heady Seas a-swell
Leviathan bestirs below!
Toss'd Sailors trim the Sails to quell
The brutish Draw of the Undertow!

Yet Heroes toward the Wind's Eye turn
Weigh Anchor, sail, pursue the Whale!
Tack toward the Storm and shirk Concern
Sublime their Fears into the Gale!

What of the Damage to the Rigging?
Of what Concern a splintered Mast?
A Hero's Pride scorns all reneging
His Ship has sail'd, the Die is cast!

During the meal, nobody appeared to notice the unusual silences of Masters Entwistle and Bramble. After three days apart, and with a race forthcoming, one would have thought there was something to say. But then who could speak over the high-spirited younger Brambles so dominant at table? Moses was such an incorrigible jokester. And who could help but monitor Anne? The proposal was the open secret everyone knew of but must not mention. She looked so very torn and tormented, and her father so eager for her to accept. Parson Bramble noticed the young men swapping significant looks and supposed it was somehow in reference to her. At one point, Hugh emptied his port in one go, smirking rather impertinently, and James appeared to catch the smirk with a twitch of his mouth.

After supper they exited into the twilight. When Hugh began on the path towards the stables Bramble halted him, motioning them another way. "Forest is yonder," he said.

Hugh peered around. "Egad, thou perceivest excellently in the half-light. So it is! Fear not, we shall turn back to the house and soon to safety."

"It's three days," muttered Bramble, "and we planned it."

"Yes, I know, but I had believed you worrying yourself about Green Pea. Fie! Thou art a liquorice lad!"

"Call me lustful if you like; you wished it twice a day last week. You're good for six now by my reckoning."

Hugh fixed his eyes forward and continued towards the stables. "You want decorum, James. We have just dined upon delicate shin of beef, with forks and fingerbowls. Are we to have commerce out here like beasts in the field?"

"Here, or in the forest, makes no difference."

"Aye, thou art an obliging pup. And yet—"

"Leave off that damned blathering!" shouted Bramble and cut their progress. "No more words!" Hugh paused and met his eyes, only just possible in the approaching darkness. This show of spirit was quite to his taste, and when Bramble looked down Hugh took his jaw and held it. "Give us a buss," said James, but this was not to be. Leaning away to avoid the kiss, Hugh came in from the side, grinning.

"Get in those trees," he whispered, "We shall have our commerce."

Were the Chancellor of the Exchequer present to judge,

Entwistle and Bramble, too, may have merited praise for extraordinary negotiations. Hugh collapsed on Bramble's heaving chest, breathless with delirium and a job well done. Around them the summer evening glimmered to life. The stream lapped at the bank like a spaniel, the birds in their nests settled with soft cooings.

Then came the misgivings. All could not be doves and sugarplums indefinitely. For Hugh the Sailor, tossed by the stirrings of Leviathan though he often was, must once more step to solid ground. This behaviour was indeed quite dangerous, and should they ever be discovered – it was a capital offense, the penalty...

Yet the penalty could not be allowed to matter. For as they lay on the bank, Bramble's heart beat like a little rabbit – with his ear to the place Hugh heard John Wilkes, heard the pipe and tabor. Heard rebellion. For James hated the injustice of his lot, and the angrier he became, the more explosive became the vanquishing of him. He saw a world full of betrayers and hypocrites, taking fortunes, and life choices, from him. The church was to be his future, yet what was it but the place sinners went to feel good once a week? Hugh certainly had no interest in contradicting this view – the guilt Bramble carried from that institution had nearly ruined their first frolic. After they were done, Bramble had turned to him and asked if it was all right.

"*All right?*" Hugh sneered. He was, after all, still trembling with pride at his wickedness, ready to scorn any insinuation the encounter had not been perfect. *All right?* Hugh was not Isaiah Dawson going too far with Mrs Benning's daughter! But then he understood – the bold face who had offered himself for such sport was also the son of a parson. The boy was, suddenly, in fear for his soul.

Hugh sighed. "It's common practice in London, as I said before." After a moment's consideration, he added, "That is to say, not uncommon. Be discrete for love of God and country but forget holy books and sermons and all that. We're just having a bit of fun." But Bramble had remained silent, continuing to observe his companion, apparently wishing to hear something more. "You did ask for it," said Hugh, "and liked it well enough by all accounts."

Still he refused to speak. Then Bramble rolled from the bed of hay, and, pulling on his clothes, made to descend from the secluded loft Hugh had chosen as their trysting place. Suddenly fearing he might be denied future privileges, Hugh jumped up and grabbed his shoulder. "Think of it as being made a favourite," he said. "You know, a favourite? There's another way to look at it."

"A favourite?"

"Like James I and Buckingham. Every king has his favourite."

It was perhaps a mark of both their inexperience, *Constant Reader*, that neither laughed at this pronouncement. Rather, Hugh believed he had gone unusually far making his feelings known. Bramble, for his part, appeared not only pleased but keenly interested.

"King James, really?"

Hugh nodded. "Good King James was a first, a sixth, and a lover of the Duke's shapely legs. It's an open secret, upon my honour. Everyone at Evendown knew it." This, he saw immediately, was a stroke of genius; Bramble cursed, with no little colour, the hypocrisy of the church. Hugh fell back into the hay and, grinning, stuck a bit in his mouth.

"There you are – think of that next time your father opens his King James Bible."

All true. But since then, Hugh had begun to sense his friend expected him to bring him to London in September. Where else could all this be leading? So tonight, to avoid all unpleasant topics, Hugh feigned a little doze on Bramble's chest. His breath grew deep and intense. As he snored, Hugh observed Bramble's arm rise up as though to encircle him, perhaps hold him. Then the arm paused – hovered in mid-air – retreated. At last, rather in defeat, the arm fell to the ground.

"Hugh."

The word hung on the night air. Was it a question? An accusation? Whatever it was Hugh refused to touch it or claim it as his own. For a moment he even cowered from it, like it was an apparition. Then after a time, it, too, fell away and disbursed into the sounds of approaching nightfall.

At last Hugh stirred, jumped to his feet, and yanked them forward to the water's edge. Feet sliding, hands gripping, the struggle to push the other forward forced both into the stream. Running out at the far bank where stood a grassy hillock in a shaft of moonlight, Hugh halted, panting. He looked about, drew in a deep breath, and spoke aloud a favourite line from *The Iliad:*

"As when a wretch who, conscious of his crime,
Pursued for murder from his native clime,
Just gains some frontier, breathless, pale, amazed;
All gaze, all wonder!"

As Hugh strode up and down, quoting whatever of Greek thought he hoped to apply to himself, Bramble wandered the opposing bank and observed him. He stared up at the moon and dressed in its light. Then he sat on a rock and wrapped his arms around his knees, watching until his friend, at last tiring of his solitary diversions, stepped into the stream to return to him.

As the new month dawned, the air grew rich with spiced cake and ginger wine. The August sun brought women into the lanes and yards, wiping hands on their aprons as they spoke of plans for the annual dedication feast at the old church in Newbury. The progress of home brews was assessed, lids cracked, and samples taken. For the inhabitants of Newbury and the surrounding parishes, the third week in August was the focal point of summer, followed a week later by the horseraces on Enbourne Heath. Prominent members of the church met at assemblies to organise food and entertainment, and the wives of feuding parishioners sought to mend grievances before their husbands met at the events. Mrs Bramble gave Anne her recipe for raisin cake and told of a reconciliation between the exciseman and the old sporting farmer in town, who, for five months, had accused that worthy official of stealing. Anne relayed this to Margery as they checked the progress of the Clarke's wine, a full five months under fermentation. Along with cake, the wine would be set out for guests the week of the feast and was considered among the best in the county.

Margery, however, had little time for wine or farmers.

"Oh Anne, do let's speak of Duncan. Must I remind you of the tortures Miss Betsy Thoughtless endured after refusing to take the issue of marriage to heart? You think only of that brother of yours. You urged a greater interest in the parson's son, who is by all accounts a superior rider on your little pony. James bested Mrs Benning's stable master yesterday in a three-heat race. There's talk your Green Pea may well upset the favourite this year."

"Is one race enough to predict an upset?"

"For my father it is. He's put five pounds on Green Pea. When your brother learned of it, he nearly tore my father's arm from his body shaking his hand and promising success."

"Mrs Bramble regrets my pushing them together. James is no more studious or agreeable since Hugh adopted him, far less so. But the alteration in Hugh, Margery, is what concerns me. Yesterday he announced he is using Hume's *Human Nature* as a doorstop. I supposed him to be joking, but he laughed and then, as if it were the grandest joke in the world, showed me. I never imagined Hugh might be the one changed; now he is as aimless as his friend."

"He is working towards his commission—"

"And Ned does not thank me for promoting James Bramble. It quite upset him to lose the other day when they had a horse race."

The following day while the young women were strolling around the garden of Deerhurst Hall, Anne caught Hugh's eye as he watched James's practice runs. There was an attempt at a smile, but she rather looked like she wished to ride off on the gelding herself. It was becoming apparent that Miss Clarke was in fact preventing her friend from making a decision, for no sooner did Anne approach an answer than Margery reminded her of the counterarguments. Hugh had just decided to overtake them, and evict from the grounds the unhelpful Miss Clarke, when he was struck with the sound of Ned's loud complaints to Sir Frederick over by the stables.

"But Father, *why* must he be always upon her?"

"Upon my soul, Ned," said Hugh, who had sprinted over and was now working to catch his breath, "you are a fine racer, very fine indeed, but you have not the experience for the races just yet. James has three years on you."

"All very well!" said Ned, rounding on him, "But why is he not on his uncle's farm this year? His lot is herding runts and slopping pigs! He's a dirty pauper, you know he is!"

"He is just as refined and learned as you or I, Ned. He deserves our compassion."

"He deserves nothing from us, and Father agrees. He wouldn't allow you to put five pounds on him in the race because he's worthless!"

"Ned, our father has never allowed me to gamble and I should not have asked. Now I will see James leaves off early tonight. Then you can take Green Pea out and we'll see how you go."

This was sense enough to end the dispute, and after

declaring it *all very well, though I might have Green Pea this moment!*
Ned shoved his hands in his pockets and marched back to the
house. With a shake of the head, Hugh turned to Sir Frederick. He did not quite like the look which met him.

"Should I have sent James home, then?"

"Your brother is jealous," said his father. "He had hoped
for more time with you once you returned from school."

"We must be allowed our own friends. Ned has
Humphrey, and that crew…" When there was only silence
Hugh continued, "It hurts me knowing you believe I do him
wrong. I…"

A terrible moment passed as the man's eyes fixed on
Bramble, so commanding on the gelding he did indeed appear
to own her now. Had Hugh done too much for him? Was his
obsession with this boy becoming obvious to the world?

"Father?"

"You know it's my wish that you and Ned had more in
common." He let out a breath and shook his head. "Promote
a common interest wherever you find one, that is all."

Hugh promised, then returned to the house determined to
ignore the remaining practice runs. He took some comfort
knowing that, had his father suspected anything, this would
have been the moment to tell him. Until then Hugh had been
intending to place the five-pound bet despite the ban and be
damned the consequences. By the next day he had decided on
an alternative. With the money he had intended to wager,
Hugh bought two subscriptions to the dancing master.

Golightly's Dancing Academy stood on the first floor of a
dingy building off the High Street, which, despite its being
often assaulted by the noise and stench from the market below,
remained popular. This was owing to the troupe of flirtatious
dancers he employed, his sixteen-year-old daughter Cecelia
among them, present to enliven dry and tedious lessons.

Dancing with a partner, however, was reserved for Hugh, the schooled dancer. As a rank amateur, Bramble found himself relegated to a corner to pose and step and trip through elementals and proving himself entirely inelegant when deprived of his horse. And dull as was Hugh's experience with Cecelia, a dancer of only middling talent, Bramble's solitary torment was entertainment well bought, as the student was a full hour dodging the master's critical stick.

By the time they exited onto the High Street, James Bramble's inelegant attempt at dancing had utterly endeared him to his benefactor. Though a certain warm affection had been growing in Hugh's breast, this failed effort at last did him in. Though he dared not say he loved him, or even much liked him, Hugh could not resist gift-giving and gazing at him. From a bakery he commanded the stoutest, stickiest honey cake on offer simply to watch Bramble devour it. Ladies young and old, high-born and otherwise sighed and stared, for James was now universally declared the most handsome young man in the county. How Hugh ached to scale the ruins of Donnington Castle and shout that Bramble was his! And too many times the object of affection caught his looks of admiration and grinned, for Hugh had grown careless, and simply did not care.

The favourite was beginning to feel the power of favour and began to hint what might be required to keep him. When they passed a stagecoach letting out travellers from Bath, Bramble announced he had a mind to jump in when it continued to London. The meaning was clear enough – he wished out of his home and away from his future. And who better than the wealthy young man who caressed him to accomplish it?

When Hugh pretended not to understand, the boy strode a few paces ahead and, looking absently into a warehouse window, said, "And I'd be just as happy to catch it going the other way."

This inspired a touch of fear as they turned up the road leading to Deerhurst. That James might choose Bath over London should opportunity present was clear enough; but perhaps he meant something else. Perhaps he meant women. Young women, old women, *debutantes*. Wealthy widows. Neglected wives. He was just the kind to play Gallant, and there would be opportunities a-plenty in London or Bath. Women! Hugh had not an ounce of inclination in that direction. However, he suspected his friend had no such limitations, especially where his ambition to depart was concerned. And if there was one thing to drive Hugh to madness, it was this.

The parsonage of St. Timothy's was a brick-panelled, piecemeal affair, often with a dirty face pressed to the old casement windows. By the time it came into view Bramble was once more Hugh's grateful pet, thanking him for the honey cake and the dance lesson and for always being so good to him. Hugh had no sooner taken his hand for a farewell shake, than Mr Bramble stepped from inside the building and beckoned them forward.

"What?"

"I wish to speak to you both in my study."

Where was the easy-going, meek man who appeared gentle even when preaching God's wrath? In a daze Hugh followed the parson into his home as children rattled its crammed arteries, circulating through rooms one undistinguishable from the next. The novelty of seeing Bramble's home for the first time was lost to this unforeseen attack. There had been the unmistakable ring of accusation in the parson's words, and Hugh felt like an animal being knowingly lured into a trap. The ceilings stood low, little of beauty adorned the rooms. No cornice to ease the angles, no secluded corners. Poor construction had left the walls leaning in at strange angles, and only force of will kept Hugh steady as he passed through the back kitchen. By the time they reached their destination, so stupid was he from fear, a hand was required to bring him bodily into what was termed a study. This was little more than a cupboard, crammed to the hilt with books, with a miniscule square of window strangled in ivy. The door closed.

As the parson sat behind his desk, he said, "Hugh, are you unwell?"

Into the silence left by Hugh's shake of the head, Bramble, seemingly untouched by concern, said, "Worn clean out by Golightly, a mean and particular man." After a pause he added, "We've been admitted to study dance at the Academy thanks to my friend."

Hugh shot him a look – he had assumed discretion. However, this was nothing to what the fool was about to say: "You saw too, Father, the lace jabot I've been wearing, a purchase Hugh made in a mad moment. And I never showed you the leather-bound journal he bought me, and the snuffbox before that."

The blood draining from his skull, Hugh felt on the verge of doubling over in his chair. This was an outrage – the wretch was mad!

"Snuffbox?" said the parson. "Hugh, is this true?"

Cold sweats commenced. The visitor grew dizzy and feared he was not long for bringing up the contents of his stomach.

"Not a quid of snuff will ever sully it," said James, "It was only bestowed for the fine inlay of its case – every Gentleman needs a box for his trinkets. I shall fetch it and you'll see the tied-up bits of mane and odd relics I keep in it. Even hung that hook I used to catch my first stickleback under the lid."

"Hugh, this is beyond generosity. This is too much. What have you to say for yourself?"

"Sir," he rasped after a dry swallow, then after clearing his throat continued, "Sir, my sister sat me down when I returned from Evendown. She told me I must do more for others." Inelegant or not, this statement had a placatory effect. That the parson did not immediately sneer returned some of the blood to Hugh's cheeks and if by some miracle the man had not guessed… well, Hugh might just defer killing James for his fool mouth.

"Perhaps I've gone amiss to question your generosity," said Mr Bramble. "You appeared quite afraid of me just now, I do apologise. A parson, Hugh, is subject to pride like anyone else, and so perhaps… in light of the dancing master, and the continual kindnesses of your sister and father…" He lifted his quill and studied it. Then shaking his head, he tossed it onto the blotter. "A turn with Cecelia did the mischief, eh? James, did you suffer a similar fate?"

"No Sir. I was an hour upon tip-toe in a corner trying to save my shins from the master's stick."

The parson chuckled and Hugh could have fallen on his knees to praise God's great mercy. "But dancing, boys," the man continued. "How came dancing to the fore? Many subscribe to the dancing master not for his expertise in a fine art, but for the charms of his assistants, often chosen for their physical attractions."

Said Hugh: "I daresay your perception is more than common, Sir. But I assure you there was nothing indecent. Close dancing with Cecelia there must be at the lessons – I confess I had my share today. James will soon share in the fun, but he must first suffer through the elements."

A cloud passed over the parson's brow and he leant forward. "I am afraid Hugh, though you do not wish to, you betray your frame of mind completely. 'Sharing in the fun', I cannot approve. The utmost attention must be paid in comprehending motivations – in this, and indeed in every endeavour of life. A child asks innocently to stop inside Gifford's Warehouse where he may, with more efficacy, harass his grandfather into purchasing that toy previously denied him. One woman befriends another, the keeper of a spice shop, who is careless of her inventory when entertaining friends. Something goes missing.

"These examples are taken from life. I'll grant you Golightly provides an honest service, and yet in the event… the close proximity during the lesson… the hot touch of a hand, the warm breathing often fevers the mind beyond any attention to learn. Carnal urges are powerful stimulants and we do well to stand clear of those situations which bring many to the point of no return."

"We are but weak and sinful men every one," Hugh said, in fair imitation of last Sunday's sermon. He turned to James, who appeared mildly perplexed, even a little bored. "Matrimony," continued Hugh, turning again to the parson. "So much talk lately of matrimony put dancing into my mind. This proposal to my sister. When it was made, I was dazzled. He is a great and successful man, Mr Charles Sallow of Boston, well-known in the world of international trade. Dines with Horace Walpole, praised by the Chancellor of the Exchequer. What man can compete when there are such as Mr Sallow making proposals? How fare us of lesser accomplishments? And so, seeing my friend lacking an advantage, I sought to improve him as I myself have been improved, that we might at least stand a fighting chance."

Though rarely rated lower in his own estimation, Hugh had experienced too much terror not to enjoy the effect of his lies upon the parson.

"A fair observation," said the man, no doubt mistaking the beads of sweat on the visitor's forehead for earnestness. "Refining your skills in a fine art may facilitate the finding of partners. However, I must remind you it is prayer and devotion which merits a man's time the most, not social graces. Do remember that tonight when you are on your knees." Making an effort to lighten the tone, he continued, "Now listen to me. I did wish to speak to you both, though it seems we have come to the point in a very roundabout way. I wish to know your own thoughts on matrimony, James. Matrimony and hats."

Before Bramble could put his foot in his mouth, Hugh interrupted, "Oh Sir, we were so meticulous and shy in our intentions! It must be Alice has let slip, the miserable scamp!"

With a triumphant smile the parson declared, in cadences equally suited to the pulpit, "Then with one word shall I dispel thy delusions! That word is a name; and the name is Sarah. Miss Sarah Ward."

"It was not a secret," said James. "I said nothing to you as I feared your laughing at me."

At this the parson laughed heartily. "The famed cocked hat was meant to bring you to the attention to your fair cousin. She must hold a special place in your heart."

Though Hugh could have wished more from him, Bramble's wordless stare was not ineffective. And, in truth, Hugh began to pity the parson as he continued: "When you sought permission to write to the Wards, I had supposed you to mean something much different. They keep a fine stable in Salisbury, Hugh, and I had supposed James wished more time with the horses. But thanks to you, he has all he could wish riding Green Pea."

"Never was there a friend like Hugh Entwistle," said James. "I love him with all my heart."

Love! But for Hugh's contortions the parson would have damned them both with hellfire, and now to talk of love!

Said Mr Bramble, "I shall permit the dancing master, but I require your words of honour, both of you, that your master's school is beyond reproach in terms of morality."

Thoroughly exhausted, Hugh nodded and mustered his best response. "Sir, you have my solemn word nothing untoward will ever occur with any member of the fair sex – at Mr Golightly's or anywhere else I attend your son. As for Cecelia, she disdains any she is obliged to teach. We are all blundering fools in her eyes."

And after a few more words of advice Hugh was sent on his way. A more serious conversation between father and son seemed likely, and there being no opportunity to speak to James before he departed, Hugh escaped the interview in terrible unease. It would take just one slip to destroy them both.

For, all at once, Hugh realised they *could* be destroyed. This was not a game. This was that corruption of order, the vice of Turks and Jews, the most heinous crime against Nature. Title and standing were no security against downfall. This had brought down Captain Rigby and ruined the name of the Earl of Sunderland. Propositions alone had sufficed to send into exile reverends and playwrights; and Hugh had done far more than proposition.

This was the arrest of twenty-six in Holborn.

The raids in Hyde-Park.

This was the gallows at Tyburn.

CHAPTER 10

"You are deathly pale, Hugh. What's happened?"

In the music room Anne sat forward from her place beside Miss Clarke; then, seeing an excuse to rise and break from those comforting arms, she stood and went to him.

"I must request the loan of my sister, Margery. In private."

Collecting her shawl, the girl stood and smoothed her dress, announcing rather stiffly that she had not observed the hour. Something in her manner said she understood they both wished to be rid of her but declared she would leave only so long as Anne could spare her. Assurances were given. Once she was gone Anne grasped her brother's hands and looked near to kissing them in gratitude.

"High time we removed that growth," said Hugh. "Go upstairs and rest, you may thank me later for my deft performance."

"Performance? Hugh, you cannot look as you do and expect me to believe that." The look in her eyes said she had been waiting for just such a moment to speak to him, and she pulled them into the window seat.

"A bustling day and a bit of dance instruction is all it is,

Anne – disgracefully out of practice. But much obliged somebody can make use of my ugliness."

"Do leave off joking and be serious. I do not pry into your affairs unless I believe I must, and I've become concerned – of late very concerned indeed."

"As I have about you." He had believed this line of defence justifiable until the words left his mouth. They both knew that since the visit from Charles Sallow Hugh had been conspicuously unavailable to her. But before much more could be said, Samuel announced dinner, and the family sat down to a meal few appeared to enjoy. Sir Frederick seemed in a particularly stoic temper and afterwards, as Anne returned to the music room, he took his son to one side.

"Is there another lover, some secret engagement?"

Only a man who understood Anne not at all could have supposed this. "It's nothing more than indecision and the fear of change. Shall I speak to her?"

Not appearing to have heard him the man said, "Our representative, Mr Hill, has stepped down due to poor health. I was not informed as… promptly as others. It seems he suffered an attack of ague nearly a month ago and has since been under the care of a physician."

"It is not four months since the election."

"A by-election will be held."

"Who will stand…?"

"A young man of fortune and ambition who seeks a favourable introduction to the Duke of Grafton, to whose attention I have lately come. A man in whom I am so confident I will spend £1,000 of my own money to promote him, in addition to the £10,000 promised as a dowry. Else the offer of marriage shall be withdrawn."

"An American?" said Hugh, unsure if such an arrangement were even legal.

"A royal subject nonetheless."

Father and son observed each other for a moment. Then

Frederick said, "Speak to your sister if you like. Our letter of acceptance posts tomorrow." With these words he exited the room and Hugh closed his eyes to steady himself.

Smiling when she saw her brother Anne sought to bring him again into the window seat, but he opted instead for an easy chair. After a full minute, during which he made no effort to engage her, he declared himself bored and asked to hear a piece on the harpsichord. Her look of confused indignation, in danger of devolving to downright self-pity, settled him this was the correct approach. The application, *ad nauseam*, of Miss Clarke was to blame for this, and bold counter strokes were needed. He crossed his leg.

"One piece, whatever you wish, to repay my kindness extricating you from your tiresome friend."

On the point of tears, Anne flounced to the harpsichord and, after a moment, began. By its bright staccato opening and lively runs he discerned the genius of Scarlatti and once committed, she played with as much vivacity as the sonata required. At the conclusion of the piece she waved off his praise, rising from the instrument to pace the room while bestowing her most reproachful looks.

"Thank you, dear heart," said her brother. "You do, incidentally, have the answer you've been seeking."

Rounding on him she said, "My answer? What do you mean? How can you make such sport of me?"

"What says your heart at this moment? Will you meet Duncan Sallow in London or will you not?"

"Hugh I cannot decide! My life will be forever altered should I accept, and, I fear, no less should I decline. I do not wish to displease my father, and yet the thought of losing my life here in the country… oh, I cannot bear this!"

"You have proclaimed your answer a hundred times, if you will only recognise it. Have I yet heard the word *no*? 'No, I shall not meet Mr Sallow.' Yet you are a hundred ways saying yes. Just now, uncertain whether or not to play me a tune, you rose silently and played. Your silence is assent."

"I had no choice…"

"You had a choice. I asked to hear a piece of music from mere idleness, there were a hundred ways to say no, including your way, which is simply to say it." He rose and took her hands. "Do, Anne, understand the choices you have. And the choices you do not."

A cloud passed over her face, but Hugh squeezed her hands and smiled. "I admire you more for choosing to play for me. Not for you retirement into the dust of a windowsill, or a mournful lament at the harpsichord. You march to your instrument, choose a bright, lively piece and perform it as it should be performed."

"I should have looked a maudlin fool to play it mournfully."

"You did well, as you always do when you respond instantly to your heart." He released her hands. "So, I ask again: what is your answer?"

Then, with a shake of the head and an uncertain smile, tears came into her eyes and she began to laugh. "Can it be that simple? I believe… No, I know you are right. I must have said no, immediately, had that been my answer. The very day he called. And so, my answer must be yes."

Then she fell into Hugh's arms and began to cry. How easy it was to forget she was still a young woman, with as many fears for her future as he had himself. He held her small frame close, until at last she pulled away and wiped her eyes. "I must look a fright," she said shaking her head.

Hugh touched a hair into place, tilting her face towards the light, then said, "No flower is as lovely as after a rain, in my idea."

Next morning a refreshed Anne moved with a liveliness absent many days; that dead wick drowned in a pool of wax was cut new and burned strong. She was for a few minutes obliged to rally Miss Clarke, who had arrived before breakfast fully anticipating another day of low-spirited vacillation. However, she was not so mean as to wish a return to indecision and so congratulated her friend.

Glancing at Hugh, Margery asked if he were not still indisposed? He looked scarcely any better than yesterday, did not Anne agree? Anne frowned and shushed her, but no doubt she was right. Tossed between disagreeable thoughts of how to cut relations with Bramble, which he absolutely must do, and agreeable thoughts of the relations themselves, Hugh had slept very little indeed. Sometime after midnight he had at last rolled from bed, slipped downstairs and roamed the gardens and the grounds. At the memory of his endless restlessness and under Margery's curious gaze Hugh crammed the last of his plumb cake down and exited the room.

That afternoon about three-thirty Bramble arrived to take Green Pea out. When the stable hands proceeded to the house for supper at five James tossed the dandy brush at a box of grooming tools and approached. "Where shall we have it, then?"

The dandy brush had come up short and Hugh stooped to set it in the box. Then he announced his decision. No doubt owing to Hugh's tendency to tease him, Bramble took the proclamation as a joke.

"I'm to stay away from you, is it?" he said. "How can I when I know what particularly obliges Sir Hugh? Fancy the sound of that?"

"Makes no difference if I do—"

"Wind your clock, Sir Hugh? Fancy the sound of that?"

Hugh expelled a breath and closed his eyes. "This is my decision. You ignore the risks, the very great risks we run, should we be discovered. Your want of caution, your rashness – we were very nearly hanged yesterday, no thanks to you."

"I'd never tell a soul," Bramble said, with a look of genuine surprise. Tugging absently at the sleeve of his smock he continued, "I should like to know why you chose yesterday to begin fearing my father."

"I fear anyone who might discover us."

"Well I have no fear because of my faith in you. Miss Sarah indeed. You're a damned genius planning that lie for so long." James caught the eye of his friend, always dependably affected by compliments and, liking what he saw, continued, "Would you like to know my own contribution to the cause? After you departed yesterday, I was a lovesick dog in my father's study, suffering terribly from carnal thoughts of Sarah and crying into my handkerchief for shame."

A string of amusement tugged at Hugh's lip. He pinched his mouth and said, "Well done with that, but those unchecked declarations about me—"

"The same said of a tutor not overly inclined to beat me – *I love Mr Fleming with all my heart!* And of my uncle who let me ride his steed and gave me a pocket watch at Michaelmas – *Never was there such an uncle, I love him with all my heart!* I'd lay half a dozen of Burgundy that the boy who cries wolf disguises best the wolf when he does arrive."

Could Bramble, who claimed to spend inordinate amounts of time composing odes, ever know the poetry of those words? Constructed in an unknown meter, and which rang in Hugh's head until he could not hear.

"Am I the wolf?" he said.

Taking Hugh's wrist and pulling him forward, Bramble nodded. "Pity to leave such a fine disguise unused."

When Bramble came closer still, the smell of sweat and longing filling the air, Hugh nearly flinched. Then, unable to bear more, Hugh crushed his friend between the wall of the stable and himself.

"Pity to have the steps from the dancing master," he said, slipping a hand up Bramble's smock, "and nobody to dance with."

So it progressed – a continual slipping under the waves

each afternoon. Glorious August afternoons threatening to drown them both; Hugh lamented and longed for every one. Afternoons were not afternoons until Bramble could be seen approaching down the lane to the Hall, the dust rising at his feet and the summer sun in his hair. Green Pea was put through her paces until five when the staff returned to the main house for supper, at which point the stables were theirs. As a further precaution, Hugh varied their places of assignation to the streamside or a disused room of the garret. Each night in bed he lay with a hand to his head, wondering how he had succumbed again. Alone in the dark he resolved with vows and solemn oaths to distance himself, and in the light of day, as the tide rose once more, dissolved them all. He could bear no distance.

Many evenings, unwilling to let go, he joined Bramble at the parsonage to work rabbit-netting by the evening fire while the parson read stories of the Golden Calf and Potiphar's wife. How many happy hours were spent exchanging glances and watching James's rough, dexterous fingers work the rope? Pulling, tying, knotting – again and again until the parson set the Bible aside in favour of Thomas à Kempis.

The day before Hugh's nineteenth birthday a letter arrived from London. It contained an acceptance, with humble gratitude, of Sir Frederick's offer to speak on behalf of Duncan Sallow to the residents of the borough. Matilda, wrote Charles, had implied the family might return to London the final week of August. Charles trusted this was not on his account, but it would be most fortunate in promoting a connection between their children.

"The final week of August," said Hugh, as his father set down the letter. Next week. Three weeks sooner than originally planned – he might attend the dedication feast but would be departed before the races on Enbourne Heath. The immediacy of losing his friend struck Hugh with the force of lightening, and he learned it on a day James was required at the glebe lands. So, with a parcel of mutton, apples and plumb cake Hugh set out for the parsonage at a measured pace.

And soon... the final approach down the gravel lane... those running, squatting, bustling shapes coming into view on the farm land behind the parsonage... from the cloud of activity clarified to his eye, with the wipe of his hand, and the scratch of his head, those mannerisms which could only be Bramble's – the one chosen by Hugh's hand. Then the moment James observed him: that standing to attention, that informing his stepmother and coming forward. The shake of the raw, hard hand would have been enough, God knew, to send Hugh happily away. The favour of his smile sufficient to scent his dreams.

"Set the basket in the garden," said Bramble, "I have something for you."

Proceeding inside, they closed themselves inside the room James shared with his two brothers. As Hugh leant against the door to prevent unwanted intruders, Bramble produced from under his bed presents for his birthday. The first was a new poem in praise of friendship which he read out shyly – somewhat better than his previous efforts. Then he handed him a newly published, beautifully embossed travelogue of Egypt, with drawings of the Great Sphinx of Giza, bound in calf. It was as fine as anything in the library at Deerhurst Hall.

"Did you purchase this for me?" When Bramble only shrugged, Hugh experienced a pain in his chest that was, for a moment, almost unbearable. His mouth trembled, he pulled Bramble close and held him tightly. He nearly told him everything, every wish to make him his forever, every feeling too deep to own. Then he pushed him back and said, staring at his feet, "I have not said you are handsome, James. The handsomest boy I've ever known."

It was without doubt the silliest thing he had ever said, given what he meant to express. Yet he could produce nothing more in that moment. He had not the words and had less trust what Bramble might do with the information. And though it had been the aim of this visit, he could not yet tell him he would be departing weeks earlier than intended.

"And I haven't said I love you more than life," said James, staring without hesitation into Hugh's eyes, "and I wish to go to London when you go."

It was said at last, but Hugh felt such a surge of tenderness towards him he could not regret it – hearing it at last was, in truth, a relief.

"The commission brings ninety pounds annually. One might be established with that. But it will take time – perhaps months."

"I cannot wait. I shall be miserable every day without you!"

Hugh embraced him again and whispered in his ear that they must wait and see. With their united weight against the door, the offer seemed entirely reasonable and just. After-wards, however, as Hugh returned home, he knew he had been rash. Of course, those gifts were nothing more than a means to an end, produced at an opportune moment to manipulate him. And as for love – the boy tossed the senti-ment around whenever he liked, he said so himself. One must not feel the word too deeply. And yet, together with that damned travelogue... it had overcome him entirely.

Bramble was everything to him.

On occasion Uncle Barlow enjoyed telling a tale of Hugh which it might, at this point, edify the *Reader* to present:

While still in the nursery, Hugh was tended by a sour old attendant, who sweetened her existence with a sip of cordial waters secreted in a cupboard. The libation was particularly alluring in presence of squawking infants, for which the woman had no use excepting as a source of income. And on one occasion her charge was so obnoxious and the cordial so delicious she tucked the bottle into her skirts and carried it with her as she went about her tasks, uncorking it whenever opportunity presented. Soon enough, she had quite doused herself in spirts, which she applied to her lips, down her neck and as a scent at her wrists. So liberal was this application that Hugh was, from his cradle, able to snatch a dripping finger and place it into his sucking mouth. Attempting to jerk away, the attendant inadvertently baptised the infant in what the French call the waters of life. And when, upon the entrance of a maid come to bring fresh linen, the woman was discovered and ejected from the house, the maid snatched Hugh into her arms and asked if he were well.

To which the child spoke his first words, pronounced with a wily grin: "Very well indeed, Miss!"

So now, unable to face telling James of his early departure to London, Hugh reached into his riding boot to withdraw his stash of brandy. He soon found a measure of peace, then something rather beyond as he fell from his chair, drew all the curtains, and lit every beeswax candle in his bedchamber. For, laughing, he realised he was more than equal to telling Bramble he must depart. "Why the Devil had God created pen and parchment?!" He sat himself down at his escritoire. It was soon done, and he added in his post-script an invitation to call at Deerhurst the following day. Then he sent the note off with Arthur.

Next day, with a scourging headache, Hugh dozed in his room as the time for Bramble's visit came and went. Alarmed, he descended the stairs and found, of all things, Anne giving him a lesson at the harpsichord. When Hugh stepped to the door, he saw, like a picture of domestic bliss, James sitting beside her, plucking out the chords to a simple prelude. Anne turned to her brother, and with a smile informed him she had been sitting with their visitor for more than an hour, for he hoped to learn as much of the piece as possible before Hugh descended.

"Another ten minutes," said Bramble, without lifting his gaze from the keyboard.

"Just do your best, James. We seek only to improve."

The boy looked to Anne, who nodded and stepped aside. Once she had seated herself beside Hugh on the sofa, Bramble performed the piece. Bewildered, Hugh looked to his sister for an explanation, half-suspecting the visitor had wished to speak to her alone for some obscure reason. But she only shook her head and shrugged, as James completed the piece a second time.

At supper the guest remained composed, asked polite questions about the townhouse in Westminster, and had a decent go at the meal. That evening he and Hugh perused a bawdy French play, and when they tired of that, opened the travelogue. Looking at the pyramid of Giza, Bramble asked, "You will write to me?"

"The moment I am settled. Our date of departure is owing to Sallow, as I said in my note. It cannot be helped."

"How many?"

"How many?"

"Letters. Are you very fond of letter-writing?" Hugh supposed he deserved this; they both knew he had not been the best correspondent when his friend was in Salisbury – he had, in fact, been ill-attentive and careless. James continued, "You wrote before of diversification. Diversification in all things. So, I wonder: do you diversify your correspondence as well?"

"With whom, pray?"

"Your friends from school. A few live in London – that is what you told me."

"I maintain my connections. I write notes by the bye, it's only natural when you share a common history."

"A history of amusements at school?"

With particular care Hugh said, "My amusements at Evendown were got hunting up birds' eggs, playing at ninepins and a bit of cricket."

"All very innocent diversions," said his interrogator, with a dryness rather beyond his years.

"That's a mite impertinent." After a moment, he said in a lowered voice, "Nothing like this."

Only it was clear Bramble did not believe him. He flipped a page, his eyes flashing with anger; Hugh would forget him if simply allowed to run away. And despite the note, which communicated the news concisely and with regret, he had arrived today still hoping for a command to have his trunks packed in a couple days.

But then James appeared to brighten; he sighed and spoke of something else, wished to say not a word more on the subject, and was even smiling as he departed for the parsonage.

The sun rose, filling the day with soft light and billowy clouds. Hugh filled his flask and set out, breathing deep of air drenched in raisin wine, feast-cake, and spiced gingerbread. The dedication feast brought all to the green south of the old church, and after indulging his taste for roast beef and pickles, Hugh took Bramble on a saunter about the grounds with ale and long pipes, trailing long, impudent smoke around the peepshows and tuppence amusements. They were soon accosted by a lively gaggle of girls, the boldest of whom addressed Bramble with, "My, you do look purely!" then introduced herself as Miss Molly Perkins. With his tousled blond locks and wearing a simple white smock, the angelic was not difficult to see in Bramble. Miss Perkins, she announced, was available for the evening's dance should anyone fancy a partner. He accepted with a business-like grace and Hugh quickly pulled him from the admiring crowd.

Though keen to distinguish himself in the sack races, James made a poor showing against a troupe of well-practiced youths, who had been weeks honing their skills. Newly of an age to compete at back-swording, Hugh ventured onto the stage unable to resist the lure of this manly endeavour. His adversary was a carter, a Mr Childers, whose knotted and scarred legs declared him well-versed in another manly art, the mean sport of kickshins.

Hugh approached him in pristine white stockings which drew howls of mirth from the faces pressed against the stage rails. He smiled and gave a deep bow. Then, with his rod of stout ash, he shuffled forward in the sawdust strewn about the stage, covering his eyes with one arm, while Childers extended the blade at the end of his rod hoping to nick Hugh's forehead. With the outcome never in doubt, Hugh having never taken up the stick in his life, he made the best of the moment by strutting about the platform in search of laughs; feinting, striking out blindly with his blade, and at last calling 'Hold!" as blood tricked down his forehead into his left eye.

"An inch of blood from Mr Entwistle, match to Mr Childers," pronounced the moderator, whereupon Childers continued to his next opponent and Hugh announced triumph to the crowd.

"Yes triumph! Not a drop of blood has spattered my stockings!"

He was touched to receive a cloth from Ned, who had watched with bated breath. His brother had warmed considerably as the departure for London neared. He and Alice were to remain with Uncle Barlow until Christmas, when a break from school would allow them to come to London, the unforgivable sin of promoting another in the horseraces apparently forgiven.

With cloth to forehead, Hugh's battle wound was tended by his brother and sisters, as well as the swarm of little Brambles. All but James, whom Hugh discovered again in a throng of girls, who were intent on quizzing him about the sack race. Hugh tossed aside the bloody cloth and as soon as he was able took a sting of brandy down his throat, determined to find other amusements until the revellers proceeded into the tent at the call of Mr Golightly, master of ceremonies.

At dances Hugh made it a policy to partner any girl who would have him, none more than another. But in one pretty face after the next he saw disappointment, boredom, even irritation; he was stiff, distracted, and produced not a single *bon mot*, with which he was well known to regale his dancing partners. For Bramble was each and every dance with his Molly and, by all appearances, becoming ragingly drunk. At the conclusion of the minuets, the chairs were set back for the country dances, and Bramble continued with his choice. Revolted, Hugh swung his partner the other way, stamping and clapping past Isaiah Dawson and Miss Benning. Oh, the happy pair! Congratulated by everyone on their forthcoming marriage – the endless accolades nearly turned Hugh's stomach.

At last grown sick after so much stomping about the floor, Hugh excused himself and walked over to where the tireless Bramble was spinning his partner. When the opportunity presented, he snagged the waist of James's breeches and tugged him back to where he could face him. Then, wishing to scream with jealousy Hugh stared into his eyes and pleaded silently: *Please God! If you an ounce of pity for me, do not betray me like this!*

James understood none of it. He pushed Hugh aside, declaring he would continue his dance, indeed he would! humiliated to be handled in such a manner before his peers. Indeed, the incident was going over famously, the young men and women who observed it were howling with laughter. Hugh, however, had become so enraged he left his own partner waiting for him on the floor and stormed from the tent knocking over chairs and sending a jug of water to the floor in his wake.

The next day, his last at Deerhurst, was misery Hugh had scarcely imagined. Such was his rage he felt nothing else, not even the aftereffects of alcohol. He waited until four for Bramble, though he had been invited for noon, growing angrier each minute he was late. God only knew when he had left the dance. God only knew what he had done with that trollop who had all but...

At last Bramble arrived. One look and the reason for the delay was clear for a finer representation of post-debauch illness there never was; Hugh was pleased to see his very eyes nearly throbbing out of their sockets. And for once Hugh felt a blessed distance from him.

"Supper is at five, James. You cannot stay tonight, and I haven't much time..."

"I shall stay only a few minutes."

Then Bramble walked into the music room and sat on the bench staring at his feet. No doubt he remembered little of the night before, no doubt his parents were highly displeased with his behaviour. Hugh was divorced entirely from it, and it felt wonderful. Bramble was a spoilt child who had been unforgivably horrid to him. Did he not understand these had been their last days together, perhaps for months? And to spend them sick and chattering with silly village girls?

"I shan't be at the races," said Hugh, with every word feeling stronger and more independent. "I'll see you are admitted here whenever you like, see you have access to ride Green Pea, of course."

"I cannot bear this..."

Hugh repeated what he said of his commission and promised to remember him. He would see what could be done about bringing him to the city in future. A tear slipped down

Bramble's cheek. Hugh continued methodically, rationally, and while it appeared of no comfort to his friend, it was a great comfort to himself. For what had happened all these months? When had this poor son of a parson, entirely dependent upon him for any prospects, taken the reigns of control? It was an outrage. For the next fifteen minutes, as Hugh spoke of his own plans and prospects, he reminded himself of this, becoming increasingly aware that a separation was just the thing to set things to right.

The time approached for supper, which was to be a small family gathering. When Sir Frederick's carriage pulled into the drive to let out Uncle Barlow, Hugh stood to let his friend know he was being excused. The boy quickly descended into sobs. He looked about the music room as if he did not know where he was or if he should ever see it again.

As the house stirred and began to move toward the dining room, Hugh did the only thing that could be done. He stepped out to the drive and ordered the coachman to delay putting the horses away. He wanted Bramble driven home. Bramble was ill. Then he retrieved the wretch and, fearing a scene, perhaps too roughly pushed him out the front door and into the coach. James had scarcely taken his seat and was on the point of saying something when Hugh said goodbye and slammed the door. As the coach pulled away he proceeded to the side of the house and into the garden, walking briskly, maintaining his composure, pleased to have it done.

"There – I've pushed you off-shore. My letters from London will, from the first, set a new tone. I shall bring you to the city, as I promised, only on my own terms, and when it can be done rationally. You will not expect more of me. This is the moment I retake control – of you, of myself. Our skins are scorched, but they will heal. No one knows. And no one ever will."

CHAPTER 11

On a humid day in August a carriage bumped eastward toward London. Before departure the Entwistle's machine had received in whitewash a large and conspicuous 45 across its boot, rather a right-of-passage for any vehicle travelling during the summer of 1768. Newspaper editorials wondered at the continuing national obsession with John Wilkes whose supporters had only grown during his incarceration. The carpenters, weavers, boatmen, and apprentices who, somewhat inexplicably, connected their poverty and poor working conditions to the plight of a decadent MP. This was, after all, the man who had written the filthiest piece of pornography ever published in England, *The Essay on Woman*. Though printed for a private Gentleman's club, a copy had been stolen by his enemies and read out before Parliament to humiliate him: "Life can little more supply, than a few good fucks and then we die…" Yet, as so often happened with Wilkes, this did nothing to diminish him in the eyes of his supporters. For the man had a voice, and a rebel with a voice might be the only voice for a silent class.

To Anne Entwistle, however, the cry of 'Wilkes and 45!' stood for nothing but profligacy and misbehaviour. In her own brother she had observed the hazards of profligacy, of laziness, much as it pained her to admit it. How happy he had been living under the directives of Evendown – with curfews, intellectual improvements, daily readings of the Bible and required appearances at chapel. For, however vague her understanding of Hugh's activities that summer, she saw clearly his lack of duty and consequent discontent. If she had her wish, she would install him for a month in an alms-house. Or, failing that, send him to work in one of the timber yards they passed as they rattled towards London. Such was the devilish side of Anne Entwistle, as far as it went, when she observed the manicured nail of Hugh's middle finger tapping his lip as he stared absently out the carriage window.

Lady Highborough, however, had little time for quiet contemplation, or thoughts of 45 – she was in high spirits. Before departure she had received a long, lovely epistle from her dearest correspondent Mr Charles Sallow Esq.

"Only imagine, twenty-six years in the America – the daring, and the sacrifice! He departed Wiltshire a humble distiller, and returns utterly transformed – a nabob, and his sons foreigners!" Flipping through the pages of his letter she continued: "Where are they established? ... he wrote it somewhere... ah! 'My eldest Benjamin and his wife have a home in Mayfair (Mayfair Anne!), and Duncan and I have taken a house in The City, a lease of one year, after which Duncan will have the option to continue – and by which time I will have discovered a place in Surrey or thereabouts (he is a widow, you know, dear man). A country estate near town has been, dear lady, my ambition since a boy (oh Anne how charming! What vision!). The love I bear England maintained me through the trials and many deprivations of life in Massachusetts. But the commitment to my dream never wavered. It is that same drive and determination which courses through the veins of my children; which saw Duncan through his experience in the Seven Years' War to produce a man of courage and endurance equal to any I have met.'"

By the second day of travel Anne was showing signs, some happy, some a little beyond happiness, of heightened nerves.

"You fear you will not like Duncan," said Highborough. "You fear he will be absolutely ugly, which few men are, so on that account you must be pleasantly surprised. Only moderately ugly (bad teeth, scars from the smallpox) and you fear you must hurt him with a refusal. Remember, your being distinguished by his father demands he make himself pleasing to you, and that must always go a long way. If, in the end, he proves incapable of inspiring anything but contempt, he is twenty-nine and you cannot be the first to deny him."

"Yes Anne, cheer yourself," said Hugh, crossing his leg, "A hundred to one he is ever so plain."

"Listen to your brother. Should he be plain, as most men are, he is well bought at ten-thousand."

"And if he is a handsome man?" asked Anne, with a sigh.

"Should he be handsome," said Matilda, "say no more than three words, and deign to meet his eyes but once. He must be a Coxcomb, a Rake, or a Fox if a father is required to make the introduction."

Smoothing his travelling breeches, Hugh stared out the window as the east-bound carriage rattled gently to the north. From Bagshot into Brentford tendrils of smoke from the city drew travellers into the growing network of streets and lanes, dissipating into the gloom of an indifferent sky at Kensington and onward into Westminster. The glory of the stench and sprawl, the squalor that sucked at the heels of the weak yet supported a splendour unimaginable – London.

The eye was lost in the broadening expanse of smoke to search out the fire, for it was said that at all times a house, a business, a church, or a neighbourhood was, somewhere in the metropolis, aflame. Newcomers admired spires and churches, bridges, and thoroughfares, but what of sheer vastness? – that a city could support such destruction while continuing to produce, thrive, and, indeed, grow.

Delays began as the coach navigated steppingstones placed pell-mell in the mud for the benefit of ladies on foot. These stones tripped up chairmen carrying a merchant's wife in her best day-dress, nearly sending her into the mud, much to the delight of chatty fishmongers hallooing for business. Butcher's boys harassed the slowing coaches, bantering and occasionally fighting with apprentices who were forever milling about scouring soot and grime from brick and stone façades. A hastily closed window saved the travelling coach from a thick spray of mud − the castoff of a galloping horse whose cursing owner sought rapid recourse around a drove of oxen.

From Charing Cross, a turn off the Strand led the carriage to Beaufort Buildings. With just three days' notice a troupe of city servants had opened and stocked the place. Spacious by city standards, the townhouse must for a day or two feel like a pocket-watch compared to the grandfather clock of country sprawl. Judging from the calling-cards, billets, and notes which greeted them on the vestibule table, Highborough had been busy promoting their arrival, no doubt with hints of secret and newsworthy negotiations. By their second day in the metropolis, the messages ran in drifts onto the mantle of the drawing room, which, with its lacquered surfaces and Oriental wallpaper, gave the impression of winter in Peking.

One took particular notice now of Jasper Sharp, whose tall, lanky frame fit less well into the confines of city dwelling. To the scurrying city servants, he was sometimes heard to shout "*Suffiamina*, you louts!" for he was proud of the Latin he had got up and could proclaim as *ignorami* any who failed this command to put on the drag chain. The city domestics made shift to avoid him, and in secret moments amused themselves with pantomimes of country sloth as he ambled by.

The following morning, he sat Hugh down and brought his dripping straight razor into the yellow light of day.

"I am missing summer mornings in the country so much I like to open a vein."

"Are you?"

After making a first pass at Hugh's neck, Sharp continued, "Just now yer father leapt from his seat the moment we completed our shave – back home we had a habit of reading an item from the paper and speaking on the news of the day. But here there is such rattle and commotion in his apartments, servants in and out and a summons from her Ladyship, I scare had time to wipe the suds from him before he left me."

"I daresay he will need you again."

"I've been told he will not until this evening so much obliged if ye'll bring me yer errands and what have ye."

Hugh allowed him the next pass at his neck before saying, "There's a list on the escritoire for an errand boy. Diverse enough to inconvenience you the better part of a day."

"Not for me. For little Arthur, Jenny's boy. After he shines up my shoes nobody wants him, so I intend to teach him the layout of the city."

This bit of consideration cemented what Hugh suspected of a fondness for Anne's maid, and he agreed.

"A considerate man is your father," said the valet. "A right shame we're once more under petticoat government..." which is how he referred to Lady Highborough's seizure of household affairs whenever the family were in the metropolis. Yet without her, they would likely be confined to the intimate dinner parties Sir Frederick arranged, never receiving a tenth of the invitations to balls, drums, concerts, and ridottos stimulated by her Ladyship's particular style of self-promotion.

Next morning a letter from Margery Clarke lie on the vestibule table – Hugh took it up in the hope of distracting his sister before Charles Sallow arrived with his son. But Anne had no interest in a letter. She stepped by to her mirror pinching her cheeks, which were threatening to introduce a most unbecoming grey into her complexion.

"Pray leave off the Protestant Pinch, Miss Anne," said Jenny. "A touch of rouge today will not send you to Hell. There's a bit right here her Ladyship left on your vanity – sit and I shall apply some."

"Fetch a glass of sweet wine instead," said Hugh, "See she drinks it before the guests arrive." Jenny looked between them, then to the face-paint on the vanity, as though judging which should have the final say. Then with another look at her flustered mistress, she shrugged and left the room.

At one o'clock their city footman, Philippe Gallante, escorted their visitors into the drawing-room, where the family were waiting. The younger Mr Sallow was tall with russet coloured hair, and an uneven complexion. He was of a type inclined to excess weight, though as yet encumbered by no more than an extra stone. Good teeth, and like his father had cheeks quick to redden and was possessed of a particularly masculine musk.

Hugh glanced at his sister, who exchanged just one look with the son then directed her gaze to his father. After compliments and the presentation of refreshments, Charles Sallow said:

"Thank you for this warm reception. I trust you have had opportunity to settle after your journey."

"Now Charles," trilled her Ladyship, "I must stop you there if you mean to learn the date of our arrival. As I said in my letter, our perambulations are always of a very haphazard character – very Bohemian, you know."

"Very well," said Charles with a grin, apparently willing to humour the woman's insistence that this appointment was not their first order of business, and that their prompt appearance to meet his son merely serendipitous.

As a way of easing introductions Sir Frederick began speaking of the differences between the city and the country, then, after relating an amusing misunderstanding between Jasper and Philippe, the topic of managing domestics was introduced. Speaking with a deep, slightly nasal inflection, and clearly wishing to suppress certain aspects of his speech and manner of phrasing, Duncan drew on his military experience for examples of how to run a household. He concluded by saying, "I trust, Miss Anne, your own domestic conflicts are rare. From all my father has said, I imagine it is a pleasure to work for you. And with you."

Appearing wholly unprepared for the compliment she looked to Lady Highborough.

"Nicely done," said Matilda. "Let us have another topic – you may choose, Duncan, only you must use your imagination – refrain from all direct questions regarding Anne's upbringing, schooling, and hobbies."

Tapping stout fingers upon his knees, Duncan raised his eyebrows and said, "Necessity is the mother of invention, as they say. Very well. A question about your brother, Miss Anne, whom I understand you hold in great esteem. I would have an event from his life which you believe most informs your feeling of sisterly affection."

Hugh shifted in his seat beside her trying not to cringe as his sister took a moment to consider.

"I own, Mr Sallow, you could scarcely ask a question to touch me more deeply. One day about five years ago my brother was brought home from school, into this very drawing-room, in a piteous state indeed. His eye was swollen, his cheeks and forehead torn and scabbed. He was all over bruises of the cruellest variety. A bundle of bloody, shredded clothing was placed into my hands. I shall," she brought her hands together, "never forget that. Even at fourteen, my brother was a Gentleman and refused to tell me the details to spare me. To this day he never has. But I saw the fear, the embarrassment, and the hundred other things that the eyes lay bare. I realised it is left to me to remember the child he was, as a mother would. This event in his life, more than any other, most informs my feeling for him."

The room had fallen quite still. Could Hugh have imagined this old and very personal story would figure into Anne's marriage negotiations! *Well done Duncan, you rat, who will verbally ravish and leave us bare to your scrutiny.*

"But your brother will tell you," said her suitor, appearing concerned by her emotion, "this is but the natural path to manhood. Trivial misunderstandings will ever make boys fight like cocks and are quickly gotten over. Many friendships are born in the settling dust. Do relieve your sister's agitation, Hugh."

Would nobody put a stop to this? Did nobody but Hugh believe this was inappropriate? On the contrary, the company appeared quite pleased. Here was a suitor petitioning on behalf of his intended, and a young lady aglow in the very flattering light of motherly affection.

"My sister," he said, "does not consider I spared myself under the guise of sparing her. You will agree, Sir, that the male animal is possessed of a most pernicious tendency towards selfishness. A tendency which women would do well to remember."

The look of discomfort this produced was some measure of recompense – Duncan worked to phrase an honest answer without tarnishing the un-tarnishable metalwork currently on offer.

"Man must always work against his baser inclinations," he said, "and value that honest nature which precludes the thought of deception by others." After assuring himself Anne had comprehended his compliment, Duncan took direct aim at her brother: "Won't you tell us how this deception was practiced, Hugh?"

The looks from Hugh's relations, who had never been

satisfied with the explanation for the fight, showed him how much this incident still meant to them.

"I shouldn't wish to offend you or your father."

"Not at all," said Charles. "Honest, open conversation is why we are here. Our first order of business, as I see it, is getting beyond polite reserve. I wish you to continue – and continue truthfully."

So, with a look at Duncan, who had less of a real interest to know, Hugh began in these words:

"While attending Mr Harvey's Academy, the scene of the misfortune, I adhered to a set of principles. One of these principles held that a Gentleman of my station should not be suffered to construe vulguses with the likes of a fishmonger's son. Then one arrived; a boy named Wharton. New money. Shortly after he enrolled a violent sickness went around the school which laid up the school ushers. At which time I lured Wharton into the yard out back which gave onto an open field. It was there, with the aid of a loyal faction, where I provoked the wretch into a fight which eventually led to the injuries my sister observed. And so," Hugh glanced at Anne, who sat in disbelief, and then at Duncan, whose lip was twitching, "I trust she is relieved of that unwarranted compassion for me."

"Well Duncan," said Charles though his eyes remained fixed on those of Hugh, "what do you say to this tale?"

"What do I say? I say that, had I been present, I would have rubbed that schoolyard bully down with an oaken towel." Duncan's smile gleamed, but the glint of teeth said he was not his father's son in all things. He did seem to have a real distaste now for Hugh.

"And you, young lady?" said Charles. "What do you say?"

"This is a surprise to be sure," said Anne. "And I... should like to have the conclusion of the story at a more appropriate time."

"Well that can never be," said Charles, "for this honest,

unpractised discourse, and our honest, unpractised reactions, are precisely what we must have. Now I insist we have the end of the story."

"There is little more to tell…"

"Come now, we have yet to hear how the fishmonger's son withstood this unfair assault. He found an advantage, did he not, and taught you what a son of trade can do?"

Duncan, too, nodded encouragement, so Hugh returned to this dangerous recital, which he performed in these words:

"You wish to hear it was Wharton delivered my retribution; if I had less respect for you and your son, I daresay that is what you would hear. But I learned that day what can be accomplished by force of character. I took sole charge of Wharton, though he was a year older, and both taller and larger than myself, because I appeared superior – popular and the leader of my pack. Nothing more was needed. And so, after a brief attempt to parry my blows he submitted rather sadly to my abuse."

Nearly fit to come out of his chair, Duncan almost shouted, "But did he not try to defend himself? Did he not get in a few good jabs?"

"He attempted to avoid the worst of my blows, that is all. Had he perceived I was younger and slighter no doubt I would have measured my length upon the ground soon enough. But I was too confident and appeared too important as a leader of the other boys, to fail. And so, he failed to see it."

"And had he no schoolfriends to come to his defence?"

Hugh shook his head.

At this unfortunate turn in the story Charles gave vent his confusion. "And yet your sister described you not as victor, but as a wretch badly beaten and laid up for days."

Matilda took this opportunity to interject, "But enough of this childish story, we forget why we are here——"

"I am in no way displeased," said Charles. "Bad conduct at fourteen gives no offense when one has the courage today to admit it. But I must insist upon the conclusion of this encounter at Mr Harvey's, young man, which you have now three times avoided relating."

There was nothing for it but to continue: "Very well, and so here it is: a party of young men, singing and on a bit of an early rake, were crossing that overgrown field behind the yard, and chanced upon the fray. As I recall, most encouraged my behaviour, as Wharton and I were no more than a pair of fighting cocks competing to the death. However, one of the group intervened, dived between us, and appealed to my reason. He appeared no less drunk than his confederates, yet he would not allow an unfair fight, or the continuation of a pointless beating. He bid me leave off." Hugh glanced once more at Anne, who was looking increasingly disheartened. "You see I had every opportunity to avoid what came to me. But I thought only of earning the admiration of the revellers. And so, taking not a word of his counsel to heart, I broke away and redoubled my efforts upon the fishmonger's son.

"These fresh offenses, Sir, rather than any meanness, provoked what my counsellor did. He tugged me up by the lapels and lent me a shove which knocked the wind from me. His friends, laughing riotously, passed him a bottle of Geneva and began goading him to 'shave the fuzz from my lip'. And somehow in the hullabaloo, I managed to clip this brawny young man on the jaw, much to everyone's surprise, and everyone's fury when the contents of the bottle were sent to an unceremonious burial. With a right hook my counsellor sent me into a tree, splitting my head open. I would have fallen to the ground had he not held me up and pummelled me until he could not hold the dead weight of me. That is how I received my injuries."

Sir Frederick remained unreadable, the ladies appeared duly shocked, and their visitors quite gratified. Duncan, in particular, appeared well-pleased that Hugh had been beaten to a pulp at some point in life. With a shake of the finger

Charles declared that the boy was a better man today for that intervention.

"But now Anne," said her Ladyship, exchanging a look with Sir Frederick as she rose from her seat, "We must take our handsome young visitor into the music room where we may relax and perhaps have an air on the harpsichord. Come Duncan, just us three, all very snug."

Hugh understood the two other men wished to speak in private and so found himself unceremoniously excused from both parties. At about three Arthur tapped on the door of his apartments and summoned him downstairs to bid the Sallows farewell. Though there were smiles and good wishes, and an invitation to dine in a couple days, it was apparent nothing had been settled. Charles extended his hand to Hugh and said it had been a pleasure; Duncan merely extended his hand.

After promising to be up shortly to speak with Anne, Hugh turned to his father.

"Are matters at all delayed by my behaviour?"

Settling into an easy chair, Sir Frederick said, "It is Anne's reserve which delays us. Charles took her aside and said he wishes her to take her time – he wants to be convinced of her love and admiration for Duncan."

"I had come to believe admiration was secondary to obtaining the seat at Deerhurst."

"It is, but a man of such… faith in his own abilities believes a match of his choice will fulfil both ambition and the requirements of marital bliss. Go upstairs and remind Anne how very attractive wealth and political influence is. See she understands the power Charles wielded in negotiating the repeal of the Stamp Act, and how crucial his Boston connections continue to be as we work to promote peace in the states. Deerhurst is not the only borough with an opening – such is that man's influence any number of MPs might *become* ill and be obliged to step down, do you understand?"

"Of course." Hugh turned to leave.

"We do not provoke those bigger and stronger than us, son," the man called after him. "Else we are knocked against a tree and carried home in bloody rags."

After a moment, Hugh nodded. "Yes, Father," he said, then, bowing his head, departed the room.

CHAPTER 12

With grease smeared into his wig Hugh ducked behind the face-shield and bowed to the bellows. As the powder room blanched, Jasper shouted to remain motionless, pumping until Hugh, capped in snowy white, fled to the first-floor corridor. Tossing shield aside and dropping his robe, he slipped into gleaming shoes cut in the French fashion, then cantered in a clockwise rotation before the looking glass. After examining the floor for residue, he took a turn anti-clockwise before pronouncing himself pleased. The valet emerged, wiping his face as he stepped from the powder room, and said, "Aye, nary the hint of a trail when Jasper Sharp is at the bellows," and with a fresh ribbon secured the tail of Hugh's wig.

A week of dinners and concerts was to be capped tonight with a grand ball, of which there were precious few prior to November when Parliament opened, and the season officially began. Arriving at the Haymarket assembly to waves of music and shine the family were introduced to a cortege of visiting foreign ambassadors, in whose honour the evening had been organised. During the high season such as Lady Highborough would not have rated the invitation. However, at the end of

August, being the widow of a Baron involved in Prussian affairs twenty years before, had sufficed. Anne, faint with nerves, appeared ready to follow a group of elderly ladies into the card room for whist. But she bowed to her Ladyship's order to proceed into the Grand Ballroom and not be a "silly, silly girl! Charles Sallow will not hear that Anne Entwistle sits with the decrepit. He will hear she is upon the dance floor, demanded for every set!"

But it must be a hard heart indeed that would condemn a pair of uncertain, occasionally downcast eyes at such an assembly. At first blush, the spectacle and circulating guests must inspire dreadful uncertainty in oneself to the exclusion of all that is meant to dazzle. As her Ladyship scanned for a partner, Anne sat at the wall and scarcely looked two feet before her. The candles, the chandeliers, the sparkle – it was rather like looking too long into the sun.

Hugh chose to observe his father – did he actually know all the men he nodded to? Taking a turn with him about the room he had to wonder. Most looked right past them. One man, seeing Sir Frederick's expectation of acknowledgement, clearly did not know him, but bowed and said something of warm regard as they passed. Then there were the women. Painted, sparkling, and voluminous in hooped gowns. Not the city's finest, but at any gathering some must rise to be celebrated, leaving those of less standing or finery as so much wreckage upon the shore of men's indifference. The bucks and stags came forward to assess them, pivoting with hand on hip. They glanced from one woman to the next, then out to the dancers to make their comparisons, before continuing on, laughing. Many were heard to say, that other men might know they were well-bred, that there were 'but two beauties in the place', and it was for these that their praise was reserved.

Anne, dismissed entirely: an outrage! So Hugh, that these men might feel the punishment of his neglect, tried to prevent his eyes from lingering too long upon their figures. Their confident, pouty sneers, their beautiful, bejewelled hands, the shapely calves in snowy tights.

One handsome man in yellow, rubbing râpée into his gums in thick applications, was paying his addresses to the young woman immediately beside Anne. Yellow had a friend in lime-green who laughed riotously at everything Yellow said. When Yellow bid his young woman for a dance, Lime-green got her friend for his trouble – however not one of the party appeared contented with their partners, or indeed happy in the slightest. Increasingly desperate for something to do, Hugh offered to retrieve his sister a glass of punch and again set off into the crowd to observe the men.

Where were the nerves, the misgivings, the uncertainties which must be every man's portion? All displayed confidence; all glittering in offerings to others glittering to receive. Beautifully turned curls, gleaming black of silk bagwigs, voluptuously embroidered coats over cloth-of-gold waistcoats. A slipper turned absently to fourth position bespoke a grace sufficient to make those sensible of such things swoon. And Hugh was sensible indeed. These men were everything he wished to be and, in some instances, to possess.

He was an inordinate amount of time standing in the refreshment line and could not but blush to recall the final dance in Newbury, where, miserable though the experience had been, his confidence was never in doubt. In the Haymarket assembly, he would not dare speak to a potential dancing partner without an introduction. And as for the men, he'd already received far too many reproving looks at something in his manner or dress to dare attempt a conversation.

And, of course, this was to be expected. And, of course, her Ladyship might find a girl for him to dance with. Yet when he returned to his party to discover Anne speaking to the handsome man Highborough had found for her, his heart skipped, and he was suddenly unsteady on his feet. Timothy Everett was a fair man of about twenty-four. Taking his hand as they were introduced the touch of his palm brought to mind another… another handshake, another of the fairest…

For, however it may appear, in the week since his arrival in London, Hugh had not forgotten James Bramble. He was yet to take up his pen or, after the initial pain of separation, lose much sleep over him. For he could afford to take his time writing, and, indeed, must, if he intended to regain control of the relationship. The upper hand was his in having left for London. His for his wealth and connections. And until he chose to thaw him, James would remain frozen at their leave-taking, just as he was when the coach door closed…

In his reverie, Hugh had heard nothing at all of Mr Everett's introduction, or Lady Highborough's jibe which he 'must not deny', and the good-natured insipidity which followed. Hugh turned to Anne, who was blushing and giving Timothy Everett shy looks, for she had just assented to join him to the set. Then Everett, with sparkling brown eyes, placed her glass to one side and led her to the floor.

For the entire set Hugh could not pull his gaze from the handsome blond man. Lithe and lilting. Bramble – as he had appeared on the High Street or upon Green Pea. And what of the horseraces on Enbourne Heath? Earlier this very day had been the event. How had James fared, and what had he been doing in the days since their departure?

At the conclusion of the set, Anne returned with her partner to seek out Timothy's people in the Petite Ballroom. Here Hugh was introduced to Mr Everett's younger sister, Hannah, all wide, dark eyes, darkly arranged ringlets and a mouth given to frequent explosions of feeling. Somewhat numbly he exchanged a few words with her, then escorted her to the next set.

"Forgive me for a silly schoolgirl," she breathed, "I own I am but four months graduated from Miss Marianne's

Academy for Young Ladies, but dancing with a boy, that is to say a Gentleman, *more* than answers the dreams we entertained at school! Upon my soul a girl is too yielding ever to partner correctly! You cannot image the incongruity: there is nothing at all to support one! and I must confide your posture inspires, for you lead divinely…" and so forth.

When they were seated again the conversations diverged into that of the chaperones, Hugh with his partner, and Anne with hers. And Anne, for her part, appeared uncharacteristically starry-eyed. Timothy Everett's attractions elevated as his manner grew familiar. Hugh attempted to listen, to catch his eye as the man's silly sister prattled on. Then Hannah's voice was lost entirely as her brother uncrossed his long legs, leant forward to be heard over a loud passage by the orchestra, and clasped Anne's hands affectionately. Something in that strong, protective gesture was, to one onlooker, a direct blow to the gut. Hugh grew near sick with longing to have such a hand clasp his.

"…I must apologise, I will go on," continued Hannah. "Do tell me about your lovely sister; or indeed about yourself; or Oh! I am informed you have been to Brighthelmstone, pray tell me about that place…"

Little was required to maintain Miss Everett in raptures, and, indeed, little effort was expended. For Hugh was now in a freefall towards foul humour. Timothy Everett was *not* James Bramble, that is why he did not return his look. He was *not* James Bramble, that is why he spoke to Anne. But he was similar enough in appearance, by God and all the Saints, that Hugh began to shake with regret and heartache. How he missed, how he sorely missed, his friend.

By the time the coach departed for Beaufort Buildings Hugh had descended into a raw, overpowering grip of emotion. He was angry, nearly furious, with Anne. It was an absolute, ugly feeling. He could scarcely look at her. Flattered all night, now with a glazed look in her eyes, all the while knowing a man like Duncan Sallow waited for her.

If that were not enough, there was the warm intimacy now between their father and Matilda, who found they could, despite their constant bickering, occasionally like one another. Anne, Hugh smirked to himself, had she even been in her senses, could never understand that small liberty their father took with her Ladyship, confirming everything Hugh supposed about their private relations. For Hugh knew physical passion like that. What it was to have. And, tonight, what it was to be deprived.

Once home, Anne drifted up the stairs into the darkness of the first floor, with hardly a word to Jenny, who had waited up. Sir Frederick thumbed through the post on the vestibule table while the lady, warm from sweet wine, nuzzled up to him and tugged playfully at the tail of his wig. His face blackening, Hugh pounded up the stairs to his apartment where a fire burned bright. There he stripped jabot, stock, wig, frockcoat, waistcoat, shoes, and stockings, then sought the brandy bottle from inside his riding boot, the contents of which were quickly exhausted. Resorting to the next best on hand, he set free the waters of Geneva, and, taking great, burning mouthfuls, took his quill in hand and began:

My Beloved Friend, or,
as you are in my Heart, My Bramble,

Would we had not met, that I should never know what it is to
part. How much misery can be Man's portion? I know the
answer tonight, James. And I, doubtless, the object of your envy.
You wish to know of my Most Illustrious Adventures in London
but Hark! These diversions do but powder for a night and rub
away! Tonight, in this raucous city I see nothing but an empty
bed. How I need you with me! How many Delicious Summer
Nights were spent apart because I dared not keep you in my

arms? How I hate my cowardice! And now this thirst, this agonizing thirst... I would risk any discovery to slake it! O how devious our delights! I taught you to find me in dark corners; bless my father for keeping the stable hands to a schedule! I was your solemn guardian against trumpery; bless the parson for coun-selling us against Miss Golightly: I had just had his son panting in the garret of Deerhurst Hall! Fools! One and All!

And now tonight I am suffered to stand beside Anne, Hateful Creature, whipped frothy as a Syllabub! Oh, to be brought to ecstasy by a word, and a gesture of some handsome man; she who lives in darkness and knows not the Sun at the Horizon! You asked once what would oblige me James: would to God it had been discovered to neither of us! For to be sure I am well punished for it. I had not the depth of these feelings discovered to me, as I found with you. Even as I fell, I prayed someone would catch me, or save you from me; and yet opportunity was bringing in the carriage, and I could not resist her.

And yet, my beautiful boy, for all my ranting, here is what I know tonight: it is the afterglow, your laughter, and our sweet friendship I need, even more than that bliss between your thighs. Friendship so tender cannot be wrong, and I do ache with bitter remorse: I should have been kinder to you. I should not have rallied you so hard, for my own amusement. I love you. Why could I not say it, as you did? I LOVE YOU – more than Life and Liberty. You think I make a habit of this. You do not trust me. TRUST ME. I swear on the memory of my mother: as these things are concerned, I only ever had a kiss. One time, before you, and that is all.

I frank this letter now for, without the aid of vast liquor as I now enjoy, I never shall. I want the misery of your reading this upon my conscience, until you deign to write, if you ever shall. Alas, I cannot bring to decorous conclusion that which

commenced in vulgarity, and must leave off now that you may
think no worse of

Your humble Servant, and Ever-Affectionate Friend,
Hugh Entwistle

Folding and sealing the letter with wax, Hugh snatched a candle and descended into the vestibule. He set the letter with the outgoing post then, determined to take no rest until it was gone from the house, retrieved the bottle of Geneva and sank into a high-backed chair. There he awaited the sunrise in wretched remembrances through drafts of numbing medicine.

At the first stirrings of the house Jasper descended, followed by the light footfalls of Arthur. After thumbing through the letters Jasper handed the boy the stack and told him to ask for help should he have any trouble with his deliveries. After they had departed Hugh ran to the table. Everything, including his letter to Bramble, was gone.

He awoke, it seemed, immediately to find the valet in his room bidding him rise from bed. More than three hours had elapsed.

"Leave me as I am Jasper; I am ill, truly ill this time. My stomach."

"Balderdash, I smelled ye at the door."

With palpitating heart Hugh sat up, shielding his eyes.

"Make my excuses. I am much obliged for any but overindulgence." The plea was met with silence. "I entreat your compassion as a fellow mortal. I am not the first to fall. Never shall I ask it of you again, you have my word. Only nobody can have a hint of this, not family nor any of the servants. You will have a gift of my gratitude, but only upon successful concealment today."

At last, after another interminable silence, the man

relented. He opened the windows to air the room, exchanged sodden bedlinen for fresh and produced a ceramic basin in which to spit after gargling cologne, the performance of which nearly brought up the watery contents of Hugh's stomach. Then he lay back and fell quickly into oblivion.

Jasper, bedclothes in tow and the lid tight upon the basin, stepped quietly from the room.

CHAPTER 13

A disagreeable morsel of meat took responsibility for Hugh's illness. Sharp related the news before the invalid made his late appearance. Sir Frederick, the ultimate test of a deception, looked up from *The Auditor* when his son arrived and recommend pectoral balsam of honey, his recommendation for most ailments. Anne bid her brother sit next to her on the sofa and stroked his hair, at which point the bile rose his throat, this time not from jealousy, but from the memory of his monstrously unjust condemnation of her.

He spent much of the day dozing in the drawing room listening to plans for an upcoming dinner with the Sallows, happy for company which kept him from his own confused thoughts. He was pleased even to see Jasper, who did not bother to conceal his smirk when Arthur returned home with the bottle of pectoral balsam. Hugh grabbed the errand boy and sat him down. Was he mastering the layout of Westminster? *Yes, I am quite expert now at delivering billets and fetching packages and should Mr Entwistle require anything more for his stomach Arthur Mapplethorpe is at his service!* And the letters on the sideboard this morning? Had he delivered them?

"The post office is just up from London Bridge, on

Lombard Street – sure it's the easiest to find of any place in the city."

That evening they were joined by the son of one of his father's creditors whom they were occasionally obliged to entertain. Mr Heaton Marvel was a libertine who had pickled himself into age rather beyond his thirty years, tonight in a suit of sea green foaming with lace frills at the wrists and pockets. At dinner he brought Hugh from his distraction speaking of the many Gentlemen's clubs he belonged to and declaring that Hugh, now he was a man of the city, must join something.

"I myself," said Marvel, "am member of the Society of Misers, in which our elected officials organise the cheapest evenings to be had in London; I also belong to The Wanderlust Club, which meets when no less than three members experience the urge, always at a new location; The Club for Complainers, with a monthly prize for the wretch saddled with the worst home life, the most encounters with the magistrate, you understand. And The Puffers and Poets Guild, no doubt the worthiest of the lot. I write, you know, and write very well."

"Poetry, Hugh," said Anne.

"Does your brother compose?"

"He does, though he is shy of admitting it. And he has lately taken to puffing a pipe. Is that what is meant by puffers?"

"It's settled," said Heaton, not answering the question. "I initiate you, Hugh Entwistle, and shall stop for you once I have achieved your admission."

By the following morning Hugh was once more himself and vowing away from drink for a good long time – perhaps for all time. Yet the alteration in the valet's treatment of him had become highly provoking – this condescension of manner, this smirk which only increased as Hugh improved. As he rose from bed, the valet wished to know if young master was *able* to do this, recovered *sufficiently* to do that? As Jasper went about his duties, he stepped gingerly around him, as though he were liable to break in two, raising him into morning half-dress with agonizing sloth. Once the torturous shave was complete, Hugh, now almost beside himself with irritation, rose to fetch a pair of guineas.

"Much obliged," said the valet, taking his payment for silence, however Hugh retained his eyes.

"Your service, Mr Sharp, is not of so scrupulous a character as to preclude dismissal, at will, upon my recommendation." Observing the hint of fear, Hugh continued: "You boast of six years' service with us, when not one, but two interruptions of employment occurred during that time. One was due to mere waywardness. The other was owing to your debauching the scullery maid, then refusing to marry her when she came with child. After the upset this caused the entire house, my father was rather beyond generous to take you back. Even so there continue to be rumours of indiscretions with the prettier girls who enter the house."

Never more than wan, Jasper went quite pale. After a moment he said. "As regards liquor, it is what many men will do. Reminding ye, it is not my own, but at the desire of yer father that I bid ye rise no later than eight and relate any behaviour unbefitting a Gentleman. Drink is his aversion, ye know it is." He cleared his throat. "If ye harbour misgivings about me, I had not this of ye." He held the guineas between them and nudged Hugh's arm.

"I promised a gift for your discretion and am good on my promise. Put them away."

The guineas vanished from sight. Some moments passed collecting the items of the shaving kit, then Jasper said, "Pleased to say Arthur is a great success about town. Have ye anything to deliver?"

"Nothing at present," said Hugh stepping to the window. Then the valet was gone.

For the first time in months, Hugh experienced a great desire to apply his mind, follow some course of study and improve himself. Yet the old methods held no lure for him. *Human Nature,* the Greeks, every volume he opened savoured of other men's experiences. Books seemed the things of the country once one arrived in London, which was newspapers and pamphlets and current events.

For he *was* in London. He might step out to the Exchange, might observe the progress of the new bridge at Blackfriars, set out for Marylebone, or Hyde Park. When he did step into the fine September day, though it was with the intention of seeing St. James's, he found himself on Church Lane going in the direction of St. Martin's Fields. Just a few months on, little could be guessed of the riot and murder which had fired a national discussion. From there he proceeded to King's Bench Prison, where a subdued gathering lingered about the places Wilkes was known to show his face. Somebody shouted, "45 forever! Liberty forever!" But was there not more liberty in remaining silent? In proceeding through life unnoticed? For surely airing one's views could not be worth a prison sentence of two years.

Then suddenly a fear descended upon him, so hideous Hugh nearly staggered on the spot – had he, in his wretchedness, written his own *Essay on Woman?* Might what he'd written to Bramble be somehow used against him? Had he been more cross with Jasper than was necessary? ... But no, it was madness to believe anybody knew the contents of his letter home – Sharp had handed the stack of letters to Arthur, had perhaps seen the direction but had no reason to look at it before it left the house. His father certainly had not seen it, and Arthur had confirmed its delivery to the post office.

But what of its arrival at the parsonage? Would Parson Bramble open a letter addressed to James? Why had Hugh not directed the letter to the chocolate house in Newbury, as he had done with letters far less damning to him? How could he be so reckless, so stupid? He must be more careful. Because should that letter be opened by anyone but James it would be...

"45!" came the shout from the crowd at King's Gate. "Forever!"

CHAPTER 14

Next day Hugh began executing his plan to dine with every prominent military family in London. As such families were few at the end of summer this was not as ambitious as it might sound – still, he had the satisfaction of sitting at three tables the following week in quality of a particular acquaintance. He was welcomed into homes, caressed, and given the names of Lords or Ladies he might bring to his cause. On each occasion, however, he was informed that petitioning for a commission into the Guards, never easily accomplished, was exceeding difficult after the Peace of '63, and upon hearing this for the third time he found the news quite sobering. Frederick, however, remained undiscouraged. He held any achievement possible given a passionate desire and the ability to position oneself well.

Six days had now elapsed since the letter home, and not a word from Bramble. Trying to prevent the worst of his fears from overpowering him Hugh became convinced the letter had somehow gone wrong. Arthur, he discovered, had twice lost his way in The City, and had held for an entire day a hand-deliverable placed in his charge. The boy was by many accounts careless around the house and had broken a tea cup of bone china. This was more than enough to convince Hugh of his having mislaid the letter.

"No Sir! A letter placed in my trust is as good as arrived, you have my solemn word of honour!"

But after their summer together Hugh simply could not credit the notion that James might forget him. His letter, wretched though it had been, deserved at least a bewildered response. And, more likely, compassion for his misery and a pledge of everlasting love. The following morning, Hugh awoke in a room cool with notes of autumn and an idea he must now seriously consider. What of that bold hussy at the dedication feast? Had she continued to pursue him? It was not inconceivable, however addicted to Hugh's caresses, the boy might betray his King for the throne of the Paphian Queen. This so enraged him he was in a right state when Sharp entered the room, and despite their now shaky relations began badgering him in the hope of betraying Arthur. However, the valet would speak no ill word of Jenny's boy and grew obdurate in his defence.

"You've a cruel streak, Hugh, layin' blame for unanswered letters on a good honest worker."

"Cruel? I'll thank you to keep a civil tongue when you speak to me. Is that understood?"

"*Intelligenti pauca.* And yer not beyond making mistakes yerself. Ye know whereof I speak."

Hugh came forward and said in a low voice, "And you've put my patience to trial since that day with your knowing looks. One more show of petulance, Jasper, and I'll slap that smirk off your face. Think I shan't?"

This to a man of Jasper's dignity was a bitter pill. "Aye, I believe ye."

"Christ Almighty, let us have no more words about this. You know I wouldn't do it."

Into a gusty September morning Hugh struck out for Smithfield, desperate for whatever amusement might take his mind from his imaginings. He chanced upon three school-friends from Evendown among the revellers at Bartholomew Fair. Among the party were the brothers Grey, two loud, rather arrogant braggadocios, and with them none other than Horatio George, whom Hugh had been hoping to avoid until the boy returned to his torturous career at university. Immediately the grateful, lumbering child threw himself into his old friend's arms, told him how much he had missed him, and could he believe it was nigh on two years since they had been together? And Hugh, after his initial irritation at seeing him, smiled at this bit of warmth now so lacking in his existence.

Were he an option on a bill of fare, Ratio, as he preferred to be called, would be a round tower of plum pudding, no everyday fare, but oddly attractive on occasion. With skin like scalded milk, and snub, childish features, he was that good-hearted boy who would never be a man. Even dressed and presented at Court, he would not fail to pick his nose and could never be better amused than by the breaking of sonorous wind. In short, he was that son of nobility who dared even wild wealth and influence to help him on in life.

Still, with no aim loftier than the prevention of melancholy, Hugh grabbed his arm and joined the group. For two hours they strolled about the fortune tellers and watched the merry-andrews jest. Saw the Real Rhinoceros, and attempted to see through a small, grubby opening in a tent the Genuine Pegasus, who was said to be light sensitive. With their bellies full of dainties and palates slick with ale, the Greys sallied up to every pair of unattended girls with unsavoury, and unsuccessful, propositions. During these absences Hugh pulled Ratio from one food stand to the next, transfixed by the boy's face, which was particularly communicative of the subtlest shades of delight or displeasure.

"Here is an epicure of rare decadence, a connoisseur of all!" Hugh bellowed at a group of street urchins who had fallen into step behind them, apparently believing Horatio to be one of the sideshows. To them Hugh bestowed samples of whatever Ratio found particularly agreeable, tickling and prodding the large boy into obscene raptures. "What voluptuous pleasure it is to watch you indulge!" Hugh cried, himself sacrificing liberally to Bacchus. Then he planted a kiss on Horatio's sweat-beaded forehead and led him to the hot meat sandwiches. In the midst of this frenzied display Hugh experienced moments of catharsis; as he gulped his ale, pushed Horatio forward and tossed samples to the ravenous ragamuffins, he realised they were none of them so different in the furious pursuit of happiness – indeed, one must envy any taste so easily entertained as Horatio's palate.

In a foul mood the Greys returned to them after another unsuccessful sally. They declared Hugh a drunk, Horatio a buffoon, then said they were taking their leave to sample delectables of another variety – those on display down the Strand: "Where those jolly damsels who serve brutish appetites may be found."

"Aye," shouted Hugh, "and where are found the best Gentlemen's surgeons!"

"I know what let's do, friend," said Ratio, and Hugh saw in his eyes the look of a child experiencing the happiest day of his life. "Let's tell my father of our adventures today, then you may stay and sup with us."

They arrived at the large, stately home on Fleet Street whose walls and floors were, from Lord George's obsession of all things which smoulder, liberally doused with soot and ash of every variety. This was an exquisitely male domicile. What were everywhere feminine flourishes at Sir Frederick's townhouse was masculine bravissimo on Fleet Street. Hugh stepped with Horatio into the dark, smoky drawing-room where were maintained, like pets, live coals in a chafing dish. Tobacco pipes were pressed upon them by a fastidious footman, who stoked the boys expertly until they smoked like chimneys.

Dregs of a poppyseed cake and cold tea stood testament to some earlier convention. Upon seeing their interest in the aging delicacies, the footman distributed silver toothpicks, then as a matter of course laid out râpée with ivory graters and spitting boxes. Shortly thereafter Walter George arrived and took in the scene, appearing pleased with everything save the cold tea; he slammed a bottle of cognac in the centre of the table sending the tea set to the floor with a crash.

"A bumper for your nineteenth birthday," he said, filling snifters before settling down in an easy chair. Hugh tended to forget the overwhelming presence of his godfather – a great edifice, imposing as Westminster Bridge and rather frightening in an old-style long wig which descended down his back.

Narrowing his eyes at his visitor George said, "That father of yours invited me up last week, but I was every day *indisposed*." Hugh had no idea what were his godfather's indispositions and did not quite care to know. The man sucked bitterly at his pipe until, pausing, he said, "You like that, do you?" for Hugh had just withdrawn the snifter from his lips and exhaled.

"Christ do I! Where does this brandy come from, the vineyards of the gods?"

"That is no brandy pup, it's cognac! Trebbiano grapes of the Fins Bois, from soils of clay limestone. And let me tell you, at your age, your father fell into a faint at anything stronger than sweet wine. Vomited up his guts at every application! It was me drove him to it again and again, but I ask you, was I such a tyrant to try to build up the old dog's constitution?"

"Sir," said Hugh with reverence, "that one must be *taught* to enjoy this!"

"So said a serving wench I knew up Wheatfield. Went on to become a famous dasher in Madame Kelly's Temple of Venus."

For an hour they spoke of Hugh's activities since leaving Evendown and his ambitions for the future. Imbibing liberally,

Hugh awoke from the haze he had, at some point, fallen into, finding himself at table and obliged to bow to Lady George.

Over roast beef and sheep's trotters, Hugh inquired into his godfather's friendship with Frederick at Oxford.

"A forward, insinuating chap was Freddy – had to beat the public school from him."

"How so?"

"He understood no distinction between currying favour and fagging. Told me his right arm had been broken at Rugby after his protector was expelled; then I understood he'd sought me out as the biggest, ugliest, and meanest to fag for at Queen's College. The great blockhead! I toyed a good deal with him, let me tell you, stopping just short of having him wash my feet with milk-warm water... I did, by then, have another to do that for me..." he laughed uproariously, and puffed his pipe. "But by our second year he was dear as a brother to me. Bestowed counsel with a cool head and kept me from many a foolish endeavour. To him I owe my moderation and decorum," he said tearing into a side of beef, then tipping a measure of claret down his gullet.

"No doubt without you, Sir, my father had never learned to enjoy himself."

"No doubt, and lucky for him. I could tell you of some occasions pup... occasions of, shall we say, rare fun."

"Must be in the family, Sir!" declared Ratio, "for I recall years of rare fun when Hugh and I were together at Evendown! A merrier companion there never was! He would get me laughing most often during our forty lines of Homer, when we were sleepy and restless of an afternoon. And I never stopped laughing till our instructor Mr Matthews would strike me! And I had but just stopped laughing at what was Hugh's freshest antic, and then there would be another, and I would be all night laughing!"

This pronouncement served only to stop the flow of conversation and there was for some moments only the sounds of chewing and swallowing. Ratio urged another bowl of sheep's trotters at his guest.

At some unknown point in the evening Hugh was again in the drawing room where Walter's eldest son Allan had settled down at his viol. Standing before the chafing dish Lord George was confiding that he found great solace staring into his dish, and reckoned the hot coals, which he nudged with a poker, looked rather like kittens at play. His godson's eyes remained steadily on the glowing kittens, then drifted from this soothing performance to where Horatio lay sprawled upon a settee. Then his eyes blurred and without knowing why or where it had come from said, "Bramble."

"And who is Bramble?" said George.

Hugh started, and in a slow, cognac-panic stammered, "You will laugh, Sir. I have begun to name your bits of hot coal."

This confession was so agreeable the man fell into a violent earthquake of laughter. "Damn my eyes if I haven't done the same! Could you but be my son Hugh, I would be a contented man. Look at my own, the useless clod. Is there any hope for him?"

"Allan?"

"No, the other one. Can you get him a woman?"

"A woman?"

"Come now. I hear how you get about with the ladies. And I ask you – is Horatio not surrounded with all the accoutrements to make a Gentleman? Damn, if he would not take a game of Spilikins over a wench. Have I not given him everything he can require, everything to instruct him in manly ways and boost his libido?"

Hugh stared about this room of impressive masculinity. "Everything, Sir, save a bowl in which to soak his sheep's gut."

"If I could trust him to use it, or even understand what armour is for."

At this point they were interrupted by Allan at his viol, for he had commenced a Sarabande. Hugh felt his knees waver as he was brought from rife vulgarity to the high art of Allan's performance. Shuffling to the settee, Hugh collapsed beside the insensible Horatio, and found he was just able to command himself until the end of the piece. But he was not long in safety for Lady George joined to lend her fine contralto to the sonorous strains of the instrument. Together they filled the rooms with Italian songs of the most aching expression. Oh, that such beauty was suffered to exist in this brutish house was unfair beyond enduring! It quickly became too much; Hugh threw his head into his hands and began to sob like a child.

He was losing James. And what was left but a strange exis-
tence in a strange world, in which he could never have a moment's solace lest his true nature be discovered? As Lady George sang, Hugh heard Horatio rouse and grow concerned for his friend, felt the pounding of Horatio's meaty hands upon his back as he asked his father what could be the matter? To Hugh's tearful apologies Lord George nodded, took his godson's shoulder, and wished his 'other' son might have enough experience someday to feel as deeply.

The night wore on; Hugh's tears dried. He lit his râpée for a third time as Allan commenced the reading of some original poetry. Hugh grew heavy and introspective, nursing his cognac and the deepening fear of what might be lost love. When he awoke, he had remained in the drawing room with a now snoring Horatio and a clock striking one.

He pulled on his overcoat, crept from the house into the chilly night and ran across London. In moments during his flight he was certain, absolutely beyond doubt, that a letter awaited him on the vestibule table. But when he arrived no letter was there, and as he worked to catch his breath, he could only stare at the empty space.

And wonder.

CHAPTER 15

The following Tuesday brought another glittering assembly. Lady Highborough gripped Hugh's forearm as Duncan Sallow announced himself ready for the floor. Anne stepped forward, gave him a demure smile, and they strode forward hand in hand for their first dance together.

Said Highborough: "And if she withstands after tonight, with that fortune and that lusty embrace, I take my bow in the whole affair – she is not of my species."

Hugh said what was appropriate, then fell silent the better to greet the gloomy thoughts which now often took his arm. After a time, he was introduced to a Miss Sanders, reputedly worth twenty-thousand pounds, and they joined the dancers on the floor. But dancing failed to rouse his interest, and the girl herself offered nothing but schooled civilities and the requisite female parts to shift about the floor. Suddenly she declared herself quite flushed, said she could not complete the set and must, in fact, go home. Whether or not this was owing to his abysmal mood Hugh was relieved; he held her hand until an appropriate moment, then she scurried from the floor as he turned for the refreshment table.

To one side of the punch bowl stood a man whose eyes

met Hugh's, his arms drawn behind his back in a thoughtful posture. He looked down and then up to the dancers, as though to say he was available to be approached but would allow Hugh to pretend not to have seen him. He was about thirty-four, smart in a deep brown coat, and a ruffled jabot nearly as white as his wig. The shock of dark brows over the bridge of his aquiline nose lent an air of earnestness. And though Hugh rather admired his understated elegance, he possessed too much the air of a chaperone to provoke a second look. Choosing the other side of the refreshment table for his exit Hugh crossed the room to observe the progress of his sister. Not surprisingly, Duncan was a lusty dancer, sweeping her along with unflagging energy.

After the set Sir Frederick beckoned his daughter and her beau to one side – Hugh was beginning toward the party, when he was confronted with Lady Highborough in great distress. Joined to one arm was the man from the refreshment table, her other arm extended dramatically before her.

"Pray do not vanish again, child! I conjure you, take my good Gentleman from me. He asked to be introduced earlier and you were just then off to the set. I have an engagement in the next, and crave a *petite refresh*, if you take my meaning, so I trust you will entertain in my absence." Then she withdrew, dancing in some discomfort and cursing the punch, and forgetting to first make the introduction. As their hands came together Hugh offered a curt smile.

"Beg pardon, Sir. I saw you by the punch bowl and perceived an interest, but in the crush etcetera. You are a friend of her Ladyship?"

"Lady Highborough is a friend of my father. You know my younger brother Duncan and I trust you will know my name. Benjamin Sallow."

Perhaps it was forgivable that with one son the very image of his father another might be expected to make a third. Still, though not large with virility, he possessed a variation on

Charles's engaging manner which was difficult to place, and so distracted did Hugh become attempting to distinguish the resemblance, he forgot to release the man's hand after greeting him. He withdrew with an apology.

"Not at all," said Benjamin, smiling. "It was I held your hand too long; I who was a little lost. You see I fail to recall when last I introduced myself. Do you observe that the task of introduction is, in the normal course of things, nearly always performed on one's behalf? By a mutual friend, by a spouse. We live in a world in which even one's Christian name may sound foreign once one is tricked into pronouncing it."

This was not for a moment to be believed, but the skill of the subterfuge was admirable. "I never considered it," said Hugh, "but no matter the introduction it is a pleasure to know you. Your father is a remarkable man. We are much obliged to him for bringing our families together."

The man inclined his head though declined to add anything to the remark. Something in the mildness of his gaze, and the maddening evanescence of feature led Hugh once again to stare at him. He was like a text brought into English from Latin by way of Greek. It was so very odd, it was...

"Again Sir, you catch me out," said Hugh, now actually angry at himself. "Forgive me. I thought to distinguish the exact source of the resemblance. I cannot say why it should quiz me so."

"I make comparisons whenever I meet the family of friends."

"No doubt without vulgarity."

Looking about the room Benjamin said: "The fashionable set loves nothing so much as a masquerade. True novelty, Mr Entwistle, is more often found in a face which will withdraw the mask. Would you agree?"

"I would and do. The name is Hugh."

Benjamin inclined his head, and by his silence made clear

his partner must continue, a tactic both flattering and unsettling. "I suppose," continued Hugh, "my behaviour just now was owing to the consciousness of having avoided you. I understood your look at the refreshment table though am embarrassed to admit it. We do not always know why we make the decisions we do. I assure you it was from no disinclination to know you. I suppose after the heat of the dance... you might say I had not yet found my sea legs."

The laugh was a throaty baritone. "Allow me to fetch you a glass of punch."

"Sir, there is no need—"

The look which came into Benjamin's eyes silenced him. When it passed he said with a smile, "I insist."

When the beverage arrived, Hugh put a palm to his suddenly damp forehead. "Much obliged." And in less than a minute, hardly hearing what the man was saying he had finished the beverage.

"I must fetch you another."

"No, I beg you. I drink as easily as I breathe... that is to say, I was not thirsty..." He closed his eyes. "The servers will bestow their harshest looks upon me, for having to refresh the bowl so soon."

Benjamin laughed. "It would be strange indeed to begrudge anyone anything in a room of such prosperity. 'Tortured Tantalus stands parching in his pool...'"

With these words Hugh was brought round in a fire of disbelief. What could he mean quoting *The Satyricon*, that most notorious of Ancient books? Hugh had never yet met one who would quote it in conversation. Casting his eyes about the room, then down to the floor to recall the passage, he said:

"Unhappy Tantalus, with Plenty cursed
Mid-fruits for hunger faints, Mid-streams for thirst
The Miser's emblem, who of all possessed
Yet fears to taste, in blessings most unblessed."

Then he delivered his gaze once more to Benjamin. The man's irises had dilated to saucers, his cheeks like two flambeaux on a moonless night. But here, *Dear Reader*, our Hero's perceptions failed him. For though Hugh had searched out *The Satyricon* specifically to read those passages describing carnal union between men, he believed he was the only one who might do this. Anyone else would know it as a work of Antiquity, valuable as an historical document but utterly deplorable. And so hardly crediting what they might have communicated to each other, happy only that the man had not called him a filthy reprobate, he laughed:

"The red cheeks, bright as two apples – there, Sir, is the family resemblance! Now we can be easy, so long as we conceal our scholarship of even the naughtiest works of Ancient Rome. Shall we find our party then?"

With most of the house out on errands Anne sat pensively with her tea waiting for Duncan to pay the call of courtesy due her morning after a dance. As Matilda had promised to be home in time to chaperone, Hugh saw no reason to remain once he had finished his plate of eggs. He had an interview that afternoon with a decorated war veteran and in any event, his presence could do little but irritate the suitor, who appeared capable of tolerating Anne's brother but no more.

When they heard Philippe open the front door and escort two men into the drawing-room, brother and sister exchanged a look. Duncan was not only forty minutes early but sounded to have brought his father. Anne rose and hurried from the breakfast room to greet the guests, and Hugh, after another glance at the clock in the passageway, dusted his breeches and followed. Upon passing through the drawing-room doorway Hugh discovered it was not, in fact, Charles, but Benjamin Sallow who had accompanied Duncan. Benjamin appeared somewhat altered from the night before – agitated and slightly dishevelled. When Duncan asked Anne for a private moment in the music room Hugh directed the man's brother into a chintz armchair and sat opposite him.

"Pleasure to meet with your lovely charming sister once again," was Benjamin's rushed announcement. Hugh blinked, unable to believe this was the same eloquent man of the night before. After one or two false starts the man, to Hugh's utter amazement, was obliged to take a moment to collect his thoughts. "She is as lovely a representation of female, as you are of male charm."

"Thank you," said Hugh, no less baffled now the man had recovered his powers of speech. "I am put in mind of our conversation last night on language – our common lament about thoughtless hyperbole, and how it deprives speech of so much force of expression. I know you are not one to use words of praise carelessly, and so must feel your compliment very much."

"I come," Benjamin continued, appearing not to have heard, "at the invitation of your father; that is, should I find myself free and in the vicinity, he instructed me to call. I come particularly to ask after your health, and to thank you for your company last night. I trust you have recovered from the heat of the dance, which for a time affected you so much."

"Well Sir," Hugh laughed, "no girl after an assembly could feel more flattered at this uncommon concern. It may amuse you to know that, by voice alone just now, I took you to be your father. Is that not incredible? And certainly, this very gallant interest only increases the resemblance. You come not as far as he did to my sister in the country, but it is far enough for the likes of me."

Though Benjamin did not laugh, Hugh observed his every word was having a strong effect. The visitor was sitting forward, his jaw working silently as he clasped and unclasped his hands. And though Hugh was gratified he was, alas, still no wiser. At this point, one might wonder how the young man,

not entirely innocent of the world, came so slowly to understand the crux of the situation. Perhaps the unexpectedness of
the approach, perhaps low spirits. But at last he was given
pause when his guest said, "I woke last night several times,
almost continually in fact, first from the fear you would not be
well this morning, then from a terror you should be abroad
when we called."

"That is... quite..."

"And do you wonder that Duncan should arrive nearly
three quarters of an hour before he was expected? And that
he should bring his brother, who was not?"

Some strange dread began to disturb Hugh's digestion, for
this man was approaching mania in his obscure frustration.

"Yes, if you must know, I find this irregular and a little
thoughtless."

"But you see it was not thoughtless. It was entirely at my
insistence that we arrived so much in advance. My brother
was concerned to give offense, of course; still I could not run
the risk of missing you." His dark eyes widened, pleading
silently for comprehension. And comprehension, at last, began
to dawn.

"Good God..." whispered Hugh, "do I understand you?"

"Has nineteen yet understood four and thirty? But I
expect, if you have not proved quite supernatural in your
comprehension, you come to know my words now as I would
have them known." Hugh could only stare. "I say no more
myself at present..." for voices, issuing from the music room,
were growing gradually louder. "Only answer me ...are
you...?"

The weight of the confidence crashing down upon him,
Hugh nodded. "Yes, Mr Sallow. Yes."

"Then pray," said Benjamin, his cheeks ripening to scarlet,
"send a note to my home that I may receive you there, or at a
place of your choosing."

Hugh rose and walked to the window as voices filled the

corridor. Upon the couple's re-entering the room, he grew so hot he dared look at neither of them. But the pair were too occupied in their own affair to observe any alteration in the men. By her manner it appeared Anne had received the man's latest tribute with cordiality and no more. Nevertheless Duncan, having said his piece, appeared gratified. He had wished this visit not merely as a call of courtesy, but to state his position without family present and on his own terms.

And so, it appeared, had his brother.

CHAPTER 16

That afternoon, in full dress, Hugh called at the Charing Cross residence of Captain John Musgrove to discuss his commission. The Captain, who had served under General Murray of the 42nd Regiment, was known for his valour during the siege at Cuba, his interest in recruiting the next generation of fighters, and the half hour he bestowed upon young men of ambition. Rumour had it, if he could be persuaded to even one minute beyond this strict allotment of time, to which he was accurate to the second, a soldier's career was as good as made.

With this in mind Hugh arrived at the meeting, hoping to be one of the privileged few. In a suit of grey silk with gold piping, and a sword from Mr Jefferies, Sword-Cutler to his Majesty in the Strand, he was indeed *un homme complet et puissant*. And could Bramble but be here with him, what could he feel but even more love and admiration now Hugh was the declared object of Benjamin Sallow's admiration? Only James was immature and sought the power of a couple of weeks' silence – had Hugh not told him ten times it was his father's silences he admired most, for their power to persuade? This, then, was the explanation for Bramble's silence.

So ran his thoughts, and with them his first fifteen minutes with the dry and serious Captain. *Would not Mr Entwistle consider an ensigncy in a marching regiment? This was a far more practical place to begin.* Well Captain, as my wish is to remain in England, I desire a position which will keep me at home. *But an ensigncy, once obtained, might be exchanged for a cornetcy, and so in a few years make a position in the Guards more likely.* Your advice is much appreciated, Captain, but my father knows Lord Halifax. His Lordship returns to open Parliament in November, and the commission, if it cannot be secured before this, is nearly assured at that time.

When the grandfather clock showed just five minutes remaining of their allotted time, Hugh began interrogating him about the siege at Cuba which must needs have taken many hours to relate. For three minutes his questions were answered and even encouraged. Then the Captain stood, told his guest his time was up, and wished him a good day. Hugh was deposited outside a full minute early, but he found, with a laugh and a stretch in the bright sun, he cared not one fig.

This was a happy day. Happy that he could tell his father of Musgrove's grudging promise of assistance. Happy to at last understand Bramble's childish games. And happy that he was a tall, dapper man in full dress, who could boast heart-rending admiration from a rich and very well-connected man. That Benjamin held no attraction but as a sympathetic friend signified little. That the man might wish him for his own hardly crossed his mind. Hugh Entwistle was admired – that was what mattered.

From Charing Cross, he proceeded to St. James's to take in this bright, blue day. Along the way he observed a look or two in his direction. And why not? He had a good figure shown to great advantage in the suit. Why, once or twice he even saw reflected in the windowpanes a face quite tolerable to look at.

Then, a slight commotion in the direction of the Palace

drew his eye — a Gentleman bedecked in cream brocade attended by a large retinue. Hugh advanced for a better look. It couldn't be… no, it *must* be… this was Christian, the nineteen-year-old King of Denmark, whose tour of England had been noted in the papers. And, as had also been reported, His Majesty appeared decidedly unhappy. The stories must be true. For it was said the young man was entirely neglected by his royal hosts, who viewed this visit from a spoilt relation as something of a nuisance. But that *royalty* might be neglected! As with so much in Hugh's life of late, the idea of it was utterly absurd, and yet somehow true.

He determined upon a dignified approach. Christian remained motionless. After a blank look at the greeting in English, spoken at a respectful ten paces, Hugh came another step closer. He bowed deeply and announced in French it had been his hope today to glimpse His Majesty and pay his respects, for his arrival had been noted in all the papers. This appeared to please the young man, handsome in a bug-eyed way, who asked to whom he had the pleasure of speaking. When Hugh answered he was Sir Hugh Entwistle, a Soldier in the Guards with a house in Westminster, Christian strode forward and withdrew his sword with a cry of *"En garde!"*

Without time to think Hugh's own weapon was drawn and he had parried three wild jabs from a gleaming sword. Then his assailant returned the weapon to his belt and walked in a large circle. Heart pounding out of his chest, Hugh knew not how to flee, or even if he even could flee. Might this not be some foreign show of respect? Then the young King wiped his nose on his sleeve, fingering the hilt of his sword, and appeared to consider another attempt. One of the King's middle-aged protectors, with a reproachful stare at Hugh, approached his charge with a few low, soothing words in Danish. This appeared not at all to the King's liking. The words were answered with a hard slap across the face, sending the attendant staggering with one hand to his cheek. Christian advanced and, pulling aside the attendant's hand, delivered a second and more brutal slap then pushed him aside. Then, returning to Hugh, who lifted his sword again in terror, he said in English, "Tell me where finds the jolliest, best whore in London?"

"Your... Your Majesty will find her at Madame Kelly's Temple of Venus. In Piccadilly."

A broad smile spread over the King's lips. A look of elation – of relief! Then he said a number of things in his own language accompanied by some provocative animation. For better or worse, it appeared Madame Kelly herself was to be his aim. Knowing nothing of Madame's age, demeanour, or availability, Hugh contented himself in the knowledge he would not be present when Christian made the discovery.

There was by then a crowd of young men gathering, the same who love a cock fight or a boxing match. They overtook Hugh, eager for a chance to greet Christian, though with nothing but fists for defence. Hugh retreated as the boldest of them bowed deeply to introduce himself. At this King Christian hurried forward and leapfrogged over him, sending him headlong into a hedge, which assured Hugh that the encounter, amusing though it had been, was best ended at this time.

At home Hugh fell into an armchair with a bundle of the week's newspapers – the Danish King was in the city for an undetermined period of time. He had a history of saying odd things, acting strangely, and appearing mentally deranged. He was now, it was widely believed, quite mad... Hugh set the papers aside and thought how very sad was the wild King of Denmark. What was he but another man of nineteen, let loose into the city of London and fancying himself neglected? And were there not countless just the same? Arriving in the metropolis to imagined fanfare, made monstrous by indifference? Yet still he was a king, somewhere.

The townhouse had grown still. No strum of the harpsichord from the music room. Only distant clattering on the back staircase used by domestics. His father arrived home and proceeded into his study. A moment later came the clamour of Arthur, who scurried past asking if the Master were not just arrived? He was keeping a letter for him – a letter from Deerhurst. Hugh was out of his chair before the child could say any more. He snatched the letter from him, certain he was mistaken.

He was some time reading the direction. The hand was that of his uncle and, indeed, directed to Frederick. Hugh kept close to Arthur's heels, hoping for a note folded inside the first, or some mention made of the parson and his family. If there was not, Hugh must apply to his uncle himself, this very night, for he could bear this not one day longer. Withdrawing a volume from his father's set on Roman history, he flipped the pages as the man read his letter. Upon finishing the second page, he returned to the first with an increasingly grave air and read it through again. At last Hugh set the volume aside and proceeded to the desk.

His father had gone ashen.

"Tell me what it is."

He set the letter to one side, declining to look up, or in any way acknowledge his son. After a full minute of silence Hugh continued, "It is only my agony to know which compels me to ask – I must know what has happened."

At last Frederick said, "You will know the contents." Then he rose and, walking passed Hugh, slammed the study door. "Have a seat."

He knew. He knew everything. Hugh lowered himself into the armchair and understood he would rise no more. His throat closed, and he found the words to speak only from the fear he would be despised more for silence: "I displease you. Send me away if you cannot look at me."

After a sharp exhale the man said, "There are things you

must explain, for I cannot… but I do not hold you responsible for this."

Hardly knowing what he did Hugh fell forward to one knee. The man's hand was seized and kissed, Hugh professing himself a faithful servant forever at his service. After he was reinstalled in his seat Sir Frederick said,

"I find the world tempts one in nothing so much as to be selfish and heartless. One despairs at ever finding a man who will not betray a kindness shown… I depart in the morning for home. We shall say nothing of the reason; you must help me contrive a story. Will you do that?"

"You may depend upon it."

"I insist, Hugh, upon a better relationship with Ned even allowing for your differing tempers. Write him tonight. He has suffered, and I fear may need to leave Deerhurst for a time. You know James Bramble continued to tend and ride the gelding after we departed. This was a favour shown him as your friend. Ned never liked him – and Hugh, if you had only taken more time with your brother…" He shook his head. "After we departed it seems James was at some pains to mend the relationship. Professed he never meant to offend and was grateful to our family and so forth. Knowing how prized James was by you, Ned jumped at the attention as quickly as he had been used to hate him. I don't know where James went wrong, for he has, among other things, developed a taste for spirits. Runs about breaking windows, stealing. He brought Ned into all of it, even the drinking…"

"I'm sorry for it if they brought it to Deerhurst. He knows the rules. And his father preaches drink is the gateway to Hell."

"So it has proven to be. You understand that drinking and breaking windows alone do not oblige my return. James did not seek a friendship from Ned; what he wanted was best accomplished by rendering his victim insensible. I confess I am shocked that the Devil could invade a pious family like the

Brambles and produce such villainy. I trust you understand what the world offers of vice."

"Yes. He… would make Ned his Ganymede."

Sir Frederick went ruddy and shook his head. "Ganymede… we make pretty the vileness of that practice, the filthiest perversion under the sun. Did he never try this with you?"

"Never."

"Look at me, Hugh. I want this honestly. Your word of honour this was not the nature of your relationship this summer."

"Certainly not. What more can I…"

"Our troubles are this: James took Ned to the granary." Hugh closed his eyes. "I cannot conceive why, only its being disused and a far point from the house… but of course Mr Colfax is our tenant living just down from the granary and with four children running about. He saw what was going on, and stopped it, though apparently with two of his children present. He swears Ned was not a willing participant. Colfax went to your uncle and this letter was composed. The parson, when it was told to him, collapsed in grief."

Hugh opened his mouth, but no sound emerged.

"Bramble's always been a weak man. And he raised a weak son, open to vice. Their name is ruined, his son has no prospects and will be prosecuted. You look pale, Hugh."

Regardless Hugh had, at that moment, the sword of the King of Denmark run through his body, he managed, "I… am shocked, and saddened."

"James is seventeen. This is not a childish misdemeanour. By its very nature it is not. We shall seek justice."

"I will begin a letter to Ned, lend encouragement, and offer whatever advice you wish."

"And James?"

There passed a long silence, after which Hugh said, "I say

to the Devil with him." Then in a lowered voice and with particular care, "And yet…"

"Yes?"

"I read once of a similar incident. When it was brought before the magistrate, the victim, by seeking justice for the wrong done, himself became an object of condemnation. Many saw fit to condemn both equally." His father nodded. "You have the power to contain Colfax."

"There are rumours already of something serious having occurred. The parson's health has declined dramatically. His curate has taken on most of his responsibilities. Your uncle says there is gossip in Newbury, even schoolchildren are speculating. I don't know if my presence there will help, perhaps it will do more harm…"

"I take your meaning."

"My meaning?"

"As you say it is a contest between the country and the city. Who knows, but we are construed the very representation of city vice."

After remaining silent for a long moment Frederick said, "I had not thought quite in those terms." And yet Hugh understood he had been thinking precisely that. Overnight visits with her Ladyship had made him the punchline of gossips around the common well for years, his family's kindnesses to the Brambles scoffed at as penance for a guilty mind.

"It will be in James's interest," said Hugh, "living his entire life in the country, to plea seduction to the practice by one of us. By Ned. Or even by me."

The man's grey eyes flashed. "No," he said, suddenly at pains to contain his anger. "No, I must think further upon the matter. It will not be decided tonight."

"I shall go home with you. I insist on being of some service, even if it is only to box the thing about as we are doing now."

Frederick rose and, with an oath, snatched the letter from

his writing desk. "That is out of the question if you will but consider what relies upon a presence here. Matilda has told me things to make me hopeful where Duncan Sallow is concerned. Anne is stubborn and will not listen to her, but she trusts your judgment." Frederick came forward and took his son by the arm. "As do I. We are at a crucial point, and Charles will not delay where others would answer his purpose just as well. You must use your influence, every moment of every day if need be, to see this matter to conclusion."

"Yes, Sir."

"You will maintain the household in my absence. The women will be told there are matters to do with the by-election. They must hear not a word of this until I decide to bring it before a magistrate."

With this Sir Frederick departed to order his trunks. The cloth was soon laid for dinner, the excuses presented for the departure. Detailed instructions were composed for the maintenance of the house and servants, except Mr Sharp who would attend his master home. After dinner Hugh retired to his apartment and withdrew pen and paper. He had composed the better part of a letter to Ned when, mid-sentence, he set down his quill and looked up at the ceiling.

"I cannot see you. I cannot write you. I cannot own you…"

But whatever else he intended to say was lost to grief so violent it lynched him of the power of speech. He shoved his chair from beneath him and fell to his knees beside the bed praying for forgiveness. He screamed into the bedclothes, clawing at his head until he felt a pair of hands on his shoulders. These belonged to the chamber maid come up with his warming pan.

"You are fit to do yourself in! You must have your father, do let me fetch him."

"Do not call him! Do not tell him what a wretch his son is! Pray leave me!"

"But Sir, I cannot leave you lie upon the floor! I must do something."

"You can do nothing – nobody can. I cannot tell you, so leave me in peace and say not a word to anybody on pain of dismissal," he cried hoarsely, and then doubling up upon the bed, wept into his hands. "I think I should rather die than continue in a world so baffling and cruel!"

CHAPTER 17

In the beige light of morning Hugh read his father's instructions for the maintenance of the house, a calendar of upcoming duties, his fingerpost through life. He read it again and again and again, like a love letter, and was still. No Jasper to wake him at eight. Nobody to answer to at all now. Until Sir Frederick returned from the country, the place was his.

"This is my house," he said into the silence. "My house."

He descended to the ground floor in half-dress nodding at the footman before continuing into the breakfast room. Placing the instructions beside his plate he drank his tea and perused the pages. He spoke few words to his sister or Matilda, aware of their uncertain glances to each other and happy to ignore them. They made no mention of the departure, Hugh's taciturnity, or swollen eyes. When he asked her Ladyship to explain his father's direction regarding a trade bill, she was business-like but kind. After exchanging another look with Anne, she returned to her breakfast.

The instructions were organised to accommodate his introduction into the art of stewardship. Tradesmen to settle with, accounts to reconcile, along with reminders to apply daily pressure on Anne. The centrepiece of his duties was the organization of a dinner for the Sallows, which Hugh quickly determined to accomplish without the assistance of Lady Highborough. That dinner would be his production, and he would plan every detail to perfection.

The new duties, however, failed to occupy every hour. A walk in Hyde Park was performed demurely and with head down. He wished to see nobody and wished no incident. Bitter regret scourged his belly, ripped down his back and blackened his mind. *You suppose I hate you, James. I do not. Yours was a desperate attempt to find a benefactor elsewhere because I tested something fragile. For vanity. If prosecuted, it is the loss of your freedom and perhaps your life. I shall wear the scars from this for the rest of mine.*

Slow, methodical action saw the first day's duties to completion. He hired Louis Gallante, the footman's brother, as a personal *valet de chambre*. The position was little more than an extended trial to serve in Jasper's absence, but it was an accomplishment to have secured him.

Yet his melancholy was never long returning. He turned to considering a response to that strange dream of Benjamin Sallow's visit, though utterly at a loss how to proceed. At last understanding the dinner party he was to give the man's family afforded the perfect excuse to meet, he jotted off a note asking for advice. He did wish desperately to speak of his pain. If the spirit moved them, perhaps they might confess a little of themselves and their experiences. An invitation came almost before it could be expected. So, in frockcoat, cocked hat and riding boots Hugh set out on horseback to the home in Mayfair.

An aged butler in sombre livery escorted Hugh through the dimly lit vestibule. They passed down a corridor to a parlour of comparable greys, for heavy curtains allowed in only the necessary light. Here was none of the modish mahogany of Beaufort; each piece was of aged, well-hewn oak which stood monument to a style from fifty years ago. The house was almost entirely silent, both from within, and from without. When his host emerged from the dusk of the interior, he greeted his guest with some reserve, bidding him wait five minutes as he spoke with the footman in a low voice.

At last Hugh was bid follow him to the first floor, a floor flooded with natural light, at which point the visitor became keenly aware he was come to see a stranger, and perhaps a strange man. A shaft of illumination slanted over the study desk to a chair set before it. Into this chair Hugh was shown. Around the chair Benjamin paced, stirring dust motes up the thick beam of light. He set a pitcher of water on the desk then apologised for keeping him waiting.

"I was very much at my ease, and admiring your furniture," said Hugh. "I find it remarkable that a home in Mayfair may be so entirely divorced from noise."

"Good construction, and we maintain silence and subdued lighting inside for my wife – she has a room downstairs and suffers bouts of nervous agitation. As to furnishings, I know they are passé. The place was furnished when we took it last year – after the ordeal of a move across the Atlantic I had little desire to replace anything immediately, and Rosamunde said the style reminded her of her childhood home."

"Why replace what is useful?"

"I see no reason."

Benjamin poured a glass of water and had he not betrayed a laboured swallow during the operation, Hugh would have believed him nearly indifferent to himself. The glass was offered, and Hugh was put so much in mind of taking sacrament in a shaft of divine light he asked to move to the sofa.

"And you continue in health?" asked Mr Sallow, his eyes following him.

"I do, and of late have been vastly occupied. My father was obliged to leave London and I find myself master of a household. A prodigious endeavour."

"I see. And what in particular challenges you?"

"It is the minutiae of each, rather than any one, task.

Maintaining provisions and delegating tasks with judgment and clarity requires a resolute character. And my father's insistence upon scrupulous ledgers occasionally confounds. He makes a matter of principle an intimate knowledge of household affairs and keeps no steward."

"I trust you felt no obligation to neglect your new duties to come here."

"I neglect nothing which cannot wait."

"May I ask why you answered my invitation?"

Trying for humour Hugh said, "I am made specimen under your close examination, Sir." When his words produced nothing he said, "You had occasion to pay me a tribute and I seek to continue the conversation. Was I remiss to wait so long?"

His gaze passing over Hugh's tan coat and breeches, Benjamin said, with an edge in his voice, "Rather fearless, are you not, to receive a tribute so naturally? This is not the first you've received."

"No matter what I have received your own address struck me most singularly."

"And yet not the briefest note to communicate that interest. Three days of silence means, at best, indifference. At worst, the time to secure a witness for the magistrate."

"Can you actually think that?" Hugh said, horrified. Could the man ever know the cruelty of these words at such a time? "But for a sequence of events which upset the peace of my thoughts I must have written sooner. Surely a friend, which I hope you will be to me, may wait a day or two to receive an answer."

"Are not young men impatient for the things they like? Perhaps my address was just one of many. Another bouquet of flowers to feed your pride then toss aside."

"Certainly not. And even during days of terrible turmoil for me you never left my thoughts entirely."

With a sigh Benjamin's reproach appeared to slacken, and

he took Hugh's hand. "I'm sorry. I've longed for you to come and now I..." he shook his head.

"Rather than speak of me, tell me of your own experiences. I should like very much to know."

His host laughed. "If you mean what I think you mean there is nothing to tell. I have no experience and am late to try. It was always our wish, my family's I mean, to return to England when the time was right. Everything has centred on our returning. So, too, this other part of my life. The very thought of attempting something back home..." He raised his brows, "quite impossible. However, in London, where one may be anonymous. The winding lanes, the dark corridors into which one may enter and never return. It seemed the natural place."

"But things have not gone to plan?"

"The best way to know one's self is to travel, Hugh, that is what I have discovered. I am not a prude or a Puritan but have never felt more of one since arriving. London is glorious and filthy and wild, as I knew it would be. Yet I was so overwhelmed when I arrived, I scarcely ventured out the first three months. One night I gathered the courage to caterwaul in St. James's but very soon sensed danger and departed. I have since determined there must be a better way. Now I may be found at every ball, drum, or rout in the city, developing my tactic with people of Quality. Until you, my approach has been either too elusive or too abrupt or made to the wrong sort entirely." That he laughed so easily at this confession warmed Hugh considerably toward him. "Then with you I struck upon the quote from Petronius which had such... implication. And then to have you answer it so completely. Even when you were slow to understand me, in that moment I understood you perfectly. I could not sleep for thinking of you... and now you are here, in all the blow of youth. You are so very lovely, Hugh."

The look coming into his eyes was a warning, and a reminder of what most certainly were his expectations.

"And now what I must tell you," said Hugh. "You do not know me yet and so I must believe your interest in me lies primarily in what I represent." Benjamin's brow furrowed though he attempted a smile. "Which is to say, by no fault of your own, I must decline to be more than a Platonic friend with whom you share a bond. Do not be offended – let me be that friend. Perhaps I may even be that conduit through which you discover what you want. I do wish you to have it. Only it cannot be me, I'm afraid."

"Nay, Hugh," said Benjamin, withdrawing his hands, his eyes flashing, "I cannot take *more* offense than to be told I do not know my own mind. It is you, and not what you represent, which inspired hope, and which after a torment of three days, after as many decades, cannot but inspire the most exquisite pain in my breast!"

"Will you not understand what is difficult to say? My heart has been broken. Just a few hours after you called saw the end of my happiness." The silence which followed stirred Hugh's anger; the man actually suspected the truth of this story! "And had I sought a pretence to evade you, Sir, I have the wit to find a better one than this. There have been moments I would rather have died than attempt to repair myself. I lost all my hopes and dreams with him, and yet I must not stop hoping and dreaming. You are the first I can tell it to. Not a sister, not a father, not a friend."

Benjamin was for some minutes unable to look at him, rather twisted in the other direction and staring at the floor. Hugh expected every moment to be thrown bodily from his house by an aged servant.

"*What you represent*," he said at last, "I understand what you mean, I suppose. It is what I took particular offense to. I maintain it is *you* who inspires this affection – but I own a poverty of… willing specimens may, of itself, have inspired some awe."

With a smile which said Hugh had not lost a budding friendship he said, "Very well. You succeed in convincing me, though at the expense of personal excellency." Then in a good imitation of brightness Benjamin said, "Shall we have a look at the garden?"

Pleading wordlessly for understanding Hugh said as humbly as he could, "If I may," and began to rise.

"Sit. We have nothing but a dingy courtyard here. Close your eyes."

A look into Benjamin's face said he was serious, and Hugh settled back in his seat.

"My family has come up in the world. We wish great things and have, I believe, earned them. My father has begun his search for a country estate, a place he hopes will be passed down to generations of little Sallows. The estate will be mine in the future, but I will take on the design of the gardens from the outset. What is the name of the horse you rode today?"

"Jupiter."

"Picture yourself on Jupiter, cantering up a long approach through a tunnel of dogwoods in dappled light. Tie your horse. I am round the back, on a patch of earth walled in by boxwoods, with rows of vegetables and a place for herbs. Now begin down a path of yews with an underlayer of laurel. As you proceed there are glimpses of secret and delicious paths you must return to another day, for you cannot take them all in at once. At last, you cannot resist; you fall into one and so are lost in private, winding turns. There is a brightly lit glade around a blind turn. This glade might contain you for an afternoon's reading, or perhaps it contains a special friend. You link arms with this friend and continue into circuits of snug walks. Through beds of Apothecary roses, in fuchsia and plumb, all very fragrant. Madonna lilies and peonies, hibiscus, and some impressive figs. You recline on a bench, pluck a fig, and look out to a hill. On this hill stands a grotto with a tumble of ruins, very old, and evocative of a time out of mind."

After a moment Hugh opened his eyes, a smile playing on his lips from the curious intimacy of the interlude. "I should like very much to see the garden in Surrey, or wherever it will be."

"Then perhaps I shall invite you. But first we have your dinner to plan, and that is best hashed out over a dish of tea in the parlour." He bid them rise but before they reached the door of the study Hugh placed a hand on his arm.

"Are you very disappointed?" When there was no answer he continued, "Because I wish you to kiss me."

"Kiss you? That is a strange request."

"Not strange; as the first specimen for your collection."

After a sigh Benjamin said, "I think not. Such a fine specimen must lead me to hope the next will be as fine. No, Hugh, I must decline."

"Then do it if you believe you can relieve, for one minute, my sadness."

A shadow crossed his face and he shook his head.

"Then kiss the one you met at the dance, the one who refused to release your hand. Kiss him because you were happy to meet him. And because he was, I assure you, happy to meet you as well."

It was not what Hugh had imagined. With unforgiveable gentleness the man came forward and took him not for a kiss, but into an embrace. He held him with surprising strength, and for some time until Hugh grew uneasy at the emotions being disturbed. Then, like an afterthought, Benjamin drew back and pressed his lips to Hugh's, then again, then inhaled deeply as he withdrew.

"First specimen for my collection − speared and boxed," he said, smiling.

"Will you not kiss me properly?" said Hugh, wiping wretchedly at his eyes.

"I will not – and I see it is right I will not."

"I do not come to your home to disappoint or bring misery. You agree to help plan my dinner and must be so little repaid for your kindness."

"I shall be repaid in time, Hugh. Let me know you slowly."

Over the next two hours a dinner was planned though with digressions into too many other topics to count. Benjamin owned a small bookstore on Charlotte Street, which led to a discussion of literature. His only child, a girl of about nine, made a few appearances, curtsying whenever she entered the room, in total about eight times under as many pretences. Otherwise his was a household of servants slipping in and out of rooms, and pretty dust motes hovering in this bright, peaceful glade within the city.

At Hugh's departure, Benjamin pressed into his hand the ninth and final volume of *Tristram Shandy* as the merit of the work had inspired some genial disagreement.

"Though I never continued beyond the second volume," said Hugh, "I suppose the ninth must begin more or less where I left off."

"Never continued beyond the second, and dare criticise the work as a whole? Hugh, when you said you had not yet read the last volume I assumed... wait while I retrieve the third."

But when Hugh mounted his horse it was with the ninth, and a prediction that he would understand every word of the story even omitting the other six. Upon his return to Beaufort Buildings he composed the invitations to dinner, then fell onto his bed with the book. The novelty of attentions from an older man numbed some of the pain, and he began to recognise an evolution in himself. Gone the aimless lay-about of Deerhurst Hall, lovesick to distraction. Hugh in London had made a new friend and was running a household moderately well. Even his thoughts of James had altered – gone those longings for physical passion. He prayed only that his friend might continue in this life, no matter where, and no matter the trials he must endure.

About eight o'clock there was a knock on his door and Arthur announced a caller downstairs. When Hugh descended a letter was placed in his hand by a servant from the home in Mayfair.

Dear Friend,

The impression of a rider upon a black stag, with my book in tow, lingers so strongly I must write or remain forever distracted. I have accomplished little since his departure, for I look up every five minutes and say: 'Who was that beguiling visitor in my home, who quizzed but did not condemn me, who beheld my heat but never wavered?' Stand on no ceremony should you ever seek solace or an ear to listen. You will be admitted day or night here. Let us cultivate prudently what has begun; it would be wrong to ask for more, at present. I trust you will remember this as I proceed:

You mentioned something which, had you not said it, would hardly bear introduction by me: that you might be a conduit for what I seek. If I misunderstood, or misheard, I beg you will disregard and think no worse of me. But I am a man like any other and continue the pursuit. I cannot have my first choice, leastways not yet, and I am reconciled to this. My wish for experience has not waned and, if I am honest, has now only increased. I fear very much making a mistake. I ask your advice in this matter.

Send a brief note to say either yes, or no, and a time you are at liberty to meet tête-à-tête. I trust nobody but the members of my staff, who are long established in my family, and ask that you burn this letter upon reading.

Your ever Affectionate, and Humble Servant

⁂

The return note, sent back with his man, read as follows:

You will wish to know if I have begun upon the ninth volume. The answer is yes. As is my answer to any other question asked and requiring an answer. I propose next Friday at eleven, Salt's Coffee House in Chelsea. As I expect to see you at the dinner on Thursday, we may modify the plan then as necessary.

Yours Affectionately
HE

⁂

The afternoon of the dinner Hugh received a letter from Sir Frederick which read as follows:

Dear Hugh,

Upon receipt of yours of 26ᵗʰ Sept and regarding affairs at Deerhurst.

After meeting with the parties concerned, I have determined prosecution would promote nobody and serve only to harm and humiliate. My interview with the Brambles I will not relate; your imagination will suffice in a most painful encounter. I would have you to understand that, whatever my fondness for the parson, I would have sought redress had I not believed it would bring more trouble to ourselves. Nevertheless, there are many rumours about town. The parson goes about pale as a ghost, James has been disposed of with some far-off relation and will not return home, and I am returned from London unexpectedly – this is all the gossips need to talk.

Ned is uneasy here. He has spoken for some time of an apprenticeship in the city. He is settled upon Finance as a profession, and your Uncle Barlow is, for once in his life, proving useful to me. We seek something immediately in a London bank or brokerage. I suggest this as a topic for your next letter to him, as he is certain to have much to say on the subject.

Regarding affairs at Beaufort, I draw your attention to the following matters:

1. Payment should not have been made on the haberdasher's bill, 1 frockcoat/2 waistcoats, ordered 12nd Sept. Mr Jones sends a man to collect as a matter of course but will extend credit for six months. The mantua maker in Ludgate has similar terms.
2. Dismiss Anne's maid immediately. She has become belligerent. Matilda can recommend another.
3. Retrench on candles. You sought to supply the overage from petty cash which is not its purpose. Use tallow if you must but only in the bedrooms. Candles, beeswax or tallow, should not exceed three pounds a week.

Matilda complains of little to do in the running of the house. I am told the dinner is planned for Thursday and it has been organised entirely without her counsel. Make use of the resources at your disposal and hazard no insult or oversight regarding the Sallows in the gratification of vanity. Her Ladyship will intervene where she sees you going wrong and I will be most displeased at any attempt to override her judgment. This dinner must decide the matter of our connection with that family. They will wait no longer.

Post a letter to me Friday morning regarding the dinner and the three other matters. I do not yet know the date of my return to London.

Yours Sincerely,
F.

Hugh set the letter aside.

His breath had come faster, there was a restriction in his chest, but he would not break down again.

"I must be satisfied, James," he said, "I must. More could not have been wished for. You do not lose your life, whatever else you lose. Allow me to believe I helped you a little."

CHAPTER 18

"I am put in mind of a curious event from my youth," said Lady Highborough as the three Sallow men settled at the dinner table. Now the trio were together, Benjamin's resemblance to his relations was more apparent, and this had led the discussion. "A likeness in a pair of old portraits brought my people into an affair with a very illustrious family. My great uncle painted portraits and had the good fortune to paint James Stanley, 10th Earl of Derby when James was a young man. This portrait was much prized as it was the only one of him to survive a terrible fire. One day my aunt, a nuisance-some climber worse than I ever was, saw this portrait hanging in the home of the present Earl of Derby. She proclaimed an uncanny resemblance to a portrait of her own father and begged a comparison.

"The portrait was brought, and to the surprise of everyone it was, to use the common phrase, the spitting image of James. The Earl's family were so struck they began looking into old rumours of foundlings and illegitimate offspring. With irregularities in an early marriage, and the complex succession of earldoms and baronies by writ, we were for a time quite sure something would be discovered to bring us a title, an inheritance, or perhaps a great estate."

Said Charles: "Matilda: relation of the Earl of Derby! Most extraordinary!" The room was by now warmly diverted and the very observant noted a look between Anne and Duncan which signalled common affection for whatever irreverence was to come. Did they not, in that moment, appear the very picture of a united couple?

"Yes Charles," said her Ladyship, "my aunt made the extraordinary commonplace and the vulgar habitual. She began to dig for more portraits, in her house and in my father's. My great uncle was discovered to have been quite prolific, for he had hundreds of canvasses stashed about in many a dark and dusty corner. Many more pictures were produced, and more likenesses found. But when one portrait, of the family spaniel, showed the same striking resemblance to the Earl of Derby it was, I am sorry to say, the end of our hopes of a turn in fortune. My great uncle was not a very well-known painter nor greatly celebrated."

This story produced quite a riot of mirth, and Anne fell into a peal of just-controlled laughter. With one hand pressed to her mouth, her eyes wet and she lost that formality which only ever dulled her charm.

"Give me your hand," said Duncan, and in a curiously intimate gesture reached across the table. The hand was released after a moment to make room for a haunch of venison, but Hugh caught Matilda's eye with a significant look. With the venison, the table was soon overwhelmed by a parade of Charles's favourite foods – sweet and savoury puddings, a beetroot salad, and a fricassee of frogs which had been his earnest desire for some time. Duncan looked sidelong at Hugh's supernatural dinner-planning abilities.

And, quietly, Benjamin Sallow observed them all. The politely interested looks he gave Anne's brother were so convincing Hugh himself began to doubt anything had ever passed between them privately. Even with no possibility of observation, he was only ever the polite brother of a suitor, asking questions the answers to which he already knew. Hugh attempted to provoke him into a smirk with an impertinent question, but not once did he fail or show any sign of special comradeship. Alcohol loosened him to an expected and entirely appropriate humour, and he looked duly impressed when Matilda insisted the meal had been orchestrated entirely by Hugh. It was, in short, the most consummate and subtle performance Hugh had ever witnessed, on or off the stage.

With his every appetite sated, his every thirst slaked, Charles Sallow rolled hither and yon like a Roman Emperor. With alcohol he grew belligerent: he was determined to know how his young host had done so well planning the meal. And *that pineapple confection so particularly to his taste, he believed he had the breeze of the West Indies once again on his skin!* When Philippe produced a chamber pot from the sideboard and showed the man behind a screen, her Ladyship produced Rhenish and sugar for the guests. Whatever remained of formality dissolved with the mixture. Charles went to one knee to debate with her, of all things, breeds of dog, and Duncan had the good fortune to cut his finger playing a bold knife and fork. Immediately Anne rose and sat by his side to staunch the flow and dress the wound, the flute-like notes of her cooings accompanied by the steady bass of Duncan's gratification.

By the time Bishops' fingers and apple creams arrived Anne had returned to her chair, and Duncan looked more affected than Hugh would have believed possible. Then he said, in a moment of perfect quiet:

"I have not enjoyed such happiness at table since my mother passed. Supper was a special time for us, Anne. My father can tell you, so can Benjamin. As you know she passed some years ago, and I believed we would never have that experience again. However, I place this evening with you and your family among those treasured occasions with her."

To purchase a moment Anne said, "My brother takes credit for the menu. Her Ladyship for the amusing conversation." Then, looking into his eyes, she added, "The greater credit, however, belongs to the natural warmth of your family. I come to feel a strong affection for your father, whom I find more accomplished and interesting with each meeting. Your brother Benjamin is the very essence of a Gentleman, truly. And in you, I see a man shining with a very bright future, and whose achievements will only be limited by imagination."

Duncan received the words with an incline of the head. "Have I merited such praise from Miss Entwistle?"

"My words are nothing to what you just said but they are given from the heart. And the high cost of your compliment, when uncertain what, if anything, it would purchase... I feel the praise as much as you could wish me to feel it. And I do share your regard."

At the end of the evening, Duncan kissed her cheek, and held her hand to his heart, and left her appearing quite radiant.

At the door Hugh took Charles's hand and congratulated him. "It is congratulations then?"

"It is. I know my sister."

Charles looked again at the pair he had been observing all evening and appeared to see it himself for the first time. He grinned and patted Hugh's hand before releasing it. Then Benjamin stepped forward and took Hugh's hand.

"Tomorrow at one?"

"Tomorrow at one."

Next day Benjamin rose and held Hugh's chair in a corner of Salt's Coffee House. Long, slender windows descended from the lofty ceiling to reflect a blazing fire. Strung over and set before the fire appeared all varieties of vessel and pot – squat, tall, and bulbous. At long tables set about the room, as wait

staff flew and newspapers rustled, sat patrons of sizes compa-
rably squat, tall, and bulbous, descanting upon hot topics of
the day. *Which factions were fuelling these vicious title disputes? And
was not his being of the Opposition the true motivation for that suit
against the Duke of Portland?*

Sipping his thick, piping hot brew, Hugh said, "And your
brother wishes to be a part of that crazed world of politics?"

"He does. Let us hope it is not all title disputes of the
prominent and John Wilkes."

"No doubt there is more of drudgery representing a
pocket borough."

"His election is assured then?"

Hugh hummed. "My father must first furnish the voters
with banquets and a river of libation. They don't have much
choice in selecting their representative, but most will not care
once they are fed and watered in a show of eternal gratitude."

"I see. And is that all?"

"No, not all," replied Hugh, with an edge in his voice to
answer that of his companion. "Your brother must ascend the
hustings for an afternoon, make a speech and answer the
voters' questions to the hazard of whatever rotten eggs or
stinking vegetables they wish to throw at him. After *that* the
thing is done."

"Thus, the noble system of representation is corrupted."

"Why Benjamin," said Hugh, "you've never sounded more
American."

"I am an American, whatever that means."

"It means one must leave home for the privilege of bribing
oneself into politics. Berkshire seems a long way to come, but
you Yankees will have your representation."

"Your Irishman Edmund Burke speaks passionately as any
Yankee of it, and with more eloquence. The idea is entirely
relevant in this endless debate about deeming every one of
Wilkes's elections illegal. *No taxation without representation* is not
merely an American sentiment, Hugh."

"That may be, but you will learn that *no taxation without misrepresentation* is the true Englishman's creed."

Benjamin laughed then inclined his head. "Very well. You do glow when you speak of power and influence. What I wouldn't give to have you represent my interests."

Hugh grinned. "I never supposed the power of flattery, Sir," he said. "I was used to say, 'What stuff and nonsense men spew at women.' Now I know why so many fall." With a wink, he continued, "And how is your little Paulina, and Mrs Sallow?"

"Well enough," was his response, "and Paulina very well. Though she just nine she wishes to marry you. And what I say of you is no flattery. You are and always shall be my first choice. That I will divert my interests, for the present, does not alter that."

"Understood."

Not quite knowing where to start, Benjamin returned to the dinner. "It was quite an argument last night between my father and Matilda. I never learned if the foxhound, dalmatian or mastiff was to be preferred. Last I heard they were at an impasse whether aggression or defence should be most prized."

"Your father settled upon aggression and the foxhound. Her Ladyship, defence of her coach and the dalmatian. I regret the pointer made neither list."

"Or honourable mention made for the collie."

"And do you prefer the long-coated rough, or the smooth and short?"

"I prefer a long coat on a collie."

"And as to hue: dark or fair?"

The man took a quantity of his beverage into his mouth, swallowed, and stared across the table. "If we speak now of hue, I knew one of late tending toward fair. Sandy-haired to be precise, a variety approaching perfection. Perhaps dark hair for contrast."

"Very well."

"Is the thing so easily arranged?"

"And as to figure," Hugh continued, "perhaps the long, sinewy lines of the dalmatian?"

"I value a good temper over figures. But if can I choose, slim, and smaller than myself."

"I saw a toy poodle once in St. James's Park—"

"Indeed no."

"There are bulldogs in the Arcades, seeking a master for the day."

"Bulldogs, or Water-rats?"

A somewhat prolonged pause. That they had descended to speaking of rough day labourers and equally rough prostitutes was getting to a place neither wished to go.

"Dark hair, a fair complexion, and blue eyes," said Benjamin. "Small and obedient, and as free of crudeness as possible. Not above twenty. But is this all conjecture? Is there such supply one may command at whim? I wonder you can actually know."

"One has only to learn the location of the pillory, always faithfully reported in the papers, to know the neighbourhood in which criminals do their mischief. Nine times in ten it is the same place. Read an editorial denouncing activities in Moorfields or Holborn, and understand they are the best places to explore."

"This is how you know?"

"Yes, mostly. But I can personally attest that St. James's Park, after dark, overflows with lusty specimens from the army barracks. Many appeared quite promising, and I have other ideas."

This produced none of the effects Hugh had foreseen, and he was quickly commanded to forget the matter entirely.

"I beg your pardon," said Benjamin, tugging at his stock, and looking about the coffeeshop. "I open the topic and place a young man in terrible danger. I will hear no more of this; and am indeed ashamed of myself."

"I wish you to have what you desired in your epistle."

"Piss on my epistle and listen to me. Anyone of a like mind has recourse to the same conclusions from the same evidence. I, too, in a weak moment, placed myself on the same walks in St. James's, with the same aim, and departed before I made the greatest mistake of my life. Later that night there was a raid."

"But—"

"I will rise and take my leave of you."

"There is no need. Very well, I shall say no more of the matter. At present." The man pleaded silently to be spared this torment. "Of what worth life," said his friend, "if what you propose can be called life, if it is to be endured in fear and self-imposed oppression?"

"I have a *good* life," said Benjamin. "A very good life, one for which I am grateful – will you not believe that?"

"I wish more for you."

The man cast his gaze heavenward and was, for a moment, at pains to restrain his emotion. "Let us postpone difficult and dangerous topics. Wait for me to raise the subject again. I have been overwhelmed by too much and too soon – and perhaps too late."

"Not too late, Sir."

"It is enough to have met you, dear boy, is what I mean to say. Do you believe that?"

"Of course I do," Hugh snapped. And when Benjamin smiled and said there were no hard feelings, his companion knew there was nothing for it but to relent. He sighed and nodded. "We shall postpone for now if you wish. And all my discoveries into the Thames, with the other jewels of Fleet Ditch."

CHAPTER 19

The falling temperatures of October saw an influx of Lords, Ladies and MPs returning to open Parliament; the city came to life as the streets and thoroughfares darkened. London became a pulsing heart, lit by the flambeaux of footmen lighting chairs up and down the Strand, linkboys with lit tapers leading couples home as robbers emerged from alleys of broadening night. Duncan Sallow exited the city to attend the by-election and was elected member for Deerhurst. Hugh continued to perform his duties about the townhouse, which many days lifted him from bed at dawn, and kept him toiling over ledgers by candlelight.

From the haze of trade bills and changing seasons, Heaton Marvel arrived in a hackney coach to lead Hugh to The Puffers and Poets Guild. The guild met every fortnight at a chocolate house in Temple Bar, and when they came to Wren's Gate Marvel, today in a riotous suit of orange, proclaimed, "Your entrance, Capricorn, into the City of London!" This announcement, slurred by an incorrigible drunk, nevertheless captured Hugh's imagination and he wondered what, ultimately, might be his fate in this city.

Marvel's illustrious guild turned out to be mostly embittered hacks only a step above Grub Street, condemned to compose everything from advertisements to obituaries at a pauper's rate. Nevertheless, the organization benefited members who produced anything approaching art, be it a poem, play or novel. Upon publication one's fellow members, always under assumed names, set about 'puffing' the piece, this being the writing of impassioned, sometimes outraged, responses to a performance few had heard of, in an effort to inspire conversations in coffeehouses and so stimulate sales. The official seal of The Puffers and Poets Guild was a stylised Wind with puffed cheeks prompting a boat with a single sail out to sea. Hugh gained admittance with a poem in imitation of Juvenal, taking as his theme Persephone's retreat into the Underworld.

Late October saw the return to London of Sir Frederick, Duncan, and Ned. After a brief appearance in Beaufort Buildings, Ned continued to lodgings in Exchange Alley where he would remain during his apprenticeship. Their stilted correspondence had done little but gratify their father, and Hugh could not meet his brother's eyes without seeing the duel accusation of neglect and betrayal for having introduced him to James Bramble. Better to think of Anne's forthcoming marriage, set for the following Spring. Frederick's handshake upon re-joining his daughter was perhaps a little cold, but Hugh cornered her soon thereafter with an embrace. "Well done. You have made him exceedingly proud."

And well done his own efforts directing the dinner which had seen the two engaged. Or so he believed, until he learned it was general knowledge that Benjamin had authored the entire bill of fare.

"Let's not look so bleak," said Frederick. "I have my ways of discovering the truth."

"I wish you to believe me of rare and supernatural ability."

"I believe you will employ the resources available to you without the need for supernatural intervention."

Hugh nodded.

"No trouble, I trust, discharging Miss Mapplethorpe?"

Hugh assured him none at all, however the woman had departed with no letter of recommendation and so in a storm of harsh words. The sight of Arthur hauling away his small portmanteau had nearly broken his heart. With his father's return, Hugh had also been obliged to dismiss Louis Gallante, although his service had far exceeded that of Jasper Sharp, a man now exceedingly angry by the dismissal of Jenny and her little boy.

Next morning at five after eight, Sharp was threatening to strip the bedclothes and pour water into the bed if Hugh was another moment rising. The wash and shave proceeded without a word. At last, Jasper stepped back, threw his instruments into his bag, and said:

"I'll have a word now. Ten minutes shall suffice."

Buttoning up a new cream smock, Hugh stepped to the looking glass not trusting that his face and neck had been left unscathed. "After twenty minutes of silence, Jasper, I wonder you do not employ your time better."

The man's look betrayed not just his usual surliness, but quite a lot of heat. So much so that Hugh paused with his buttons and waited for him to continue.

"Regarding Miss Mapplethorpe: Jenny was a good woman. She was five months attending yer sister and happy in her employment when I departed. Then I received a letter from herself to say she had been dismissed. I desire to know the reason for this."

"Her fitness to wait upon Anne was the issue. One may be dismissed without one's personal character being called into question."

"I ask again: was it yerself or yer father decided it?"

Pulling on an emerald embroidered waistcoat Hugh said,

"And if I had cause to displeasure in the services of Jasper Sharp would I be correct to relate it to all and sundry? Jenny's dismissal is none of your concern. You took a fancy to her, I am aware of that, and I am sorry for it."

"Aye, and so must be concerned in her affairs even more, now she's lost her livelihood. And without a letter of recommendation she and Arthur were obliged to seek support from her relations in Portsmouth."

Snatching his frockcoat from the back of a chair, Hugh turned to Jasper and said, "Let us end this, while I am still of a mind to do it cordially. My father and I are of the same mind in these matters. We decided it was for the best."

Jasper wiped his hands and forearms with a cloth, then he strode forward, placing himself between Hugh and the door. "Yer father was right pleased with your handiwork here in London; sold the seat in Deerhurst a second time in a year and your sister too into the bargain."

"How dare you speak of her like that?" said Hugh, coming forward. "She has never had a word to say against you, or Jenny, though with no shortage of reasons. Now you will begrudge her her good fortune?"

Jasper smiled. "I begrudge nobody nothing, what merits it. I am *Philogynus*, a lover of women, and Miss Anne is a right meritorious lass."

His heart pounding in his chest, Hugh said, "I shall breakfast now, then I shall see my father. After my recent successes my influence with him cannot be anything less than decisive. I can tell you your performance quite pales to that of the one I hired in your absence, and it is high time my father hears it."

"Aye, Mr Fancy Gallante let you lay about till eleven and who knows what all."

"Get out of my way," said Hugh, moving for the door.

The valet stepped in his way and favoured him with a grin.

"You have but to run forward and pass me," he said. Then

with one hand he pushed Hugh backward until he was sitting on the bed. "It's beyond formality and respect now, ain't it?"

"I know you are unhappy about Miss Mapplethorpe and I don't doubt she is a deserving woman. She will soon find another position, in another family."

"Everybody deserves a good position, Hugh. Even James Bramble. What position did you have him the first time?" To Hugh's silence Sharp continued, "Well, never mind that. Such is often the way of Nobility. Aye, and Half-Nobility, wishing themselves finer. And a baronet's son must have his fun. It was no fun for the poor son of a country parson, I can tell you."

"What?" said Hugh, hoarsely.

"He was right crucified by yer father. Daresay Sir Frederick loaded the letter with a good deal of perfume before he sent ye his account of it, but that is how it was. I got no sympathy for an Invert, but James didn't deserve to be brought to the gallows for yer Turkish Delight. After infecting him with it, ye left him to pay the price while ye prance about London with yer sword and jewels."

"What happened to him? Where is he?" When there was only silence and an incredulous look Hugh said, "I am more miserable than you could ever wish me. No matter what you think of me I think tenfold worse of myself. Tell me where they sent him."

"I'll tell ye what, I'll leave ye here and continue on with my duties." Quite ready to be left to his misery and shock, Hugh did wish him gone, so was confounded as the man lingered by the door, as though desiring to hear something.

"I shall inquire for my own valet, that we need not..." Then, looking at Jasper's expression, Hugh said, "What do you mean to do?"

"Proceed to the study. What the Devil else would I to do?"

"You will not tell him. Do you have my letter?"

With a groan of contempt Jasper said, "I had a higher

opinion of ye, leastways as a conniver. Course I have that letter."

"Did James never receive it?"

"Ye blamed Arthur when it went missing, rather than yerself, for writing the filthy thing. Had my suspicions ye'd do it."

"You kept it from Arthur's delivery that morning?"

"And it's a damn sight less than your crimes, my buck. Ye kept that dalliance obscure this summer, even from me, until the end, when I saw ye gazing at each other. Then that last day ye had an enormous carriage drive him a few steps to his home. Put the coachman in a right fit for the trouble of it and raised a few laughs down in the kitchen. Laughs, but not eyebrows I don't think, other than mine. And so, if ye can still mistake my intent, I had rather bypass the middleman and seek yer father directly, who will value concealing a family's shame." He turned to go.

"Christ's Sake do not open that door! I'm… I'm not in my right mind. You know I value discretion, I proved that once before. And I will prove it now. Return my letter and we shall have an end to this. What's your price?" The words had only to leave his mouth to wither in the air.

"Price for silence. The letter is safe."

"What do you want?"

"First I'll say what I have. A letter detailing the mischief. I've held it a while. Now we have Sir Frederick half-suspecting yer proclivities, and his petticoats all in a twist denying it. Two copies have been made of the letter. Not *Pamela* but sufficient to bring a modest income. The original lies not with myself, nor with Jenny, and if any wickedness comes our way, the letters will be made known. To yer father, to the magistrate, and to the good parson, who would relish the chance to prosecute ye, if he knew. So put from thy imaginings pistols or poison or overturned carriages, or you will have upon ye a

charge of murder to add to sodomy. It's in both our interests
to keep dear Jasper Sharp safe and sound."

"How much?"

"Only what should be: the wages of a lady's maid and
errand boy, plus thirty pounds for the room and board they
were used to enjoy. In twelve parts. Beginning first of
November. Five guineas additional for myself, today, and a
letter of recommendation for Jenny what'll be wanting this
week." When this was agreed to, Jasper extended his hand –
not for the money, but for a handshake. "Let us leave things
civil," he said, and smiled. It was some moments before Hugh
took the hand, unable to meet his gaze. "There it is," said
Sharp, "a thing done every day. *Per angusta, ad augusta.*"

Hugh released the hand and retrieved the money.

"Now then," said Sharp, "Yer father will have a pleasant
October to think about the happiness of his daughter and feel
pride in his son. Is any price too high for that?"

Some time later the chamber maid entered Hugh's room,
observed him ruminating upon himself in the mirror, and
swept carefully around him. She put the room to order, said
his suit looked very well, and, departing, wished him a good
morning. Yet it was not his suit he was regarding; in the mirror
behind his image stood the freshly made bed. The bed was
canopied with large mahogany posts and curtains left untied.
Through the fall of those dark curtains there had appeared a
deep, black cave. No doubt the angle of his position before the
looking glass explained the effect, and yet Hugh resisted
turning to find it out for certain. What happened if the cave,
when he turned, failed to disappear? What if it remained and
beckoned him inside? And once it had him, refused to
surrender him?

He proceeded to his father's study, searching the man's
face to assess the likelihood he had been told anything. Once

he was certain he had not, he made his request to re-hire Louis, this time permanently, as his personal valet. After making his argument the request was approved, however he was not allowed to leave before his father added: "Let me ask you something, and give it a moment of consideration: do you sincerely wish a commission in the Guards?"

Sitting forward in astonishment, hardly equal to another shock, Hugh said, "What do you mean? You desire me to consider it, and I shall, only I wonder you should even ask the question. It is all I have wished, and what we have planned."

"Very well. But should you doubt, though it would be a difficulty, allowances would be made. And I urge you to consider what lies beyond a commission."

"Beyond?"

"Perhaps politics, travel, university… in short, you need not think of a commission to the exclusion of everything else. But at present, we do think of it, and Lord Halifax is just returned. We shall see him on Friday. Now go, send your note to Louis before breakfast. The securing of a servant, if he is as good as you say, cannot wait. The best ones never want employment for long."

After sending the note Hugh spent the remainder of the day alone in his room indulging the fantasy he was a castaway on a deserted island. He made a new attempt at Hume, then after lunch brought out Virgil in the original, as deciphering Latin never failed to consume his attention. By day's end the sea had brought two bottles from the outside world. The first was Louis's assurance of availability and wish to return. Hugh could have wept and wished no more. His man, his alone, and distance from the one he did not wish to see.

The second note to arrive, from Horatio George, read as follows:

Jesus College, Oxford
19th October

Dear Hugh,

How often do I think of you, my good friend. How very lonely I am here. And so, I do tonight elope to London. You may write to me at my father's home in Fleet Street.

Bartholomew Fair, I believe, was the happiest day of my life. I crave we may have more like it, now I am eloped.

Your most obliging, and humble servant,

Horatio George Esq.

After Hugh folded the letter and placed it on his escritoire, he paused. In that moment he understood he had ceased entirely to expect a letter from James Bramble.

CHAPTER 20

On the 28th of October Jasper vanished from the house unusually early for his pipe and can. Louis sent a spy, who traced him to the 45 Tavern in Gray's Inn Passage, Holborn, where he was seen waving a flag in honour of Wilkes's forty-second birthday. Sharp was home again before the crowds came down the Strand bellowing and playing French horns. They had been hours prowling the city and by the time they arrived at Beaufort Buildings, threatening fire and vandalism to any house that remained dark, Jasper had seen to it lights on every floor were lit.

Upon ascending to his bedchamber Hugh stepped to his window, his eye drawn to a fire in Whitechapel. Common enough though on this night appearing of rather more significance. Was Wilkes at a window in King's Bench observing the same thing? Was he waiting for the return of the mob who might make good their threat to overtake the prison and set him free?

As winter neared Hugh read whatever he could find about Wilkes, increasingly uncertain what he should feel about him. He sat in coffeehouses, venturing into conversations where he could, and listening to the arguments for and against. Though the hero of scoundrels like Jasper Sharp, he was not universally detested by men of parts, indeed some of England's brightest had lent their support. For though Wilkes abhorred the idea of an aristocracy, that class Hugh admired and wished to please, if the House succeeded in ejecting him merely because they did not like him, the Commons was in danger of becoming a self-electing body.

At the end of the year, with his prior elections officially null and void, rumours began that Wilkes intended to stand as alderman for the ward of Farringdon Without, one of twenty-six wards in The City.

"Can he actually be elected from prison?" Hugh asked a man in the Bucket of Brews coffeehouse.

"More remarkable if he is not – he is so popular no man dares stand against him, in or out of prison."

And so it was. On January 2nd, 1769, John Wilkes was elected by a cheering crowd of liverymen in St. Bride's Church, later receiving the traditional alderman's gown trimmed in fur. It remained to be seen if he would ever be allowed to wear it.

By the new year Horatio had returned to Oxford, had escaped again, and was again returned. A wedding dress was ordered, and Benjamin's home in Mayfair had become a cherished refuge. It was here Hugh voiced his frustrations with Halifax, a man who could only be found in the gaming parlours, and who assured him a commission in the Guards most probably could be obtained, only there was no way to predict when this might be and so why not relax and consider his next play at piquet?

The visits to Mayfair were both judiciously advertised and judiciously concealed. No one was to know he called there any more than he called upon the Greys or other former schoolfellows although he and Benjamin had remained Platonic friends. And yet whatever might be his comfort in having found such a friend, Hugh had determined not to sully their time together with talk of the extortion, and so kept the entire affair a secret. So too he discouraged talk of Bramble, as the pain had scarcely diminished, and his brother-in-law surely wished him to forget what came before.

For as snow fell outside, Benjamin began taking Hugh into lingering embraces. Kisses on the cheek edged, while feigning careless brevity, towards the mouth, as his arms drew tighter around the slope of Hugh's back.

Then came professions of love. On one occasion he fell to begging just one night in discreet lodgings, wherever Hugh wished, and whatever must be his limitations. Hugh refused. There was anger, they reconciled, and Hugh fled home to his bottle. Under the sway of this seductress, he called on the Greys to skip out with the nymphs and swains of Piccadilly. To gorge at Chapman's eating-house in Oxford Road and ravish the early nightclubs before proceeding to the gaming parlours. When enlivened by a bottle of Old Hock, Hugh could rile a rowdy room, could be as lewd and obnoxious as his friends, and laugh off the ridicule for saving his shillings while the Greys lit up the tables at Hazard.

It now being too cold to stroll the Strand, evenings with the Greys often concluded in music-filled Temples of Venus. On his first night, Hugh ripped white, snowy breasts from their stays, buried his face with fierce determination, then slid to the floor and passed out. The next occasion saw the trio in a wilder, somewhat menacing bawdy house, whose air sung not with fiddles, but marrowbones and cleavers. After the Greys retired with their choices, Hugh took a girl to her apartment, sat her down, and made a confession. Would she not regale him with her adventures, of which her profession must be an inexhaustible source? For though she could not see it, he was, at that moment, artfully contrived to accommodate a gleet.

"La!"

Yes, and his friends were not to discover he was four weeks more under a surgeon's care for gonorrhoea.

"And you appearin' innocent as the babe unborn," she cried, tossing her shoes. Then she drew up her petticoats to massage red, swollen feet. "Aye, I've a tale or two to tell ye. But it'll be a trial to ye, if yer to keep things calm down there."

Upon his assurances they passed a pleasant evening, some of which passed in unconsciousness while the girl continued to talk. When the Greys came pounding upon the door, threatening to leave without him if he was a moment longer, she brought Hugh to his feet. His clothes were pulled apart, his face smudged with painted kisses, and he was pushed out the door to exclamations of passion and prowess never before endured! So convincing was this angel of Venus, Hugh was sought his advice in the art of love. For the next month he made her a regular partner while out with the Greys until, of necessity at the expiration of his supposed gleet, he abandoned her at the end of January.

It was now four months of petitioning for a commission, and he was beginning to fear becoming a nuisance. He suspected he was quietly smirked at, seen as a fool who did not merit the favour in a city of so many richer and nobler worthies. Jasper collected another payment and Hugh ceased calling on the Greys, for though his nights with them were contrived always with their bed to sleep off his sickness, and so disguise them from his father, his self-loathing became so acute he feared one day he would be unable to recover. For after a debauch came the most vicious, wrenching moments of weakness, when he could only sob remembering James, and tear his hair for not knowing what had become of him.

Duncan now dined twice a week at Beaufort Buildings.

Exceedingly busy after the election, he made time for Anne even at the hazard of falling asleep at the dinner table. Hugh would have welcomed anecdotes of life in the House, but the new MP had no interest in relaying such mundanities and absolutely forbad talk of Wilkes. He was, however, glad of any opportunity to tell Hugh where he was wrong, not only as regarded politics, but in his continuing wish for a commission. When the subject was broached one evening, Hugh observed he and Anne had disagreed about this in private and she had requested the subject be left alone.

"Now Hugh," said Duncan, as his bride-to-be went skinny in the nose, "everyone thinks the world of your merits. But really, petitioning for a commission in the Guards is, I can say it no other way, a fool's errand."

Hugh dismissed this with *fortune favours the bold*. However, Frederick's expression remained impassive, and Hugh wondered if he were not secretly beginning to side with Duncan. This awakened his Spleen, and so, sure he could push the smug man into making himself look bad, he said:

"I declare I should rather *enjoy* military life during peacetime. I do not apologise for it."

"You are aware," said Duncan, "that many of our best soldiers are without employment and subsist on half-pay. Men who risked their lives for their country are now relegated to stand sentry outside taverns, quarrelling with belligerent drunks and blackguards. And worse if Mr Pitt is to be believed. Do you know Mr Pitt?"

"I know *of* the Earl of Chatham," Hugh snapped, "though am not personally acquainted with him. Nor by knowing of him, can I be expected to know everything he says."

"Then I will tell you. Peacetime, says Mr Pitt, has sent the bravest men the world ever saw to starve in English villages, doomed to languish and forget their prowess. The military is quite a serious matter, Hugh, I assure you. Not a sinecure to fund a gay life in the *Beau Monde*."

"One may always wish another war," said Hugh, sipping his port. To which Duncan, unable to believe his ears, stood from the table, incandescent with rage, and excused himself. Hugh had but to see his sister's look of astonishment, and Sir Frederick's frown, to know he had gone too far. He rose to his feet.

"What do you mean to do?" said Anne.

"Apologise." And unable to look in his father's direction, muttered, "I'm sorry, Sir."

He found Duncan in the tiny garden plot behind their home. The light of a waning moon sufficed to show a look of distaste Hugh had rarely countenanced.

"I have come to apologise. That was wrong of me, very wrong indeed." Lines of mist from the man's lips rose on the icy air. "I know you do not like me. I often do not like myself, and now tonight am as low in my own estimation as I ever have been. Allow me to explain."

At last betrayed into a sneer: "Let's hear it."

"If I had to insult Jesus Christ himself to win a point in an argument I would do it. My family sit inside, utterly disgusted with me, wearing expressions of contempt I should not wish to see again. I assure you I have the highest respect for our military, and do not wish war. I said it to provoke you. And if I have not attempted to make myself more pleasing to you, it must be that I resent you a little for taking Anne from us. But I always supported your suit for her hand, even when she was not convinced. Do not doubt she is worthy of your family, even if her brother is not."

"And have you nothing to say of your military ambition? Your *deplorable* ambition, Hugh."

"I know it is." And then he realised, in the time it took to draw a few breaths, not only what he needed to say to win Duncan, but what he had been unable to admit to himself: "I should have left off months ago. To tell the truth, I do not know what I wish for myself. But was I to turn down what sounds well? Turn down what comes with an income and prestige, and which I understood might be obtained through our connections?"

"You are a child Hugh; spoilt with praise, and too many toys."

Hugh swallowed this with difficulty, more hurt than he would have supposed. "Come inside," he said, "before you catch your death. But I beg you not to torment me further about my commission. I must try a little longer out of respect for my father – Halifax told him May bodes well for potential openings. I haven't the faintest idea why – nor have I the foggiest what I might do if I don't get it."

"You would do well in law, or politics, if you wish," said Duncan in a huff. "You need not actually *do* anything, you know that. Do not let your father go on indefinitely."

After a nod, Hugh at last led them inside. As they resumed their places at table Sir Frederick looked them over. "And so did not come to blows?"

Duncan looked at Hugh and raised his eyebrows.

"It did," said Hugh. "Only he hit me every place that does not show."

Next afternoon a letter arrived:

3rd March 1769

Dear Hugh,

You will know first what happened, my good friend. I am expelled from Oxford and shall be returned home. As of this date, you may write to me at my father's home in Fleet Street. He will be, I fear, dreadful upset and in a rage when he knows.

I believe I only joined the Methodists to be expelled. I never much

*understood what I heard of their Methods and do I daresay still
follow you entirely in howsoever you observe your devotions. To
tell the truth, I am not entirely sure that I joined, only I told all
the fellows, and anyone who would listen, that I had. Oh, for
another day with Mr Entwistle at the waxworks, or at the Fair!
I do crave we may have more of the same, now I am expelled.*

Your most obliging and humble servant,

HG Esq.

Horatio George was again returning to London, but Hugh
had not the patience for this anymore; he had his own
concerns, his own future to consider. The boy was soon
sending notes hoping for *a dish of tea, or adventures.* He was
denied at the door as a matter of course, but one day
Philippe handed Hugh a note which was little less than an
order to receive the boy that afternoon. Throwing the note
into the fire, Hugh began his steely reply, informing Ratio of
engagements every day through July. Midway through the
note Sir Frederick walked into his apartments and told him
to expect Lord George and his son at five. Hugh nodded
and set down his quill. What could this be about? His godfather was notoriously busy, and little inclined to travel when
he could summon to his home. Perhaps he had learned of
Hugh's refusal to see his son and now came to reproach
him.

"He says Fortune has smiled upon him," said Sir Frederick
with a shrug.

When father and son pulled to a screeching halt before the
door of Beaufort, Hugh dashed out to the street, eager to
admire what appeared to be a gleaming new curricle, embrace
Ratio, and put to rest any suspicion of neglect or mistreat-

ment. However, this could not be until George left off braying at his son for almost overturning them during the drive.

"Sir," cried Horatio, after he had scrambled to the ground, "this is why I can never think to drive one. Sure, it would be a disaster, for I am far too scared of wild horses!"

"You are grown far too fat to be pulled by them," said Walter, throwing the whip across the seat and just missing Horatio's sweating head. The man had a point, for though large himself, he was now surpassed in girth by his ungainly child. "Throwing your weight to oppose every turn in the road very nearly killed us Horatio!"

"And being doused by all the filth under those accursed stones they cover the streets with. They are not sound! They squirt up every ounce of piss and dung when run at the wrong way!"

"You tell him, pup," said Walter striding toward Hugh. "A man runs headlong into that thing, he is most coward to face. Brought us nigh-up upon a coach and six, the young mammy-sick, and himself almost cast under and ox-cart."

Hugh felt the familiar stab of shame for having neglected his friend. Why must this world be so hard on the likes of Ratio? For all he was the son of prestige and wealth, there was not a humbler soul on earth. More pride could be found in night-men and beggars, than in this boy, who never betrayed an ounce of resentment toward one so unjustly preferred. Horatio ran forward and pumped Hugh's hand, all fresh anticipation, all happy reunion. He began to hint at some great news, but George pushed him back and presented Hugh to him at a few paces.

"Look, Horatio, at my godson; what a Gentleman should be. Tell me what makes him fine."

"Ever the most handsome man in London, Sir, and my very good friend!"

"And do you think it is improved looks, of all a Gentleman's accomplishments, that I wish you to have?"

"But Sir—"

"Handsome? You blockhead, Hugh is not handsome, never was. Till he was sixteen he was downright ugly. A boy needs but three things: wealth, social graces, and connections. Any shortcoming in one, must be compensated for by the others. Good looks in a boy are harmful, for they make him an object of resentment. But now observe all Hugh has done, with a face only tolerable to look at. Would you not agree, Freddy?"

"If you judge him so," said the man, coming into the street.

"I do, and more to his credit. Frederick has only a pittance to give his son, Horatio, really, but has it slowed him? Hugh is every night on the town, making connections and making merry. He's ploughed through half our Ladies of Quality, and you last week weeping before the most patient and obliging of courtesans. Lords and Ladies eat from Hugh's hand, and if he has yet to get his commission, it's the cut to the military budget carries the blame. Depend upon it, he will soon mount his horse to the honour of king and country. And you no more able to mount a horse, or a woman, than a curricle!"

Even Sir Frederick, long acclimated to the man's insults, appeared shaken at this uncommon assault, which had comprehended every one of the listeners. But when he stepped forward it was not to defend his wealth or Hugh's looks. Addressing Ratio, he said, "Hugh tells me with the greatest pleasure of your correspondence and adventures. He had many unsatisfactory experiences in school before he joined you at Evendown. I do not forget it was your father who accomplished his admittance there, nor you, Ratio, for proving such an immediate, and constant, friend when he needed one."

Unable to take in such praise very quickly, when he did, Horatio began pumping the man's hand and telling him it was his great honour to know the Entwistles.

"The honour is ours entirely, and always has been. But you must listen to what your father tells you, for he knows what it is to be a success, and he wants the same for you."

With a fist on his hip, Walter narrowed his eyes. "The time for subtlety is passed, Freddy. I want him to study Hugh and be like him. Simple as that."

"Because you see your son as a man, equal to taking the criticism," said Frederick, to which his Lordship could not see his way to contradicting. Horatio, too, was coaxed into *supposing this must be true.*

"Now let us have a look at the curricle. I can tell you, Walter, if horses are yoked abreast, they must be perfectly matched. You see how the pole sits unevenly?; the left animal is perhaps three inches taller than the right."

The boys exchanged a glance at the great daring of this comment. Looking as much at his friend as the yoke of his horses his Lordship said, "Is it?"

"Look straight on and you will see it. I wonder your coachman could be so careless."

George looked closer at the harness then struck the pole which tilted at fifteen degrees. Appearing slightly abashed, he looked at his friend and said, "I had them latched up hastily. Any other words of advice, Freddy?"

"You may wish horses of the same shade; it is the fashion."

Walter turned to his godson. "Do you hear your father? It's advice any man should know when bespeaking equipage."

"Very good advice, I think."

"Very well. The curricle is yours. A Marquis, who shall remain nameless, lost the stupid thing to me at Hazard on Wednesday. Have it as an early, belated birthday present." His benefactor was obliged to repeat this before Hugh could be made to comprehend it. "Your father declares you must have two horses of the same exact height and shade. It is *the fashion.* This mismatched pair remains with me." The grin of his

Lordship might have been wider, were he not suffered to watch his son point out various pretty features of the curricle with jousting arms, or, for harder to reach places, a toe extended from his precariously balanced frame. Hugh caught his father's eye, fearing the expense of two horses. But the man, dignified at any time, certainly now the size of his fortune had been swiped at, agreed without hesitation to provide horses of the most perfect, identical black.

George then declared a wish to look at his godson's apartments. The rooms were tidier now Hugh had Louis, who shifted things into place with a look of disgust whenever he observed disorder. The French valet was immediately seized by his Lordship and ordered to see what could be done with Horatio's person and dress. Then Walter perused Hugh's escritoire, bookshelves, and boots, from which he withdrew a bottle of good brandy with a look of approval. After ten minutes, Louis's dexterous hands had wrought a few alterations to Horatio's appearance, and Walter ordered the man to recommend someone like himself for his son.

"Though I've always hated the French, in these things you are judged best. A Jimmy Round for himself if you please." After Louis departed the bedchamber, the conversation turned in a most unpleasant direction. "*The Sublime and Beautiful*," said his Lordship, lifting the treatise from a shelf. "Never read it. I've always hated the Irish; Burke's a terrible joy and lackey for Wilkes. But what do you think of his writing to help raise a man's libido?"

"It cannot hurt."

"Do not be shy, pup. Some advice now for my boy. I've given him every possible piece of my own, and in the event, it has elicited nothing but trembling knees and tears. One cannot imagine anything has changed from my day where relations are concerned, though looking at the painted buffoons wandering about the streets these days, one begins to wonder. Regardless, we enrol tomorrow night in another School of Venus."

"I doubt I am as experienced as you believe me," said Hugh, but, hardly willing to press the point, continued, "Engage a lady you wish to speak with, Ratio. Men often visit as much for tea and conversation, as the other." At the snort of disbelief from his godfather Hugh said, hoping for cool dignity, "His Lordship asked my experience."

"Pray continue," whispered Horatio, his eyes so wide and hopeful Hugh's heart nearly broke for him. And so, he took the plunge.

"I know whereof I speak because I was unable to myself, at first. I was afraid, and panicked, and sweaty. Find a girl whose voice pleases you, with the thought only of talking. Tell yourself you must listen, and *cannot* touch, like it is a game. Remind yourself that the girls often do no more than talk to their callers and expect nothing of you. The rest will follow."

Horatio appeared to undergo a religious experience at these words. What was not possible, if Hugh Entwistle said it could be so?

"It cost him something to tell you that," said his Lordship, with a finger in his son's face.

"I suppose so."

"Now you will do as he says and be successful."

"I must be, if he says I will."

The pair departed with *The Sublime and Beautiful* in tow, and Louis's promise to send round a man next day at noon, to see about becoming Horatio's valet. When they had gone Hugh remained in the mews to inspect what Fortune had brought him. Wheels and a frame of shocking yellow. Piping and tufted upholstery a deep blue wool cloth. Absolutely gorgeous, he'd never seen finer. Stepping up to have a seat, Hugh pulled up the black leather cover and imagined his Benjamin sitting beside him. This was a sign: in this curricle he would take his friend to meet a young man. He knew not how or from where he would find him, only that it would happen.

One need only bear a few insults from a Lord George and tell a few lies to get ahead in life. Hugh settled back into the plush seat, inhaled, and produced a grin. Rather pleased, rather revolted.

CHAPTER 21

Looking for Hustlers in new carriage

Overjoyed to see a few rays of sun, Hugh took the new curricle to London Bridge to enjoy an unusually warm day. It was here he had observed, many years before, a modestly well-dressed man without ceremony approach and thrust his hand down the breeches of another. This curious image, so brazenly performed, had clung to his mind as somehow instructive of the place, yet after an hour passing back and forth, he had discovered no curious loiterers, nor did any of the men on the arms of ladies appear willing to relinquish them. Of ill-looking young men roaming in loose, menacing gangs there were plenty. By late afternoon Hugh had become the object of their attentions, no doubt with an aim at robbery, and he soon departed.

On next to Birdcage Walk – a location the *London Herald* once disparaged as offering 'a brace of poultry for the deranged.' Commerce and bustle greeted Hugh when he arrived. He parked the curricle and within a minute observed a couple of slouching shadows on the opposing side the street. Oh, but the uncertainty! – and this the very place of downfall for so many. Still, the defiance, the dare, and the prospect of succeeding were too delicious, and even noble – for this was not for himself, but for a friend.

After a time one of the shadows stepped into the weakening afternoon light. He looked at Hugh, stuck thumbs into his armpits and began to play a lively tune upon the breast of his waistcoat while pursing his lips. This was not ineffective for conveying a like mind, and though rather rough-looking, he appeared to be about Hugh's own age. Still, even in the throes of his most brutish appetites, Hugh doubted he would touch such a man without some cleaning and restoration; and Benjamin, often fixated on Hugh's smooth cheek, and scented person, must surely balk at the prospect.

Yet Hugh felt powerless to refuse when the performer saw his spectator continued to observe him, and, nodding, slipped up a side-street. In the moments he was gone from view, the man was suddenly much cleaner and worth the chase. Hugh crossed, dodged a speeding curricle, and turned toward the side-street, where a hackney coach was bringing up behind Hugh's little bird, loitering as it worked to pass some obstacle in the road. Yet despite his urgency to pass the vehicle, Hugh saw something so extraordinary he was momentarily distracted from his quarry.

For all at once, he had a perfect view into the back of the hackney coach. The fabric, stretched across a minute before, was now gone. Inside one could observe the backs of a man and woman, their heads enveloped in wigs of voluminous curls and frizz, gesticulating and complaining loudly at whatever obstruction was stalling the coach. Then, into the mass of curls on the Gentleman's head, a small, dirty hand reached into the carriage, took firm hold, and yanked. When the wig refused to move, a second, more violent tug was executed, which produced such a lion's roar it proved, in fact, to be the Gentleman's own mane. The hand proved quick-thinking, opting for the lady's headdress, frizzed out to a diameter of three feet, and which leapt from her head like a flock of doves. Yet the management of this ungainly flock proved difficult enough to down the wig thief, bringing the better part of his prize with him into the mud. The Gentleman with the extraordinary hair jumped from the carriage and set upon the muddy thief with cries of "Devil take the chiving lay before I skin him alive! Constable! Constable!"

As the beating grew more severe, Hugh felt a hand venturing into his pocket. He seized it and flung the perpetrator to the ground, then discovered other members of the thief's gang making simultaneous attempts in the crowd. A blow to his head sent Hugh to his hands and knees, but, gaining his footing, his purse firmly in hand, he slipped around the coach and up an alleyway. It was half a minute before he had his bearings and could be sure he was out of harm's way. But by then he had lost sight of his original aim, and his little bird had flown.

Armed the following evening with a new ambition, a belly-full of good claret and his sword stashed inside his greatcoat, he told Louis to expect him back by ten and set out on foot determined to find his prize. An area in Holborn had been mentioned in a newspaper story a few years before, so in Field Lane, in a lively Inn, he commanded Huckle and Buff, then looked about the rooms as he consumed his powerful brew of gin and hot ale. Here were some raucous gatherings, some colourful intrigues, though perhaps too ordinary for what he sought. Up a winding street, then, through alleys until he arrived at an area of rather less respectability. Inside the Hook and Crook, he commanded another Huckle and Buff, and brought it into a corner.

The article which referenced this area of London had been obscure: off Field Lane, from a house which catered to 'those of Captain Rigby's fraternity', twenty-six had been dispatched to Newgate to await trial. The location of the house was unclear, said only to be near a home of prominence, and Hugh's hope was to learn if and where this place had re-established itself. But where to start?

He was soon presented with the charms of Olive, the tavern pintle-merchant, who sought to bring him into a back room. After commanding a third drink, he moved far from her to the end of a long table where he settled into a dark, noisy cloud. There he learned of a candle auction in Potter's Field. A pair of sharpers approached, offering to accompany the young libertine to the gaming tables and keep him from those seeking to fleece him. His inquiry into a *house of rare fun* brought the reintroduction of Olive, who was greatly displeased to be a second time scorned. She complained to the publican, who seemed about to approach the table with some variety of threat. This prompted Hugh to a rapid completion of his beverage, unquestionably the strongest thing he had ever ingested, and so with three down his gullet he stepped from the public house to find another means to his end. He had taken but a few steps when, from behind him, he heard:

"Light your steps, Sir? The moon is just gone behind the clouds."

Four youths stood slouched in an alley beside the establishment. A linkboy, Hugh realised, might be a valuable guide in discovering what he sought as they knew the area better than most. He waited to be approached, and his path lit, however nobody ran forward with lit taper or torch to guide him. His suspicions of this gang were then roused, for though one appeared to be about eleven, the other three were rather older than what one expected for a linkboy. Emboldened in his inebriation, Hugh was nevertheless quick to defence after being set upon the evening before, and when the group began to advance, he announced:

"One emissary only, else I shall satisfy thy taste for steel!"

After a prolonged pause, the largest and ugliest said:

"Christ crucified! Hadn't we best approach, so's ye may make a selection?"

"Advance," said Hugh, aware he was beginning to slur his words, "not one step farther, without I see thy taper."

A taper was produced, and the light struck bright, casting from four still souls dancing shadows on the alleyway walls. He selected the one who appeared least likely to attack him: the boy took the taper and, glancing at him through a curtain of dark hair, stepped lightly forward according to Hugh's direction. With a concerted effort Hugh kept to a straight line behind him, having the misfortune to know the worst of his inebriation was yet to descend and determined at all costs to keep clear of those other three. Every few steps Hugh ordered an abrupt change in direction, ever watchful they were not followed, and wracking his mind for the words to address the true aim of this outing. After a minute sailing up an obscure byway, the gentle tenor of his guide said:

"Pray Sir, might a word of advice be in order?"

"Perhaps. Once I've settled where I mean to go. Turn up there and talk to me."

The linkboy began a friendly prattle, guiding them according to his own desire. To the boy's questions Hugh told a string of lies: "Hanover Square!" cried his guide, "I knew it! I conceived by yer vast finery you *must* belong to Hanover Square. I reckon no finer dress at Court. Old Sam, he's the proprietor of the Hook and Crook, popped his head out my alley and whispered it to us."

"Did he?"

"They was right-honoured by yer presence in that place. What does a Gentleman of Hanover Square take by way of libation? I shall drink the same with the next money I earn."

"Claret at home; Huckle and Buff on this street."

"A stout belly it is takes that concoction upon the heels of fine wine. But now rest yerself upon that bench, you look rather out of sorts. And if Yer Honour allows me save my taper from complete extinction, I'll entertain ye as I have done, only in the dark, or follow yer fancy what would oblige ye."

They were by then standing in a line of dark trees, which had appeared seemingly from nowhere. Seeing they were quite alone, Hugh sat down hard upon the bench as the youth extinguished his light.

"One hears of a bawdy house in the area," Hugh began, "in service to rare appetites. It is some years since, but I wonder any in the area answer to that description."

"Well, I wondered ye were not a Gentleman of Pleasure! If I may join ye upon the bench, I shall tell ye what I know."

"Indeed ragamuffin, you may not. I'll have your information at five paces."

"Ragamuffin? Nay, but you jest."

"No jest; I trust neither you, nor your alleyway-henchmen."

"And am I to be so used, who tries to oblige, while the Gentleman prevaricates? What sort of man is it seeks a lift with one hand and punches me in the face with t'other!?"

"And are you not sent upon this errand, at the behest of the publican? Who, failed of a sally by the tavern wench, hopes to extend his reach in obtaining my purse? Lead me to a favoured place, then extinguish your light so I cannot see to defend myself?"

"But the Gentleman has, by his own whim, directed the entire journey."

"Turn out your pockets and give me your name."

"Turn out my pockets?!"

"Aye, 'less you have a taste for steel."

"I never robbed a Christian in my life! I seek only to earn two shillings that I may feed and shelter myself."

"Then tell me your business; for you are sixteen if you are a day, and no linkboy."

"Never denied I'm sixteen, which I may be."

"And your name?"

"William Dempsey Esq."

A brief strengthening of the moonlight showed a slight young man of hardly more than five feet, and of rather a comely appearance. His clothes, somewhat the worse for wear, together with open palms and pockets turned out, at last sounded in Hugh's breast a note of pity.

"Then Mr Dempsey, I bid you at your ease, once you confess your arrangement with the proprietor."

"I am a linkboy, well-versed in the lanes and side-streets of Holborn and adjacent vicinities."

Squeezing his eyes closed, and opening them wide to clear his addling head, Hugh said, "And as linkboy earn two shillings, when any other would ask thrupence? Two shillings is the cut of a Gentleman's purse, after the proprietor has been satisfied."

"Do no ask the arrangement!" Dempsey wailed, "the shame will bring about a true and honest faint. I am but a poor, humble servant, and must lose my life within the storm of your fury!"

"Tell me, or you will have my fury, and not a farthing for your time."

And so, opting for ten paces rather than five, Mr Dempsey proceeded in these words:

"Miss Olive, Yer Honour, is to have her advance upon any lone or two men who are not so ill or decrepit as to make use of her. Failing this, which will occur, a drink of great economy is pressed upon the patron, and Miss Olive is to try again. If a patron rejects her and departs, we are one of us four to offer as linkboy. We are an array of shades fair to dark, and many ages… and so by these, and other, differences, might better supply the interest Miss Olive wants, if you take my meaning."

At this Hugh fell into a peal of laughter he was some time containing, bidding the youth join him on the bench.

"Well, my comely lad, which is, I suppose, why I selected

you, it is a fool indeed who sets out on a mission, finds what answers his desires very well, and then repels with insults and sabre-rattling."

"I feared this whole long walk I should not oblige ye, not even in your stupefaction from Huckle and Buff, the fiercest of any in London."

"And a request for a house of rare appetites left my inclination unclear?"

"Oh, 'rare' is the most common thing imaginable. Equal to flogging, pampering, mothering, masquerading." As he said this Dempsey punctuated the air with his hand as though showing each vice in its place in the surrounding shrubbery. Pointing up the street he said, "You had but to ask the old molly house, which was up yonder, that I should understand. Sir, those places are much gone over; that one has stood empty these many years."

There passed a moment of silence: that of an inheld breath. For by stealth, the hand lately gesticulating, had disappeared from view. Next, into this silence, an unravelling of services and corresponding prices flew like coloured ribbons into the night. His head lolling back on the bench, Hugh snorted as he pushed the hand from his lap, declaring he would part with no money save what settled the bill of illumination.

"But Sir," cried Dempsey, "it's to this end you came out tonight. Said so yourself."

"Not quite, *damn me*," was the slurred response; Hugh's tongue was now quite unequal to expressing his thoughts. "But I shall grant you, *gratis*, an education in what obliges a Gentleman of Quality; and the first rule is this: we do not pay for petty, open-air trifles."

"But I must have bread to eat; you won't expect a favour for nothing."

"And what of the favour I do you?"

At this Dempsey jumped to his feet, clutching his head like

Hugh — Hustler Seizure

it might shatter apart, and cried: "Damn my blood if I ever heard the like, in all my years! I'll have ye know, there've been Gentlemen aplenty, *fine* Gentlemen, which every one saw fit to recompense for services rendered."

"But if you will grant my bit of sport, free of charge, I can teach you to please a Gentleman in Mayfair, the likes of which you can have never encountered. Should he be seen to properly, he will put a young man under tuition: a private apartment, a servant, all the comforts of fine living."

"Aye, and that apartment will be at the end of the garden, and I shall sip tea all day with faeries."

"I assure you, my saucy fellow," head lolling to the other side, "a living is now being held for a boy no older than twenty, with dark hair, smooth, fair skin, and above all, a sweet and obliging temper. But for blue eyes and a want of cordiality to me, you answer quite well. However, I have no occasion to make the introduction if you insist on challenging my principles. For without me, you will never know what might secure you in luxury, and happiness beyond dreams."

Two things happened, so swift and unnatural they can never be exactly described. For just then Dempsey tipped to one side, eyes rolling back into his head, and began, with all the force of nine stone, upon a thunderous descent to the ground. His stupefied head tilted at an angle to see this, Hugh stirred and leapt to his feet. He caught the boy in his arms, bringing them down with such cordiality, that, when they reached the ground, but one hand of the insensible youth was scuffed. The boy then slipped off the silk bed which was his saviour and onto the grass. Hugh, however, coat, silks and stockings tearing, sword twisted viciously in its sheath, cracked his head open to the stars. Breath, vision, sense of any kind but shocked pain were, for a time, utterly deprived to him. Even his own name had vanished. At last reviving, Hugh scrambled to the fainted wretch.

"Oh, I am a scoundrel to bring to grief with only the power of my words! Do wake and tell me you are all right!"

By this and similar pleadings the boy came at last to his senses and was soon sitting up and asking what had happened.

"Let's neither of us attempt to recall it. Take two shillings and put from your memory the entire sordid affair." The revivifying effects of two shillings completed Dempsey's physick, and he soon regained his feet.

"I shake hands with you here and bid you good evening," said Hugh.

"But Sir, there was business we had not completed, I know there was… was it… was it pertaining to a Gentleman of your acquaintance? Of Mayfair? Oh God, have I imagined it? Am I gone mad from my despair at ever leaving the Hook and Crook?"

"You are not gone mad, only I thought better to forget it…"

"After you hounded me into a faint, I dreamt I was given sentence to ply my trade forever and ever without a farthing, for in some hellish Devilment the world had changed, and I found I had no recourse even to a crust of bread!"

This was too much, and Hugh begged him leave off all such talk; he would introduce him to the man in Mayfair if he wished it.

"I wish it vastly," breathed Dempsey, "Only tell me where ye live, and yer name, that I may find ye. Then we can see that I am fit to meet yer fine Gentleman."

But Hugh would have been of another character entirely had this plea, to the overthrow of all reason, succeeded.

"At present I cannot, you understand, tell much of myself. Should you be in earnest, tell me where you may be found tomorrow afternoon at about two."

The boy gave him the location of a house, and begged Hugh would not forget the one he had been so good, and so gallant, as to save.

"And I must have some name to assign my Saviour, for I will think of him tonight, all night – and dream of him, and pray God no harm ever comes to him!"

Hugh closed his eyes. A prayer. Very well, let there be a prayer.

"Bramble. The name is Bramble. You may pray for his safety as a deserving soul."

"Thank you, Mr Bramble, I will indeed! I shall begin the moment ye depart."

The night began to spin but keeping to his feet Hugh patted the shoulder of his eager new friend. Then he departed down an alleyway that a prayer might be said.

About two the following afternoon, from the tiny window of a garret, Mr Dempsey descended to the street to meet the curricle. His was one in a line of high-built, overcrowded housing, squalid and appearing to have withstood at least one fire. The youth was dressed in his best: breeches and waistcoat three times refreshed, and last night's frockcoat, an indeterminate colour of darkness, as though it continued to live in night. He had tied his thick, chestnut hair with fabric taken from the lining of a dress, then dusted it liberally with baking flour, which, after an hour waiting in an airless garret, showed some signs of dough ready for kneading. But his figure was slim and supple, his features exceptionally fine. Lovely, unscarred and, Hugh suspected, deceptively doe-eyed.

They took lodgings at The Black Lion Inn where they might begin improving his appearance. But so dire was Hugh's condition, his head slow to recover from the acid-bath of gin of the coarsest quality, he soon proved unequal to the task. Getting no further than opening a bottle of lavender water, he was twice sick into a ceramic basin. After much shaking and sweating, and some creative curses for the dealers of vile poison on Field Lane, Hugh allowed the boy to shift for himself in the room as he collapsed into bed. At this change in plan Dempsey showed himself to good advantage, mopping the brow of his benefactor, emptying the basin, and completing his own toilette while the other sweated through a dizzy sleep.

Washed, his shoulder-length hair combed and scented, the boy sat for two hours looking through a crack in the shutters to the street below. At last the patient stirred, sluggish but with a fresher perspective. Accomplishing no more than to stretch his stiff joints, Hugh found the boy with him under the bedclothes and so quickly succumbed to his addresses. When Hugh was done, he rolled away and sat stooped on the edge of the bed, torn between an old bliss he had nearly forgotten and some rather Saturnine reflections. After assuring himself everything of value was still somewhere in view, he rose and put two shillings atop Dempsey's folded clothing.

"I'll warrant," said the boy, sitting up in bed, "the Mayfair Gentleman cannot be half what Mr Bramble is, who is in my eyes a monstrous saint."

"Quiet – I don't wish that name spoken aloud."

"The name Bramble? But why…"

"I am in earnest."

"But … is this because… or perhaps… Sir, I am too turned about to see my way to the why… Do explain, I cannot allow such strange secrets if we are to work *in tandem* to please yer friend."

Each repetition of the name, and the belabouring of the subject, were like the many little wounds which killed Caesar: "Will you not leave me in peace about it?"

There passed a few moments of blessed silence. Then, Dempsey laughed somewhat shrilly and declared he understood everything. "Bramble ain't yer name at all is it? It's the name of yer beloved!"

Dismayed, shocked, at this show of perception Hugh

shouted, "And how the Devil did you arrive at that conclusion?!"

Dempsey let slip a grin, then quickly cleared his expression and blinked doe-eyed at his companion. "Permission to tell a small joke at my own expense?"

Closing his eyes, for he had not the energy to argue, Hugh nodded. "Proceed."

"Just now, I'd settled on it's being true a Gentleman differs from other men; which, as ye'll recall, ye told me was the case last night. At the time I thought that were but a silly boast. But just now, while having yer will of me, ye shouted that very name in my ear, such as 'Bramble, O Bramble, beautiful boy!' Do you recall it?"

Through gritted teeth Hugh said, "*Proceed.*"

"Well, after the surprise of the novelty, I thought it befit very well the dignity of a nobleman such as ye are."

"Dignity?"

"Ye think very well of yerselves. And so perhaps praise yerselves, at that point in yer performance, in order to… *stimulate* yerselves on to a worthy conclusion."

This was beyond grotesque, but even in exhaustion Hugh was taken into a fit of miserable laughter, was nearly sick again at the effort, and fell forward onto the bed for support. Then summoning all his strength, and whatever dignity he had left, he thrust himself from the bed, threw on his waistcoat and said, "And so you are expecting the Mayfair Man to shout his own name when he beds you?"

"For a while I was. Is it my fault I have no other name to know ye by?"

"As long as you live, buck, tell not another soul that story."

"Even now I have no name, though I was all morning praising The Good Mr Bramble."

Throwing up his hands at last: "Hugh, Dempsey… Hugh. This I promise will not change. Now get up from bed, that you may benefit by my fashionable hands. Christ, but you are pretty. And this rich, thick mane now it is washed; how he will enjoy you! What I will not do for my friends!"

Jumping to open the shutters, Dempsey proceed to the mirror to observe this vision. "But should you not be ashamed to introduce me without a bob wig or such?"

"If one could fit a bob over that hair. If more Gentlemen had such a lustrous head, the periwig maker would soon be out of custom, and more horses would keep their tails. Now take that suit of clothes I brought you, tie your hair with the blue ribbon, and present yourself as you will to the Mayfair Man."

"You will not be vastly harsh upon me?"

"You shall never have a harsher critic. I want you fetching, amiable, diverting, and submissive; and I had best not hear of liberties with that wayward hand. This Gentleman may well find it unfit to debauch you in the first five minutes. If he does, show no surprise, and encourage him. If he cannot perform, tell him it is often the way, and bodes better for the future."

After much more of posing, conversing, undressing, and redressing, Hugh nodded, sufficiently pleased. Then, unequal to more cultivation without enjoying the fruits again himself, abruptly bid him farewell until the morrow, when he would return to bring him his destiny.

CHAPTER 22

Having told Benjamin to expect a surprise, Hugh arrived in Mayfair and invited him for a ride around the city. By 'surprise' Benjamin believed him to mean the new curricle, and as they began, he let out a tired sigh and took Hugh's forearm, simply to touch some part of him. The complaints of his wife had of late increased and the treatments could, for weeks on end, consume nearly every moment of his time. So, the most must be made of this escape from that house; fragile melancholy would never do today!

"I asked you to ride for I wish to open a new chapter to you. A chapter of happiness and diversion."

Dropping Hugh's arm at the approach of a hackney coach, "Riding about after so many days of doctors and failed remedies is indeed another chapter to me. I find I am scarcely happy without you."

"Thank you, however my vanity is not of that calibre to have meant only myself and my machine."

Little more was said as they struggled through a swath of mud, after which they were obliged to overtake a disabled carriage and a postilion searching out a thrown horseshoe. Much activity greeted them as they made the next turn:

chairmen running their fares and cattle sliding in small patches of ice remaining after a cold night. As they turned up a quieter street, Benjamin said, "I think of you… more than you know. Our afternoons in the parlour, just you, me, and Paulina. I begin to worry for the time you are no longer there."

"I always shall be here for you and what is more, shall always lead you right. And now what if I pull the reigns and put us down somewhere… upon the next street. We shall get out, stand tall, and together declare 'By Jove, we have had enough of this Existence! It is high time Existence gives us something in return!' You have endured years of your wife's imaginary complaints. She does nothing to help herself; she only ever takes large doses of the bed. Never a thought for fresh air and exercise."

"Strong words," said his companion, "like strong medicine, should be supported by a proper diagnosis, Hugh. I will admit her indispositions are often aggravated by melancholy. But she does indeed suffer from afflictions difficult to diagnose."

"Well, if I was rash to say so it was only in consideration of you. Now address that other matter."

"Our stopping to have a walk around the next corner?"

"No, for we have taken that corner and are arrived. There," he said, jumping down and tying the horses, "Let us both have our wishes."

After looking rather uncertainly around the street Benjamin said, "I believe you should tell me your wish first."

"My wish, my dearest wish, is to make you a happy man. Your happiness is my greatest wish."

"But I have no wish. And I begin to grow a little concerned."

"No need for concern, all shall be made known."

Into The Black Lion Inn they repaired, and with a deep

breath Hugh led him up the stairs to a door hewn of heavy oak. After a quick rap they continued inside.

The room was dark. Much too dark for a sentient being, so figuring the silly goose had fallen asleep, Hugh stepped round the bed. But he soon discovered the bed was empty. After running to throw open the curtains, Hugh returned, unable to believe what he was seeing.

"Upon my word, this is not the present I contrived so artfully! Do the strings of my gift fail to hold fast a single night?"

"My God..." said Benjamin, hand going to his breast – for, alas, *Dear Reader,* he understood nothing but a private room, a bed torn freshly open, and Hugh Entwistle standing beside that bed. "It beggars belief you should overturn so entirely our resolution."

"In matters of your happiness, I am the fittest judge," said Hugh. "I overruled our agreement because you must know, at last, what you should have known years ago."

Stepping forward in anticipation, Benjamin said, "I was convinced your heart was too fragile to attempt it. And then, even if it was no more than sport to you, it must be of inexpressible import to me. This is almost more than a heart can bear..."

So again, to his horror, Hugh must disappoint this man where matters of pleasure and the heart were concerned.

"I pray this is all a consequence of my fall," Hugh whispered, "and I am, in fact, hideously concussed and deluded. Benjamin, dear, dear Benjamin, though I am a fool, a sinner, a knave, and an idiot, I would not mislead a beautiful soul for the world and all its riches. I do not sport with you, in bed or out of it. I had brought another for you. A comely youth answering almost entirely what was described at Salt's. So eager, so happy to be off the streets and in fine lodgings. He was instructed, in no uncertain terms, not to depart until I brought you. What the deuce has he done with himself!?"

The man came forward and, seizing Hugh by the arm, thundered, "You hired a he-whore off the street!? When I instructed you not to?"

"We agreed only to a delay. And do not call him that. That is altogether too harsh."

The anger of this controlled man, once it arrived, was quite frightening and Hugh withdrew; Benjamin now too furious to speak, Hugh too confounded to explain. So, it was either fortune, or misfortune, that the youth in question chose that moment to arrive. Slipping into the room, he came face to face with the man who was meant to be his benefactor. Though furious upon seeing him so airy and carefree, Hugh forced a smile, took his arm so he would not run, then closed them inside the room.

"Dempsey, this is the Gentleman of whom I spoke, who shall remain nameless." When Hugh hazarded a look at Benjamin, he was heartened to see the man closely inspecting the stranger. So, with recourse to hope all was not lost, the matchmaker promised God that if he would only allow these two to come together, he would go to church every week for the remainder of his life. Dempsey, for his part, held forth a hand and gave a hesitant smile. But the hand remained suspended in mid-air, untaken.

Hugh prompted, "With hair that would be the envy of Rapunzel herself. Shake hands."

"I know you," was the man's response.

"Indeed, no Sir," said Dempsey. "We have never, till this precise instant, met."

With horror Hugh watched Benjamin's hand extend, not to take the proffered hand, but, with silky ease, to seize the boy's lapel. Turning him farther into the room he guided them to an interior wall.

Trying to keep the panic from his voice, Hugh said, "You believe you know him, as he answers so well what you requested. Hair dark as night, skin pale as the moon, small in stature and young. All you could wish."

"I know you, you rascal. Tell me how."

"Oh God Mr Hugh," wailed Dempsey, "I don't understand him, but I see ye've brought me to him that he may kill me!"

"You cannot know him," said Hugh. "Whatever you think, you are mistaken."

"I am not mistaken," said Benjamin. "He picked my pocket last year and made very clumsy work of it. When I pursued him, we came upon his gang who would have thrashed me for everything short of my life had not a constable arrived and beaten them away."

"No Sir, never, never!" cried Dempsey. "Oh, I see Christ Incarnate come to punish all my sins – on the eve of my happiness he will take it all from me…"

And with this Benjamin, thrown off balance, lurched forward – for Dempsey's lapel stretched taut as the boy fell backwards, his eyes rolling up in a faint. Together they sank to the floor, pushing out a long side table with their combined weight. Seeing the young man was now unconscious, and himself robbed of his ability to berate him, Benjamin threw the youth farther behind the table and rose to face Hugh. And the wretched matchmaker, who had remained frozen during their descent down the wall, withdrew a few more paces.

"I take my leave of you now and will thank you to keep your distance until I seek you again." For a few moments the only sound was the trembling, intermittent breathing of Dempsey, wedged between the wall and the table leg. "And you with nothing to say. Not a word of explanation, or apology for what you have done?"

"Hit me Benjamin. Break my jaw before you go, and we both will sleep better tonight."

"That is insincere, and unworthy of you."

"Because you are too good to strike me. And you are too

good to depart before you've helped me lift that boy from the floor."

"The wretch can rot where he is."

"Please. I will take the week, or the month, or however long you wish to punish me. But you must help me put him on the bed. He is not a dog, or the sweepings of a public house. If you cannot help me, you had best continue your silence to me indefinitely."

Whether this was the lowest blow or the loftiest principle, it had its effect. With an oath Benjamin ordered Hugh to take the boy's feet. Then, upon moving the table forward that he could find purchase, he took Dempsey's shoulders and they lifted and laid him out on the bed. Hands on hips, the man remained breathing some moments over the insensible lump. Then, with tears in his eyes, he departed the room and was soon outside The Black Lion Inn.

Time passed. William Dempsey continued to sleep; Hugh happy to let him, for what would he say when he awoke? He must return to the Hook and Crook, or to thieving, and relinquish his dreams of improvement. Oh, must he see the boy lying there in clothes hastily purchased for him, and with the crudest modifications made to fit? Dressed up, only to meet his doom. The realization drove Hugh's face to his hands, and finally pushed his gaze entirely from the room and out the window. To the sky, the street, the passers-by indifferent to it all. He must undertake the care of this boy. Must somehow contrive from his ruined allowance some means of providing him assistance. He must sell some of his things. Whatever could be disposed of without arousing suspicion...

His mind for some time wandered...he could not place the moment he beheld the form of Benjamin Sallow. The man stood staring up from the street below, without a raised hand or by any other means seeking to attract attention. Hugh scrambled from the room and down the stairs. After more than an hour, they were both altered, penitent creatures. Once Benjamin was reinstalled in the room, Hugh kissed his hand and put it to his chest, that he might feel a heart brought alive with gratitude. When he attempted to speak, his friend shook his head and stepped closer to the sleeping form.

"He is remarkably like my description."

"He's here for two nights, I have paid it all. He is available to be yours exclusively if you choose."

"After what he did, and where you found him?"

"I cannot answer for what he stole, or why he vanished when I asked him to remain. But I promise there is not another so pretty to be found for twenty miles. Once you have him you will not settle for another, and you must keep him once your taste is fired." Benjamin lifted the boy's hair, still tied in a tail, then let it fall. "He fainted before, and no doubt with a little effort he will be brought round again. I couldn't think what to tell him when he awoke, and so like a coward have let him sleep."

"And can you actually think I will put him in an apartment?"

"Not unless you choose. I suspect you will not sport so easily, then toss him aside. But if you do, he must go back to his life, and you to yours. He knows nothing of you beyond you are a Gentleman of Mayfair, whom it would behoove him to please."

Benjamin's eyes met those of Hugh as he listened to the terms. Then taking up one of Dempsey's hands, and then the other, he rubbed them until the invalid came around, and bid him be quiet when, upon seeing the source of his great trauma, he yelped like a puppy.

"He'll murder me Hugh! Am I dead already?"

Turning Dempsey's face to meet his own, Benjamin said, "I wish you to address me, young man. You fear me, but I hope not for long. I conquered my surprise, and my anger, at recalling that other affair. Will you admit honestly what you did?"

"Yes Sir. I stole, as you say. I am the worst wretch ever to try the profession. I was soon kicked from that gang for yer seeing my theft, and other blunders. Upon my soul I profited nothing by the watch and the sterling piece, which was taken from me more or less as they was from you."

"And how came you to meet my friend?

"Hugh? Enjoying his Huckle and Buff in the place of my employment. I am as fitting a companion for yerself as any he has seen. And very willing to oblige yer taste."

"But if he, or I, ask you to remain in a place you must do it. You left this room and caused... some not inconsiderable disturbance and confusion. That cannot be."

"That was very wrong of me and I shall never do it again."

Benjamin pushed a lock of hair from the boy's face and said, "I shall send our friend on his way then, if you will promise to be truthful and oblige me."

"We dine next week," said Hugh, rising. "Let us have silence till then. You have two nights with him, as I said. And then whatever you choose to add."

With a sigh, Hugh stepped out and closed the door behind him, trusting the week sufficient to bring the man to a commitment. Then he proceeded out the tavern door to his curricle, his mission, somehow, accomplished.

CHAPTER 23

The remainder of the week he devoted to Horatio, certain he could bring culture to his life with a bit of focused effort. After one last visit to the King's Menagerie, Hugh informed him they would not be returning and would instead work to improve him. *Henry V* was being performed at Drury Lane.

The boy's new valet had Macaroni ambitions for him, so the night of the performance Ratio stepped into Hugh's curricle in a set of powder blue heeled slippers, with a hint of rouge on his cheeks and a velvet beauty mark pasted above his lip. Not unexpectedly the play only pleased when Ratio could join the gallery screaming or booing at the players. He fell to stroking the beauty mark for diversion, often with rapt concentration. Sipping coffee afterwards, Hugh complimented him on his looks of deep contemplation during the play, declaring he was already halfway to a true appreciation of The Bard.

"Am I? I understood no more than two words the entire performance."

"Nonsense – I shall tell you those sequences I saw you take particular interest in."

After this Hugh asked for the details of his recent visit to a brothel and was pleased to see a smile light his friend's face. Ratio had met a jolly girl who had in her possession eleven volumes of Joe Miller's *Jest Book*. Oh, she had read wonderfully, and he had laughed until his sides hurt! And what was best, the following morning Lord George had observed his happy stupor and supposed complete success. Hugh toasted the boy and told him this *was* success. For were not joke books and velvet beauty marks the basis of Hugh's own perceived successes?

"Well done Ratio. You enjoyed yourself in the presence of a young lady, with not a tear shed but from merriment."

"Ever so merry, though I attempted the other and was ten times failing! But I don't take it hard, nor worry at all anymore. For I am only impotent like my very good friend Hugh Entwistle. Which is what I told Miss Lucy."

"It was only once," said Hugh, quickly. "Soon got over and long ago. Understand?"

"Yes… I suppose I knew that. Is it very bad, d'you think?"

Hugh considered a long moment. "Between us, the longer you keep from all that the better. It comes to nothing but heartache in the end."

The dinner at Charles Sallow's was to be his first news of Benjamin since leaving him at The Black Lion Inn. Hugh entered the drawing room in great expectation to hear of his happiness, but he had not yet arrived. He was soon immersed in conversation with Charles about the travails of Wilkes, whose elections to represent the ward of Farringdon Without, now two in number, had produced two different outcomes. The first win had been declared illegal. The second would not be challenged, and so he was expected to be seated once released from prison. However, the House was now proposing its own candidate for the county of Middlesex, the seat won by and subsequently denied to Wilkes three times the year before. A Mr Luttrell was the lucky man and with over-whelming government support he was assured success. Charles laughed at it all.

"Let the free market of ideas sort it out."

"Have we one?" said Hugh. "I mean, yes we do of course but – can it?"

"It must, for the system is healthy. We squabble over whether to allow criticism of a king or to publish Parliamentary transcripts. My people in Massachusetts wish representation, perhaps they should have it, but let us thank our stars we have a system of representation *from which to be excluded*. You've to look no farther than across the Channel to praise to High Heaven our own imperfections. France has no system to improve. What exists there must either remain as it is or be burned down entirely."

"But a structure must collapse which is under continual reconstruction."

"Not when it is established upon a sound foundation. Let our great minds hash it out. Wilkes puts it well by declaring a government must be from the people, rather than for the people. Dr Johnson counters that the House of Commons can be the only judge of itself and has the right to overturn elections of an illegal candidate, which by all accounts an outlaw is. Wilkes returns by saying such power to determine legality is endless and must eventually be abused. I say this is perfection – wholesome as an apple from Arlington."

"But in your opinion which argument is the stronger?"

"I am won over entirely by the last until the next is made."

"In your opinion, which argument do you *hope* prevails?"

Charles chuckled and patted Hugh on the knee. "Very well. Johnson's, in the end, should prevail."

"I am surprised to hear it."

"Why should you be?"

"Your having represented the interests of America in trade might more align you with Wilkes."

"Until a current system absolutely cannot continue, Hugh, side with conserving what has worked. The Stamp Act was new and would likely have broken America from Britain entirely. A system of representation in the states would also be new, so I am, for now, opposed. Do not forget my family has succeeded under the current system – Duncan's promotion into Parliament is enough like that of this despised Luttrell I should be a hypocrite to criticise it. I do not judge the system good or ill. I operate within it and believe I have done so quite well."

At this point a man entered the parlour livelier, and appearing more youthful, than Hugh had ever seen him. Laughing at something his father's butler said and chatting up a lady who looked vaguely familiar, Benjamin appeared transformed. The lady on his arm moved with liquid animation and when she was introduced as Rosamunde, Hugh was momentarily at a loss for words. This lovely, elegant woman, no more than a rumour for eight months, was not at all a wreck of her old oil and canvas representation in the dining room. Upon her graceful neck rested an elevated chin, and her eyes had the pretty squint of one looking to a hilltop on a bright day. Her delicate hands were like butterflies alighting here and there, pretty though to little effect. When Paulina ran up to position herself between her parents, they were the picture of a small, rational family of fortune nurturing one hothouse orchid of extreme value.

As Charles and Sir Frederick wished to speak a few minutes in private, Hugh took the opportunity to pull Benjamin to the fireside in the back parlour. At first, he would only speak of Rosamunde and how well she was looking. Hugh listened for as long as he could, but when he moved on to the weather, whose dismal state had already been well-canvassed, Hugh lost all patience and took him by the shoulders:

"Benjamin! Suffer me to hear of drippy eaves, when it could not be further from what I desperately wish to know?"

"Now?"

"Yes! I am wild to hear it. I cannot wait."

A moment passed in which it seemed possible it had all gone wrong, for the man simply would not speak. But then Hugh's arm was grabbed, and his forehead kissed, and under the roar of the crackling fire:

"He is an angel; I wonder he is not done in pastels. I summon a handful of those wondrous locks here where we stand simply by rubbing my fingers together. Observe," he said demonstrating. "If I press a hand to my mouth, I recall that warmth of his cheek, or his soft, cool forehead. I must apologise for so entirely honouring the request to neglect you. I have devoted myself to him all week, as you wished, and am diverted beyond all imaginings."

"I expected nothing else, if it was a success." Hugh could only shake his head in wonder. This met, and indeed surpassed, his ambition for the match. This seemed almost like love. And as such, it must be a cause for caution, for Dempsey was an established pickpocket and who knew what else during his career.

"Has he kept to the agreed upon price? Does he remain at The Black Lion?"

"Until next week, registered as my stepson. Then I shall put him in an apartment in another part of town. Yes, the price remains what you told me. He is at liberty during the day, and at four remains with me until I depart."

"And I trust all will be reduced to pin money when an apartment, clothing, and food are provided."

"Yes," he said, somewhat absently, "Yes, I suppose so."

"All payment, Benjamin, but the most trivial allowance, must end..." Hugh wished to hammer every detail out of him, for it seemed to him something was amiss. He was not acting... this was not quite how a man would behave, even in the best scenario. "He must leave off running about town. You must sometimes have a morning or afternoon to yourself and he should be there to receive you."

"You would not have me gotten the better of, but I do understand business and maintaining terms. He is not showered with presents, or money beyond what was agreed upon."

Forced to relinquish a fight which seemed not to merit one, Hugh could only shake his head and try to let the matter be. Perhaps he could no longer recognise happiness when he saw it.

"You are an altered being, one sees it the moment you step into a room. You speak of him, your colour rises, and you smile so naturally; I feel like an old man by comparison."

"I have even taken to reading to him. Rosamunde is entirely unmoved by what moves me. But William curls up by my side as I stroke his hair. Listens, asks questions when he fails to understand, and says I have a lovely speaking voice. Trifles – I am brought to joy by trifles!"

And Hugh, having not entirely relinquished his hunt, at last sniffed out his rat. Placing a hand upon his friend's shoulder he said gently: "I want you to answer me truthfully. Will you do that?"

"I will never shy from you. The mask, as it has been from our first meeting, remains down."

"Tell me then, for I begin to suspect something about your arrangement with Mr Dempsey. Can you guess my meaning?"

The man's look was one of defiance. "You are a mature young man, wise in many things and I will defend it to anybody. But there are things in this life you may not yet understand. I bid you observe my happiness and let the matter be."

"Do you mean to tell me," said Hugh, his eyes flashing in the firelight, "the meal I prepared for you has remained untasted now seven days and nights?"

"Tread carefully. He and I have a bond more beautiful

than I can express, each supplying what the other desires and needs. I would not force this happiness into a mould it will not accept."

"And will you deny," Hugh said, at pains to suppress his voice, "your first intention has always been that experience so long coming to you? For which I had myself been taken to bed had I allowed it?"

Bringing them into a far corner of the room Benjamin said, "It was much more than that. Billy is no whore, as you said yourself. I admit, that first night after you departed, I was on the point of… taking what I believed to be mine, and the poor child fainted dead away again. After I brought him around, he clung to me and kissed my hand most tenderly. He declared he saw in my eyes what he could love − saw goodness and felt like a son in his father's arms."

"You had sought a son of Rosamunde if you desired one. Or, I daresay, found somebody to sell one," said Hugh, unable to believe the stupidity of this man, or the connivance of that horrible Mr Dempsey. "He has tricked you out of the experience you must have to take possession of your own Character. He has no business selling a body he will not give. He is no virgin I assure you, if…"

"That is enough. I wish more of course, and I hope someday to have it. But I am not nineteen, nor do I believe that that is all there is. What I have is an intense fulfilment of other, and exquisitely subtle, desires. I hold him for hours. I kiss his cheek, and smell him, and sleep with him warm in my arms."

Oh, the foolish, hurtful wretch! Accomplishing little more than the pittance tolerated by himself. The Platonic holding, the caring for… it should be Hugh he was loving, if it was anybody!

"But Benjamin—"

At this point they were summoned to dinner and chastised for antisocial behaviour. Hugh spent the first part of the meal fuming at Dempsey, then at Benjamin, then at himself. Yet as the meal progressed his annoyance turned to apprehension. If Benjamin had a new toy he could pet and read to, who could listen and soothe extremely well, what was left for Hugh? Even a maudlin like Rosamunde appeared raised by the great lifter of spirits that was William Dempsey. Hugh had never been able to do that for Benjamin, though by doing no less! Oh, the violent, boiling hatred of the Pretender, who extorted money through as much craft as Jasper Sharp. But Hugh dared not press the matter further. He must not displease Benjamin for he might now very easily lose his friendship. And by the time the dinner drew to a close, he insisted upon another moment with him.

"You are not angry with me?"

"Angry? I am indebted to you."

"I demand happiness for a friend beyond what I expect for myself. And you are a dear friend, Benjamin. My best friend. Do not turn your back on me."

The man took his hand. "I shall never turn on you, dear boy. Come to me day or night; do unburden yourself at last. You have grown sadder, even than you were, these last months. Tell me more of him, the young man you left back home. What caused the break? Can the pain still be so raw?"

"I cannot move beyond it," Hugh said, suddenly understanding he had not moved forward with Benjamin for the thought of Bramble. It seemed obvious now – and he had known it, at some point...then, somehow, forgot it. "I *cannot*—" He stared a moment at the wall, then shook his head and said, "Good-bye."

"You will come to me soon, Hugh. Promise you will."

Hugh said what was necessary, re-joined his family, and was soon gone. At home he paced his apartments. Would that he could slam a fist into his Hepplewhite cabinet, throw a chair through the sash window, or himself through it. He tipped a dram of brandy into his mouth. Then a second.

"At last Our Hero's footing has begun to slip," he said, pacing the floor. "An inclination of the ground seems to draw him, gradually, down a strange slope. His spark flags. He drenches in liquor and sets himself alight. When he shines it is only to light the steps of the Greys down dark alleys. To burn the hands of Benjamin when he gets too close. To heat to milk-warm that cider meant to intoxicate people of power and persuasion. And he can bear it no longer."

After only a moment's deliberation he proceeded downstairs to the study where his father was speaking to Jasper Sharp. The man who everyday drove his eyes to the floor, who made Hugh cower in his own house; he now favoured the domestic with a look of such loathing the man straightened, and, for a moment, appeared concerned. As Sir Frederick pointed his son to a chair and stowed away a few papers, Hugh held Jasper's eye and grinned.

"I need to speak to you of a letter I wrote, Father. A foolish, ill-judged letter, and a situation I can no longer abide. We shall require no servants."

Sharp appeared unable to summon his habitual sneer. Instead he said, insipidly, for it was already eleven o'clock, that he was at the master's service should he need him.

"You are not wanted, good-night."

Once the door closed Hugh began:

"It is a matter preys upon me, and so I do not wait until tomorrow. A letter, or rather letters, increasingly foolish and ill-judged. For they are, each one, less sincere. They are dangerous to my reputation if they inspire a service to me which I must now decline."

"You were speaking to Benjamin about it this evening?"

"Yes... indirectly. We are grown good friends. He was in a similar situation at one time, as regards his father's military ambition for him. Only he was not like his brother and never had the desire. We have spoken of life he and I... of finding one's true nature. You see, I... I no longer wish to pursue the commission."

"Yes, I know."

Hugh blinked dumbly, finding the words constricted to his throat. His father looked at him with an arch, albeit passing, look and nodded. "If you've persuaded yourself that you do wish it, I'm afraid you are the only one you've persuaded."

The words took his breath. All the petitions, the sparkling interviews, the notes, most of which Sir Frederick had approved before they were sent. All ill-conceived? All lacking conviction?

"And it is inaccurate to compare your desire for a commission with Charles wishing his sons into the military. You returned from Evendown with that ambition and I lent my support. Did I seek to purchase the commission?"

Hugh shook his head.

"That was not frugality, but from a wish to see your commitment to the endeavour. You've demonstrated commitment, and tried, though I saw within a couple months it was not to be. I provided the opportunity to leave off last October, did I not?"

"Yes Sir. Only... I confess I am terribly confused. Have you seen me as grossly deluded? I pride myself upon a level of perspicacity and judgement I supposed beyond my years. I have wasted your time, the time of Lord Halifax and many others."

"Halifax is fond of you and enjoys your company. As to the others, had I seen you making a fool of yourself I would have intervened. You are well-liked, and if you were deluded it was seen only as rather endearing. You are beginning to be talked of as a desirable match for some very wealthy young ladies in a few years."

Hugh let out a wet, rather uncouth breath, and laughed. "Am I? I put myself into your hands entirely regarding that. Now I am proved a blockhead too daft to understand your hints, do counsel me. On everything. Tell me what I should do and what I might reasonably expect for my future."

"Advice is given as required," said Sir Frederick rather like he was clearing his throat. Then, appearing to think twice, said, "Do mind your drinking, Hugh. I know you keep it to your nights with the Greys, and with your godfather. But I should never like to see you drunk at the dinner table, certainly never in good society."

With an absent nod, trying to recall an occasion of late when his father had *not* seen him drunk, he waited for him to continue.

"Now what has occurred between you and Jasper? I have observed you do not like one another, but your look to him just now would like to take off his head. What has he done?"

Do not tempt me. For I could, I really could, destroy myself to take him down with me.

"He is at war with Louis. And I have always disliked his manner with Anne."

The petty pranks and squabbles between the two valets were common knowledge, but a comment about Anne was nothing Hugh had dared say before – and by his father's look of alarm, clearly nothing he ever expected to hear.

"Was he inappropriate with her?"

Oh, what could he invent to get Sharp thrown from favour, and from the house.

"Impertinent. Observing her figure too long. Smirking whenever her marriage is mentioned, and a snide comment about the wedding night."

Frederick nodded, and when nothing more was vouchsafed, pressed, "Do not believe he is so favoured as to admit actual wrongdoing. There is more, I see there is."

Hugh said as forcefully as he could, "There is no trusting him. He would sell a man's secrets to the highest bidder and is a menace to every member of the female sex. The longer I am in the world the more I distinguish those of his trim. I have no actual charge to make, beyond the latest trivia with Louis. He is too devious to be often caught out."

After letting a long moment pass, Frederick changed the subject as he did when he wished more time to consider. It was his way to come at a question at another time, unexpectedly and mercilessly if need be, and by then Hugh would have contrived something to suit his purpose. Still, Sharp would feel the effects of his displeasure, and understand the power he still had in this house. The money he received by way of Hugh did not equal what Sir Frederick knew he paid him. So he must, even now, be concerned with retaining his position.

"Tell me you have other schemes for me," said Hugh. "Where free will is concerned too much generosity has already been shown."

Though declining to tell the particulars, his father gave assurances that things were in the works, some rather remarkable things in fact. He stood, and though Hugh understood he was being excused, he felt once more like a well-cared-for child. He took the man's, soft, smooth hand and brought it to his lips.

"What son ever had such a father?" he said.

Sir Frederick sighed and sent him on his way.

CHAPTER 24

By breakfast something had changed in the house. Some reprimand must have befallen Jasper for he was not to be found and the domestics were nearly shiftless for their hushed whispering in corners. Lady Highborough, too, appeared particularly pleased. While entertaining friends at breakfast, her godson was seized and celebrated to her guests as only she could do, praising him to the heavens then releasing him like a sparrow into the Spring day. And there Hugh remained until late afternoon, not trusting to meet the valet just yet. After dinner he exchanged an indifferent glance with Sharp in the corridor, but no more. A short time later Frederick called him into his study to say they were expecting guests in two nights' time.

"Guests?"

"A small gathering of the known, unknown, and unexpected. It is a dinner of some consequence."

That night Hugh sank into bed in no little expectation and rose early when the new chamber maid entered the room. In the house just a couple days, this Eleanor was a pert thing in a white bonnet which held her face like a new rose. Chatting merrily, she dallied here and there, quite sure of her attractions and looking to climb if a man could spare a moment to look at her. After she had swept, dusted carelessly, and stoked the fire, which she proclaimed she was 'quite skilled at', Hugh ordered a pitcher of water after which he intended to step outside for a walk.

He was looking idly into his wardrobe when Jasper entered the room. Hugh had only a moment to note the oddness of the visit when the valet came forward and fetched him such a slap with the back of his hand that Hugh crashed full on against the wardrobe. He was for a moment blinded to everything but stars – he then rounded on his servant to repay the blow, with interest, when Jasper held up one finger: "One word and I fetch the letter. I know what is planned for ye tomorrow night, and one word from me ruins those plans. And may well ruin yer father."

"You don't dare, you dog! You need this—"

Jasper seized Hugh's ear and nearly dangled him off the floor. The pain was so excruciating Hugh could scarcely breathe, unable to trust his trembling nerves in a counterattack, which might serve only to detach that orifice entirely.

"Pull a stunt like that again and ye'll have much more than a twisted ear to trouble ye," Jasper hissed, no more than a watery mess before Hugh's swimming eyes. "I've never yet been subjected to such scrutiny in this house, as happened after your talk with Sir Frederick. And if—"

"*Go to hell, you swab!*" hissed Hugh.

"Lord bless me what's happened?" The chambermaid had returned, at which point Hugh was unceremoniously released. Shuddering, he attempted to regain his dignity while blinking furiously and choking on an overabundance of spittle.

"I shall call here at eight this evening," said Jasper, "and ye'd best be here. None of yer prancing about the city tonight… I want ye here and ready for me. Understood?"

"Yes, whatever, leave me."

Sharp turned. "What say ye pretty Miss, or should I bastinado him here and now?"

"But that's the master's son ain't it? You'll be turned out er'e nightfall."

"Possibly. But if I'm still here come bedtime ye'll know who holds sway and where it pays to be attendant and supplicant. It'll never happen with that one there," he said. Then, seeing the chambermaid overly cautious to keep her pitcher of water upright, he pinched her taut bum as he departed. Eleanor was that manner of lass to squeal and pretend to scold, quick to understand who, for whatever reason, held power in this house.

"Well I never!" she said, and after setting the jug down hurried across the room.

Hugh swatted her away miserably. "You'll want to leave this house if you know what's good for you."

"La! I've withstood much worse. But will ye really not tell yer father, Sir, after being so savagely used?"

"No, I will not, and that should be a caution to a girl of sense. The balance of power is strange in this house and pretty girls do not last long. He'll be up your petticoats tonight if you let him, and you'll be seeking employment this time next month when he tires of you. Without a reference. Leave today and you will have my reference before you go. A glowing reference if you can recommend a good, reliable girl of the plainest and dowdiest."

Tugging at her bonnet, Eleanor made a great show of confusion, flounced from the room, and Hugh was content to resign her to her fate. But come noon, her bonnet tied tightly, she came forward with an odd set to her jaw as though unsure how to crack a chestnut. She wanted the letter, a glowing letter if he pleased. She would send the Entwistles her own Olivia, an unfortunate relation.

The day was clear, damp with melt and those notes of freshness and heaviness instructive of a new season. The folly of Spring had already provoked the anger of a blackmailer. Jasper would certainly ask for more money now and must be denied. To make the February payment Hugh had asked a loan from Horatio, and in the process gave in to his pleas to return to the waxworks. When Jasper departed for his pipe and can that evening, there was a hope he might simply leave Hugh waiting all night. He was capable of it. But then came noise on the domestics' staircase. Steps sounded, the apartment door opened, and Sharp was inside.

Two chairs faced each other in the middle of the room. Hugh was determined to lead this conversation and directed the valet to take a seat. After perusing it for needles or other unpleasant traps, Sharp took the proffered seat and looked him over with a twist to his mouth. The gleam in his eye declared him a little drunk, which might be Hugh's best chance of bringing him to something like compassion.

"It's good of you to see me Jasper."

"'Twas my own command," he said, "not yer hospitality."

"I wished to speak to you about our business, because that is all it is to me. I see it as any other transaction or trade bill. In a moment of anger, I made those comments to get a reaction from you. I said nothing to my father of our agreement."

"Said nothing but what got me interrogated for molesting yer sister and her Ladyship. And raping that chambermaid bore a baby last year, what had been ten others' as much as my own. What, ye didn't know about that?"

"It isn't true?" said Hugh, eyes widening.

"Course it ain't true. Only I had the best establishment of her many beaux, which is what I told him at the time and which he believed until last night."

"And have you no feeling for the man who employs you? You are not taking my money; you are taking his."

It seemed a mild enough rebuke, but Jasper slapped one palm upon his thigh and leant forward: "Feeling? Yer father would do the same in my position, don't you know him at all?

I knew that country school did little for yer head but leave you an utter dull-swift I hadn't supposed. How's that conveyed in the Latin lingo: dull-swift? Do you know it?"

The man was in such a wayward state of drunkenness he actually seemed intent upon learning it. "Let us return to business, Jasper. I observe you are in your cups."

"And I observe ye are a Catamite. Tomorrow I shall be sober."

The sting of this rebuke was nearly too much to endure, and suddenly all the indignity of being struck by an inferior returned full force.

"I take my hat off to you, Sir; thy wit is well placed."

"Aye, and so here's the lay of the land: yer sister Anne netted a big fish and is soon off to live in happiness. And I daresay a rich wife's being organised for Hugh himself as we speak; Papa's been on the hunt for years. It's every man's due to have a dutiful lass to call his own, and raise legitimate offspring, whatd'ye reckon?"

"If he merits it."

Jasper sat back and nodded. "It's his due, long as he can support 'em. So, I'll have an increase in my benefit," he said, inclining his head, "beginning next month. Jasper Sharp ain't destined to be an old, lonely bachelor with bastards running about. He'll have a wife, and legitimate male issue, and a good living for their maintenance."

"I am not the man of unlimited means you appear to think me. My father grants no wild allowance and requires a ledger. I'm in no position to pay more."

"But I am in a position to require it, my buck, and let thee handle of the details. Else I shall bring thy love-letter to the eyes of your father and hope it doth not kill him."

"I cannot make any payments at all if I cannot disguise them. I shall continue to make the payments as I have done, which already obliges me to sell my belongings and take loans.

But I cannot work a miracle in a ledger beyond what the laws of mathematics will allow."

"And so take yer hat off to me and send me on my way. Hadn't ye better know the amount before trying to deny it? Take yer hat off to me indeed," he said, his voice rising, "*and send me on my way.*"

"How much?"

"I am a man likes clean lines, in a shave and dressing and all such. A hundred annually, in twelve payments." Seeing Hugh begin to protest he said, "And nobody's cryin' roast beef with a hundred: it's for a nest egg. Rest assured it'll be no more during that time."

"I cannot, there's no point asking."

"Had you not better retrench, then? The services of Gallante for a start?"

"Without a replacement? Our arrangement will only work if I can meet your demands without raising suspicion. How is that to be if a man of my station lives without a valet?"

"Then seek out employment, say, as footman or postilion."

Much as Hugh tried to endure it, the effrontery of this man was blinding him to all but a red rage.

"How much closer to a solution by tomfoolery?"

"Tomfoolery is it? To suggest ye might work for yer bread? Ye might try it, then tell me if it's yerself won't have the job, or the job what won't have yerself!"

"And so you attempt to disguise the impertinence of saying it?"

"I never was impertinent. I had flogged your ass a few years ago had you called me impertinent then, and your father would have handed me the stick." There passed a rather strained silence. "I'm in earnest wishing to see ye at a day's work; I had suggested *valet de chambre* as well, were it not placing ye so often near a Gentleman in a state of undress. Now then," he said, with a little grin, "there's a bit of whisk."

Well beyond anger now Hugh was becoming quite frightened. "Seven years and you would use me so cruelly? Seven years in which, as I have heard you say many times, you have been treated better than anywhere in your experience?"

"Fortune brought me to it."

"Fortune accounts for many things, which are otherwise not in our control."

"I agree. And it was Fortune *only* gave ye the wherewithal to hire a valet, and not serve as one. What have ye ever done to deserve yer money and clothes and Grand Tours?"

"Grand Tours? I expect no Tour, though I might see it as my due. Certainly not if I might employ the money to come to an understanding with you. That I promise."

Hugh thought this well played, but to little effect, for Jasper said only, "Then I say what have ye ever done to deserve yer money, and fine school, and parties and clothes?"

"One had better ask God so esoteric a question."

"God places the low classes low, eh? 'Tis the Holy Order of his Plan." This sounded like a quotation and Hugh saw too late his misstep. "It's what Gentry always say but I will not believe it of any Christian. God placed me in this family that I might seek my fortune same as Hugh Entwistle: by proximity to a wealthy Gentleman. Frederick's a devious son-of-a-bitch, but he's got the means to fund us."

"Leave my father out of this," Hugh spat, leaning forward. "You who had rather cut his throat than shave him."

Jasper rose from his chair and produced the bottle of brandy from the riding boot, which place appeared to be an open secret, and tilted a fair amount into his mouth.

"Up with ye; wantcha to have a wrap in warm flannel with me," he said holding out the bottle. He was on the point of coming to tug him up when Hugh stood.

"Put it away, I don't want it."

"I knew that. Never sully thy palate after I tasted of it. It's fine brandy, finer never tipped over tongue. You never was one to retrench where libation was concerned. So fine puts me in mind for a woman." He laughed and swished another mouthful around before wincing it down.

"Christ's Sake, how will I get you out of here and down the stairs if you are falling down drunk?"

"...Aye, ye would have me on my way, I know, I know... 'I take my hat off to ye Jasper,' that is what ye said," he muttered, dropping the bottle into the boot, and kicking it aside. "A fine way to dismiss a loyal servant. I'll tell ye what, Hugh. Forget hats: I'll have yer breeches off here and now."

He came forward and, seeing Hugh's hesitation, grabbed his shoulders and hissed into his face, "Get those breeches down, Hugh, and bend over yon table. I shall take my payment another way if you refuse me pounds sterling."

"I'll get you the money – only leave me be to think how to do it!"

Jasper laughed, spraying him with a good deal of spittle and pinched his cheek. "But that is not the way of the world. And it is not for the want of hush money I'll have this. Ye dispatched my pert little Jill, or whatever her name was, before I could get to her, and I'm in mind for a woman, as I said. I don't imagine it's unwelcome attention, for such as ye are."

He shoved Hugh at his writing desk and commanded him again, or would that moment fetch his evidence and read it out before Sir Frederick, her Ladyship, and their illustrious dinner guests. Hugh found enough anger to conquer his fear; he tore at his buttons and, stepping to the table, dropped his breeches with a flourish. After considering a moment, Jasper came forward, pushed the contents of the desk onto the floor, and with an extended hand presented the space to him.

"Lay across it, turn yer face to the wall; and I promise, ye won't be smiling like that in a minute."

Hugh's swagger at last faltered, and he was unable to lay forward without his knees betraying him. He folded his hands, in an attitude of prayer which seemed unavoidable, and at last turned his head to the wall. Footsteps came close and stood beside him. A hand in fabric… Then a long, long silence. Too many moments came and went, in which Hugh nearly turned his head, but could not. But at last, though nearly too frightened at what he would discover, he turned his head.

Jasper was standing a few paces back with a pocket-watch in his hand. His eyes went to the timepiece, and he commenced a low, rumbling laughter somewhere in his gut.

"One minute, eighteen seconds."

That this was meant to humiliate was clear enough, but Hugh was too relieved to escape the fate he could only feel something like gratitude.

"I'll tell ye what," said Jasper, as Hugh scrambled to pull his clothes up, "I'll take a guinea for thy cheek, and find a real woman tonight." Unable to wish for anything but an end to the interview, should it cost him fifty guineas, Hugh scrambled through his drawers to scrape together whatever he could find. He placed it in his hand.

"I swear on my life that is all I have at present."

"Aye," said Jasper, "that'll do. I'll rough it with a fifteen-bob wench. There's compassion for ye." He pocketed the money, then came in so close Hugh was obliged to shrink away. "But I'll leave ye with food for thought, for I can get much nastier than that, doubt me not. Fail to make payment first of April, and you'll get that poke against your will, and far more into the bargain." He brought Hugh's face up to his. "Ask yerself, is it commerce against yer will, or commerce with a servant, a low, dirty servant who is beneath yer notice, bringing tears to yer eyes? Ye get yer money same as I do: from Sir Frederick. And excepting you haven't the skill as would qualify ye to find my employment and had rather a boy than the woman to have your will of, there is, as I see it, little distinguishes one from t'other."

When he departed, Hugh returned to his desk. From the floor he collected letters and papers generated over the better part of a year. Notes he'd kept to reference in his returns.

Drafts, second drafts which had never achieved the post – he tossed the entire bundle across his desk. Then, struck with the sheer volume, he leant forward placing his hands over them, and laughed so hard he was obliged to sink to the floor, all the time wondering if he was beginning to lose the battle for sanity.

CHAPTER 25

Hugh had heart for little the next day. Evening arrived and with it the dinner for which he was to dress and expect some surprise. On went the wig, the silk stockings, suit, and solitaire. After the bellows frosted him white, Louis applied a touch of rouge. What signified any of it? He had been outwitted by a servant. Now he lied for him, took loans for him, feared him. All to construct a house of cards that would collapse the moment Jasper chose to bump into it.

A note had arrived from Benjamin the day before, telling of his presence tonight, and he was first to arrive. Hugh was working himself up to asking a loan, which he feared must include a confession to the blackmail. Benjamin would be shocked, compassionate him, then no doubt become fearful himself. To know Hugh was to be in danger and he must certainly back away.

Hugh poured a dram of Geneva, then a second, dropped the gin bottle into his boot and descended to greet his brother-in-law. When he arrived in the drawing room Philippe was setting out tumblers, brandy, cognac, and a box of râpée. Benjamin was lifting a cordial to his nose when their eyes met, and from the look on his face, one might have thought he had not seen his friend in a year. As soon as the footman departed, he came forward and said, "You know then?"

"Know what?"

"You looked a bit awed. A bit pale."

"I do not know whatever it is. I'll ask Louis to apply more rouge, shall I?"

Benjamin smiled and shook his head. "I don't mean to concern you. Will you take a tumbler of something?"

"Not presently. I am just returned from Geneva."

Looking as though he had never heard the euphemism before Benjamin said, "Could you but know what you say…"

"What is this about? You act as though… am I going somewhere?"

"You look terribly innocent right now Hugh. Let me look at you."

"Christ! I *am* being sent away."

But his friend refused to answer. Hugh accepted a large tumbler and toasted his good fortune, whatever it was. Could this be a Tour? Christ almighty, and if it were, would he be granted an allowance for the journey? Could he meet Jasper's demand with that allowance? It seemed too much to hope for, and yet what else could this mean?

After a few minutes the Entwistles' carriage stopped on the street. A modestly dressed man stepped out. Of medium build, somewhat darker than sandy, with dark sparkling eyes. Rather than proceed to the front door, he remained speaking with the coachman and postilion. Two expressive hands were used in short, precise gestures as he spoke. According to Benjamin, this was a Mr Snodgrass, a Scotch Calvinist. A distinguished man of letters, and though Hugh could not make out his words, the lilting cadences of his native-wood-note-wild somehow gave hope. It stirred the air like birdsong this Spring day.

A second coach deposited Walter and Horatio George. The former dressed in his habitual dark suit and long wig, the latter an astonishing, teetering confection of Macaroni achievement. The Entwistles' coachman stepped back to comprehend Ratio, the postilion unable to retrieve his jaw from the ground. Mr Snodgrass, for his part, took a step back, that his sermon might encompass them all, but took no pause, nor betrayed any reaction as he drove toward his point. As the party turned at last towards the house, curious as he was to meet this North man, Hugh's attention must be first and foremost for his Horatio.

For what were Hugh's concerns now? What were his melancholies and apprehensions? What can concern, in the face of one in still more pitiable condition? The voluminous young man, normally so lively, now carried himself with great formality in torturously stiff packaging. Into the vestibule stepped one pink slipper. Horatio came forward in an elaborate waistcoat of cloth-of-gold strained to burst, silk coat and breeches of a dashing mauve. The furniture of his head: a bouffant wig loftier than any yet seen this season, with cascades of lavender curls and bobs. His face powdered white as a Japanese geisha's, the better to enhance his cheeks, two bright red circles garnished with silk beauty marks.

"And what say you to the touch of his Jimmy Round valet?" said Lord George, whose wish for his boy's success appeared at war with his disdain for what might be required to achieve it. This desperation must mean he had learned that the only success Horatio had enjoyed in the brothel was a better knowledge of Joe Miller's sense of humour.

"But for lack of a sabre," said Hugh, "and a wig of perhaps two additional inches, to balance the overall proportion, I think my friend has done very well. No son of Lord George will ever be a shrinking violet; he will be at the centre of any fashionable assembly."

Walter scowled. Said his godson might be correct in his assessment, given modern tastes, and added that Horatio might even fell a brace of pigeons when his fastenings let free.

Pursing his lips, Horatio set one toe forward, and turned his foot. Now in fourth position, he tipped forward in a bow with all the grimace of a ballerino. One felt positively under-schooled, and under-dressed, in such company. Hugh attempted to catch Ratio's gaze, staring from atop this tower of pouf, and hearten him that the evening would not last forever. There was, as ever, that familiar regret of having neglected him, and, occasionally, denying him when he was at the door. And now look what he had become, it seemed to Hugh, merely to attract his attention.

Next forward was Robert Snodgrass, about twenty-eight, whose ease of stance, and indifference to anything in the phys-ical realm, appeared from another world. Even in a plain brown suit he was strikingly intense. After the introduction Hugh said, "Well Sir, and what do you think of our gay young fellow?"

With a gaze which asked why everyone could not see the Gates of Heaven through their earthly enclosures, as he did, he said, "I take you to witness: that as to his silks, and brocades, and every contrivance of powder, they can have no bearing upon his immortal soul."

"His soul, Sir?"

Snodgrass took his hand, quick to distinguish any who did not immediately sneer at piety, and fixed Hugh's tipsy gaze with dark passion. "His *immortal* soul. For those like yourself, lad, who tarry in Babylon, and stew their senses. And Master George, grown fat like a Caesar, filling his belly, but not his—"

"Come Snodgrass," said Benjamin, "these boys are come to celebrate a new venture."

Mr Snodgrass turned to Hugh: "Do I insult you by plain speaking?"

Squeezing his hand, in the vain hope of eliciting a reac-tion, Hugh gazed into his eyes. "On the contrary, I feel your words to my core, and am pleased to know you."

Proving as unmoved by approval as by reprimand, Robert Snodgrass favoured Benjamin with a blank look and waited.

"What you said of growing fat, Sir," said Benjamin. "It must give pause to guests arriving for supper."

Said Snodgrass: "You may accept my apology, then, but I am not done. Now I am called to take these children to my breast, and lead them through temptation, and suckle them on the milk of our Saviour, I will not fail them. And if we are to kill the Fatted Calf, let it be in honour of the return of our Saviour, which may well be tomorrow, look you."

At this point Sir Frederick and Lady Highborough arrived to greet their guests. And in the sparkling, domed vestibule, with a feeling of much grandeur and state, Hugh gazed down his arm to where it was swallowed in the hairy, strong grip of his religious adviser.

"Are you ready to find your Laird, Hugh Entwistle?"

Like a thunderclap Hugh understood this was just what he needed. A dour Calvinist to restrain him and show him the path to follow.

"I am ready," he whispered, "I want you to show me."

"Then it will happen. Under the guise of a Tour through France and Italy, of whose histories and tongues I am scholar. Two years I studied at the Sorbonne, and three more at diverse appointments in Italy. I know the cultures, the music, and those accents of vice tender lads must be trained to parry. When you cry for salvation, day or night, I shall be with you. I shall teach you the ways of righteousness. When you falter and go wrong, I shall lift you in my arms. When you doubt yourself, I will make you whole."

"Sir," said Hugh, his eyes dilated almost from their sockets, "I believe you are come to save me!"

Snodgrass reached for the hand of Hugh's painted Jezebel.

"And you powdered fellow. Join hands."

"Had we not better on with the ceremony, Walter?" said

Sir Frederick... or seemed to say. "Our sons are together at last."

Snodgrass took the hand of each young man, and by having them join to each other, a circle was formed.

"We are come together, under the direction of Lord Walter George and Sir Frederick Entwistle. They have settled upon a match between Mr Hugh Entwistle and Mr Horatio George. This match, first proposed by Lord George, remained under consideration for some time. Sir Frederick, while not opposed to the connection, is of that considerate nature to wish an interest first be shown towards a suitor. And so, to Hugh many invitations were given, of which hardly one was accepted, and Horatio George, smitten since his schooldays, despaired at ever having his heart's desire. But after the collapse of his son's military ambition, Sir Frederick feared his son's tendency to debauch and debase and saw fit to reconsider. Under the persuasion of a most eloquent Lord George, at last he gave his consent. Now, at the approach of his sister's wedding, another union is announced, and another fine connection won to the house of Entwistle. And so, I put it to you, Hugh Entwistle: will you take your blushing bride?"

"Yes Reverend. I come to know Mr George as a fine young man and diverting acquaintance. And he is more ravishing tonight, than ever I beheld him. I believe I must have this creature for my own."

"And will you consent to the match Horatio George? It has been determined you will take the name Entwistle. You shall be remade Mr Horatio Entwistle."

"I had not," cried Horatio, at last breaking free from his restraints in the production of passion, "for the loss of my own name, betray my craving for this Gentleman! I have loved Hugh these many years, and desire him for my own! I hereby accept the name: I shall be Mr Ratio Entwistle. And in the event he is Sir Hugh, Lad Entwistle suites my fancy with equal pleasure."

"Sir Hugh and Lad Entwistle, it sounds very well," cried Lord George, and two meaty palms descended to clap each young man on the back...

This brought Hugh around from his reverie. This was, in reality, not quite the matrimonial gathering he had imagined, and Lord George was awaiting a reply to his extraordinary invitation.

"A Tour of Europe with your son, Sir? Can I be so fortunate?"

Hugh looked at his father, who inclined his head and lifted his glass.

"Horatio has taken what he will from university. Now he seeks a greater education and requires a companion for his travels. You, son, of course, must be the obvious choice. A thirteen months' trek through France and Italy, with Mr Snodgrass, a man of great learning and piousness, to guide you and act as your governor."

BOOK TWO

CHAPTER 1

To Benjamin Sallow, Mayfair, London 17th April 1769

Dear Benjamin,

*After a bleak week in Boulogne, we have continued on to Paris.
Robert Snodgrass believes an education of the Continent lies
primarily in preventing us from encountering much and
disparaging what we do. 'France,' he declares, 'is nothing but the
foppery and theatricality of its religion, promoting ignorance,
poverty, and idleness with its endless Catholic holidays'. In
Boulogne he quite terrified my new bride, as I sometimes call
Horatio, as he does rather cling to my arm. We wandered the
village from end to end always stopping to observe famished devotees in hoods and camblet cloaks animated from their hovels only
to stagger across the streets and kneel in church. Horatio screamed
whenever these downcast devotees stumbled into him, certain he
would be transformed into a living wraith doomed to a life of
devotion.*

Snodgrass is decidedly less content here in Paris, as we possess

*letters of introduction and so are many nights in better company.
Monks and devotees in cloaks have been exchanged for swaggering Lotharios, longer ruffs and larger buckles than one ever
sees in England, and wig tails dangling to the waist. These too
are disparaged as symbols of degeneracy. 'The long, suffocating
shadow of King Louis the Beloved is cast over the land!' cries
Snodgrass, and in this I suppose he is correct. This extraordinary
gap between rich and poor does occasionally sicken, as does an
increased understanding of the laws which promote it. And I
wonder, should Snodgrass die, Horatio and I might not ourselves
be assessed King Louis's belongings under the 'droit d'aubaine'
and confiscated for the State, like all property of a traveller
unlucky enough to die while in his Kingdom.*

*We fight being overcharged at most meals and must resist the
services forever pushed upon us. Yet I will say having a Scotch
guide has proved to be an asset. Good feelings remain between
Scotland and France from the days of old alliances. Robert's
woodnote-wild brings a storm of contempt back home, but in
France, the Scottish accent is like a little umbrella which often
exempts us from some of the despotisms of this place.*

*You ask about the food here. Mornings I have a dose of scalded
milk and a plate of fricasseed eggs, and come supper, a brace of
pigeons and a glass of Burgundy. My bride's taste is entirely for
fromage, morning, noon, and night. Wine is her aversion, which
Snodgrass proclaims is her greatest virtue, and with a stare in my
direction suggests is my greatest vice. I am condemned for even the
very thin Burgundy I drink (the best is all exported). To Snodgrass wine is, quite literally, the blood of our Saviour. So, I must
be content to partake socially and perhaps this will please you to
know. Drink tempted me too much while at home and I do strive
to be better. Happy the bride who contrives to get drunk on
French cheese — still, I may propose a prohibition on Sundays*

*when such intense pleasure appears particularly offensive to
Snodgrass.*

*I discover my lady's figure is of some concern to her. Our first
night in Boulogne, Horatio was three times failing to attain his
mount upon the bed. He took no comfort in knowing the French
bed does stand uncommonly high. I was half the following day
dandling him upon my knee with promises he would leap like a
rabbit once the weather warms and we fall into a regular regime
of exercise (I am afraid he found no true comfort until the
evening produced a ragout uncommonly rich and toothsome). But
I do not despair – I do claim as my hobby horse the task of
making of my little Weed, if not a Rose, then a bright and lovely
Dandelion.*

*I am sorry to hear you grow concerned for the health of your
wife. I trust Rosamunde will recover as she always does.*

Ever your faithful servant,

*Hugh Entwistle
Paris, France*

To Hugh Entwistle, Paris, 2nd June 1769

Dear Hugh,

*After a week of small improvements, Rosamunde is again in
decline. Many have questioned the sincerity of my wife's
complaints, but she does indeed suffer in a way no reading of her
Humours can alleviate. She was blooded heavily yesterday afternoon to no apparent effect. So, you will imagine my joy this*

*morning when Geoffrey handed me your wonderfully thick
epistle…*

Ever your most loving and affectionate servant,

Benjamin Sallow

To Hugh Entwistle, Marseille, 16th July 1769

My Dear Friend,

*I have just received your last. Forgive the quality of my penman-
ship. Having allowed more than an hour to the restoration of my
nerves I can delay no longer. The shock of what you confess and
the trials you have suffered at the hands of your blackmailer
inspire such a fury I cannot well see the paper through my
emotion.*

*What is not clear now regarding your behaviour? Your declining
spirits, your secrecy? I can only think of the nine months until
your return and shall be upon the rack the entire time for not
seeing you. This sudden increase in demands, contrary to what
was agreed upon with Mr Sharp before you departed, of course
left you little choice but to confide in me. I do wish you had
earlier, Hugh.*

*I shall seek out the lawyer who makes the payments in your
absence. Do not worry for a moment. The shortage will be
supplied, and every demand met.*

Ever yours

Benjamin Sallow

To Hugh Entwistle, Nice, 20th August 1769

Dearest Brother,

I must prepare you for a sudden and sorrowful piece of news. Mr Charles Sallow, my father-in-law, was seized suddenly of an apoplexy and passed from this life yesterday evening about nine-thirty. I can scarcely believe the words as I write them, so soon after learning of my own joy. But even the coming child must come second to this terrible news.

My husband is inconsolable. Comforting him must be my first duty, but his brother, as your particular friend, I fear has it worse. As you know Benjamin's wife is often in a cycle of decline and improvement; however, I am given to understand she is now in some danger. With the funeral and her health on his mind Benjamin must now think of taking possession of his father's estate in Wimbledon, Sallow House. My hope is you will receive this letter before you depart for Italy and send him words of comfort.

I miss you terribly. My only joy is planning for the child who will arrive about a month before you return.

Death does make us keenly aware of life, Hugh. Do go and experience all you can. Each day brings you closer to home – your home and your family. We need you here.

I am, as ever, your devoted sister

Anne Sallow

To Benjamin Sallow, Mayfair, 10th September 1769

My dear Benjamin,

Yesterday, upon our arrival in Italy, I received a long-delayed letter from Anne informing me of your inconceivable loss. Now this morning I received two letters from you with news of even more misfortune. The loss of your father in the first, and your wife in the second. My dear friend, how do you support this tragedy? What can I say at this late date to give you comfort? ...

I am as ever, and ever,

Yours, H.E.
Genoa, Italy

To Benjamin Sallow, Mayfair, 23rd September 1769

Dear Benjamin,

The news of your losses colours everything but here is something to cheer me – just seven months remain until I see you again. Now more of our journey into Italy:

From France, we prosecuted our journey to Genoa by boat – a baptism by sea into another culture, language, and country. At dawn, we set out from Nice in a felucca with our letters of recommendation for the English Consul. As we rowed, I observed a subtle tilting of the light which everywhere graced us. The shores of Italy appeared to glow in anticipation, the sea warming to brilliance.

Our first stop was The Annunziata – much anticipated by my bride. We had no sooner stepped from the felucca than she led our party at a run into the celebrated cathedral (much to the irritation of Snodgrass). I did not merit the ornamentation as she did (all appeared rather vulgar to my eye I am afraid), however our passing into Italy has marked a change I can only call Horatio's long-delayed passage into adulthood. There is an attempt to appreciate art, and indeed the world, around him.

In Tuscany, he wished a little villa of his own nestled in a forest of thick oak. My surprise was only heightened as he confessed a great wish to master the language of Italy (he is already far better than I am in this language). He has been studying secretly, and I could scarcely believe my ears when he traded a few barbs with our coachman in that language! If allowed a phrase or two of his Oxford Latin to stop up the gaps, he approaches fluency in Italian.

Apart from some wonderful white bread in Genoa, our repasts in Italy have been middling fare, our meat indifferently dressed. Perhaps I am grown fanciful, but this, too, appears owing to my Dandelion's preoccupation with other things, as his immense delight in meals, of any sort, has often been my only delight in them. His figure is already a little improved, his colour no longer that of scalded milk now a buttery dollop of Italian sun has been cast into the mixture.

You will ask where is Snodgrass during all this brilliance? On the journey to Florence our cicerone began to experience the symptoms of an influenza which have only worsened since our arrival here. I tell him he must repair himself now and leave off seeking to repair our souls. He resists my advice in all things, but in this he has no choice. Poor man.

I hope the news of our adventures brings some pleasure and diversion to you. That is always the first aim of these epistles. I am, as always, your most loving and faithful servant,

H.E.
Florence, Italy

To Benjamin Sallow, Mayfair, 14th October 1769

Dear Benjamin,

It was with the greatest happiness that I read of this strange contentment you have lately experienced. Perhaps 'resignation', Benjamin? You begin to heal. Sorrow, I think, is never entirely sorrow; there must be some light, some relief, or some art produced. Some pleasure at the change difficult to admit to. In Spring you shall move to your new estate – your father's greatest dream upon returning to England, and so now it must be yours.

Regarding Snodgrass, the preacher is recovered from his illness but is subdued and does not disturb me, nor the great happiness of my Horatio. My bride and I are too full of spirits to care we are the most immoral creatures upon earth. I imbibe a bit too much, I admit, and Horatio... well –

As you know he has long wished to discover a deep and true friendship with a lady. At long last this has come to pass. One night, in the character of Pantaloon, I escorted him to a Ridotto where he struck forth in an attitude of a bon vivant. *I could scarcely keep to his train! and more than once believed I mistook him for another in cloak and domino. Once or twice I was obliged to lift his cloth hood to confirm his identity: yes, it was indeed my Dandelion.*

He was at first a source of general amusement. The Gentlemen rallied him mercilessly. The Ladies tittered for reasons too obvious to require explanation. However, by his unrelenting merriment and marvellous assays into Italian, they quite fell under his spell. By night's end he was the toast of the event. And so, hoping this boded well, I informed one of the guests my friend had an earnest desire to play at 'quadrille' in the company of 'good-natured ladies'. I need not remind you the difficulties Horatio has always had playing cards, his trouble recalling the rules of the game, etc. But this night, this marvellous Florentine night, he took his place at table, recalled the rules, and was a success. He is now many nights, and indeed many days, at quadrille with Signora Tosetti, a motherly local in the fortieth year of her age.

And so, a husband is obliged to entertain himself in this city. Florence is said to be a 'welcoming place', Benjamin, so I set aside my apprehension and went for a stroll in the Parco delle Cascine. This park is known as a place of diversion; and after an hour or so of strolling, so it proved to be.

A few days later I proceeded to that triumphal arch outside the city gates. At this place, when the weather is fine, ladies stop in open-topped carriages to enjoy the day and converse with their male companions. I was a week passing them before I understood the men were no ordinary escorts, but that odd species of Italian, the cicisbei: fine, lusty men escorting their married companions about town. One can scarcely believe the practice in a country of such machismo. Yet it is met with everywhere and, somehow, accepted.

One meets, as well, with the Improvisatore – a street performer of impromptu poetry. One day at the arch I was observed by a cicisbeo standing on the footboard of his lady's coach. He summoned an Improvisatore and at his direction began verses upon 'errant youths looking at ladies forbidden to them'. I quickly understood this was meant to mean me, as I had been observing the goings on. I came forward and managed enough in Italian to say this reprimand was odd coming from the companion of another man's wife.

The lady's escort, a handsome man about my own age, took his lady's hand and informed me the office of cicisbeo was a noble one.

Then the lady, Lucia, brought me forward not to condemn but to praise both my fair complexion and my fair attempt at Italian. I was bid stand on the other side of her carriage and, I must say, I burned with pride at the honour! I praised her beautiful city, and when she saw I had exhausted my vocabulary completely, she patted my hand and glanced at her friend.

Domenico, she informed me, was allowed to escort her because he was 'trusted not to abuse the privilege'. Did I understand? I said I believed I did. Lucia then announced a fondness for afternoons of quadrille; Domenico, however, was much more a player at billiards. Was I, asked the signorina, also a player at billiards? For if I would entertain her friend for a few hours and leave her to pursue her own amusements, she would be much obliged.

As you may imagine, my urge to play billiards was too great to be denied. Domenico, though possessed of almost too much frippery to bear, answered all my other requirements. We were four hours at his lodgings – after which I was dismissed without ceremony. Afterwards, I believed myself well-pleased with my adventure and so strutted about the city for a time. But my purse, I discover, is not always equal to this variety of gaming; there is a cost my budget does not easily support. I was obliged to take a seat in a park to wonder at my growing sadness. To yearn for, and very nearly regret, my handful of afternoon diversions which had, for a time, felt quite real. How was it they had meant nothing at all to my former companions?

I returned to my lodgings, laid down and stared at the wall wishing not just to be anywhere else, but anyone else. Even Horatio, who would see his courtesan that evening. I wished, even, to be Mr Snodgrass with the comfort of his holy book.

Such are our exploits in Florence.

H.E.

To Frederick Entwistle Bart., Westminster, 10th November 1769

Father,

I have the honour of setting pen to paper in none other than Roma, Italia. Could I have imagined a year ago I should have this experience before the age of twenty-one?

I am saddened to know our time in Beaufort Buildings draws to a close. After so many years it is home second only to Deerhurst Hall. I am happy, at least, that I shall return a few weeks before the end of the lease and so in good time to organise my affairs.

Your son-in-law is generous to provide you with a room in his home in Brunswick Square whenever you are in London. You anticipate my concerns and assure me my travels did not contribute to the decision to give up the townhouse. I must accept this. I understand Lord George did a great deal in accomplishing this Tour for me, but that gift upon departure of two hundred pounds was not his. That came from you, Sir. The day is coming

I shall bear fruit and bring a good return on your investment once upon the marriage market.

We were five days longer than intended in Florence that Horatio might remain with Mrs Tosetti. At departure he was inconsolable. When Snodgrass chid him for his fornication, Horatio beat him until a constable was called. We may be obliged to winter in Florence after our time here in Rome, perhaps forgo Venice altogether if he insists on returning to his love. He calls Mrs Tosetti his Sleeping Angelica, after Reubens, and insists he will bring her home to England. Trust I will set him to rights, whatever it takes.

I have yet to write to Lord George regarding his son's romance; you know it all first. I welcome any advice in the matter, but until I hear from you, I shall use my best judgement.

I am, as ever, your dutiful son,

Hugh Entwistle
Rome, Italy

To Hugh Entwistle, Florence, 17th December 1769

Dearest Hugh,

You have begun your long journey homeward. What can I say that I have not said? You know it all, and my heart is overflowing at the thought of your return.

Before I proceed let me first tell you this: you notice I have not spoken of my 'stepson' for some time. He has been run off these three weeks. I am reconciled to it. No doubt you are surprised and even saddened. Do not be. This is how it should be — all will be explained when you return.

Now on to more important things. You ask after my daughter. Paulina is as well as can be expected …

Ever yours,

Benjamin Sallow

CHAPTER 2

"Sir, I hear Wilkes will be discharged from King's Bench today. One can scarcely believe it. What do you think will be the fate of the world?"

Hugh was not an hour returned to London when, so overcome by the festivities up and down the streets, he was obliged to duck into the Bucket of Brews coffeeshop in Temple Bar. The patron he addressed peered over his newspaper. "You've heard he will be released from prison, have you? Imagine that. Did you just recover from a hibernation, to ask the state of the nation?"

"Sir, I had not heard the exact day…"

"Six o'clock in the afternoon, 17th April 1770. The ministry's put Guards and Light Horse in readiness should there be rioting at the prison. Thoroughfares are at a near standstill for the merrymakers. I cannot say what will be the fate of the world, but it's a damned fine thing for our nation, if the will of the people is to retain any value. Many believe, myself included, that Wilkes will be returned to prison before nightfall, on some pretence, and we will be planning another celebration in two years. I suggest you mark your calendar." Then he returned to his newspaper.

"Sir, I am just arrived from thirteen months on the Continent. I was so eager to see London I left my governor at Calais and crossed alone. I have yet to see my home or my family, I sent my trunks on that I might proceed more rapidly on foot only… having never imagined such a sight on these streets, I was compelled to stop in here to sit, for a few minutes at least, with my countrymen."

"There," said the man's companion, who took this opportunity to touch his low-set spectacles up his nose and motion the newcomer closer, "is that not the finest example of an Englishman you've seen today? My name's Andrews, young man, and the pert oaf you've been speaking to is called Harding."

Andrews was a solicitor in a flowing wig dropping bits of cake to a circling terrier. Beside him on the bench sat Harding, a smaller, more quizzical-looking man in stars and garters of dubious authenticity.

"Entwistle."

"Now Entwistle," said Harding, tossing aside his newspaper, "let us first establish why you eloped from your governor. Deep feeling for your homeland? Perhaps to escape some mischief?"

"The love of an Englishman for his country," said Andrews, "Did you not hear what he said?"

"A loyal subject of England might misbehave in France," said Harding, "And perhaps bring with him a half-anker of brandy?" Seeing disapproval, he added, "For our coffee, Andrews!"

Andrews sighed, inclining his head to return the floor to the newcomer.

"Sir," said Hugh, "I did not introduce myself as Richard of Runswick − I did not smuggle a hundredweight of tea into Rye at my arrival, neither do I wear an eye-patch. I am a Gentleman returned from my Tour. My governor remained at

Calais with my travelling companion who was not well enough to make the crossing."

Said Andrews, looking over the tops of his reading glasses, "Now, Sir, consider the motivations of your smuggler before employing him as shorthand for aimless impudence. You imply many things about Richard Brent by what you say. Should you like to be judged in five years for mischief done this week in France? No doubt there was some?"

"I take your point, however—"

"Let me ask you, Entwistle – why do caricaturists, to this day, draw an eye-patch and a parrot on the shoulder of old Brent? You understand these were both inventions of the *London Herald?*"

"You speak of ancient history," muttered Harding, "Our traveller was still on lead-strings."

"Five years ago is not ancient history," said Hugh. "And as to what I recall from my lead-strings, here it is: when Richard of Runswick learned he was smuggling not just tea and brandy in his lugger, but muskets, ammunition and three of the most dangerous political exiles residing in France, he changed course from Rye. He pistol-whipped two of the exiles, then held the entire crew at gunpoint as he brought the lugger straight up the Thames and into the Pool of London. He was wounded during the conflict which ensued at his arrival, and though the exiles were arrested, he spent five months in King's Bench before he could prove the plot against the royal family. His overthrow of that lugger, though it was his own, is why he is fancied a pirate; his service to the Crown why he was pardoned for smuggling."

"There you are," said Andrews, "much more than a rebel making mischief on the high seas. And his smuggling, as you call it, was, in my opinion, non-violent protest against the import tax here and in America."

This was answered by a finger in his face and a stern look

from Harding. "Now *that* I will not allow. Next you will be defending Sixteen-String Jack or McClain."

"Brent is no highwayman, he's a national hero," said Andrews.

Turning to Hugh, Harding said, "Let me ask you – how does one come by with the name *Brent*?"

"Come by with?"

"Aye, you did not know some names are come by with. Richard Brent comes from people in Yorkshire long associated with theft and wrongdoing. Whatever the name was before, *Burnt* became the family name when some forefather had his hand branded as a criminal. With time the name was corrupted but make no mistake – the family fortune was got by smuggling rings between Runswick and Denmark, and later with France. Everyone says his father was a secret Jacobite, and the turning in of his smuggling compatriots a cynical move. A fleet of revenue cruisers had just been dispatched to put an end to it. He should have been transported to a plantation in America or better still hung at Tyburn. How many men," he said, lowering his voice, "are called out for a duel by the Chancellor of the Exchequer?"

"That never happened," said Andrews, sliding his glasses up his nose.

"Upon my honour it happened! Mr Grenville, our Chancellor, called him out and his Second was to be the Treasurer of the Navy. It was Brent who declined to meet them in Hyde Park."

On the floor the terrier was jumping from side to side, driven to mania by the elevated tone of the conversation and the thought of another piece of cake.

"By 'never happened'," said Andrews, "I mean the duel never happened. That was due to Brent's good judgement."

"But Sir," said Hugh, "Brent is an errant poltroon to refuse Mr Grenville satisfaction. How can he show his face?"

"Because it was Grenville, Mr Entwistle, who refused to meet in Hyde Park. It lay with Brent to choose his method of prosecuting the duel; he selected not a brace of pistols, not swords, but rather to *box* Mr Grenville – and so was declined. Bless me! a show of courage and a bit of wit!" Andrews let out a throaty laugh, and was some time shaking his head before he continued. "Brent's become quite the renowned boxer since then you know. I saw him in a match once and I'll say this: he's no less fit to stand for Middlesex than your Mr Wilkes. Sensational performer – because he knows the people. We are coming to a place, I'm afraid, when that is all that matters. One need only charm the public, as good Mr Wilkes does, and one may do very nearly anything. Boxing indeed!" Then he tossed a morsel of cake and the terrier flipped in the air to fetch it.

Harding shook his head at his companion. "He's a regular merry-Andrew. Well I haven't met old Brent, nor wish to meet him. Neither do I wish to meet John Wilkes. I hear stories of both that'd make your skin crawl, only nobody cares a fig for infamy anymore. Wilkes is a member of something called the Hellfire Club, which each Sunday holds a service to the honour of Satan. You think I quiz you Entwistle?"

"No Sir, only…" Hugh blinked. "I am a little shocked that you can be in earnest. You were defending John Wilkes when first I asked about him."

"Yes, I was, and I'm a better Englishman, if not a better Christian, for it. It's a question of liberty – I will never support a government that installs its own lackey, this Luttrell, in the House of Commons over the duly elected Wilkes. Wilkes *is* the will of the people, no matter what he wrote about our king, and no matter his other blasphemous activities. So too one must support a mob in Boston, and compassionate that massacre of angry fools, who will cut their own throats in the noble demand for representation. Perhaps we *must* support our radicals. Perhaps we must make deals with our Wilkes's and our Brents to secure ourselves against utter corruption."

Hugh was momentarily speechless by the passion of what had, at first, appeared a rather idle character strung about with cheap decorations. "Very well. In the interest of upholding the law, perhaps one must support lawlessness."

"*Yes*," shouted Harding, made only angrier at this agreement, "but do we risk excusing vice and riot to affect our aims? Do we give our crown not to a King, but to the most charismatic and diverting? Are we nothing but mindless papists like you saw in France, idolising the patron saints of Sedition and Smuggling?!"

Now stirred to frenzy by this speech, the terrier spun across the floor like a child's top. Harding aimed his boot at the dog, and instead struck a chamber pot which rang like the bells at St. Mary's against a neighbouring spittoon. Cursing the dog, and with stars and garters swaying, he shouted:

"*Welcome home, Entwistle! Out of the frying pan, and into the fire!*"

Sometime after six Hugh exited into the streets to the sound of skyrockets set off every forty-five seconds. A table forty-five feet in length stood in the middle of a congested lane, where revellers had set, among the victuals of the oddly situated feast, forty-five place settings with forty-five pints of ale. Houses far and wide illuminated, and tales began to circulate that John Wilkes himself had begun parading up and down the Strand with his alderman's fur-lined cape and sceptre. Once or twice, when he was rumoured to be approaching down this lane or that avenue, couples broke into the Wilkes's Wriggle, a country dance imported from Northampton.

By sheer coincidence Hugh met the coach with his trunks he had jumped from some two hours earlier as it neared the Savoy – he jumped in again as it made the turn to Fountain Court and so on to Beaufort Buildings.

·   ·   ·

Next day, through streets still congested with revellers defying a gloomy, chill dribbling, Hugh arrived at Benjamin Sallow's home in Mayfair. Relieved of his overcoat, he was shown to the fire and, as Geoffrey announced his arrival, looked about a ground floor so altered as to be unrecognisable. Even on a rainy day it possessed a new lightness, both freer and, somehow, eerier. The seal on the dark curtains had been broken and there hung about the windows and wall sconces that rawness after the black crepe of mourning has been removed. The knowledge that, for a time, the mirrors had faced the walls lent a queer quality to the reflections, as though the surfaces were straining to perform a duty rarely asked of them. Hugh stepped around fat oak furnishings dislodged from their former positions, fancying this was not just in expectation of the move to Wimbledon, but from an earthquake which had dislodged nearly everything in London.

Then with rapid footfalls the lady of the house arrived and was in his arms.

"Let us look at you," said Hugh, trying futilely to extricate himself from the embrace of Benjamin's daughter. When at last Paulina drew away, he smoothed her hair and kissed her tears. In her eyes he saw the remnants of hope that his arrival would return to her all she had possessed when they were last together. Her mother, her grandfather, a home, and existence she knew. This hope was now fading, for she understood, as she looked into his eyes, she would never have that life again.

"You know about my mother," she said, looking at him in some confusion. "And Grandpapa."

"Yes, darling, I learned of it in Italy. You cannot think how I have mourned our loss. They wait for you in heaven and watch over you every moment." She nodded as though she had heard this too many times during the months of mourning.

"Papa says you visited a convent in Boulogne where I might learn French."

"Nothing I saw could justify the separation it require. And you are so beautiful now I cannot think, but nuns must lock you up all day and night."

"Why would they do that?"

"For fear all the men of Boulogne would try to marry you and bring you to Paris."

"Really! I should love to go to Paris; what would I do there?"

"Who can say? You would not be there long before King Louis himself learned of you and carried you off to Versailles."

"Versailles! Oh Hugh, did you see it?"

"Versailles, Fontainebleau and all the places in between."

And so, he regaled her with stories for ten minutes until Geoffrey bid him upstairs. With a deep breath Hugh followed the butler to the first floor where Benjamin waited for him in the upper parlour. The butler had hardly closed the door when he grabbed Hugh and with tears of joy pressed them close, kissing him until Hugh's mouth, cheeks and forehead were a series of raw, red burns. Then gratified smiles as they studied one another in that unsteady mixture of natural light and firelight which illuminate dribbly days. The amber glow of brandy danced into tumblers and Hugh was directed into an armchair.

"My condolences. You have seen your daughter through the worst of it. She is recovering remarkably well."

Sitting in a chair pulled close Benjamin placed a palm to his friend's cheek. "I left you ten minutes speaking to Paulina simply to hear your voice and savour that unbearable torment of not yet seeing you. Thirteen months. Thirteen months, Hugh. Do speak."

Determined to strike a new tone of maturity, Hugh said, "You will know a man now, Ben, and not the boy who departed. I was a child in many things, but in nothing so much as in my hasty judgments about Rosamunde. You cannot think

my fool mouth when I am alone with my
God she can forgive. And as to your father
believe such a life force has departed this

appeared around Benjamin's eyes and
across his forehead, and after months of death and funerals,
he appeared eager to relegate to an attic room his bereave-
ment. "Let us speak of happier things now. I would not have
you return only to grieve – we must celebrate. You are
matured – my God, Hugh, what an extraordinary continu-
ance of your boyish beginnings. You do accelerate my
heartbeats."

Hugh was momentarily at a loss for a response. This was
not, after all, quite the Benjamin of old.

"But how is Master George? Does he prowl for another
lady in Calais? Now the beast is unleashed, can Snodgrass
possibly contain him?"

"The women of the Continent are nearly as safe with
Horatio as they were with me. In my efforts to break him from
the grip of Signora Tosetti, a quality courtesan, I introduced
him to harpies, herpes, and a bout of gonorrhoea. He is
another three weeks in Calais with a gleet, which, he insists, is
punishment for his sins and a sign he should not return to
England. He is terribly cross with me for having introduced
him to other courtesans. He longs for Florence and his
Sleeping Angelica. He is *in love*… Now, what else would you
like to know?"

"Anything. Everything. All afternoon and evening. You will
not depart before I would let you?"

"I shall remain as long as you wish. I saw to everything,
and everyone, yesterday. My father was… slightly reserved.
That is to be expected. You have heard about giving up the
townhouse?"

Benjamin nodded. "Such places do become expensive."

"Highborough cried and nearly ravished me on the Turkish rug. Your brother Duncan gave a good imitation of pleasure at seeing me, but I find him so altered now. Ever since he began in Parliament, whatever he had of rugged, American spirit appears to have been beaten out of him entirely. And a stauncher adherent to our new minister Lord North I daresay there never will be."

Smiling, Benjamin said, "Yes, I know."

"And Anne – she glows. She is a mother now, truly and completely; the fulfilment of everything she ever wished to be."

"Your sister has been so kind to me, a fine surrogate in your absence." He brought Hugh's hands into his own again, "You understand why I waited to see you. Why I wished to meet you here, privately? It wasn't just the Wilkes madness in the streets." They looked at one another a moment and Hugh nodded. Then with a sigh, he continued, "I must ask if you have seen the other. Your father's valet?"

"Yesterday."

"Did he make any demands?"

"No demands. We had no real chance to speak. If I remain occupied, I can avoid him entirely."

"Ignore him at your peril. At the very least confirm all payments have been received and there has been no misunderstanding on any point."

"Very well." Hugh waited until he had secured his friend's eye, then said as forcefully as he could, "I *will* see you have every farthing back that you have lent me." After an acknowledgement the man clearly wished to continue to the next topic. "Speaking of scoundrels, Ben, your own has departed. Your 'stepson', silly Mr Dempsey. He was only a rented punk, remember that; they cannot be trusted. But do tell me there was passion at last. Many months of passion."

Hoping to bring forth a little swagger, a little boast, Hugh was dismayed to see no more than a meek smile and a look of regret. At last he said, "He told me you two had a talk about his being *friendlier* with me before you departed. He was, eventually. What we had lasted eight months after you departed, then ended with a note informing me he had found a benefactor to suit him better. Such is the way with these things, I imagine. I had considered how to end the arrangement, though I doubt I would have done it myself. He had stolen money from me here and there, furniture and paintings when he departed, but it is a small price to have the thing ended cleanly. I left not a shred of evidence that I put him in that apartment or ever knew him."

"But you would not undo the experience?"

Benjamin smiled. "No. For my part, it felt like love."

"The bloody fool; he might bit his blow with the drunkards stumbling out of the Hook and Crook; but it beggars belief that boy discovered another who could set him up as you did."

After a sip of brandy, under whose exquisite effects Hugh had already sprawled back in his armchair, Benjamin said, "Is it so hard, anymore?"

"What do you mean?"

"Let me ask you… well no, you've been home less than a day."

"Ask me what?" When Benjamin would only shake his head, Hugh gripped his tumbler in both hands and leant forward. "Egad Sir, you do pique my curiosity! What can you mean?"

But there was a devilish side to good Mr Sallow, and if he ever had opportunity to torment his friend, he would use it.

"Perhaps it is merely the circles I mix in now," he said. "However, one hears things one cannot quite… place. There is a word, you see, a word which one hears spoken occasionally, though not a new word by any means. I can think of three common meanings off the top of my head. And yet, to make any sense of the context in which it was said, I am led to believe there must now be a fourth."

Hugh's eyes widened. "Will you bring a poor, weary traveller to his knees Benjamin? For I shall bow and scrape and all manner of inconvenience before I leave this room uninformed!"

With a small smile Benjamin said, "Do not trouble yourself just now, it's unimportant. We've a hundred other things to catch up on. Discover it for yourself, then we can speak more about it if you wish."

The dismissal of what was, in that moment, the greatest desire of his heart nearly took Hugh's breath. "When Samuel Johnson claims there are 43,000 words in the English language, damn me if I shall ever discover the one you mean!"

Benjamin laughed. "Very well, I will say this – your sister has made a very illustrious connection in a Miss Julia Motley." Hugh blinked stupidly, never before having been so well-manipulated by his older friend. For, despite this unknown word now set to drive him mad with curiosity, the mention of the wealthy and superbly connected Motleys gave him pause.

"*Motley?*"

"Yes, quite the girl about London these days. Though not as beautiful as her celebrated cousin Chloe, Julia is London's premier socialite. She has rather adopted your sister – I don't suppose Anne has mentioned it to you."

"No, she has not! Benjamin, are you joking?"

"It doesn't surprise me; Anne's head is not to be turned by well-connected people."

"But explain how any of this pertains to my discovering this damned word with four meanings."

"At least four meanings," Benjamin said with maddening punctiliousness. Hugh kept his mouth in check until his friend continued: "It was in conversation between Julia and a Miss Dalrymple that I last heard the word used, in that particular sense. That it should arrive in the conversation of two young women, decided me incontrovertibly that something was afoot."

"And may I ask which of the two employed this word?"

"Julia Motley."

"Then I shall make an intimate friend of Miss Motley and have that word of her as though my life depended on it. You cannot imagine how this torments me."

Benjamin grinned. "Yes, Hugh, I can imagine it."

His head spinning with spirits, that evening Hugh set off from Mayfair in his curricle with a bursting heart. Oh Motley! Brent! Wilkes! A mysterious word! – how he loved his city! How he loved the people he was to meet in this city! He charged up a merchants' alley in the absolute certainty he would find his elusive word around the very next turn. Under his wild direction the horses stamped and skidded across the cobblestones, Hugh jumping from his seat to slap a tailor's signboard swinging in the wind, before continuing.

As he proceeded south, his fingers extended while maintaining the reigns in the cradle of his thumbs, his fingertips trembling to touch something in the darkening evening – but no! he must seize the reigns tighter, must wrest from the twisting, writhing leather this grand gesture he so yearned to make in the world! The gesture one could only make, and only if one were lucky, in London:

Wilkes's sedition in the *North Briton*! Brent's hijacking of the lugger! Pope's *Essay on Man*!

The lights of Vauxhall ignited!

It was the *air*, the *everything* one could not see in the metropolis! It was just *there*, under the night watchman's repetitive call, lurking in a dark corner waiting for the law to pass before leaping out to mesmerise the city! It was the moment a handful of the Elite understood a new scandal was about to descend upon Society, as they rushed to organise friends to hushed teas! Evanescent and around the next corner, up Maiden Lane or down Threadneedle Street.

Formations and constructions, deformations and deconstructions, relationships dissolving, then resolving…

As Hugh turned off the Strand and came near home, he passed a tall, ambling figure that could only be Sharp, returning after his evening in a neighbourhood tavern. After hastily stowing his horses and curricle in the mews, Hugh swept up behind him and took his arm.

"I meant to have a word sooner, Jasper, but have been quite occupied since my return."

The man withdrew his arm. "To be expected."

"Although I have been assured by my lawyer, I wish to hear it from you – have all the payments been received?"

"They have," he said, in a tone not much above street level. "I'd have written if they wasn't."

"You understand it was not easy to meet your demands while I was away."

Said Jasper, narrowing his eyes, "'Twas a rather obscene fortune bestowed at yer departure. Yer father wouldn't tell me how much, at first."

"It was meant to sustain me for more than a year. The last five or six months I had scarcely a shilling to my name."

Jasper had no answer for this, and as they neared the front door of the townhouse his footfalls quickened.

"Congratulations to you and Jenny on your marriage." Sharp halted, looking down the quiet, enclosed street as Hugh continued, "You and I have known each another a long time. Despite – our differences, despite everything, I do wish you happy."

"Much obliged," he said, then ascended the steps of Beaufort Buildings and held the door until Hugh followed him inside.

This exchange appearing to have been a success, Hugh ventured to his father's door, supposing it time they spoke of the future. He knocked and put the question to him: would he remain in London, return to Berkshire, or perhaps something else? But Frederick, who had been unusually occupied since his return, said only that they would speak within the next few days, then closed the door.

CHAPTER 3

Next day Hugh arrived at Anne's residence in Camden. They took a tour and she presented him the room she was preparing for Charlie's return from his wet nurses in Islington. Then Hugh introduced the topic of their father and his decidedly cool reception since his return.

"No doubt you have seen far fewer of his moods than the rest of us," said Anne. "But I assure you he has always had them."

"Have I been such a confounded fool my entire life?"

Tucking a stray dark hair behind an ear she sighed, "Oh dear, I must choose my words more carefully."

"I *have* been a fool, for far too long – always so ridiculously favoured. Do not make me one a second time. Highborough tells me our creditors have been continually at the house. We are losing Beaufort Buildings, I can accept that, and I expect to see signs of distress and yet – he looks at me differently now."

"Perhaps it is you who has changed. You are at a crossroads in life, and you believe the alteration to be in our father. How can you find your direction in the world without the compass which guides all things? Come to church with me this Sunday. Open your heart to the Lord."

This was expected, and Hugh, on the point of making his excuses, found he had at his defence no more than a shrug: "Oh, very well."

It was almost worth enduring a long, dull service to see his sister's look of astonishment. She jumped up, holding a finger in the air at him, and almost skipped into the next room. As she returned, she stopped to look at the grandfather clock in the passageway, then came forward with an item in each hand.

"Unless my eyes mistake me," said Hugh, "you hold in your hand the Protestant Manual." Then he sat forward, for in the other hand she held a necklace of sapphire-coloured glass in remarkably bad taste. "Upon me 'onour," he said, "jewels to choke a queen."

"Cleopatra," she said, placing the Manual in his lap, then holding the necklace across her bosom where it rose and fell in the afternoon light. He jumped up, quick to catch the falling Manual and set it gingerly on an end table before advancing.

"Is it a masquerade?"

"It is. You see? Your sister is not so very dull – yes, I know you thought that she was. Have I told you about my friend Julia Motely?"

"Yes?" Hugh said, nodding.

Anne stepped to a mirror. "Now Duncan is a part of public life he does occasionally mix with the so-called Elite. Julia was at one of these dinners. We were not two minutes arrived when she approached and told me I looked like a scared chicken. She has since decided to adopt me. Duncan and I will be attending the assembly at Mrs Cornelys's – Julia knows just about everyone in London, and somehow gained us admittance. I only do it for him. I wish him to be a success and this is important to him."

"*The* Mrs Cornelys? Of Carlisle House?"

"Yes, one of her grand gatherings."

Hugh worked to catch his breath. "Is this not rather… rather too much? No offense, but your husband is only an MP."

"An MP with the last name Sallow. A name still associated with Boston, and so believed to be useful. Who else do you think will be at this masquerade?"

"One can only imagine."

"Among others they tell me Mr John Wilkes has been invited."

"Holy Chr—!" Hugh choked. "Anne! Will he really?!"

"Yes, he will, among others. Would you like to know who one of those others shall be?"

Hugh nodded.

"*You*, you goose. Julia detests every man she knows at the moment and has agreed to do me the favour. Are you happy?"

Happy. Oh, happy.

But Hugh had hardly a moment to comprehend his happiness when his sister was ordering the coach. "Let's continue to Julia's then. Her seamstresses are arriving at two in Grosvenor Square. We must fit our costumes then find something for you."

As they arrived, Hugh grew quite dizzy. Never had he mixed with the likes, but he was determined to engage and fascinate. Perhaps begin by telling Julia of the Coliseum. Or of the new fashions in Paris – she *must* wish to know that. However, upon introduction, he was far less sure of immediately securing her attention. She appeared rather a fierce creature, with a long face and a rudely shaped mouth which appeared liable to unfurl whip-like and strike anyone who crossed her. The siblings arrived on the heels of the seamstresses, and Hugh had no sooner bowed to introduce himself than Julia seized Anne's arm and commanded him to sit for a cold collation of chicken and champagne and tossed *The Vicar of Wakefield* at him. They must, that moment, have a fitting, and pausing just long enough to tell Anne her brother was exactly as described, Miss Motely hauled her friend from the room.

Medusa, at least, once Julia had changed into her, paid Hugh a bit of attention, seeking his opinion as to the drape of her gown, and the placing of twelve fabric snakes upon her head. Anne, as Cleopatra, emerged behind her in little more than a petticoat and a twisted swath of indigo, perhaps the least Hugh had seen her in since they were children. How very fetching she appeared, blushing, and for once in her life disordered and in dishabille. Bully or no, Julia seemed rather good for her.

"We have rehearsed attitudes," said Miss Motley to nobody in particular as she stood before a mirror. "We shall make a marvel of our new-married lovers."

"Hardly new Julia," said Anne. "Duncan and I have been married nearly a year."

"But with little Charlie with his wet-nurse, and you looking so well and fresh, nobody would ever suppose it. I have no feeling for anyone I know lately brought to the alter, all for one base reason or another, so you are the new-marrieds of the fashionable set for my purposes."

Hugh stepped forward. "What can you tell one, Julia, so long in parts unknown, of London? What makes the freshest *ton*? What scandalises? I must know."

"Nothing at all I assure you," said Julia, and after a full minute, in which she twisted and primped before the looking glass, Hugh understood the complete dismissal of his inquiry. Glancing at her brother as if to apologise, Anne said, trying for the lilting, cultured girl about town:

"The freshest *ton*? – an ingenious head cushion from France, which adds six inches to almost any wig. There was an MP who fought a duel in Hyde Park then ran away to Amsterdam with his mistress."

"Is that all?" said Hugh, still smarting, though quick to give her hand a squeeze. Julia came over with a fall of ten snakes carefully cascading down one side of her head and asked for an opinion.

"Do tell Hugh something of the town," said her friend. "I can have no opinion on fabricated snakes until you do."

Holding a pin between her teeth: "Come to my box at the opera tonight, love."

"The opera?"

"The Handel production in Drury Lane. You wish to know about the town? The town shall be placed before you. We arrive at seven-thirty."

But if Julia Motley were inattentive in her home, she was the height of gracious company at the opera. For into her box she also welcomed her fair cousin, Chloe, and so Hugh, and indeed Julia, were cast utterly aside in the constant stream of guests who came to see one of the wealthiest, and certainly the most ravishing, girl currently on offer in London. And a more egocentric, sneering brace of companions there never was. The opera was dismal, ruined by performers even more affected than Hugh had witnessed in France. But this was nothing to residing inside a box containing Chloe, the prize of the season, and her legion of admirers. Had he been asked to suffer it again in the retelling, Hugh could not even say he was unwanted, for one must be noticed to be unwanted. Julia did what she could to bring him into the fold, sat him in the chair next to hers and introduced him. Here, a visiting Viscount, and there, the Earl of Leicester; neither of whom said a thing to Hugh, and hardly anything to Julia.

All was Chloe – a dazzling ruby set on a bed of silk. The interest in her a fire-breathing dragon. The girl said hardly two words to anyone, rotating her gaze around the titled finery wherever it seemed most required.

"You believe I am neglected and suffer," said Julia, whose elongated face did seem to imply such treatment. "I see it in your face, Mr Entwistle. You are thinking how I must envy my darling cousin."

"When I was at boarding school," said Hugh, "my window looked out upon a tree much favoured by the local dachshund. A fine tree, but when a second canine made it the beneficiary of its *occasion*, I observed that the combination of their rank emissions drew a third, and then a forth, and then a fifth, for no other reason, it seemed to me, than that others had pissed upon it. I did not, however, think to envy the tree."

This drew a snort of appreciation from Julia, and she warmed considerably until an important-looking man came into the box and towered above them. By his undisguised stare at Julia, Hugh was made to understand his own seat was desired. He rose, though not before Miss Motley took his hand and squeezed it, and when it appeared the new arrival would remain with her, Hugh fled the opera at his uncommon show of humanity, vowing not to return for the remainder of the season.

On the final night in Mayfair, under Benjamin's appreciative gaze, Hugh invented story upon story of '*Paulina's Adventures in France and Italy*'. The girl begged he would accompany them next day on the move to Wimbledon.

"No, darling, Uncle Hugh must be a tiger tomorrow evening."

"Like in the King's Menagerie?"

"The very kind. I shall have a porcelain mask, but otherwise you would not know me from an actual cat. I pranced about Florence too many nights as Pantaloon, and so tomorrow I shall exhibit my inner, animal nature."

"You can roar at them!"

Hugh nodded and turned to Benjamin. "I may if they are

coarse or cruel to me. But I know your father's thoughts on masks, and so perhaps should not go."

"Whose rout is it to be?"

"Mrs Cornelys's, at Carlisle House."

"A lofty event indeed. How came the invitation?"

"From Anne – by way of Miss Motley." They exchanged a look. In his study after dinner they resumed the subject. "It was only an invitation to a masquerade – I have not discovered my damned word with four meanings just yet."

"Why not write these stories of yours down, Hugh? All these tales you tell my daughter – challenge your talents, apply again to The Puffers and Poets Guild. Become involved with something beyond parties and masquerades."

"Don't worry about me – I intend to challenge myself, one way or another. And don't talk to me of masquerades, I wonder I have any desire at all to put on another mask."

"Do both. I should be sorry to see a man of twenty talk himself out of the pleasure of a masquerade."

"Very well. So long as you know I would prefer to be in the moving carriage to Wimbledon tomorrow." On the point of rising to find the brandy decanter Hugh was suddenly back on the sofa with Benjamin's mouth upon his – his friend had apparently consumed more than his usual two glasses. Hugh pulled instinctively away before he realised what he had done and was immediately angry at himself.

"Ben I... Really. I'm not averse to it... I was caught off my guard."

"My apologies."

"You may again."

After a moment, Benjamin said, "Someday." Then he smiled and patted Hugh's shoulder. "Let us first fix the day you shall come to us in the country. To Sallow House, as my father wished it to be called – does that not sound grand?"

"Name the day Sir, sooner rather than later," and he extended a hand for Benjamin's empty tumbler. When their

eyes met Hugh paused. For the look which met him said something in Hugh's tone had betrayed desire of another kind, the
kind he himself had failed to understand until he saw it
reflected. Together. In the country. Could it be just the three
of them? Could Hugh retire from the world, withdraw into
the country, and mentor a child? And would not their differing
personalities make them parents ideally suited to produce a
happy, well-rounded young lady? *in the country*

Benjamin read every word of this interior dialogue in
Hugh's face, and understood access to his heart ultimately
more profound than physical passion ever could be. He said,
"And when you come, may I lock you in a room and never let
you go?"

Hugh looked at him, wiped his mouth with the back of his
hand and thought, *Why cannot we be that to each other?* He was
utterly confounded by his continued resistance. *It's your fault,
Ben. If you would only be more aggressive with me. Or more aloof. Or
more something! For I do love you – then we would be happy in the country. Just us three. Why could not we?*

Through the grand entry to Carlisle House, Mark Antony
held the Tiger on a lead, Cleopatra stepped regally forward,
and Medusa worked a hand mechanism to enliven the snakes
nested upon her head. Then, into the crush of seven or eight
hundred guests the Tiger, free of his constraints, romped
about the gay set, quickly drunk on champagne and that
freedom only to be found in concealment. Liberty, too, came
in the form of not one, but three John Wilkeses, all with masks
displaying his well-known crossed eyes, protuberant chin and
the Devil's horns Hogarth had painted him with. The real
Wilkes was rumoured to be somewhere concealed in an
anonymous blue domino pretending to be nobody at all. And
oh, thought Hugh, reeling about the many rooms of worthies,
what could one *not* accomplish in a mask? Who could one not

be? No doubt here tonight were some horrors from Julia's box at the opera, but in a mask he could not have cared less.

For tonight, the Tiger rode a tide of champagne in a merry footrace to the end of the garden! From there, he crept back through box hedges, up promenades, around fountains, speaking to anyone he chose, with myriad affectations and under assumed accents, receiving attentions from endlessly curious, blinking eyes – for this animal might be *Somebody* and a guest might be ten minutes discovering he was not. The strings of the orchestra pulled him off the grounds and into the ballroom where a thousand candles glowed, and a thousand flirtations danced like moths around the revellers.

Through the press a diminutive Shepherdess was leading a sheep three times her size across the room, and was heartily laughed at by many in the crowd. Duncan confided that the Shepherdess was none other than Chloe Motley, and so one had to wonder at the unknown sheep, who, once his identity was discovered, would be the envy of the room.

Medusa would know, but was much in demand, for she had a stage actor's bent and was working her snakes to great effect. Guzzling even more champagne than Hugh, Julia was well soused when he at last cornered her and demanded to know the companion of the Shepherdess. "He must be torn limb from limb once his identity is discovered."

"My Lord Allenby attends her. And rest assured, he fights with only one since his duel last week." And she laughed merrily for a reason known only to herself.

"Lord Allenby is her chaperone?" She hummed assent and held two snakes to one side to better douse herself with her beverage. "He had a duel? With whom?"

"The Marquess of Argyll – over there in the corner, with his Shepherd: the Marquess is the ram with those two rather ungainly horns."

It was an odd coincidence; were Shepherds and Shepherdesses so much the *bon ton* now?

"A duel? But you take my breath, Julia. Can nothing shock you?"

"Nothing!" she cried.

"Duels are common enough, but between a Lord and a Marquess? This is worthy of some report. Why have I not heard it?"

Miss Motley was some time working the device in her hand, cursing her inability to make one of her many snakes dance, then she said, "My innocent *Hugh-go-not*! That is what I shall call you whenever you prove such a dull-swift. You claim Gentlemen of such note cannot quietly have a duel. And I declare, they are the only ones who can."

"But what do you mean?"

"Oh dear, allow me one second to think, hmm? One *Second*?"

"Second?" Hugh repeated. Then again, "Second." This, then, was his word with four meanings. So obvious, and yet... so clever he should never have guessed. But how to use it in a sentence? For it was something to speak an old word newly. "Lord Allenby," he said, "is the *Second* of the Marquess of Argyll?"

Applauding raucously Julia bowed to him: "*Was* the Second, yes. Thank goodness you understood at last – I was nearly obliged to fetch a piece of Greek pottery and show you."

Hugh was sobering so quickly the room came rather crashing into focus. Here then, an unmistakable reference to what must not be spoken of, or even known. Was it possible? This relationship between Lord Allenby and the Marquess of Argyll was known, and accepted? He grew suddenly terrified Medusa might be swept away before he could ask everything he must, this moment, know.

"And their costumes," he said, clutching her arm, "They are meant to – oppose one another?"

"After a fashion, though only a quarter of the room

discerns it. And I can tell you, now you know, Lord Allenby remains the Marquess's Second in terms of wit as well, for there is a great deal there. They broke a month ago when the Marquess discovered him with that youth you see beside him, dressed as a Shepherd. In revenge his Lordship bragged to him that he did not care because he would be the chaperone of Chloe tonight. And so, Argyll made himself a Ram, and his new Second a pretty little Shepherd, for the occasion."

"His new Second," Hugh said faintly, and looked again at the small, slim man in country clothing and a porcelain Shepherd's mask.

Soon Julia was swept away, and Hugh too fell back into the crush. Orchestral diversions grew boisterous, dances lively, couples fled over the Oriental Bridge to places unknown – Hugh joined, or attempted to join, drinking, dancing, chatting, and observing, whenever he could, the Ram and his Shepherd. Yet he did not approach, for tonight they represented far too much – they were the people he might someday become. Might he have a companion to go about with? Might he deviate from the path which had been set from infancy? Might it be accepted?

For there were so many people to be in this world, and most of them were here tonight. The painter Hogarth, spattered in oils from head to toe. Next, a man in the character of Voltaire, complaining of French opera, of which Hugh gave a lively defence, based not on received wisdom, but, wonderfully, upon personal experience. Hugh seized the hand of Voltaire and marched him toward a peasant with a basket of eggs, clearly intended to be the royal rustic Marie-Antoinette, and asked that she help him defend her adopted country. The companion of the queen, however, disguised but in no obvious character, interrupted her to berate France in a muttered lisp. To which Hugh cried:

"And have you this knowledge at first hand, Sir? I am just returned from that place, and find your judgment lacking."

Mr. Dempsey – Pact Out

"Apologies to France, if she has changed entirely while I was away."

"It cannot have done; it has only been two years," said Marie-Antoinette, turning to Hugh. "And before he departed my friend was five years in that country."

Hugh's heart skipped, as the entire room appeared to hear them. For the man he was addressing was, of course, none other than John Wilkes. Concealed in an anonymous blue silk domino and, very quickly, snatched away.

Toward dawn, Hugh realised he knew someone else at this assembly: the Shepherd on the arm of the Marquis of Argyll. For at one point there was a commotion – all eyes turned to see the pair emerging from the ballroom. Guests parted, and the Ram strode forward carrying the Shepherd in his arms. His Second, it appeared, had just fainted and must, that moment, have recourse to fresh air. There was some confusion, many were too drunk to care, others tittered behind their fans. However, Hugh, though too tired to think much of coherence at this point in the evening, could yet say to himself: "My. You have done well for yourself, Mr Dempsey."

The morning after the masquerade he opened his eyes at what felt an ungodly hour with Louis Gallante standing over him.

"Your fazer, Hugh. He want you in fifteen minute."

It was nine-thirty when he arrived at the study door, only just presentable. The man's look of disapproval was acute, and there was the added insult of observing Jasper at one wall assessing him as well.

"You are a mess," said Sir Frederick, "You look ten times your age, you stink to high heaven – you shan't be attending the concert tonight in Covent Garden, as you had planned."

Jasper took his cue and departed the room, and when no word came from behind the desk Hugh said, "I know you are displeased. What can I say?"

"You don't come here to stand and look at the floor. Take a seat and look at me. You were thirteen months on the Continent. You have been to London assemblies many times and this is not your first rake by any means. But the occasion, Hugh, dictates the behaviour, and you were raised to know the difference. Carlisle House is *not* the place. You are already upon the marriage market, think how a misstep may affect your reputation, and your prospects. People will always remember first those things we wish they would not."

"I overindulged; I own it. I—"

"Neither is this a Catholic confessional. I had the details of your brother-in-law an hour ago in a note. Do not blame Duncan, I requested the report. He wrote of falling, of elevated, slurred speech, and being sick into a pitcher of water. Identities were not universally known, thank God. That the misbehaviour of others far exceeded your own is a piece of good fortune you did nothing to merit."

"I escape the scorn of the city, perhaps, but yours is almost more than I can bear."

"I have heard those words before. You will tell me more now. I want to know your experience with women, and I want an honest answer. You whore like a sailor on leave, do you not?"

"Yes Sir."

"Or do you?"

After a pause, his son said, "Sir?"

"Do you not inflate the truth, Hugh? Whoring as much as I am made to believe does not agree with the behaviour I observe before women of Quality. Men will always show it, if it is in their character, regardless the station of the woman. And the stories which make their way back to me savour rather of the fantastic. How many street-girls?"

"Five."

"Have you had a girl in our service?"

"No Sir."

"Have you absolutely escaped distemper? I insist upon the truth, the absolute truth, if you might infect a lady."

Hugh gripped the arms of his chair, attempting to maintain his vision, and said, "I always employ armour."

"You flirt with everyone, but never one more than another. Why has there been no girl you wish to put forward, with passion, to propose for marriage?"

His head still spinning from his debauch, Hugh said, "I have fancied myself in love. While at Evendown, I admired the sister of a schoolfellow, though of no great fortune. In Newbury, there was the dancing master's daughter – not to be considered for obvious reasons. In Florence there was an Italian Contessa, already engaged. It seems I have aimed either too low, or too high, or too late."

This speech, long rehearsed, had been contrived to inspire a laugh and perhaps camaraderie. Yet Hugh knew, as did any stage actor, when his performance failed to impress. His father knew he was being lied to. Then, like the fulfilment of every nightmare Hugh had ever had, the man, closing his eyes, at last said, "Did you seduce James Bramble?"

That Hugh maintained consciousness was uncertain; an eternity seemed to elapse in the space of a moment before he could produce a response.

"What?"

"Are you asking what I mean? Should I be more specific?"

"No! Why?"

"Was I foolish to believe you before? Are you lying to my face?"

"Should I leave you, Sir, and go to my apartment?"

"Rather than answer me?"

"I answered you – the answer is no. But my presence must indeed be odious, to accuse me as you do."

"You sent Anne to inquire after him while she was in Berkshire on her wedding tour. She badgered his stepmother, on your behalf, as to where her eldest son had got to. While you were away, I had a very angry letter from the parson. He believes that whole affair back home to be your doing. His son never had a thought of the kind before he was driven mad with attention and presents from you. The expensive gifts I knew nothing of. You promoted James over your own brother in the horseraces. You were everyday together, and often off by yourselves. And after what he did to Ned, and the disaster which almost came to us because of it, you sent Anne to ask where he has got to?!"

"I swear I never touched him like that. On my life, and honour as a man. Yes, he was my closest companion that summer. I confess I have wondered if he is in any way happy, or repentant, or a productive member of society. Anne said she would ask for me and was refused any kind of meaningful answer. I do not absolutely hate him, as you believe I should do…"

At last Sir Frederick sighed. "Wipe your eyes; come now, enough of that."

"I do not bring a girl forward for marriage," said Hugh, "because I promised you, long ago, the decision would be your own. I shall have my own choice, in time – is not that what mistresses are for?"

After a long moment, Frederick fell into a fit of laughter quite unlike himself. Then he stood and extended a hand over the desk. "Put it from your thoughts," he said. Taking the hand Hugh nodded. Nevertheless, he understood this was the moment he had been discovered. Only they were never to speak of it. Hugh was to repent and change his ways and there would be the end.

"Nearly exactly as I had supposed. In any event, no man should consider marriage seriously before the age of twenty-three. It is not, however, too early to secure an engagement to a family of fortune, should the opportunity arise. I have a few in mind, so it will not surprise you if I make an introduction when the occasion presents."

"You must be a much better judge than I have been. In every way."

Frederick turned up his palms and smiled. "How many fathers may choose for their son, without some word of protest on behalf of a rosy cheek, or a buxom frame? Ten thousand is to be the dowry upon your engagement, obtained in no more than three years."

"A sum indeed."

"Required for Alice's dowry, and the promotion of Ned in a few years. Ten thousand is not a luxury, Hugh: we require it. We give up the townhouse now I have a superior place with Anne when I need one. Still, there is not much room to retrench. We are not, nor ever have been, extravagant."

"I shall sell the curricle; it is the logical thing."

"You shall retain the curricle. It was a gift, and it is precisely what you should go about in."

"And remain in the city?"

"Yes. I must divide my time between London and Deer-hurst. I depart for home in three weeks once the lease has ended, however you shall remain in view and promote your name in places of fashion. I trust you will do well, if only you will pry the bottle from your mouth."

"Yes, of course."

"You shall have £250 a year in twelve increments for an apartment and expenses. Well above what is required."

Stunned, Hugh said, "It is too much. Indeed, too much."

"Provide me a ledger; I must have it monthly. Should you ever need a reminder how not to behave those former friends of yours, the Greys, are an excellent example. They are nowhere to be seen anymore. They have nigh on bankrupted their father. Their debts are legion. Wild for Hazard, but you never followed them down that path. Whatever else there was of carousing, it was that exceptional self-control in the gaming halls which persuaded me in favour of your trip with Horatio, else I never would have approved it."

"Thank you."

"I shall always discover the truth of what you do, Hugh. One way or the other."

"Yes. You always do."

Hugh departed the interview with a smile tacked to his face, his jugular pulsing nearly to suffocate him. He had promised himself he might vomit as soon as he was released, but as his father rang for Jasper and he began up the stairs, he was pleased to discover the feeling passed. On the landing he was well enough to command his lunch of the housekeeper, before continuing down the corridor to his apartments. As he turned the knob his elbow was taken, and he was moved silently into the room. The door closed, and Jasper set a hand on his shoulder.

"The money is mine. £250, in twelve payments." The bell rang again. "Every farthing." That Hugh neither protested, nor acquiesced, appeared to stimulate Jasper's Spleen, and his gripped tightened. "He *knows*. What might Robert Snodgrass remember of handsome *ragazzi* boys loitering about your lodgings? I shall ask him when he returns."

Hugh pushed the arm aside. "Ask him – you will hear of visits to Temples of Venus, and my romance with an Italian Contessa."

"But your father *knows*, my buck. The parson told him."

"He is too smart to know anything which is not to his benefit. I am his prized investment and am about to repay him. So, I am innocent as the driven snow."

The valet leaned in. "Does he know about Benjamin Sallow?"

Hugh's silence was too long to be anything but an admission.

"No need denyin' it, you have confirmed it. He is your special friend, that is a fact. And there is always means to prove a fact. Benjamin has a daughter, does he not? Her future prospects must be protected. And Duncan is an MP:

always rather precarious where scandal is concerned. Benjamin Sallow is a wealthy man; you shall need money now and I have a good idea how you reckon to get it. And how you have been getting it."

"You can prove nothing when there's nothing to prove."

"I can prove it. Will you hand over the money?"

"Yes."

"It's twenty-one pounds each month. Starting the first of May."

Then he released Hugh and exited the room, to the wild ringing of the bell.

CHAPTER 4

On occasion, *Dear Reader*, an Author is tempted to colour over faded porcelain, raise a primrose over an unsightly fracture, or leave unrecorded what fails to ennoble. We seek a Saint, on whom to bestow sympathy, in its entirety, for the brutality practiced upon him by a cruel world. Yet who does not love Tom Jones, despite his occasional slip? Or Peregrine Pickle, his many slips? The Recorder of a History must ever be a Tom Tell-Troth, and so the following describes two days in the life of our Hero which do him little honour. For, from the moment Jasper released his arm, Hugh felt a fury he had never experienced – a pure, blinding panic of rage.

Laughing madly, he dashed off a note to Benjamin, announcing his triumph at discovering his mysterious word!, and demanding to be received next evening at Sallow House to tell it to him. Then he pushed passed the errand boy, and took the letter to the post himself, waving to any who would look the Free Frank and the signature of his brother-in-law, an MP! Yes! Hugh Entwistle was well-connected! Next, he stalked The Bedford Coffeehouse, inquiring after the Marquess of Argyll, then, with a well-placed bribe, the location of an apartment in the West End his Lordship had occasion to frequent.

Next morning Hugh strode to the door of the ground floor apartment and rapped sharply.

"*Damn* me," hissed the young man, "how are ye come here?" However, the unexpected visitor, ramming his foot inside the door, gave Dempsey to understand he would not be suffered to leave, not if he knew what was good for him. Hugh strode into a dark, gleaming apartment furnished in rather too much of the best – vases, fat, lacquered furniture, and large statuary at the expense of functionality. Without waiting to be invited Hugh was soon master of every corner of every room and, amused by Dempsey's red fluster, came forward and grinned.

"And you need not fall into a faint, love. That worked twice with me, but it will not again."

His host straightened and stuck out his chin. "I would not play that trick on ye, nor any other. I was used to like ye, until ye threatened my 'worthless, conniving neck' last year on account of that other chap."

"After you refused to sleep with him and so made a fool of me, who brought you up in the world and saw you well-established. But praise where it is due: there are not many could ascend as swiftly, by so often descending upon his ass."

"That is unfair, but pray be sweet to me, for I have always liked ye. And I know yer last name now. Benjamin slipped and told me it's Entwistle, just like his is Sallow. I am terribly lonely here and am a changed man, and not so much given to my faints as before."

"Only at a masquerade, in front of all of Society."

"Was you there? I rather thought ye'd gone away from London, else I would see ye."

"Thirteen months on my Tour, just returned," Hugh said haughtily, flicking the damask drapes aside to observe the street. Dempsey begged him to stay and tell every detail of his journey.

"Won't the Master discover us?"

"The Marquess never has occasion to visit on a Wednesday, though he claims he may, so I am not to leave. I am always to wait for his discharge, like a station in the military. He can be monstrous unpleasant, not like your friend Benjamin. Mr Sallow was vastly more sweet to me, 'pon my everlasting honour. Pray don't go on the Marquess's account."

"I shall unless you give me a reason to remain."

Hugh took a liberty then, and, as it was but feebly resisted, soon attained full success of his aim. It was only with his villainy accomplished, his host sweaty and subdued in bed beside him, that the scarlet rage which had blinded him for an entire day began to cool. Hugh basked in this newly aggressive and heartless vision of himself – what could not be accomplished by force of a nasty temperament? What pleasure not extorted? For anyone could see this inmate was lonely: he tried repeatedly to kiss his visitor, making shift to be held, and, at last, tired of being rebuffed, curling possessively around him.

"I shan't pay," said Hugh. "Do not ask, else I will not return."

This was at first a tough pill to swallow. When there was an attempt to play upon his sympathies Hugh had the happiness to say, "Best take as recompense, you little fool, the money and furnishings you stole from my friend."

After this no mention was made of pecuniary remuneration, and his host was reconciled to being what he termed *friendly*. "Very well," he said, "I don't forget you plucked me from squalor. Because you fancied me. And still do, ain't it?"

"How came you to find your Marquess?"

Propping himself on an elbow, the boy said, "Stealth. And hard work, unlike those rotten wenches got it so easy. With the money I was earning I got some new suits, then I did what they wouldn't dare, which is stroll for trade in St. James's Park like a Gentleman at leisure in prime sunshine. Many a fine afternoon was thus employed, with the liberty afforded by your kind friend. I learned that few prowl before dark, but then Moll Dowager saw me strolling and invited me back to his brandy shop. She's the one turned me out of his molly house for my being so much handsomer than her other rickety bollocks, who all hated me, and made out I was stealing. That's what sent me hard up to the Hook and Crook."

Hugh motioned for him to continue, at which, pushing his long dark locks from his face, and smiling sweetly, he continued, "With me departed Moll weren't fit to supply a Marquess with anything to strike his fancy. Told me she often regretted turning me out after Argyll called, the daft pullet. Once she found me again, she contrived a pretty note to introduce me, for half my earnings, which terms she included in the letter. For pin-money at first, that was all because I told her I was happy in my establishment with Benjamin. Which I was, till I got a better offer."

"The night I found you," said Hugh, wondering how many lies it was possible to have heard in the short time he had known Dempsey, "you told me those molly houses were all gone over. I was not so drunk as to forget that."

"So's ye would patronise me, of course. They ain't all gone over, dummy."

This comment was not well-judged, for in his fragile condition, this bit of impertinence drove Hugh to a fast rage. A battle ensued which ended in Hugh's again ravishing his companion, in the sudden heights of which he actually screamed in ecstasy and confusion. Then he pushed the boy away with something like fear, for his vision had, for a moment during his thrashing about, gone entirely black. *God Almighty,* he thought, *who am I becoming?* But his companion applauded the performance until Hugh, wishing desperately to believe the praise, began to burn with pride.

"Ye were a boy before," crooned Dempsey. "Yer a man

grown now, ain't ye?"

Hugh snorted, then hissed some rather rude things into Dempsey's ear, to the effect of much laughter. His victim thus plied, the boy began again to complain of being a prisoner in his quarters; he had not seen light of day for weeks.

"If you will consider bringing me under your own protection, I should leave the Marquess, in a trice. 'Marquess', as you know, is a title you have not yourself, but I would be your obedient inmate, and never stray as I just have with you. You are just as rich, I daresay, and would never make me miserable, for you are not fat at all, nor so very old."

"I have no money for that at present, so you had best think of another way to support yourself. You say you tire of the Marquess — what happens when he tires of you?"

Dempsey answered this with a flip of the hair then reached for a crystal pitcher of water. "He has no means to find another so charming as myself. He wore me proud on his arm at Carlisle House — a dare as had never been attempted in London. All eyes were upon the Shepherd and his Ram, and everyone in a panic to know who I was. I did once, but to rally them, withdrew the ribbon from my hair, and all the ladies fell into encomiums upon me. And half the men as well, declaring I must be a girl underneath. Then Lady Newcastle, the finest lady of them all, christened me First Arched Duke of the Nubility, which scandalised everyone into peals of laughter, for they had never seen such as I Second a Gentleman at masquerade!"

"It is... accepted? I scarce conceived such a possibility."

"Have a lofty title, and what is criminal becomes *au courant*." At Hugh's dubious look, Dempsey added "Well... not entirely — for there was many would not speak to us. And Lord Allenby they said would have liked to kill me. Still, I got more praise than would an African Negress, I am certain of that."

Hugh departed the apartment with half a promise to return, wearing a foxy grin and relishing his wicked performance. He proceeded on foot to Blackfriars Bridge, chin tilted higher than was his standard, sneering at all the men he wanted, and all the women he did not want, certain, in his youth and virility, that he might bully or seduce whatever he wished.

Arriving at the bridge he recognised a poet of his acquaintance called Chambers, a member of The Puffers and Poets Guild. The young man had been staring intently at the bridge until Hugh strode into his sightline, then seeing him scurried forward in a bulky overcoat asking if Hugh recalled him from the few meetings he had attended the year before.

"You are Gilbert Chambers. Graduate of Pembroke College, an aspiring poet of an undistinguished family with only the dubious claim of talent to recommend you."

Finding more of praise than contempt in this, Chambers nodded, shook his hand, and welcomed him home from his Tour, claiming Blackfriars Bridge, the city's newest marvel of engineering and convenience, as his to present. This annoyed Hugh, who retired to a nearby bench, with hardly a look at the structure.

When Chambers followed, Hugh crossed his ankles and said, "Still puffing and poeting then, are you?"

"After a fashion. I am a member now of the Society for the Arts…" he paused for a response which failed to come, "The Puffers and Poets Guild is no more, most of our members now belong to the High Scribblers. You are a member now as well."

Hugh raised an eyebrow. "Am I?"

"A long and tangled history, but the dues were transferred, and you are paid through February, as those things are reckoned. They read out two of your poems one afternoon, while we were organising our library," continued Chambers, wiping his nose which had gone blue at the end. "We meet at Hopkins' every Sunday at two, Hatton Garden, by Grey's Inn Gate. No street numbers yet. Will you know how to find it?"

"I know it," snapped Hugh. "And I suppose they were reckoned of some worth? My poems, I mean."

"Certainly. Scholarly, if a little irregular in terms of measurement; and yet I understood, to a one, what motivated the breaking of a few rules. I felt the glow of the Ancients in a couple of your lines, Sir."

"No doubt you are more master of them now than I am – I scarcely recall writing anything." Hugh was in danger of feeling some regret at lately having been so unproductive, when Chambers asked if he might present him something he was working on. "Please."

This required the young poet to extract himself from his bulky overcoat, lay open the garment on a dry spot and remove from a buttoned enclosure the precious, folded sheet of parchment. As he waited, his legs stretched long from the bench, Hugh knocked his beautiful leather shoes together, thinking forward to his departure in a couple hours for Wimbledon, where Benjamin waited to welcome him. Sallow House was sixteen miles from town, so he would certainly be invited to stay overnight in the guest room...

When the poem was at last exposed to air, Hugh snatched it, the parchment still warm from proximity to the overheated author. Hugh had already determined what he would say by way of congratulation, but his eye was caught where it had begun, which was the second line – he paused and moved up to the first.

"This is quite good," he said, and was a full minute reading. At the conclusion, with a shake of the head, he said, "This is your composition? It is the very essence of this bridge, both in a literal and a metaphorical sense. The second stanza is worthy of Johnson's poem of London. Better, by far, than my own compositions last year. I'm sorry you ever found them if you are capable of this."

With tears in his eyes Chambers extracted every scrap of praise before Hugh cut the interview short, sure the next five minutes would bring mention of a subscription. He left Mr Chambers on the bench with a vague promise of seeing him sometime in Hatton Garden and continued on his way.

Yet encountering a poet of ambition and talent, while in a self-satisfied state of aimlessness, never fails to unsettle. Once at home Hugh fell into an ill-humour, lamenting how little he had written, or even read, of late. He was half an hour considering his former ambition, that dazzling ode he had hoped would write itself. But as the time for his departure for Wimbledon neared, he had the good fortune to hear a piece of low, discordant music issuing from his father's study – an argument, with Jasper Sharp as the object of displeasure. Little of the disagreement was clear, but it sufficed to improve his spirits as he set off on his horse at an easy trot.

The estate of the newly christened Sallow House met, and indeed surpassed, expectations. A grand place, with an extensive prospect, a park of still-forming walks and alcoves, and a disused cottage much overgrown, which Hugh fancied more truly romantic than the false grotto situated upon a nearby knoll. It struck him that Sallow House was not just a home, but a new home. Not the house one had been born into, but a place of one's choosing. He had never lamented the passing of Charles Sallow as he did now. How he should have liked to ask that extraordinary man how he had achieved all this, the product of thirty years' focused ambition and sacrifice.

And so suddenly the loss of Beaufort Buildings meant more, far more. Examining all that was Benjamin's, Hugh felt a constriction in his throat, and once or twice as his host led him about the place tears stung his eyes. He was happy for him, and yet so unhappy for himself. There remained Deerhurst Hall; Hugh's one day, but did he want it? In his current mood he believed he must sell it and look for a place entirely new to him, a place he could name just has Charles had done.

Then he would have accomplished something, truly left his mark.

His melancholy was not improved to observe Benjamin, newly made master of this beautiful estate, and with every reason to be happy, more than a little subdued. He rather tiptoed around the grounds, even saying, "I do feel I am only the caretaker of this place. Why was he not with us longer to enjoy all he had worked to build?" Hearing this once awakened Hugh's compassion. But by the third time he had grown tired of the maudlin sentiment. Later that evening, as candles flickered to life in the back parlour, Hugh said, "Rest assured, the house answers every expectation your father ever had. Such intimacy amid such grandeur."

Touching their brandy snifters together, Benjamin sat quietly and looked into the fire. Hugh crossed to the large, Palladian looking glass, reminding himself of his personal attractions, his youth, and his vigour. Gone that amount of baby fat he was used to carry about his cheeks; Benjamin had noted it and complimented him on the improvement. But if the man admired him, why not take this opportunity to welcome him here in an intimate way? How easy it would be to rattle off, 'Hugh, my love, your presence here at last makes Sallow House a home'? Praise overflowed on every other occasion, and tonight, if Benjamin would only wake up, he would be well recompensed for his effort.

"The garden is intellectual," said Hugh, "so well-considered, but with touches of whimsy which feel the product of sudden inspiration. Free and open – I am quite at home already. Even with the bustle of your move from town, my every wish, my every possible whim has been anticipated."

But rather than saying what a joy it was to pamper his friend, Benjamin said, unforgivably, "I suppose I am grown skilled after so many years caring for my wife – foreseeing her needs before she knew them herself. One grows fond of performing a task well."

This was too much, and with a flash of anger, Hugh said, "Indeed. And it must comfort you to know your infatuation with William Dempsey last year was more of the same. Not really love at all. Just another object to care for and keep from harm."

The comment drew the man's attention, and he remained silent a few moments looking at his guest. "Was it?"

Hugh hummed off-handedly. "I trust I don't err in declaring what you have yourself said in so many ways." Benjamin frowned. "I mean it as a compliment. Your greatest joy was caressing a lock of hair and reading to him from Pope. True Platonic affection. The scamp can even be forgiven for employing those faints to avoid sleeping with you."

Benjamin's insistence that not all the faints were a pretence, and that he and Dempsey were, eventually, more than just friends, bespoke regret which had not passed, and Hugh quickly regretted having introduced the topic. Tonight was their first night together in this house, and it should have been Benjamin's triumph with him! Tonight was the night, and it would ease asking for the money Hugh so desperately needed now.

"Do forget him, Ben. You know he never deserved you and must be miserable now wherever he is. Think, rather, upon a Second."

Somewhat hesitant to relinquish the unsettling topic, Benjamin smiled and inclined his head. "Well done. You have your damned word with four meanings. And how came the great discovery?"

"At the masquerade, the natural place to hear it."

Then launching into a colourful description of Mrs Cornelys's assembly, Hugh's hopes for the evening began to rise. But he was dismayed by his friend's immediate condemnation of the antics of Lord Allenby and the Marquess. "Ben, I must be of another species altogether. Can you find no pleasure in the thought of such a relationship being known? It was only a spat between lovers, and you will condemn such a little—?"

With a hasty look to the closed parlour door, his host whispered, "This *little?* One can scarcely believe this *much!* Don't believe for a moment titles will prevent prosecution, and a complete downfall. It is a wildly dangerous game Hugh, make no mistake!"

And so, again, they lapsed into silence. This evening was proving to be the most unsatisfying they had ever spent together.

"We are to give up the townhouse," Hugh said, hoping to snap him from his fugue. "Our lease is up in three weeks."

"Yes, I know."

Where was the concern he might not find an apartment in London and so be obliged to return to Berkshire? Nothing! Hugh cried, "And is passive acceptance the most I am to inspire at the prospect of my departure!? Will a couple of weeks, after an absence of thirteen months, suffice before I fall again into the realm of ink and delayed post?"

"What is this hysteria? Your father wishes you to take an apartment in town, I know that. There are plenty to be had and I shall continue to see you often."

"Then why must I despair aloud before I hear it? It hurts me exceedingly!"

The man rose, and, closing his eyes for a moment, took his visitor by the shoulders. "If my attention is occasionally diverted to other matters, you must not believe it indifference towards yourself. You must allow me some moments of reflection."

"But imagine how I have longed to see you today; I had never come so far as this for anyone else. Think of the endless, lonely nights last year, when I could but think of the many miles, and the many months, between us. I could scarcely endure it!" Hugh tossed back his drink and poured another.

"I suffered no less," said Benjamin, holding out his own

to be refilled. "You seem to feel a great passion for me at the moment, when you suspect indifference. I'll abide no talk of my coolness, when it is you who have resisted these two years. Perhaps I am content now to enjoy our friendship, seeing you in London or in my home to converse with. Forgive me, but you take on a different air tonight. And speaking to me in this tantrum of thoughtlessness, you do show your age."

But Hugh was far too fired to listen, taking the man's hand, and placing it upon his own cheek. Then, discerning a slight tremble, Hugh pulled them together. As Benjamin brought them to a kiss, their teeth knocked together, both with his bafflement and Hugh's grin for, clumsy or not, it had been a real and honest kiss.

"You will not doubt my interest now," he said, stepping back.

"I do doubt it," said Hugh, "if you push me away again. Come back and see how obliging I can be. Hm... a passage comes to mind. You recall *The Satyricon*, don't you?" And, grinning, he recited:

"*Who hath a Pathic lust*
With Delian vice accursed?
Who loves the pliant thigh
Quick hand, and wanton sigh?"

"That's enough. I'll do no more in this house."

"*Come hither! Come hither! Come hither!*
Here shall he see: gross beasts as he!
Lechers of every feather!"

"Open your eyes, Hugh, remember yourself. You are in my house, my father's house, and you will go to bed now in the room prepared for you. The fire is lit; I'll send up my man with a warming pan if you wish." Then he took a drink, licked his lips, and looked away.

Growing nearly mad from the need to succeed, Hugh said, "Can you actually wish that? You accuse me of being twenty; I am, if I am uncertain in myself, and seek to understand in a passionate way. Desperation for happiness has given me to a few endeavours, in the hope of finding that one. But there is something which I have not yet given, and do not know. You shall be the first: I swear on the memory of my mother."

"Christ Almighty!" hissed Benjamin, a vein threatening to burst pumping blood into his forehead. "Two things never to be mentioned of a day! My daughter lies under this roof, and the servants whom I trust, and who trust me. This is my *father's* house, Hugh, even now, as I keep telling you; I fear it always shall be. I will not do that to his memory. You cannot ask me."

And, at last, Hugh must begin to feel disgust at himself. His hopes now grossly maimed, he bowed his head and stepped to the door. "I must respect you more, of course, if you stay away. Only stay away for your own reasons, and not what you believe would be the wishes of others."

But no matter the noble thought, Hugh dozed for hours tossing, waiting, expecting the footfalls which never came. Next morning over tea and brioche Benjamin said, somewhat dryly, it looked as though Hugh had been up all night waiting for something. His guest was obliged to a sheepish smile, and the knowledge he had appeared a right ass. Any attempt to ask for money now would be proof he had actually tried to prostitute himself, and he began to suspect Benjamin did not, in fact, really want him anymore. By the end of the visit Hugh had mentioned his intention to ask for the annual stipend in a lump sum but dared no more than to hint his finances were in disrepair.

There remained only one week before the new, larger payments were to begin. And he had not a clue how he was going to manage it.

Next day Hugh awoke with the sun lighting the tepid memory of his recent behaviour. He washed his face, employed a drop of tincture to sweeten his breath and stood listlessly about his bedchamber in half-dress. He had behaved repulsively, with Dempsey, with Chambers, with Benjamin. Still his troubles remained. Upon observing Matilda somewhat listless after breakfast, and complaining of still less to do that afternoon, Hugh treated her to a walk about the shops and warehouses of Cheapside then into a teahouse.

"You are a cloudy day, child. What ails you?"

So over tea and dainties, Hugh confessed to a few of his concerns. Firstly, replacing his valet, who had decided to return to France. Immediately her Ladyship jotted the name and address of one Mr Kilmister who was coming available and came highly recommended.

"Next."

Tucking the card inside the skirt of his frockcoat, he proceeded to general concerns about money, and finding reasonably, very reasonably, priced lodgings in a good area.

"Forty pounds annually? You name a very small sum. East End."

"Eighty was my idea initially. Only now it appears rather more difficult. One is not obliged to the East End with forty, surely. I need only a neat box, tucked away, where I am no more tempted to go than for sleep and refreshment. No one I might bring home might not just as easily meet at a chocolate house. I shall host no dinners."

"A finer place," said her Ladyship, "must raise you in your own estimation. Set it at £60. You shall be nice for £60. When you emerge each day, you shall radiate this niceness upon the city, and bring nice people to you." At his look of helpless protest, she turned a ring which had fallen off-centre, and narrowed her eyes: "You believe I do not understand a budget. You do me a great injustice. Here is what I tell anyone, male or female, as regards finance – forget ledgers.

You may retrench, conserve, whatever it is without one. Only take one quarter of what you forego, in this case about £5, and buy a hat or a ring, or some bobble at auction which you may take with you when you walk out. It must be a thing you can present to the world, and show to yourself, every day, as a piece of your ensemble. You will never regret a humble lodging; rather, you are indulged in deprivation, and you will smile at that."

He had not five pence to waste on a bobble, but the defiance of the gesture appealed to him. They jumped from the teahouse to discover his bobble, quickly deciding upon a walking cane of silver and mahogany at auction. Upon stepping into the street beside her Ladyship with his staff to guide them, he was hard-pressed to believe he could have gone another day without it.

CHAPTER 5

Next day Hugh scoured the city for those apartments requesting annual payment in advance – this would permit him to request his allowance up front, then, he hoped, negotiate privately with the landlord for deferred payments. By the afternoon he had winnowed the search to three and was riding about The City when he saw Gilbert Chambers departing a bookseller's in a dejected attitude.

For two days he had taken his poem about, unable to sell himself or his writings as he was never quite able to speak of his work in the presence of a professional. The unfortunate poet had something in him of the untied; as he walked, he appeared a loose collection of limbs stitched up like stockings which have undergone coaxing, that operation to prolong useful life. Hugh took him by the arm into the curricle, rallied his spirits and that evening took him to a new performance in Drury Lane. This did much to distract the sensitive young man, though it enraged his benefactor, who had spent even more of what he did not have to watch a dreadful production made even more reprehensible for its pretensions.

"Will you not scorn it?" asked Hugh afterwards in The Bedford Coffeehouse, perplexed by the mild manners of his companion. "Will you not rail against injustice? A world which is deprived performances of promise, like your *Ode to Transport*, while the public at large is subjected to such trash?"

Said Chambers, "That play is the production of a man's heart – it is his issue, his sweat and toil. If it fails to succeed it can only inspire my compassion."

"The deuce!" said Hugh. "Compassion for a cynical production which stole nearly every situation from *The Beggar's Opera?* The only thing more offensive was an audience so ignorant they failed to perceive and condemn it. I shall issue a condemnation – in writing."

This he did, and next day produced a document in pamphlet size for the inspection of Chambers, who was too much a serious artist not to see the justice of the critique. Hugh had chosen as his target not the production itself, which he praised to the heavens for its calculation, but rather the audience which cheered, applauded, or sighed at each shallow contrivance. His portrayals of five spectators were vividly drawn, each describing a type of theatregoer so immediately recognizable, that Mr Chambers was betrayed into howls of laughter, his eyes watering and his nose leaking even more than on chill days.

"Now we shall take our productions for publication," said Hugh, which produced a look of terror and a rapid drying up of Gilbert's fountain of mirth. Nevertheless, Hugh pushed him into the shop of Mr Flexney, bookseller in The City. The bookseller was perched on a stool behind a counter, within a mountain of pamphlets and errant papers, his look announcing if he was never approached by another fresh, eager writer in his life it would be too soon.

"Good day Sir," said Hugh, relieving himself of his hat and presenting his friend. "I am Mr Entwistle – permit me to present my friend Mr Too Soon."

Mr Flexney paused, his hawk's eye studying them until, to Hugh's great admiration, he understood the joke. He presented his rebuke in a pinched, nasal voice: "Wrong – I am presented with two Mr Too Soons. You both hold samples of your genius for me to inspect."

Hugh turned to his friend. "Gadzooks, sharper than my razor after an application of Packwood's Razor Strops!"

"New faces are allotted five minutes, Mr Entwistle," said Flexney, "to be spent on stuff and nonsense if they choose. It was your mistake to enter this establishment as a couple, five minutes must do for you both. Now whose work am I to feast my eyes upon first?"

Hugh took the *Ode to Transport* from Gilbert and presented it.

"*Bon appetit*, Sir," said Hugh. "When you are done with your feast, you may have my own as a napkin with which to wipe your mouth." Hugh stepped back to join his friend, whose eyes had expanded and whose hands trembled violently now they were deprived of those lines he had toiled over for so many weeks. Each moment of suspense was like a dagger in the heart of poor Gilbert, then the bookseller returned the ode.

"Which of you decided Flexney should publish this?"

Nearly suffocated with apprehension Gilbert pointed at his friend. "He did, Sir. Because of your fine reputation."

"Has Flexney a fine reputation?" said the man. "That is news to me."

"Flexney & Flexney, booksellers," said Hugh, "brought out Richard Brent's discourse on boxing, not only the finest treatise on sport since Mr Parkyns's on Cornish Hugg-Wrestling, but the only one, to my knowledge, written in iambic pentameter."

"You are fond of boxing?"

"Upon reading Mr Brent's performance. All the more to its credit, and the publisher who understood the promise of it."

"Brent's book has been ridiculed by those of a poetical bent. Most disdain uniting two distinct genres."

"Not all Sir. I assure you, not all."

"I publish little in terms of pure art – political polemic, American pamphlets, volumes on sport and travel. And devastating indictments of Parliament and various public figures in my periodical, the *Public Inquirer*."

"Which does not prevent you from recognising poetical talent."

"It does not."

"What did the publisher Robert Dodsley feel when first presented with Samuel Johnson's *London*, I wonder? It established the names of both."

"Now see here—"

"I do not say my friend is Johnson just yet. But Sir you cannot deny the comparison."

At this point Gilbert Chambers piped up with his ambition and willingness to begin taking subscriptions. When Flexney, rather grudgingly, agreed to meet him the following day, the poet nearly collapsed from excitement and began pulling Hugh toward the door.

"The napkin, Mr Entwistle," said the bookseller, extending his hand with a sigh.

Hugh had nearly, though not quite, forgotten his own composition and promptly handed it over. The man was halfway through the piece, growing redder with each paragraph, when he began to shake with laughter.

"Lord help the poor sod who finds himself the object of your condemnation," he said, returning it.

Flushing with pleasure, Hugh bowed and said he hoped this meant he would run the pamphlet.

"No. Cut it by a third and I will put it in the *Inquirer*. If it succeeds, I would like more of the same on theatre, public figures, politicians upon the hustings, whatever you like so long as there are sufficient pretentions to dispel."

"Let us pray I find some in London," returned Hugh, a bit dizzy at the thought of the eyes of the metropolis reading his words. "Very well. You shall have the revision before nine tomorrow."

Upon returning home, Hugh stepped immediately to the closed study door, from behind which was issuing two low voices in conversation. The visitor was Benjamin. Hugh was for a moment concerned that Jasper should know of the visit, but Philippe informed him Mr Sallow had arrived at ten minutes after seven, just in time to miss Sharp. The study door opened.

"The Devil himself," came his father's voice, and, bringing Hugh into the study with them, closed the door. "Your brother-in-law."

"Hello Benjamin."

Frederick pointed his son into a chair and pursed his lips. "Ben was regaling me with this charming practice they have in America. Let us see what my son makes of it." Hugh was a minute listening before he understood Benjamin was offering, at a reasonable rent, three rooms in a very good location on Charlotte Street.

"The charming American practice to which your father refers," he said, "is my belief that family should look out for one another whenever possible."

Said Sir Frederick, "And so seeks to excuse the pittance he is asking. £55 for a place we both know would fetch £80, if not £85, annually."

"As I said—"

"I shall not bargain you up − accepted. Upon Hugh's seeing the place and approving, naturally. Ben has asked payment for the year in advance − because of this I have decided to give you the stipend in a lump sum. You have the option of a linen service, an evening meal from the landlord and his wife, who live across the street... he will tell you the details. It will be a blow to your budget at the outset, and you must plan carefully for the remainder of the year."

"This is a business decision," said Benjamin. "Many advise against any mixture of family and business. I believe I know better in this instance and trust you will make a good tenant."

Hugh looked a long moment at the visitor. "Let us see the place then," he said.

"It has stood vacant for a time, but it is furnished."

"Take the curricle," said Sir Frederick. "He asked particularly to take a turn in it. It is a very fine thing, Ben, upon my soul I never saw a finer. Lord George does dote on his godson."

In the darkening evening, as they crossed Dirty Lane, they joined hands under Hugh's cocked hat, which was propped between them.

"Then I am forgiven? Or will the roof fall in during the night?"

"I expect you will like it," was Benjamin's reply, after which they remained silent until they arrived. The first-floor apartment was of brick with two white sash windows, originally intended for the owner of a bookstore directly below, which had since been converted for use as an art gallery.

"Art for the home is very much the thing these days," Benjamin said as he lit the fan lights and led them about the rooms. "Mezzotint prints of any portrait you can imagine may be had. We had West last year, in a little exhibition. You will find a little garret room above for a servant – all very snug." This last betrayed a slight tremble in his voice. Hugh regarded him, then stepped forward and took his hand.

"I cannot in good faith accept a reduced rent. You fulfilled every hope I had simply by convincing my father to give me the money in a lump sum. I already owe you so much."

"Do not think of that now," said Benjamin, putting his hands in his pockets and striding about the small, well-lighted drawing room. "Take the extra £30 as a precaution against an increase in... your expenses."

"Then you admit the rent should be £85?"

"That is what I would ask, but until something can be done to resolve your issue, this should at least ease the fear of a potential increase."

Taking just a moment to consider, Hugh said quietly, "My expenses are already increased. Twenty-one pounds a month, beginning Tuesday. He's taking the entire £250. This is why I needed the money rather sooner than later."

There was an oath, and then a long, considering look, in which Hugh was certain the man understood exactly what had motivated his terrible behaviour that evening in his house. But if he did, he made no mention of it.

"Say you accept. I want to hear you say it."

Hugh looked about the rooms and shook his head. "I accept. Of course. This is beyond anything I could have hoped for."

"Have a look at your prospect then. You've a little court-yard out back."

When Hugh proceeded to the window Benjamin drew up behind and slipped an arm around his waist. When the arm was accepted, he ventured closer and whispered, "I have done well by you?"

Hugh nodded.

"Then may I remind you?" he whispered, touching his lips to Hugh's ear. "There were some promises."

Hugh smiled, for he could always appreciate irony, even when he was obliged to go to bed with a friend he wished only as a friend. But it was not Benjamin's fault. And so, he led them into the next room, with something like acceptance, and something like relief. And soon, all the power he feared to have lost by his foolish recent behaviour returned. Within an hour, he had returned the man's adoration to what it had been when he first sat trembling before him the morning after they met – when he had risked everything to confess his interest.

When Hugh rose to piss into a chamber pot, Benjamin could scarcely release him. He sat up in bed, and watched for him until he returned, pulling him back into the bedclothes with kisses to the hazard of suffocation.

"I nearly came to you ten times that night in the country. I *did* stay away for my own reasons, as you bid me, and not for those of my father. My daughter was in the house, and the servants."

"My punishment fit the crime. Which of us did not benefit as a result of your ethics?"

"Have I still any in your eyes?"

"I daresay we share the same ethics."

"You command me utterly. And have always been my first choice. How right you were about Dempsey. I only ever wanted you installed in an apartment. And now I have you. How do you feel?"

"Safe. I know you will protect me."

"I will. I will. And I shall take not one farthing for this apartment. Not now."

"Benjamin…"

"Not after this. You are proud and wish to feel like an independent man. You are not yet reconciled to the arrangement – only give it time. Soon you shall feel much better."

"Feeling better is a luxury one often cannot afford," said Hugh, with a sigh. "Not when there are so many ways, to so easily feel regret."

Next day at two Hugh received Mr Kilmister of Gloucester, a tall, pear-shaped man of about forty-five, who came from the service of a noted London physician. That he saw to a Gentleman's personal maintenance was everywhere advertised, and though his figure was not good, his contrivance in dress did

Read

much to obscure, fooling the eye into believing many of his shortcomings were, in fact, moderately long. What he could not, or cared not, disguise was his strong effeminacy, which quality, though Hugh was inclined from the first to like him, he feared must disqualify him. Would it not be dangerous to hire an advertisement of what one worked each day to conceal? Yet he seemed an honest soul, an earnest, modest man who wished only a stable home and fair treatment. Hugh considered – did not a lady of an olive skin, or inclined to tan, hire a Negro maid for contrast?

After descriptions of his move to London years before and his unusually long periods of employment, the applicant detailed his heartbreak at the misfortune which had seen the death of his most recent employer. Dabbing his tears with a lace handkerchief, he told of the overturned curricle which had taken the physician. He then produced letters of recommendation from the man's family, glowing with heartfelt praise, to which he added testimonials from his two previous employers. Believing he would look inexperienced if he agreed too soon to take him, Hugh searched for some way to buy time. He complimented him on the ruffles at his wrists, which were possessed of much buoyancy and not, as his own were on such a damp day, hanging in a dead droop.

Said Kilmister in floral tones: "You observe how a Gent shines under proper care, as I am under my own. My mother, God rest her, always dipped lace in milk just taken off of cream, and after a brisk stir. Laundried lace, Sir, must keep a trace damp, though not too damp, then have its swim in milk before set to dry entirely. The milk lends that bit of brightness from its own native collar, and the lace in its dried structure catches the light like a flower in fresh blow."

"A very pleasing effect; indeed, everything you say pleases me."

"Splendid."

"I can begin you at eighty percent of your previous wage, one hundred after three months."

"Superb."

"I possess nothing by way of cast-offs, nor do I foresee my wardrobe in a state of overflow anytime soon. The residue of my apparel was sold in France before returning. I needed the money and continue to retrench wherever I can."

"Then necessity has bestowed upon you a virtue, my Prince. As to cast-offs, I declare before my Lord and Saviour I never did serve a man of a similar unfortunate size and shape to myself. My stars, what could Mr Entwistle have ever possessed which is not cut to those slender lines of a youth in the very pink of fashion."

Tempted to succumb to the flattery, Hugh continued, "I will insist on my privacy, Jerry, and trust you understand the line. Growing up we had servants who grew too disposed to know our private affairs. Unless otherwise stated, I will want you only from ten to seven each day. I think it only fair to inform you I must retain a distance, however fond of you I become."

"Oh, a great many things I've taken with silent modesty would get another into a combustion!" cried the man, apparently pleased the subject had been broached. "What a power of scandal have I had to incite, had I not this immense stock of natal discretion. When about eighteen, and first employed in London, I saw my Lady of the Bedchamber, benefited of the regalest cast-offs, grow chatty at the slightest inversion. Got herself dismissed tellin' how the manty-maker let out two inches from all her Mistress's garments for gainin' of pounds. Aye, the poor wench was obliged to a position hardly above squalor, all for the mischief of an unleashed tongue. Merited no letter of recommendation, as I mentioned I have of all my employers in straight concession."

Upon agreement to a trial, Jerry Kilmister asked to see his attic abode, which communicated with the drawing room through a steep staircase, closed by a door. Finally, he requested to hold that walking cane he observed sparkling in the candlelight and the reflection through the window of falling rainwater.

"A lovely piece, Sir," he said holding it with the tips of his fingers. "Indeed, I have not seen one more to my own taste in years. Was it the gift of a Lady, or selected of your own hand?" Hugh admitted it was of his own choosing. "Then you have the taste, and the figure, of a Prince, Sir. It will be a pleasure to keep you always at your finest."

"A Prince," muttered Hugh later that evening. Dining in Brunswick Square, under the sobering gaze of his brother-in-law, he felt more the spoilt King of Denmark. Julia was present to receive the man's abuse as well, and when Anne asked about Charlotte Street, her husband interrupted the chewing of his partridge to have the first say:

"We are fortunate to have someone in that apartment at last, even reduced from £85," with a significant look, in case there was any chance Hugh failed to understand the very good terms of the agreement. "Never understood why my brother kept it vacant so long."

Anne said, "Perhaps that was why Hugh was so generous with the nosegay for me and the clothes for little Charlie. I did show them to you?"

"Your husband is right to chastise me," said Hugh, "I know I am uncommonly fortunate in my family."

Not believing for a moment Hugh's sincerity, Duncan said, "I was concerned your brother might have been obliged to leave town after his performance at Carlisle House. Return to the country, hide away in Deerhurst Hall, rather than receive a sinecure and a fine apartment."

"Duncan—"

"Didn't you hear?" continued her husband, "just last

Sunday the Archbishop of London came out strong against masquerades; I have it on good authority it was those two," he shook his fork at Hugh and Julia, "which prompted the decree."

"La!" said Miss Motley, "I'll have you know I received an offer of marriage from the Earl of Wessex on the Oriental Bridge of Carlisle House. On bended knee, dressed as Don Quixote, and professing that he observed in me, through all the snakes I wore on that occasion, his Dulcinea. I promise you, Sir, he was in no way disappointed by my performance that evening."

"I daresay he was not."

When brother and sister retired to the drawing room, Julia remained in the dining room with the sole purpose of preventing Duncan from enjoying his newspaper. Anne took her brother's hand and brought him beside her on the sofa.

"Don't distress yourself about our banter," said Hugh.

"He can be so unfair. You understand it is all in jest."

"And what is not, amuses me, and keeps me humble. He does not forget what I said of our military, among other less serious offenses."

With a small smile Anne said, "He can be stubborn, and headstrong, and he is far too harsh upon you. But he gave me my Charlie, and I do love him. He is a good provider and allows me my little freedoms. I feared to miss our home in Deerhurst. We were there about two weeks on our marriage tour, and I was not absolutely heartbroken to leave it. London is my home now."

Hugh brought her hand to his lips, and they were a few moments longer before Duncan entered the room with his paper. When Julia followed on his heels, he made a great show of presenting the thing to Hugh and sitting down resignedly to his pipe.

"You must get ready for your evening with Lord Halifax Duncan," said Julia. "He expects you and Hugh to make a *investigate Loyds Ins.*

rubber of whist and does not like to be kept waiting. Anne and I will be here at our needlepoint, trusting our men to be good admirals and keep the soldiers, and their wagers, in line. Oh, do leave off trying to snatch back that newspaper from Hugh, one should think you hear enough of Wilkes all day in Parliament."

"One hears of no such thing anymore," said Duncan. "Now he is released from prison, Mr 45 and Liberty does nothing but bask smugly in his fame. Sitting soberly at Guild-hall, gorging at City banquets, while the government worries about the next great showing of patriotism, or vandalism, whatever we are calling it this week, by the motley crew which follows him about. Perhaps Hugh and I shall pop in at Lloyd's Coffeehouse on our way to cards tonight. Do you know Lloyd's, ladies?"

"Should we?" asked Julia, fluttering her lashes.

Lloyd's underwrites a variety of insurance policies, including those 'life-for-one-year' policies issued on Wilkes last June. They are all coming due, and there is some despair. Perhaps they think to extend them for one, really and truly, final year of life. With so many enemies about, there is reason to hope—"

"Deplorable," said Anne, taking up her knitting basket, and as Hugh looked like he did not intend to return the paper, Duncan said he would change his shirt and they could be off.

"Do keep him under control tonight," said Anne, "he likes to get snug with Halifax, and that means gaming."

Hugh nodded absently, for the *London Herald* had a report on Richard Brent, accompanied by a particularly large portrait of him in court. It was an uncommonly detailed etching, a likeness for once without the ridiculous eye-patch and parrot. Hugh returned to it often as he read the article. What was it about him? Perhaps it was merely Hugh's continuing fascination, but he seemed somehow familiar…

When Duncan returned he set the paper aside and they were soon off.

These days Lord Halifax was on the arm of a vulgar thing called Miss Delacour, having, as these things seemed to go, relinquished his former companion, Miss Dalrymple, after just one season. Both women belonged to a troupe of courtesans called The Three Graces and Hugh had met Miss Delacour at the Carlisle House masquerade in some rather indecent postures.

By the warm reception to his card table, Halifax appeared to have forgiven the work he had done towards Hugh's unattainable commission the year before. To him there could be nothing wrong in the world when one sat down to cards, with a bottle of Old Hock and the hand of a doting courtesan to dandle upon one's thigh. As Halifax was a friend of Sir Frederick, Duncan believed sitting beside the brother-in-law he despised and praising him might gain the man's attention. And so, as soon as he could, Hugh put forward another topic.

"Richard Brent, I was reading, wins his case against Lord Somersby, and so takes half his Lordship's land in Cornwall. It was reported today in the *London Herald*."

Halifax scratched his nose. "Not half, and not actually Somersby's lands. Otherwise you are correct."

Somewhat abashed, Hugh pressed, "Hence my motivation in asking, Sir, for I understand you have been present at the proceedings and one can never entirely believe what one reads in the papers. Most people admire Brent and his handling of affairs. And yet it comes at the cost of many enemies. Was you inclined to like him?"

"I should like him more if he ever suffered a loss," laughed Halifax, "or was made less work about. But one sees all sorts made much of during these periods of Wilkes's retirement. I suppose we should be thankful there is a Richard Brent to

341

report on, or the papers would resort again to celebrating our debonair highwayman Sixteen-String Jack, who is, I own, better dressed than Brent."

"You will laugh, my Lord," continued Hugh, "I have only ever seen a likeness of your plaintiff with an eye-patch and a parrot on his shoulder, upon my honour. But there was a pretty portrait in the *Herald* today, uncommonly large and, it seemed, well-rendered."

Seeing his chance to interject, Duncan said, "Reckon he need only ask to be drawn without those silly items, and the papers would oblige him. Take my word for it: Richard of Runswick, like any with an endless thirst for attention, *requests* to be drawn in keeping with his most outlandish adventures."

Somewhat distracted by his ongoing flirtation with Miss Delacour, Halifax said, "Terrible move by Somersby; he provoked Brent into bringing this suit for the land in Cornwall. He is a vengeful little bug; he knows the likely outcome of his own suit against Brent, that endless puppet show, which is now in its second, or is it now a third, year? Most suppose Brent will win that case as well."

"How very droll!" cried Miss Delacour. "Each suing the other simultaneously. How do they remember which suit is which, and what seat to take in court?"

"Will you listen to this lovely creature?" crooned Halifax, "I never thought of that!"

Hugh prompted, "So it is believed Brent will win the case which seeks to disinherit him of the family land in Yorkshire? There is no proof his father had Jacobite allegiances?"

"It seems not. And really, all that land was taken from old Loyalists twenty years ago, and the families long since exiled. But Somersby has a grudge against Brent from his smuggling days and has the power to put him through hell. What he does not understand is that this will be remembered as another win for Richard Brent." The man chuckled. "By Jove, the man never seems to lose. But for all that, I'd like to go a round with him in that famous boxing ring of his," he said with a right hook at nothing, then leered at his lady companion, who fanned herself at the thought of her lion against the famed Samson.

"Did you know, Hugh, Brent invites visiting Viscounts, wealthy merchants, anyone at all to bludgeon at his estate, a place out in Chessington which he calls The Farm? And they all, from Viscounts to day-labourers, come away worshiping him, all with black eyes and bloody noses. Getting thrashed by Richard Brent is something of a right-of-passage."

Miss Delacour said, with arch earnestness, "But pray my Lord, how on earth can he be liked, if he is so vicious?"

Patting her arm, "Because he is not actually vicious. Many men wish passionately to be cracked on the head, thrashed, or punished, every now and again." Pushing forward his fox face into hers he murmured, "Methinks Brent something of a flogging cull."

"I simply won't believe it!" shrieked Miss Delacour, pressing a hand to her throat, "You do talk a scandal!"

After considering his hand, his Lordship continued, "Upon being pardoned in the smuggling affair, Hugh, Richard Brent wished to show the world he was more than a naughty rabble-rouser. I understand he published some mediocre poems, then he began entering prize fights. For three years he was the undisputed champion of the sweet science, the finest England has had since Jack Broughton. Won every fight he entered and had the good sense to retire before he met his James Figg."

"But that he wins the public, Sir," said Hugh, "with his endless trials and travails, must be his greatest triumph. People never speak of him without a secret smirk or smile. Quite extraordinary."

"You need look no further than his suit against Somersby to understand why he wins the public. After the grant to his grandfather of a piece of land in Cornwall, over the subsequent decades, Somersby's family had come to usurp adjacent land. If any encroachment upon Crown land is suspected, a man may apply to the Treasury for a new grant, if he can prove title to the Crown. This is what Brent did. It went no further than this for a year: his Lordship was sent a letter to inform him that title could be proved, and if he would leave off attacking Brent in the papers nothing would be brought before the courts.

"Nevertheless, a few months ago, Lord Somersby told the *Gazette* that clemency shown for spawn of old Stuart Loyalists was a travesty. This 'nameless man' was probably a supporter of Wilkes, of American rebels, indeed any who seek to undermine the government. And so, Brent brought the suit. Somersby made an impassioned speech to the court about the history of his family, and the good they had done the freemen residing on his land for eighty years, but to no avail." Halifax laughed. "Something you will read in the papers tomorrow is this piece of impertinence: I am told Richard has made an offer to Somersby – if he will admit Richard Brent has not now, nor ever has, had anything to do with Wilkes the land in Cornwall will be returned for just forty-five pounds."

Miss Delacour let out a shrill peal of laughter.

"He is not so very infamous, then," said Hugh. "I gather he has some manner of heart, and a stock of wit. He appears entirely unmoved by the continual threats and slander. I should like above anything an interview with him."

"Low ambitions are often achievable," muttered Duncan, unable to resist the jab.

After clearing his throat, Halifax addressed Miss Delacour in a low voice: "Young, impressionable men," nodding toward Hugh, "would do well to stand clear of Richard Brent, I think."

Duncan looked up from his cards. "Must Hugh be persuaded to support old Jacobites, or begin smuggling, upon meeting this fellow?"

With a saucy smile at Halifax, Miss Delacour said, "But I must defend your young friend, my Lord. During that night of utter debauchery at Carlisle House, Mr Entwistle met my Lord Allenby, and by all accounts, went away entirely *unpersuaded.*"

Duncan, understanding only that Lord Allenby was an outspoken supporter of the Opposition, said, "Who could be persuaded by anyone dressed so absurdly? An enormous, lumbering Sheep, my Lord. Can you imagine it? Looked a rank fool."

This piece of stupidity produced a simper between the lovers. Duncan, for his part, appeared a little annoyed that his description had gone unappreciated. Hugh, however, was too shocked to take any pleasure at his folly.

CHAPTER 6

In July, Hugh penned a piece in opposition to that practice of the navy termed *press-ganging*, upon which that branch of the military relied to build their ranks in time of need. This was his first serious piece of writing for the *Inquirer*, stimulated by rumours of a worsening of the unrest in the Falkland Islands. As a boy he had witnessed the pressing of three men, and, when told they had essentially been kidnapped, had laughed, failing to credit such a thing as possible in England and in broad daylight. He concluded the piece with a petition to John Wilkes to take up the cause.

Then for a time H Entwistle disappeared as a contributor of the *Public Inquirer,* to re-appear as the topic of a *fait-divers* in the *Spectator*.

"Leave that damned terrier be and look at this!" shouted Harding from his table in the Bucket of Brews coffeehouse. "The rascal is no better than he should be!" Coming forward, Andrews pushed his glasses up his nose and sat down to the paper. "Well?" continued Harding. "You see his name there, joined with that of Miss Coates? Entwistle took her to the races in Newmarket. Starkey! Haul your carcass over here. You are just back from Newmarket, are you not?"

Mr Starkey was that variety of gamester termed a *blacklegs*, never to be seen, on or off the turf, without he was wedged into a pair of tall black riding boots.

"I am, with regret. London never was so cussed hot."

"Then you observed wandering about the horseraces that wealthy young lady, Sylvia Coates. Richard of Runswick's cousin, you must have done."

"A swinging good fortune that one has, though I must say she is a big lass. Aye, she's a heavy one."

"She was reported on the arm of a spark named Entwistle, a baronet's son shows his snout in here now and again."

"Was she now? I do not know but Miss Coates is still pursued by her famous boxer cousin," said Starkey, with some reverence.

"But you could distinguish the man on her arm as either a muscular pirate, or a tall slender chap something of the plainest. Which was it?"

Starkey tugged his beard. "The plain one, I suppose."

"You are certain?"

"Yes, in company with another tall and plain, no doubt Miss Coates' brother acting as chaperone."

"I wonder," said Harding to Andrews, "if the brother were there to protect Sylvia's reputation, or to protect the person of your Mr Entwistle from an angry boxer – do you see what I mean?" He laughed riotously.

Andrews sighed and snapped his fingers to rouse the terrier. "*My* Mr Entwistle, as you term him, came into this establishment a month or two back to inquire what is known of her engagement to Brent. I told him what is generally said of the Coates family – there is a faction wishes them united, but her parents broke the engagement and Brent does not appear to pursue it, at least not openly. That is what I told Mr Entwistle when he asked, which is the best of my knowledge."

Starkey shook his head. "Brent'll bastinado him sure as I stand here – snap him in two!"

So, it appears, *Constant Reader*, that in order to pursue his growing obsession, and appease the ambition of his father, our young Gentleman has commenced Gallant, with an aim at attaining Brent's fair cousin. Just returned from Newmarket Hugh was, at that moment, leading Sylvia and her brother through Temple to hire a boat at Tower-Wharf. After the excitement of the races, he chose for their return a leisurely cruise terminating at the verdant landscapes of their landing at Greenwich.

For seven weeks, he had investigated the family and saw much to attract and encourage him. The wish for a connection between Richard Brent and his cousin was, by most accounts, the product of a vocal faction of the Coates family who valued Brent's property and forthcoming inheritance, and believed no publicity was bad publicity, so long as one remained outside the walls of King's Gate. The opposing faction, which included Sylvia's own parents, believed her considerable fortune sufficient to inspire a law-abiding suitor with whom she could exist without the riot that always followed Richard of Runswick.

But what of Sylvia herself? Her opinion was somewhat overlooked for by temperament she was of that even consistency sought by the producers of fresh butter. That moment when every lump and imperfection is beaten away under the hand of a skilled churner, rendering a product which is quick to retake its placid integrity regardless the agitation. As a girl this attribute had won her many female playmates and confidants, for she was incapable of gossip or sarcasm. Now turned of twenty she enjoyed an uncommon number of casual suitors, including many an uncertain, timid, or ugly young man too terrified to speak to most females, and so fallen at the feet of this motherly enchantress who accepted all equally.

Once Hugh understood this, he reckoned a man of his own charms particularly well-placed to make exclusive that which she bestowed upon everyone. Sometimes he fancied himself a little in love, such was the power of his platonic fascination. Oh, odd creature! A painting, a flower, a female friend, an admirer – all were smiled at mildly and welcomed, and just as easily turned from. One day Hugh gave Miss Coates a puppy – this produced kisses for the animal and appreciation of himself, however the gift, though something wished for since childhood, did not prevent her afternoon beauty rest only ten minutes after receiving it.

For seven weeks Hugh had led the agreeable young lady about the metropolis on parties of pleasure, always accompanied by her brother Simon, and culminating in the outing to Newmarket. In this time, he worked to arouse her ability to distinguish wheat from chaff, or at least introduce to her the concept of having a preference. He caressed her maid, letting drop hints of his wild attachment to Sylvia, and (dare he say it?) love! The maid confirmed her lady had, in private, grown more opinionated where some things were concerned, and occasionally appeared in the listless manner she associated with the lovelorn.

It was not long before Hugh saw this for himself, and yet in the event found more to unsettle than encourage him. The evening in question he had been regaling the Coates family with tales contrived to portray himself as the object of pursuit in Paris. By her parents he did quite well; they appeared ever more open to the connection, even to encourage it. However, Sylvia's habitual evenness had tonight rather sagged into listlessness; she poked absently at her food with a fork and was often looking out a window though nothing could be seen at that dark hour.

Hugh cast Simon a look of annoyance. This mad whim to pursue his sister had, in May, felt a jaunty bit of brilliance. After two months, however, he had learned little of her famous cousin, talk of whom her parents disdained on all points. This attitude seemed to indicate their fears that the man would at some point pursue the connection again. And now today, all attempts to dazzle the young lady had fallen entirely flat. After this, and the great effort to arrange the trip to Newmarket, he was left no choice but to take her brother aside after dinner to ask the state of affairs.

"Your sister was less than attentive tonight."

"Was she?"

"You are better informed as to her personal affairs than I am, Simon – if you know why I believe I am entitled to know the reason."

The man collapsed into a chair with his snuffbox. "She has had a push this week; you notice this, I suppose, if you notice anything."

"A push?"

"An offer of marriage. You have never been led to believe you are her only admirer."

This, to one of Hugh's dignity, rankled almost beyond endurance. He expected to have done away with any serious competition weeks ago. He said, "So I am now second after her famous cousin?"

Mr Coates, after he had employed his spittoon, said, "You are no Second, I'll warrant, unless I missed news of a duel, or you've turned Catamite! No, my good man, you are now third in the hopes for my sister's hand."

Hugh nodded. "Perhaps next week we shall have a fourth and sit down to whist. Who the Devil is this third one, George Washington?"

Simon let out a guffaw and clapped his hands. "Damn me if I know a funnier fellow than you Entwistle! He is not another public figure, exactly. Only a handsome poof actor from Covent Garden. Just returned from a five-month tour so you have not heard of the rascal. My parents do detest the coxcomb, however my sister, though nobody would have supposed it, does appear to dote dreadfully upon him. We have had some tears!"

"And nobody saw fit to inform me? I had hoped you were sufficiently my friend to assist in my cause."

"Forever and always!" said Coates, searching out a fresh quid with the tips of thumb and forefinger long discoloured from previous expeditions. "Employ your pen against the silly bastard. You've jotted things before, have you not?"

"What of it?"

"Our stage actor is a base sharper and makes more stitches with women than a seamstress, all of which can be got into a good limerick. You will write it and be revenged."

"And will a limerick overcome Sylvia's preference, and place me first in her affections?" Simon stuffed a plug into his cheek and sighed.

And to his continued inelegant silence Hugh said no more.

By next morning his attempts at brilliant invective against Theodore Watts had produced little more than a hundred false beginnings. Only an actual passion for the girl might inspire his pen, and he rang, as he did now quite quickly, for Kilmister to calm his nerves. The new valet was that bit of perfection lacking in his former. Louis always let one know he was meant for better things. Jerry Kilmister, however, was prescient, but unobtrusive, quiet when he was not wanted, chatty and diverting when Hugh was lonely. It was of course absurd to disguise the nature of his relationship with Benjamin, when Kilmister was the same himself. But so must be the way of things during Hugh's constant state of unease with Sharp.

For with the new and higher income for his silence, Jasper had broken from Sir Frederick and was an independent citizen of London. The beginning of summer, which had seen Sir Frederick's return to Deerhurst, had brought a message from Sharp to Charlotte Street. Benjamin had appeared equal parts indignation and fear, until he understood it was nothing more than to inform Hugh of a change of address. Hugh signed his acknowledgement and sent the messenger on his way.

"Sharp has quit my father's service," said Hugh, "and continues in London independently."

Setting his book aside Benjamin rubbed his eyes. "Is that all? Thank God. I'll see the lawyer receives the new direction for payment. Speak no more of it."

"But is this not absurd? He now lives independently because... I feel a little ill."

Benjamin saw nothing in it worthy of comment and asked again for a change of subject. But the burden of the constant threat, and the inability to speak of it, had begun to wear on Hugh. By his twenty-first birthday, there were episodes of anxiety and strange palpations, for his debt to this man was now hopelessly beyond his ability to repay, and he could never argue too long with the person doing so much for him. Even his requirements in the bedroom were entirely manageable. For, as Hugh had supposed, Benjamin was not greatly ardent, preferring in place of passion reading together and peaceful slumbers. Mondays and Thursdays he came to Charlotte Street, remaining from six-thirty in the evening to six the next morning. In the dark inside the bedcurtains, within the man's constant arms, Hugh had remained grounded during the events of May, then June, and then July.

One night, after the man had drifted to sleep Hugh said, "Why not cancel my tenancy here and instal me at Sallow House? Every precaution shall be taken, you may trust to that. In the day, I will make an accomplished scholar of Paulina; she will have Latin and French, Harpsichord, Dancing and learn to ride side-saddle. I'm thinking of that old cottage upon the estate, overgrown with briars, entirely removed from the main house; instal me there and I shall make a proper home of it. Each evening towards dusk I shall light a candle and place it upon the windowsill. Then in the moonlight a shadow will emerge from the main house, and a silhouette cross the grounds to my door. We shall be together there. And you will be happy with me."

Determined that his second visit to Sallow House must go better than the first, Hugh arrived the following Sunday with his proposal to take up residency in the cottage firmly in mind. After lunch he would ask to take a walk about the grounds, hinting at things to confide. The first confidence would be his despair at the situation with Miss Coates. Then, after about twenty minutes, they would turn down the eastbound path and arrive at the cottage, and so on to the proposal.

But again, when he arrived at the house, Hugh sensed a slight unease in Benjamin's manner. It was so apparent he found he was unable to delay, and so asked to take a turn with him before lunch.

"You have settled upon this connection with Sylvia," he said, once they had begun. "You must be patient and work towards your goal."

"She is entirely distracted by this Watts character. How can I persuade her family we should be married, when neither of us care one fig for the other? I wish the dignity to remain a bachelor if I cannot discover that."

"Dignity? Well I do not know about that…" Then he said, "Let me ask you something: do you never suppose men of the other persuasion do not as often submit to connections nearly as unsuited to their taste? It is a thing done every day. Marriage must be, first and foremost, a sound business arrangement, and not a proof of everlasting love."

"But her mother and father do wish love for their daughter, in addition to joining a family of good standing – why should they not? And so they wonder I am not more successful prying her from her silly actor. She can have him!"

"Is that all? Cannot you weather the storm a while longer?"

"Is that *all*? Is that not enough? I grow utterly weary of it; it is a beastly burden to me!"

"This is about the wedding night—"

"It is not that—"

"Yes, Hugh. It is." Benjamin smiled. "You know I have envied your wider experience of…" his voice trailed off, and he glanced about the empty garden. Then in a lower tone he continued: "Yet I understand the problem it creates now to consider the other. Consummation will be accomplished very easily I assure you. You may have my own advice if you wish it. Rosamunde and I were happy enough in that way."

"But that is not it, not at all. How can you misunderstand me so entirely?" Hugh drew a breath. "May I tell you, Benjamin, really, what it is?"

"In a moment," said his companion. "I wish to tell you something first, before you say anything else." He gave Hugh a look that quite chilled him. For he knew what was about to be asked. He did not wish to hear it. "Perhaps this is not the right time; I have struggled to find… I must tell you now."

"Say it."

After a moment, taking on a look of determination, he reached for Hugh's hand. "I am to be married – in three weeks. My proposal has just been accepted. I informed my brother yesterday; I have not yet told Paulina – I desired you be the next to know."

Hugh's hand went limp. When the man sought to take both into his, Hugh recovered enough to yank himself from the grip entirely.

"How long have you been planning this?"

"As regards Euphemia? About six weeks, although one must think of it directly one loses the mother of a young child. I did not know if I should be accepted, and so there was no reason to announce it any earlier. I need a mother for my daughter, Hugh. The lady is my uncle's widow. She has met Paulina, and they are fond of each other."

"You will continue to call on me," said Hugh, yet the silence which met his words said differently.

"You understand why I cannot. Not for a while. We shall remain close friends, Hugh, always. And you will visit us here of course. But I must make this a real marriage. In time I suspect there will be opportunity to resume something in town. You know how much I value our evenings together."

"You are not happy with me. You have grown tired of me. As for my calls here, they must stop as well, you know they must. Paulina will not need my services once I am replaced. I shall cut my visits after today."

"You see why I hesitated to tell you? You take this to mean something it does not. I see clearly the pain I cause you and am sorry for it."

"Then avert your eyes."

With a note of irritation Benjamin said, "Need I remind you of Miss Coates? Might I not dislike her connection to my friend? You are still my friend?"

With little in his power but petty revenge Hugh left this question unanswered. "I have no choice but to submit to my father's requirements of me," he spat. "You cannot equate our situations. You are your own man, and this is your decision. Your daughter has every advantage without a stepmother. A replacement mother will only be resented – they always are. Your motivation lies in maintaining the perception of yourself to the world. You might have thanked the Lord for releasing you from that other obligation. Only now you seek a new one to maintain your mask of respectability – for you love your mask as much as anyone can, despite every lofty speech to the contrary!"

"That is not only unfair, but quite cruel, Hugh. Let us have an end to the discussion if we can do no better than this."

"I agree. And as this is your house, in which I have no place, I shall leave directly."

Without further ceremony, Hugh proceeded to the stables to fetch Jupiter, mounted, and was quickly away. During the ride home he believed he possessed the upper hand entirely – he said it to himself again and again. And again. Yet when he arrived at his apartment his hands were trembling so violently only a healthy dram of brandy could still them. Everything on Charlotte Street reminded him of Benjamin – indeed, nearly everything he looked at belonged to Benjamin.

"Only not me, anymore. He has cut me," he said, stepping to the window at which they had stood when he first arrived. "*Cut* me. I am more alone now, than I ever have been. He knew what I wished to ask and had no desire to hear it. Everyone around me moves forward. Horatio. Benjamin. Anne. Even Jasper Sharp. Yet I do not. Somehow I am left behind."

Next day, after composing some maudlin poetry, and sacrificing liberally to Bacchus, Hugh wrote the following:

Benjamin,

You send no note, yet I can scarcely think what you might write which would please me. I do not wish you to attempt it.

A day of my own honest, sound reasoning cannot explain your decision. The heart certainly cannot. Do not keep our usual engagement until I have had time to reflect. For even as I write this, I wonder this directive is unnecessary, and you have already foregone your friend for another interest.

H

Upon sending the note, Hugh finished his bottle of brandy and retired to bed. Then, taking Benjamin's pillow to his nose, he inhaled deeply and wept bitterly until he passed out. Fifteen hours later, he woke to a sun long since descending from noon, and called his valet, at last, about four.

"Oh, I am touched to the quick! Thank the Saviour you summoned me!" cried Kilmister, setting aside the empty bottle and attempting to touch Hugh's overgrown hair into place. "It is well for some folks to live in retirement for two days. But of what worth a Gentleman's Gentleman, if he cannot tend to his master's spirits as well as his person?"

"May not a man spend a day or two in contemplation, composing poetry, and not be thought ailing?"

"He certainly may, but I fancy you take such things in smaller sips. I fear the world has done you a wrong, and you take a fearsome draft."

This was said with no apparent allusion to his breath; Hugh was touched, and so to please him, for he cared nothing for his appearance just then, sat to his shave. "I have a broken heart," he said.

Once he had lathered him, the attendant began with his blade: "I am a-grieved to hear it. You deserve only the best from love."

"Do divert me as six-thirty approaches, Jerry. For I had, in happier days, kept an appointment at that time, and I feel the darkness of my loss as the hour approaches."

"Nothing is more natural, than to employ the native collar of my tongue. Let us consider, now, what will divert you."

"And do you recall who it was called Mondays and Thursdays about six-thirty?" The valet halted his work. When he resumed, there had appeared upon his wan cheeks some distinct blotching. And when he launched into the middle of an anecdote, from which he was obliged to stop, apologise, and take up again from an earlier point, Hugh bid him be silent.

"Do you blush at a discovery? Or at your inability to pretend that it is one?"

"Sir, I don't comprehend you."

"I would have us understand one another at last, Jerry."

The man stepped around to face him, with his work only partially completed, and said, "My directive, Sir, which I was bid upon our first encounter, and which has always been my guiding principle these twenty-seven years I am in service, is to retain a distance."

"I trust you. Tell me it will not be my downfall."

"Sir, it's shaming us both even to say such a thing!"

"Then tell me what you understand, so I know how well, or how poorly, I have performed."

"Pray Sir, I—"

"Tell me. You know, now, what is my persuasion."

The man fell backwards and snatched a fan from his reticule. "A moment! Spare me one moment to collect myself – O! am I not awash in my own fantasy? Is it his ears, or the very mind, betrays Jerry Kilmister at last?" The fan, of peach silk painted with an Oriental motif, worked the air about him. For a moment the man's great height and girth gave cause for concern, for any number of pieces which a fall might endanger. Hugh snatched a dusty bottle of lavender smelling salts from his bureau, and this, together with the steady working of the fan, accomplished the recovery of Kilmister's senses.

"No indeed, Sir. I never supposed it. Trollops, Sir, are known to invade many a Gentleman's sanctum, beggin' your pardon, for I have known a Baron entertain trumpery in his hour of need. And so, I supposed you did occasionally..." Then Jerry screamed to see his master wandering about the room with half a sudded face. He refused another word, even on this subject, until Hugh's right half was made to match his left.

"But is it possible you never guessed?"

"Had I been the type as would never merit three concessive letters of recommendation, I daresay I might have done. But with the particular dismissive, as I received Mondays and Thursdays, I sealed my mind, every scrap of my attention and all my senses."

"Then I am lucky indeed," said Hugh. "Not many would scruple to provide a man his privacy, and not merely feign it."

"It is far easier to remain ignorant, than to play at it! Yet even committed to ignorance as I have been all my life, still I have discovered secrets, and so must worry how to contain them. Now I know this and so I must despise the one who broke my Prince's heart."

"Do not hate him. He is a good man," then, after a sigh, "the best of men, in fact. He never intended to use me ill."

"But will tumble you when he likes, then leave you to cry for two days: that is no great Gallant, by my reckoning."

Over the next hour and a half Hugh confessed to the long, and storied, relationship with his brother-in-law, while his manservant straightened him up, prepared him a drink, and, as his wigs had, of late, become harder to fit, washed then cropped Hugh's hair. It was soon well past eight.

"Sometimes I believe I cannot survive in this world Jerry. Nor wish to." This obscenity, declared the horrified man, was little short of regicide. "I am each day debased pursuing a girl I do not want, a girl who chases one, and may be pursued by an impossibly desirable other, without even a commission to recommend me. Hunting the wife my father wishes brings me to such despair, you see, and without even Benjamin now... I am hard pressed for solace."

"Marathon Moll's up the Mint!" said Jerry, after another application of smelling salts. Hugh looked up. "Pray do not prowl the Birdcage, or caterwaul in Moorfields, or wherever they go now. She has a chapel does Moll, a private bedroom upstairs with a big, burly man standing sentinel outside named Caligula. Bless me, I had never vouchsafed it to you, but for to keep you from the gallows!"

"Beautiful man," said Hugh, "I do not deserve you."

"Promise me, then, you will keep yourself safe."

"Yes, always. Now dry your eyes. Take a late dish of tea with me."

To many protestations Hugh prepared and served the tea, and they passed a tender quarter of an hour. So soothing were the combined effects of gin, and Jerry, into his tea, Hugh was soon glorious with spirits, and so tipped back senseless in his armchair. The valet considered him, tilted his head this way and that, then fetched his blade to remove one remaining hair beneath his chin. Then, sweeping Hugh up, he carried him to bed, stripped him, slipped him into a nightshirt, pulled a nightcap over his ears and tucked him into the bedclothes. After a pat of one flushed, freshly shaven cheek, Jerry Kilmister drew the bedcurtains.

CHAPTER 7

Having withdrawn the bedcurtains one morning the following week, Jerry was setting out a tray of bread and grapes, a full minute into his news of the morning market, when Hugh realised this was not idle chit-chat but something quite startling.

"He what?" he said.

"Gives a performance in Kingston this afternoon, a venue on the High-Street. Says he wants to show the world what he intends those prosecuting lawsuits upon him."

"Open to the public? Richard of Runswick?"

"You asked any news be brought to you, as the man tends to fascinate you, and so I tell it to you as it was told to me at market. Somersby is seeking to extend the Jacobite trial another year, so Mr Brent will give his audience a display of his defiance as well as a preview of the verdict in his favour by way of demonstration. Oh dear, I shouldn't like to be in the shoes of his boxing opponent, no indeed, nor those of Somersby."

Nearly falling out of bed Hugh threw himself under the man's dexterous hands. "But this never happens Jerry! He's been in retirement some time now. A public performance?"

"And you are lucky to hear of it, my love. The announcement came so sudden it is not even in the papers, that is what I am hearing."

"I shall meet him," said Hugh. "I *will* meet him. God help me I shall discover what he is about. Has he a Second, and are the whispers true?"

"Whispers? What whispers? What is second? What language do you speak?"

But Hugh could not just then explain it to him. Everything felt so suddenly and completely right. Unable to bear the hours until Kingston, Hugh decided this was also a sign to reaffirm his friendship with Benjamin. The location of the display was just a few miles from Sallow House, and he could not leave things as they were. He set off at a steady clip, certain of his welcome in Wimbledon and certain he could mend the friendship. To his relief he was received warmly into the man's study with a wish to put the matter behind them. This was the easiest and indeed the happiest Benjamin had yet appeared in his new home, however when Hugh came forward for an embrace, it was granted with brief and somewhat stiff formality.

"For now, Hugh, I do ask that we refrain. You wish to begin again with me, this is how it must be."

The pain was sharp, he could not but remember the many, many months being pursued – but he would not be discouraged and so ran to the parlour and embraced the man's daughter with double vigour. He kissed her forehead and cheeks a hundred times, then declared he could eat ten Bath cakes, but first would she have a footrace with him? When she asked if he knew she was to have a new mother, he took her hands.

"Yes of course," he said as Benjamin entered the room. "You are twice blessed, as I was."

"You?"

"Lady Highborough of course, my second mother. A

second mother must be obeyed, and respected, for she is your father's choice. Perhaps even loved, eventually. Will you promise me to like her?"

"I shall try. Papa says I do not have to love her yet, though she loves me already and cannot wait to meet me again in Buckinghamshire."

"She sounds a very smart lady." Elevating his voice, "And when do we bring her home?"

"Six weeks. We depart in three days. Euphemia and I shall have the ceremony in Buckinghamshire then take an extended tour. Paulina will stay on with a relation."

Hugh nodded at the girl. "Everything is set then. This house is too big for two solitary souls; the lady will bring some much-needed life to the place. Go now, change your clothes, then we shall proceed outside for the footrace. Jupiter, too, is at your service for a couple hours. Then I continue to a performance of boxing."

"Boxing?" said Benjamin, as his daughter departed, "I never took you for an enthusiast."

"A display this afternoon in Kingston by Richard Brent. At last I shall know this character who may succeed in stealing my fair maiden from me."

This was met with only a mild smile. "I am glad you came to us today. I shall not see you for some time."

"No, you will not."

Benjamin studied his guest for a long moment, then said, "Perhaps I should take in a fight."

"One should do everything once," replied Hugh with a shrug.

When he received no further encouragement, Benjamin cleared his throat and said, "I trust I may accompany you as a friend."

"If you like. We must depart by three-thirty. Brent begins with a demonstration of technique, which I must be there to see − it is a thing he does for his audience, both to improve one's appreciation of the forthcoming fight, and because his fights are often quite short in duration."

"Very considerate," said Benjamin, to which Hugh shook his head, hoping they would not be out of place at such an event. Benjamin appeared to have the same thought – he stepped to a mirror and commenced an inspection of his ensemble.

They set off for Kingston in good time but found such a crush come up from London they could scarcely find a place to tie their horses. As Richard's public displays were now extremely rare, they had a quality of legend about them, and the gymnasium on the High-Street had overflowed for hours with drunk and rowdy jostling, pushing, and attempting impromptu displays of their own. Most onlookers remained outside the building, hoping merely to listen – this was, of course, where the relative latecomers from Wimbledon were obliged to remain. For Hugh it was almost too crushing a disappointment to bear.

At last something sounded to have begun, from the cheers and shouts of the men inside, from the loud protestations from those crushed into doorways, and from those who could only wish to be crushed. A shouting voice rose to quell the crowd.

Then a feeling of movement. The men milling outside the gymnasium leapt forward, as though the building had grown ten new rooms to accommodate them. They began spilling out behind and, in a great rush, commenced a retreat to their horses, mounting and moving down side streets. All were continuing to an open field where a low, grassy knoll was to make service as a ring. Towards this mound Richard Brent led the way – at first nothing but a bobbing head of red hair tied tightly back. Jumping from a horse which promptly galloped back to Kingston, he summoned his opponent forward, then in a loud Yorkshire accent began the instructional demonstration. Without a place to tie their steeds, mounted spectators swarmed on all sides, trying to avoid those who had simply run on foot to the new rendezvous, darting and weaving.

Six-foot-tall and stripped to the waist, calling out commentary while dodging and parrying and laughing a good deal, Brent was, even seen through the legs of bucking steeds, a display like nothing Hugh had ever seen. The cheers and huzzahs of the onlookers became little less than screams as the demonstration segued into an actual fight, the horses bucking in fear and confusion, stamping, and spinning.

With mania worthy of a stay in Bedlam, Brent's opponent attempted to body-slam him, grab his hair, kick his shins, and made numerous attempts to gouge his eyes. The boxer from York riled his opponent still further, continuing to criticize the man's stance and execution, long after the instructional portion of the performance had ended. He parried each blow, and though large and broad shouldered, was lithe on his feet, easy, and conservative with his thrusts.

When an onlooker was thrown ten feet from his horse, Hugh held fast to his reigns and circled by, leaving Benjamin far behind, winding closer and closer to the action in the round. Yet as he advanced and could observe more closely, his fascination grew strange. He observed a gesture, repeated, then another, which was as individual as a fingerprint. And a realization began to dawn that this was to be far more than Hugh had bargained for.

"I know you," he said, the sound swallowed immediately in the shrieks of onlookers and a sudden stampede of riderless horses. "How do I know you?"

Richard suddenly took a hard clip to the jaw, which was experienced with a gasp throughout the crowd as it sent him stumbling back a few paces. This brought him to full attention, and with fierce singlemindedness he went on the offensive. His attack was steady and unrelenting, and with a series of brutal blows he dominated his opponent until the man was nothing but a stunned lump on the ground. At the unexpected conclusion to the fight, some of the spectators simply galloped away. Many others, however, surrounded the victor as he jogged down the knoll. They jumped from their horses, shouting, and demonstrating their own right hooks and wanting to shake his hand.

When Benjamin reappeared, Hugh dismounted and bid him hold Jupiter's reigns so he could approach the boxer. He advanced, and as he advanced, he recalled. It was by will alone that he moved through the shoves and curses and base aroma of the onlookers, some of whom had descended into fistfights, as he approached the man now being commanded back to the High-Street for the first of many bumpers.

Pushing to the front, shoved, and forced forward and aft, Hugh stuck out his hand.

Richard, shouting at one man to stand back, took the hand of the next, then turned. Seeing another he traced it to a face.

"Extraordinary!" shouted Hugh, seizing his hand and pulling himself forward.

Brent held his grip. Their eyes met.

"'Tis tha, is it?" he said, his brow creasing.

Hugh knew this voice, knew every feature. He had known them in his dreams.

With an oath Brent shoved aside two shouting men and bid everyone be quiet.

"Say your name, lad. And how I know thee."

"Entwistle."

"*Who the Devil is this bastard?!*" shouted a man much the worse for drink, glaring at Hugh. Another round of shouting began.

"*Whistle*, is it?"

"*Entwistle!*"

"Send a note to The Farm and tell me where you are to be found."

Then he allowed himself to be pushed forward, lifted into the air, and carried off to a chorus of cheers.

Hugh stepped into the vacuum which remained, head spinning from the sudden quiet. Then he looked toward the other boxer, still doubled up, who had begun to shiver upon the mound, felled by Brent's hand.

The return to Sallow House was performed in a daze; Benjamin led the way, glancing occasionally behind to check that Hugh had not simply cantered down an obscure lane. At last returned, looking greatly perplexed he said, "Hugh, are you unwell? What the Devil happened back there?"

Before he could answer Paulina rushed forward, leading them to the dinner table and asking to hear every moment of the fight. And so, over the meal, Hugh gave his account, running long in his descriptions whenever he observed the question remained on Benjamin's lips.

"Funny thing," he said at last, "By the end I realised I had met Richard Brent many years before. Only I had no name back then."

"Did you?" said Paulina, continuing to eat and not particularly keen to know more. Her father, however, raised his eyebrows.

"In the yard of Mr Harvey's Academy for Boys. When I was about fourteen." Then, pausing a long moment, Hugh experienced a sensation he could only describe as fear. Fear – but of what? Then he produced a smile for father and daughter and continued.

"Brent was eye-witness to an incident in the schoolyard. He observed a fight in which I was instigator, thrashing a fellow scholar who would not defend himself. And though he ordered me to stop, I believed the demonstration of my prowess must be what he really wished to see and would admire. So, to stop me, he pulled me away and beat me bloody. Then he put me back together as best he could and counselled me to be better."

"This is how you know him?" said Benjamin, incredulous.

"I don't wonder he could not place me; he was drunk, and I have grown up a bit. But I've never forgotten it. You will imagine the profound impression he made upon me, and I have since wondered who he was."

"Richard of Runswick thrashed you when you were a schoolboy?" said Benjamin, and when Hugh chuckled, feeling as much pride as shame, he could not but laugh as well. Yet as the night progressed, he observed an alteration in Hugh's demeanour insufficiently explained by the anecdote. After seeing he was established in the guest room for the night, Benjamin regarded him a long moment, making clear he would listen should his friend wish to say anything more. When he failed to acknowledge the offer, Benjamin bid him good night and departed.

After the door closed Hugh waited a few moments, sitting on the edge of the bed, with the memory now bright before his eyes. Of course, he had not told Benjamin everything. He had never told it. And what more there was, was perhaps not much. Only, to the man he was at this moment, and to the boy Hugh had been...

...laying at Brent's boots, in a school uniform hardly distinguishable from the mud and dirt, the grass and blood, the schoolyard bully struggled to retrieve his breath and his senses...

"Tha forced my hand, lad," said Brent, stooping and sitting him up gingerly. Hugh could do little but cling to him, blinking stupidly, and wincing as Brent dragged him out of view behind some brush to prop against the trunk of a great, leaning oak. Then the young man ran to the well behind the school, tearing his shirt as he went, shouting at Hugh's school-mates to get back inside, and tell not a soul on pain of death, before returning with a bucket of water.

"Lord forgive me for a sinner," he said, going to one knee and examining the boy for injuries. "Not bad, then, eh? Thought I'd shattered thine jaw, or knocked out an eye, little lamb. But here ya be now, near a picture, cut up and fit to swell tomorrow, nothin' worse. Speak now: a tha harmed, lad?"

At Hugh's dazed silence, from which he could only stare into the eyes of his assailant, Brent grew more agitated and ripped Hugh's shirt to the waist, searching for mortal wounds.

"Will ya not speak? Christ, where have I harmed ya? Ah lent thee a reet flick…" Then he caught Hugh's eye and attempted a grin. "But tha were strong, faith, and a little wild!"

Hugh extended a hand into the air.

"Can ya see me? Touch my face, if ya can."

Hugh touched his cheek, searching his eyes.

"Take a lock of hair and give it a tug."

Hugh reached forward and yanked.

"Aye, there y' be. The colour – say what it is… Eh?"

Hugh mouthed the word again.

"Red, so it is. Dark red like my grandfather's. Kept a whole head till he were eighty-one, jealous of every strand."

Richard bathed Hugh's chest with his shirt, until the water in the bucket ran red, and he was obliged to pull up another clean from the well. Hugh observed closely. When he settled again before him, Hugh extended a hand and, while his arms and chest were bathed, pulled his fingers down the thick, full red hair like the teeth of a comb; then he smoothed Brent's hair like the coat of a much-loved Collie. The man observed him as he worked, and when he was done took the exploring hand and gave it a kiss.

"Ya forgive me." Hugh only looked into his eyes. "And here is my advice: lay off the drink if you find you like it. I've put it away rough these two days and blame it now how hard I was upon thee." Hugh remained silent, studying the panting, earnest face. He reached forward and touched his lips, his jaw, and his assailant, rather than questioning him, smiled, and appeared amused by the boy's slow, methodical actions. "Aye," Brent continued in a softer tone, "but will ya forgive me tomorrow? Tomorrow whilst turnin' first yellow, then green, then black and blue?"

Hugh swallowed, and said the first thing which came to mind – a schoolyard rhyme.

"What care I how black I be?
Twenty pounds will marry me."

"Base dog!" Brent cried, face lighting, his eyes shimmering out of their gin glaze, the fumes of his scorching breath expelled in a cloud: "Ya rascal, tha are only stunned! Felled a lively one, haven't I? A reet saucy thing, ain't ya?" And with that came forward and kissed Hugh long on the mouth, grinding his head into the bark of the tree. "Aye…" he said withdrawing, "like gettin' kissed, do ya? Like my hair? Toy with it." And he kissed him again, during which operation Hugh held his breath as though he were being held under the surface of a cold river. These kisses, the first Hugh had ever received, felt quite queer, and upon the heels of a pummelling he suspected had shifted every organ in his body, he experienced a seizure of emotions which twisted his gut and tightened his chest until he struggled away.

Brent laughed: "Heart's beatin' like a rabbit – Lord help me!" Taking Hugh's shoulders, he lowered his voice and said, "Do not pull away from me. Tha know how a man likes to be touched; come somewhere with me."

Hugh shook his head. "No Sir, do go away."

This appeared to awaken Hugh's counsellor – Richard leant back, blinked, and set a fist squarely atop his head. "Christ, what am I sayin'?! Curse that blue tape; gin will be the death of me. I meant to say, lamb, I shall fetch ya a clean shirt. It was your hands in my hair confused me – never do that to a long-haired lad. Now will ya have a new shirt to replace the one I have ruined, or will ya not?"

"No Sir. I wish you away."

After considering, he nodded, "Aye, 'tis best. What will you tell to your schoolmaster, then?"

"They were students set upon me – from some other school."

The man nodded, made to leave, then dropped down again to one knee before him and said, "Swear you do really and honestly forgive me?"

"Yes."

Richard Brent looked at him a long moment, then nodded.

"Then I shall leave ya, little lamb."

Hugh opened his eyes. Was he waking from a dream, or into one? Had he followed Brent in his bloody rags, had they searched out a new shirt? Or was he again in Sallow House?

It came right as he pieced through recent events and recalled the memory of the boxing match… the screaming crowd…

And he thought, *Can you really wish to know me? Was it only what was said in the moment? I daresay once you recall who I am, if you can at all, you will not. Entwistle is the name of your competitor for Sylvia, that is all. And a very feeble competitor, indeed. You do not really expect me to write you and must think me daft to have loved a little the man who thrashed me so many years ago.*

And reasoning thus, Hugh resolved not to write to him. For should he meet with disappointment, after lately losing so much, he knew he would not survive it.

But how to move forward? For he was shaken to his core, and understood that core was weak, and drained of courage. He wished desperately to know this man but was certain he must be rejected. Hugh returned to London in a state of deep confusion, his anger soon eclipsed in despair. He was sick indeed of his problems, his desires, and more than anything sick of his weaknesses. Waiting for him in his drawing room was a letter from Sir Frederick, asking for the next ledger and expecting a piece of good news regarding Miss Coates. This was taking too long. He had others in mind and would require Hugh to meet them if something of progress could not be shown. He understood there were increasing difficulties within the Coates family. And was it true there was yet another suitor now? What did he know of this Theodore Watts, the performer at Covent Garden? Sir Frederick concluded his epistle in these words:

"You are third in line now, Hugh, after a player and a pirate. And as the lowness of their characters must be known to everyone, your poor showing in the race is even more inexplicable to me."

This, alas, was the final straw upon the load Hugh had been long carrying; he looked in the mirror, at his befuddled face, his wide, dilated eyes. He began to laugh, and after a time was equal only to collapse in bed in little less than a fit. He reached for his Geneva. Held it to his nose, and inhaled...

"There you are Brent: my history in this one unmistakable fragrance. First buss, first booze, first beating as a man. I shall drink your health, for providing me all three. I have not the courage to write you, but give us a buss old chap, for old time's sake."

The mouth of the bottle was soon locked to Hugh's.

He then embarked upon a course of debauchery which lasted two days and three nights.

Upon his hands and knees in the lockup...

Vomiting into a bush in a Marylebone byway...

Sliding out a bedroom window, fists pounding upon a locked interior door....

In the lockup a second time, or perhaps a first...

Thrown down the steps of a residence known as The Farm...

Lying in bed in Sallow House, with Anne, Duncan, and Benjamin at his bedside, the voice of a physician as he begins the first course of blood-letting...

Long, deep, dead sleep without dreams...

Robbed of cash, shoes, wig, cane, coat, and breeches, and ducked in a body of water...

Tangled in two sets of arms and legs, as a fiddle plays downstairs...

Sprinting passed a cockfight in Hyde Park...

Anne held his hand. Hugh saw through parched eyes she had been crying. He observed from her reaction this was not the first surfacing from wherever he had been. Indeed, she did not believe he could see her even now, or speak to her, and so for a time he was silent, for he wished not to frighten her, or the new babe she carried. Into his mind arrived a physician's visit some unknown time before. So too a talk with Benjamin, telling him of the things he had done, before he fell backwards into a long, dark, twisted hole of thoughtlessness.

At last Anne, realizing there was sentience in his gaze, came in close and asked if he could see her.

"Water."

He was some time taking long, painful sips.

"Air the room."

The windows were thrown open and he drew deeply.

"Have I ruined everything?"

"No Hugh… Lord support me… but what have you done to yourself?"

"I have not the least remembrance…"

When he came to again, it was the middle of the night. An attendant sat beside him.

"May I have paper and pen?"

The items soon appeared.

Brent,

Upon finding he was abroad, I am told I made a disturbance calling at the residence of a Gentleman I wished very much to meet again, though I had not, while still of sound mind, the courage to write to him. I am told that, while at The Farm, the Gentleman's footman informed me his master was travelling, and I would not believe him. After which I was tossed into the yard, then hauled to Kingston and handed to a constable. As I was in a bad way, I fail to recall either the day, or the circumstance which returned me to Wimbledon. Pray, accept my apology, which I offer both to you and the members of your house.

This Rake, Sir, was on account of that Gentleman, for though, after years of speculation, I had learned who and where he was to be found, yet, when invited to engage, I discovered I could not face him. I do not lay my barbarous behaviour at his door, as I did my stupefied carcass, for I am no stranger to drink. But neither am I a profligate fool, unworthy of notice or friendship: only a sad man, attempting in a strange manner to understand a strange life. For my efforts, I have discovered only that I have not the constitutions of other men, who may behave as I have done, and, laughing, Rake and Riot next day even harder. Instead, I am made afraid of myself, unable to comprehend the lengths I will go in Flight, or in Chase, I know not which it is.

The Gentleman to whom this is addressed requested a letter, so here it is. I request he will send one in return, if he has ever had occasion to wonder what became of that silly fool in the school-yard – even if he can do no more than pity him.

For one curious day, long ago, Richard Brent brought me to my senses, by knocking me out of them. As I was willing to forgive on that occasion, I pray he will forgive, in the same spirit, the sinner who writes this, exhausted, upon the far shore of Hell, lost to know wither next to go.

Your humble Servant,

Hugh Entwistle
Sallow House, Wimbledon

That week a note was delivered which contained these lines:

A Herald, tis, Fair Bud, of coming Days
Thy Petals bled of Gold, to Browns and Greys
Thy Youth, alone, deceives.
O! What Confederates have of Seed!
Endurance! Nay, mean Root of Weed!
Regret, alone, will mend
And with Curious Wear relieves
Man, in one Season, lived wild
Limbs to a sudden Frost, extend
Face to the North Wind, beguiled!

O! that a Grace be thus maintained:
Thy Fragrance fired, thy Colour bloomed,
Exhausted through Night, by Day, resumed
And Virtue, by starry Eyes deranged,
Naught but a Sin restrained.
Temperance for Trivia, exchanged
A fading Memory of Home
A Snowflake taken for a Stone

R Brent

Hugh brought the parchment into the bedclothes and gazed at the words, studying the curve of each letter, each incongruity where the quill had tarried, smelling the parchment, the ink, the dead wax of the broken seal, until he could not see the words for the lines, and sank again into sleep.

CHAPTER 8

At last, with his senses better restored, Hugh saw a curious sight: Anne rose from her chair to fetch something; he saw not one but two women before him in the guest room. One moving away, his sister; one stepping to a far corner, his departed mother. When he sat up and called, the two women became one – she returned and resumed her chair.

"Am I recovering?"

Anne placed a hand to his forehead. "You are out of danger. We have had hope for a couple of days."

"Is the child well?"

"Yes. Benjamin saw I had as much care as you had. Far more than was required."

"God forgive me. And you, Anne, forgive me."

"I can more easily forgive, what I can comprehend."

"Can you comprehend the wretched indulgence of oneself? I fear too much disappointing – the world, I suppose. Sylvia will never have me."

"Have you truly grown to admire her?"

"No. Though I am tempted to a lie which might more easily explain my behaviour, I shall not say that a Miss Coates has brought me low. Rather, they are old things, melancholic years, and present expectations I cannot meet. I shall never please him Anne. It is not in my Nature."

She nodded but appeared curiously unmoved; she had suffered too much to let him off so easily.

"I have for some years," continued Hugh, "found my solace in drink. Now that solace has become a monster."

"Was that the trouble during our last summer at home? And afterwards, in Westminster?"

"Yes."

"Had you no other recourse to help?"

"I believed I did not. Do you hate me?"

"Can you honestly ask me this?"

"I can, Anne."

"I do not hate you. I never could, certainly not when you are suffering."

He took her hands and kissed them. "Where is Benjamin?"

"In Buckinghamshire. He remained until the physician declared you out of danger. He spoke to you for some time, though you may not recall it. Then he departed with his daughter."

They were an hour speaking as they had not spoken since his return from the Continent. She counselled him, begged him to speak to a priest, or to her, at least, should he ever despair again. They spoke of the small changes in herself these first months of her second pregnancy. News of Duncan, and Julia, and whatever else he could think to ask about, as the servants bathed him and washed his hair. She read a letter to herself from their father, requesting the status of his son's illness. She confessed the idea of an illness had been accomplished by her own lies of omission, however shortly thereafter she had written again and told him the truth. There was also a note from Jerry, in which Hugh understood the many hours of uncertainty that had been endured by not only the manservant, but by many others.

. . .

The following week a knock sounded upon the door, and Geoffrey announced a guest.

Anne looked up from her book. "Did he send up his name?"

"Yes ma'am. Mr Richard Brent."

Anne turned a look of bewilderment on her brother, then said, "Deny him, Geoffrey."

"Brent?" Hugh said, clearing his throat and raising to an elbow in bed.

"Yes Sir. He asked for you, though Mr Sallow wished your sister to take all calls."

"I will see him, Anne."

"We are speaking of Brent the boxer? Richard of Runswick?"

"Yes."

"What on earth could he want with you Hugh? I do not consent at all to this. It can only serve to upset you, perhaps put you in harm's way. I am a little frightened."

His heart nearly pounding out of this chest, Hugh closed his eyes and sat up straighter: "Send him up Geoffrey. I wrote and asked him to come, Anne. I spoke with him before my illness, a most civil and encouraging interview."

She frowned, shaking her head. "You never mentioned this before – it can hardly be credited…"

"Benjamin will attest to the interview, and its civility."

"My brother-in-law is not here to ask," she said tartly. "Do at least have Geoffrey in the room while he is here."

"Unnecessary. I insist on speaking to him alone." In a lower tone he added, "And should there be any danger, an elderly butler could hardly do more for me, than I could for myself."

This attempt at humour produced no sign of amusement; Anne continued to look quite displeased. But at last she relinquished and agreed to retire to her room down the corridor.

Soon arrived footsteps on the stairs, the door swung inward, and Brent entered the room.

With hat in hand, he nodded at the servant to remain in the corridor and closed the door for him. Then he turned, took in the sight of the partially aired sickroom, and advanced. He wore a pair of buckskin breeches, heavy boots which bowed the floorboards and a thick overcoat which rubbed upon itself like sandstone. As he withdrew the coat, he stepped into a shaft of light which brightened his orange stubble and his somehow accusing gaze.

At the foot of the sickbed he said, "I am come, little lamb."

Sinking back Hugh's limbs were overtaken by trembling. He covered his face, and was, for a time, unable to engage his guest. When at last he looked up, he observed Brent balancing his weight on the bedside, leaning in with hands on his knees, and looking quite grave. "Business obliged me to be away. Did you receive my letter, Hugh?"

Hugh. It was the first time he had said his name. The patient withdrew the poem from under his pillow. "I have only just awoken. Truly awoken, and so have not had occasion to respond."

Brent planted a kiss upon his forehead. "Stop thee whittling, I had been here sooner, if I could."

Hugh blinked. "Were you told I had a dire outlook?"

"Some conflicting accounts – though what I'm observing is a relief. I'd no sooner sent that poem than a bad account was sent me of you. As I am not known here, my man decided to bribe an ill-informed stable hand. A lot of good it did me." For a moment they studied one another.

"I feel just now," Hugh said, "as I was, propped on an old leaning oak in the schoolyard – with your gaze upon me."

Brent leaned in, his eyes widening. "And was I to have you

find me, then up and die? I have begun to reflect, to wonder at myself and my past behaviour… hope to God there is some way to be better. Then in a trice re-emerges an episode from my past in which I acted wrongly, which has remained with me. You asked to know me. I wrote a poem, based upon what I know of being young and daft, only to be told it might well be a eulogy. I come to Wimbledon not only to see you, but to know… to *know*, Hugh, if that is what life says to a man who asks to make amends."

Hugh nodded, unsure what to say about an incident kept so long to himself, or to the knowledge that it had meant something to the other concerned.

"And have you nothing to say of the poem I wrote you?"

Looking up, hurt that any silence regarding the merits of such an expression to himself might be perceived as anything but unnecessary Hugh said, "It makes me wish to write better."

After studying him a long moment Brent said, "Aye. That's a good answer."

Hugh continued: "You took the words I wrote in my letter… and, somehow, the words I did not write, and made music. You scarcely know me."

"I know ya," muttered the other. "For all I learned your name this week. You think I had forgot, in my drunken stupor – fair enough. But the snap of your little neck as I punched ya? Your eyes gazing up at me as you lay on the ground? Then you forgave me, and sent me on my way, without reproach. Just one moment in life, but an anomaly – a thing of peculiar kindness and beauty. No, it was not Beauty. It was Sublime."

Hugh waited for him to continue.

"Will you not stand for me?" said Brent, "T'would do me good, could I but see tha."

"If it's strength or vigour you wish, you will be disappointed. Perhaps after some food…"

"It preys upon a guilty mind, such as I have; fancying you

down where I felled you six years ago." And at Hugh's laugh, for he did find this amusing, Brent's mouth shifted.

"You have observed my legs fully functional – I strode up to you, lithe and limber, after your match in Kingston."

Brent nodded, rather like he had forgot. "It's a singular feeling, after a fight. I had it – and was glorious in it – then you stepped up." He shook his head. "It was the next day, on the road to some business I had in another county, that I thought of your surname and how I knew it. Entwistle – the lad making love to Miss Sylvia, my fair cousin." After a sigh, and an assessing look he said, "Bloody God, you're thin. Lost a stone, at least, since Kingston. You said in your letter you are done with riots and rakes. Is that so?"

"I intend to be. I imagine few men will abstain forever."

Brent looked him over and nodded. "It's honest, what more can be asked?" Then he rose from the bed and, at Hugh's efforts to follow him, held out his hand. "Rest. Was that your sister I saw peering down the corridor at me?"

"Yes."

"Semt right terrified of me; she'll want to come immediately I am departed and see you are unharmed. See she gets some gruel in ya."

"Do you mean to go?"

"I wish to call tomorrow."

"Forenoon, afternoon or night. I shall be out of bed and, as I cannot look worse, must be improved from what I am at present."

But the visitor remained unsmiling. He said only: "At noon. Write me tonight at The Farm and tell me how much you fancy me."

Hugh felt a smile spread over his face. "With pleasure."

Brent opened the door, cleared his throat loudly in the corridor, then exited toward the stairs. It was well he departed when he did; after Anne had hurried in, Hugh was fit only to sink back into bed and close his eyes, hard put to believe this was his waking life.

Next day came first steps, and a journey, in fits and starts, down the stairs and about the dining room. After eating a little, Hugh proceeded to the drawing room to await his caller. Sallow House was something foreign and strange without its master, and receiving Brent there savoured not a little of cuck-holding. But did Hugh dare think of the man's interest in him like that?

After Richard arrived in a curricle and was shown in, he quickly proposed a ride in his machine.

"Get thee boots on, let us get ya out of doors," he said, and Hugh, with some assistance from Geoffrey, obliged. As they began down the drive in the curricle Richard said, "Your last epistle pleased me very much – searchin' out my cousin to get closer to me, whom you'd admired from the papers. Read it twice through and laughed each time I came to the fishmonger's son – a reet bastard wasn't ya? Little Hugh in the school-yard, trying his utmost to impress me."

"Was it the sentiment, or the style of writing, which pleased you?"

"Come – you know you can write, you need not myself to say it. What pleased me was the content of the letter. You've broken with the last man to court ya; I shall do tha." Seeing Hugh's expression, rather blank from shock, Brent said, "Don't you want me?"

"*Want* you…?" said Hugh, faintly.

"Aye, ya must. Will you write me next in verse?"

"If you like."

"I prefer verse over prose. Break rules if the sentiment requires it, and it pleases you. You must always write for yourself. Pleasure alone merits the effort."

"You can say that having published your writing – the

treatise on boxing, which sold out in twelve hours. I had hoped to ask you about that. The encouragement of so many must be tremendously encouraging."

"Many more wished me to fail, and still do; neither do I rate myself less, on their account. One is, at heart, one's own best critic. I nigh on strangled Collins the bookseller, who told me years ago he would have accepted a volume of poetry from me, but for the uncertain connotations of the name Brent, which savoured of a pirate smuggler so he believed he could not touch it."

"If he wished to sell, should he not have valued them more for their flavour of notoriety?"

Snapping the reigns to bring the horses off the road and down a secluded lane, Brent barked, "He should have, lad –'Damn your hide for a liar, ya gret apeth.' I told him, 'How about a bit of honesty? Tha won touch my poems, as not one is any good!'"

"What did he say?"

"What could he say? Set my writings on a table, scurried to a far corner of the room, and told me to collect them. I was just turned of twenty-three – I needed to hear they were untouchable not because of my name, but because they were trite offal, the lot."

Struck at once with too many sensations of unreality, this joy, this companion, this strange life, Hugh was given over to a fit of laughter. He was brought round as the leaves of a low-hanging elm stroked his shoulder.

"Here's a quiet place," said Brent, pulling the reigns and slipping an arm around Hugh's waist. "Take a sup a this, now, it's magic for ya…"

"Take a…?"

"*Kiss me*, ya bastard—"

An explosion – of memories, and the wish to draw out of this man all his confidence and experience. When Brent withdrew Hugh immediately pressed for more.

"Nay, that shall suffice, lamb," he said, with unforgiveable dismissiveness.

"But—"

"I shan't fuck ya if that's what you're askin' for. Tha's weak as a new-born calf and it gives me pleasure to court ya." He withdrew, dodging Hugh's second attack, then finally pushed him back into the seat and jumped to the ground as the horses began to whinny. "Whistle with that puckered mouth, lad, I am done kissin' today."

Suddenly Hugh felt quite weak. He closed his eyes and for a time dozed in the seat of the curricle before eventually agreeing to return to the house. As they began back, venturing to put an arm around his companion, Hugh said, "I am desperately happy, Richard. I wish… for so much now I can scarcely see straight. Tell me I am not a novelty from years ago and you're looking to trim stray ends."

Brent grinned. "I'm lookin' to trim ya, am I?" Then he exhaled, and after a glance at Hugh, said, "Trust to what is happening. Leave off the kissin' and love for now. I'm fallin'."

"Are you?"

But Brent said no more.

Richard paid a short visit the next day, then hired a carriage for the day following to return Hugh to his apartment. He would join him on the return home, then would be required in York for no less than two months, as he had documentation to gather for what he hoped would be the final phase of the suit brought by Somersby. Somehow, Hugh could not regret it. He wished him away; he required time to breathe, time to place a lid on what had changed so dramatically in his life, step away, and observe it. That such a man had written this way to him. That he had taken possession of every waking thought left Hugh, once he was mending physically, cradling himself in the fear he could surely never retain him.

After they were loaded into the carriage and started off Hugh said, "How bright the world looks. I could jump this moment from the carriage, huzzah for Liberty, and run the entire way alongside the horses."

"Mark my words," said Brent, "even sitting as you are, you'll be dead on your back by the time we reach the apartment. You are far from well. After I depart, I want ya to write another letter – tell me how much ya love me. Tha do love me now?"

Hugh closed his eyes, and onto the window of the rocking carriage let strike his head, which rang clean through with a peal of Grandsire Triples. He could not yet speak of love, so said only: "If you left me tomorrow, Brent, I am already a stronger man."

Brent took Hugh's face in his hand. He looked into his eyes and nodded. "Aye," he said, and held Hugh's hand the remainder of the journey. At the apartment the invalid accomplished half the flight of stairs before Brent carried him up the remainder and saw him into an easy chair.

"Are you Jerry Kilmister?" he said, to the wide-eyed manservant.

"Yes Sir. It is an honour, and a privilege, to meet such an illust…"

"Never mind that. You call my lad a Prince?"

"Oh yes, and I do all in my power to see he is tended to, same as one."

"Your services are needed. Fetch him some tea, and fruit if you have any. When you return, I shall tell you how his bedchamber is to be organised and how he should be seen to until my physician arrives."

Jerry gave a bow, then a curtsey, then something in between, before exiting the room.

"I must continue to York now and you have the direction. We have established something for me to return to?"

Hugh nodded.

"This is how it is with me, often runnin' but I shall return. What is that over yonder?"

Brent retrieved the edition of the *London Herald* with his portrait from the vanity. "You put it there, before you came to see my performance?" Hugh nodded and when Jerry returned to receive his orders, the newspaper fluttered to the floor. It came to rest beside a stack of adventure books Hugh had possessed since boyhood, *Roderick Random* and *The Adventures of Peregrine Pickle* among them. From there his eyes travelled up the legs, the torso, to the top of Richard Brent.

The door slammed as the man exited for York; Hugh grabbed his head and sank back into his chair – the heights of this bliss were nearly obscene. Vanished his despair at losing Benjamin. Benjamin had lost him; Benjamin had given him away. Two months was not so long, and it was two months, at least, Brent would be his – he was certain of it. Upon the writing desk sat a stack of letters, among which the one he knew would be there, and must face. The letter from his father:

Hugh,

It was with shock, almost to disbelief, that I received your sister's last. If this is true, I have little to say, save what is now postscript and epitaph. I made allowances after that masquerade, but you appear set on destroying yourself and your reputation.

I hear you have contrived, by some means, to attain a friendship with your very rival for the hand of Miss Coates. Your motivation in this, too, is obscure. Had you not run wild to the point of death this must have inspired my curiosity to know your aim in gaining his friendship. But given the poor choices, poor taste, and poor behaviour of recent weeks, I am more inclined to believe the connection the product of his art, and you the dupe of a devious man. My guess is Richard Brent wishes Sylvia for himself, flat-

ters you with a little attention, and will send you skipping off into a field so he can have her.

I need hardly mention your allowance will be cut, and you will be disposed of at my whim, should even a hint of another drunken episode reach my ears. Test not even the door of Deerhurst, Hugh, it is not guaranteed to you.

At present I have nothing to give me pride in my son. One must hope he can rise — for should he sink any lower, he must cease to exist altogether.

Sir Frederick Entwistle, Bart.

CHAPTER 9

For two years a reporter for the *Political Register,* Augustine Wall, had been allowed to observe and report on the proceedings of the House of Commons. Though reporting was illegal, his accuracy was remarkable, particularly as notetaking in the gallery was forbidden. As such the members of the House pursued no legal action against the *Register* and at the opening of Parliament in the autumn of 1770, a handful of new reporters peppered the gallery. Most went away with headaches, and a new appreciation of Mr Wall, for they could not believe any activity deemed illegal could be so cussedly boring.

One to remain was a reporter for the *Public Inquirer,* our own Mr Entwistle. Since the summer he had written some amusing articles on Lady Northumberland's gowns, criticisms of new plays, and a limerick which hinted at the activities of public officials. His greatest success came with a piece he had contributed anonymously. As Marius he presented a sonnet which began by celebrating the Pantheon in Rome but, by its end, appeared to be condemning the squat and rather corpulent person of the Prime Minister Lord North. The piece was entitled *The Rotunda.*

After this Marius was given free rein to pursue his interests, and a place in the gallery beside the brilliant Mr Wall was just what he wished for. The separation from Brent forbad too many unoccupied moments in which to believe the boxer merely an hallucination born of schoolboy adventure stories. Fortunately, evidence was nearly daily produced testifying to the existence of Richard of Runswick as he was often in the papers in reference to the endless Jacobite lawsuit. Now enraged after losing the land in Cornwall, and with Brent in York, Somersby was seeking to extend the trial into a third year, cursing his opponent in long diatribes whenever the *Gazette* had space to fill in its pages.

As such Marius's reporting on Parliament made heavy reference to Somersby, and those known to be associated with him in the Commons. His descriptions contained less of substance than those found in the *Political Register*, favouring instead tales of belching, nose picking, odd noises, and behaviour rather unworthy of the House. Nevertheless, his reporting often outsold that of the *Register*.

This rather dubious success reached without the confines of London, as confirmed in letters from Yorkshire and from his father in Berkshire. Both men knew the identity of Marius and both men praised him. For, like the country, Hugh's father appeared ever less inclined to support any one cause or political party, which each week spidered into new factions like a terminally flawed pane of glass. "Principles be damned," he wrote in one letter. "If one cannot fashion criticism into a cudgel to amuse the public one must step aside. The wittiest, Hugh, proves by his wit his superiority of thought. However crude, however untenable the philosophy, however unhelpful to Society's ills – Marius, at the moment, is more worthy of support than any policy of Lord North."

This was the first sign one might look beyond making a good marriage to please the man. Stalled negotiations with Sylvia Coates mattered little; his father wrote with new admiration when Somersby devoted eight-hundred words to Marius himself, beyond livid at the descriptions of his activities in the House of Lords.

After turning in his latest piece, Hugh set out into the streets believing he had the very pulse of the city, the dazzling attention of the metropolis, however fleeting that might be. People *spoke* of Marius, and so spoke in support of Richard Brent, persecuted by that horrible, corrupt, profane, and disgusting Lord Somersby. Hugh bought two accounts of the Horrid Massacre at Boston and strode on to the square at Covent Garden, where an MP before a crowd was warmly opposing a new tax. He passed sharpers escorting a pair of drunken libertines into the Shakespeare's Head Tavern and continued into the Bedford Coffeehouse to observe the patrons and read about the disturbance in Massachusetts.

Brent's latest letter, however, remained very much on his mind. Richard had been pressing him for more details of his previous life, and in response to Hugh's obfuscations about the identity of the 'man lately left', Richard had written to say he required absolute honesty of a companion. Hugh saw no reason ever to divulge Benjamin's name, however honesty regarding the situation with Sharp must be considered, and perhaps sooner rather than later. If Richard learned of it while in Yorkshire, far removed and with time to cool before returning, then all the better…

"Entwistle," came a husky voice as a woman dropped onto the bench beside him. It was Julia. Though the Bedford Coffeehouse was a hotbed of men, from penniless Grub Street paupers to Dukes, the presence of a woman with a man was generally thought to imply prostitute and punter. Julia glanced around as she adjusted her noisy damask dress, commanded a coffee from a passing waiter and said, "Anne told me you are often here hunting up stories to get into an article. Well done with your last on Somersby, by-the-bye. Have you seen this?"

She tossed the previous day's *Gazette* beside his mug of

coffee and Hugh, for the first time, had the privilege to see his own likeness broadened, stretched, and celebrated into caricature. We must confess, *Dear Reader,* his heart skipped to know what of himself would be emphasised. It was with pride, and embarrassment, that he observed the lengthening of his somewhat elongated face and protuberant chin. The caricaturist chose to emphasise his best feature, his large and supplicating blue eyes, but it hardly mattered when taken into the hideous tableau of the sketching in its entirety.

For Hugh, with knife and fork, Brent, with his eye-patch and holding what looked to be a leg of lamb, and Theodore Watts chewing a rib bone, surrounded a disintegrating beached whale, smiling and placid, clearly meant to represent the wealthy Miss Coates. Hugh gasped. Brent, as the focal point of any tableau which contained him, upon closer inspection had withdrawn strings of pearls and a handful of diamonds from the bloated young woman and placed them into his pirate's chest.

"Richard has no need of her money!" said Hugh, but Julia shrugged and reminded him the point was to portray the man in a poor light. But such as Julia Motely, should she go to the trouble of finding someone, had far more to communicate than a picture in the *Gazette.*

"I can see from your reaction that you do not know."

Hugh waited for her to continue. Then he seized her arm and said, "About Brent?"

Julia paused for rather a long moment, then leant forward. "Not about him – about your love interest. I am just come from my friend at Covent Garden Theatre and he told me, absolutely confidentially, that Miss Coates, this morning, has placed herself under the protection of Theodore Watts. It is all but certain they are on their way to Gretna Green to be married."

That it was not some terrible news of Brent Hugh took a long moment to digest, then shook his head.

"Was it this terrible picture in the *Gazette* made her run? Poor girl. Watts is an idiot to believe he will get any of her money."

"Is he? No doubt he wagers she is loved enough to be at last reconciled to her family, and something considerable will be settled upon them." But Julia had narrowed her eyes and Hugh did not quite like what he saw there.

"Publicity is a fickle mistress, Hugh." Receiving no response, she continued, "Richard does well after so many years in the public eye. Exceptionally well. What happens when the identity of Marius becomes generally known? Marius: Brent's dependable bulldog again his Lordship. What then?"

"That is an odd thing to suppose; I've only told a few intimates. Nobody knows the identity of Junius. And Junius writes far more incendiary pieces than I ever could."

"Somersby knows, Hugh. Not the identity of Junius, nobody will ever learn that I daresay, but he knows yours. That is why such a good likeness of you is in the paper."

When Hugh frowned and reached for his coffee, Julia took hold of his forearm and the mug retained its position on the table.

"I have actor's bent, love. May I give a little performance?"

Hugh nodded. "Very well."

"'You are Anne Sallow, are you not? You adorable creature! Allow me to bestow my heartfelt condolences for the loss of your father-in-law, Mr Charles Sallow.

'I thank you kindly.

'Oh, my dear! You cannot imagine how he is mourned. I understand even Richard Brent had occasion to pay his respects.

'Richard? Oh no, he visited Sallow House to see my brother. Hugh was suffering from an... an illness, and he came to discover how he was recovering. My brother is so very extraordinary, you know, that even though he is, supposedly, another suitor of Miss Coates, his very rival for her hand came and sat with him while he was ill and took him for rides in his curricle!

'What Christian charity! Would that this world had more of that, Anne. Perhaps I should go oftener to church. Rides in his curricle? Has Brent a curricle? Do tell.

'Oh yes. A lovely curricle, and a lovely fellow, really. I was, I admit, somewhat frightened to let him into Sallow House. But you know, Hugh has been so very *wild mad* about this man. Really, I wonder he did not cosy up to Brent's cousin merely to learn more of the famous boxer! People say Richard is an eccentric character, so I was so pleased to see him blot my brother's sweating brow, kiss his head, and cuddle up to him as they rode about.'"

Hugh swallowed, something deep in his nasal cavity beginning to sting, and he said, "Julia, please…"

"'Oh! How he caressed my brother! Even drove him from Wimbledon to his apartment on Charlotte Street and sent his own physician to tend him.'"

Hugh had long since lowered his head and could scarcely summon the breath to speak. He glanced up at Julia, who simply stared, and at last whispered, "Christ God, was that an actual conversation of Anne's?"

"Not yet. But she is out in Society and Somersby could easily find the means to provoke it in a room of twenty listeners."

"But… is it generally known?"

"Is what generally known?"

"Brent… and me?"

"The pair? No. Brent's proclivities are known by some, to be sure. But he is accused of so much by his enemies that nothing sticks to him." Tossing her head back, and grandly taking a spec from her eye she continued, "Signifies nothing to people of extreme *ton*, I assure you."

"And myself?"

"Well, now it appears Richard takes such a fancy to you, it is not inconceivable you are willing to comply. Many more would comply than you might suppose, for that man. But as to whispers about yourself: forgive, but you merit not quite the notice of a Lord Allenby. And so concern is uncalled for, in both the time, and attention, accusing you would require."

"You will provoke as you assure, it is your way," said Hugh through gritted teeth. "But I beseech your mercy if you have any inclination to tell, in a moment of *ennui*, what would destroy me. This is a matter of no little import to the likes of me." In his passion Hugh could not prevent the trembling from overtaking his voice, and this loss of composure did at last inspire a moment of compassion. Supposing assurance of some variety was called for, Julia took a few stabs at his hand, then gave a prolonged sigh.

"I would never betray anyone so basely. I understand what should happen to you both, that is why I am warning you to be careful. If you are fond of Richard, then all the better for him. If you can please him, then please him. He cannot help but please the one he chooses to love."

Then, just as her steaming coffee was delivered to the table, she rose and departed.

Hugh's uneasiness continued as he awaited the next response from Yorkshire. In his latest, though telling nothing of what Julia had discovered, Hugh had confessed to the situation with Sharp. The moment Jerry placed the letter into his hands he tore it open:

Hugh,

Not one more payment. Tell me everything your blackmailer has by way of evidence. A letter to the boy you were trysting – this is all? Is he of the means to prosecute you? He must be sufficiently motivated to finance his prosecution. Understand that. Remind your villain of the costs of prosecution.

To be sure, a letter testifying to circumstances known only to you is harmful but discover if he has anything else. And tell me his name, for Christ's Sake. We will take him down, but we must first know what he has in his possession to employ against you.

Set a date to meet the bastard in a public place. A coffeehouse is best – a day or two after my return.

Richard

The next day Jerry handed Hugh a letter from Sir Frederick:

Son,

Do let us speak of Richard Brent. It is not easy for a man to admit when he was wrong, but I was, entirely, as regards your friendship with this man. I do not see as your failing, or regret in any way, hearing your silly Miss Coates has run off. There are many other young women I intend you to meet.

Yet somehow you have gained, by your brilliant defence of this public figure, a relationship rather above rubies in potential value. I have, I confess, remained entirely behind the times regarding the benefit of knowing such a, shall we say, unusual persona. He is not titled, and his past smuggling, regardless he was pardoned, would have made him untouchable during the reign of George II. We have a new King now.

You say he returns to London the last day of January. Your sister Alice and I will arrive the same week and I do expect to be introduced as soon as possible...

F. Entwistle

Sir,

You are surprised to receive a note from me. Do not be alarmed, Jasper, I have news to comfort us both: I have made my final payment. You need no longer fret about when, or how, to ask the next increase. Though I recall little of it, I do not believe the letter you hold contains anything to warrant the ruinous price I have paid for your silence. The cost to bring me to court far exceeds what you can afford, and there is no benefit to you in considering it. That is all.

Sir,

I received this morning a letter intended for someone else. This is the direction for Mr Jasper Sharp Esq. Your own letter, Mr Entwistle, I enclose here. He is not at this address.

Sir,

As regards the trade bill coming due, I do not believe you are correct about the terms of our agreement. As such, Mr Sharp, further payment shall not be remitted.

Sir,

The trade bill is in order, I suggest you review it. If not, payment will be requested directly from your employer.

Sir,

Star's Coffeehouse is near your place of residence, if you would agree to meet me there, or another public place, on Feb 1ˢᵗ, I would be much obliged. I have reconsidered my previous angry tone. May I request a look at the letter you hold? Do please consider extending credit, Sir. I cannot meet your demands.

Sir,

Star's. Two on Monday. Come alone.

The wintry day of Brent's return Hugh remained occupied, hoping to outrun his joy, his anxiety, his expectations. Brent had been away nine weeks, yet in quiet moments Hugh had to admit they were some of the happiest he could remember. The separation had been difficult, but the expectation of his letters, the fashioning of his own for Brent, and the defending him in the *Public Inquirer*, had given to his life a lovely framework.

The week before his return he had supped with the newly arrived Sir Frederick and Alice, who had grown rather too handsome for her age, and patiently answered her questions about what Brent was really like. "What makes him smile?" she asked, which, together with his father's continual questions, made clear their intentions. "What does he like to eat?"

In attempting to answer these inquires, Hugh found it somewhat unsettling the need to infer, suppose, and invent as much as he did, for, in reality, there had been precious little time with Richard. Theirs had been just brief interludes during a handful of days; all had passed rather like a whirlwind. They had never even dined together.

"He favours Dolly's Steakhouse in Paternoster Row in The City," Hugh told them, which he only knew because Brent would be there with his lawyer the day he returned before retrieving himself from Hatton Garden. Alice wrote this important detail in a small notebook she kept in her reticule and pressed him further about what made the man smile.

As his evening with the High Scribblers concluded, Hugh grew agitated, and, to avoid the other members' discovering who was retrieving him, and demanding to see him, he skipped out towards their place of rendezvous. After five minutes, through a swirl of January snow, a hackney coach pulled forward. Taking a deep breath Hugh stepped through the door of the carriage. Sitting inside was Richard. And beside him Sir Frederick. The pair were in high spirits and began speaking over each other to tell of the extraordinary co-incidence of their meeting at Dolly's where Frederick had, upon recognizing him, ventured to introduce himself.

"I reckon your father never was more a jolly Englishman than tonight," said Richard. "Roast beef through and through!"

A smile and a shake of the head sufficed for Hugh's response, and the evening passed in an easy flow of conversation. After taking in a play, they stopped for coffee then agreed to meet again *very soon* for dinner at Anne's the moment Brent had time to spare. *The moment.* The man was deposited in Brunswick Square about eleven and the coach continued on.

"A simpering flirt, but I love him," said Brent, and though continually looking at Hugh, he appeared somewhat within his own thoughts. This unexpected turn of events had rather upset their reunion; still, he took Hugh's hand, kissed it, and held it on his knee as the coached rocked along. They spoke of the journey from Yorkshire, then as they turned onto Charlotte Street a smile was exchanged. At the door of the apartment, Brent hoisted Hugh onto his shoulder and paraded him in and around the drawing-room. Ringing for Kilmister, Hugh loosened the buttons at his knees, tossed his wig, and kicked his shoes aside to lounge in his stockings. Brent lit the fan lights, smiling as the manservant chid his master for throwing his good bob wig on the back to the sofa, then dropped into an armchair.

"You are surprised I won your father so quickly."

"Is that how it was?"

"He wants you each day with me, he said it a hundred ways."

Jerry asked if his guest would take brandy. Brent nodded, then gestured at Hugh. "And one for Whistle, but keep the door locked that we may contain the beast when he emerges."

In the prolonged silence which followed Brent rose and strode to a mirror; Hugh shifted in his seat, cursing his father for having made the evening his own and leaving them without a place to start.

Then Brent stripped his shirt. "I appear to have doused myself in coffee."

"Oh, my stars," said the valet stepping forward. "Hand it to Jerry and I shall begin on the stain upstairs."

"You are a pixie love, thank you. Have you a spare robe? My host has not the brawn of you or I, and I wonder you have not something fresh for me."

A robe was produced, of lavender silk, and whatever of

Hugh's blood was raised observing Brent without his shirt, was lowered with remarkable efficiency by the lavender robe. He began to laugh as his guest grimaced down a mouthful of neat brandy, aware that he looked quite ridiculous and shaking his head. Then Brent extended a finger.

"Tha had an appointment to set. Have ya done it?"

"Yes. I meet him tomorrow at Star's Coffeehouse."

"*We* meet him."

"He is beneath your notice as a Gentleman."

"But not beneath a fair footing in boxing, the great leveller of all tiers. Not one in a hundred would resort to duelling, if obliged to the sweet science. Let your villain defend the right to extortion with 'is fists.'"

"A coward will always prefer a pistol."

"In the event my trigger finger, too, is at his service."

"His aim is money. He will not attempt violence, or even prosecution, so long as he can proceed directly to my father for the money."

"It's not enough to prevent him from prosecuting. He must be put in fear himself. Can he get at the lad tha were trysting?"

"No, he is gone beyond finding. But he surely knows my father is staying with Anne."

"You must take the stance of a boxer," Brent said, standing and tossing the robe into a corner. "Up." Pleased they had moved beyond the awkward reunion, Hugh stripped to the waist and cleared an area of the floor. Then, rather uncertainly, he took a boxing stance and waited for further instruction. "Camp low, toes out, eyes upon me. Body open to a secondary approach and maintain the left elbow close in at the side."

"A secondary approach? Do we expect Jerry will creep back in the room to attack me?"

"Establish the habit. We do not often parry but one opponent. Fists up as mine are."

Hugh worked to loosen his arms while mirroring the position. The oak floor creaked as bare feet described a circle.

"Take of Out-Play wrestling what serves as well for boxing: spend time liberally, lure by the head. Then make a false beginnin' while awaitin' the move of an opponent." With his head Hugh motioned subtly as Brent instructed, coming forward and drawing out the first attempt. "What are ya most fearin'?"

Maintaining a wide clearing Hugh said, "That you should send a blow faster than I can parry."

"What do we speak of?"

Reddening, Hugh attempted a surprise swipe at him, missing Brent's jaw by a wide margin. "I fear, first and foremost, my father discovering the letter."

"Right. Set aside the fear of prosecution and focus on what is most pressing."

Nodding, Hugh let his gaze fall to the floor as he considered, then felt the hair on the left side of his head stand on end, with no moment to react. "That was a knockout blow, Hugh, had I wished it. Understand what I am capable of. Have ya made a blow yet against your opponent?"

"I asked him to meet me at Star's Coffeehouse. I do not know how next to proceed."

"Turn to your own success for instruction. Are you proud of what you have accomplished thus far?"

What had he accomplished? A letter saying he would not pay? Pretending to tell his father last year of the blackmail to get a reaction from Sharp? Hugh came forward and Brent stepped aside before he had even decided on his blow. They resumed their stances.

"I have done nothing in two years Richard. Nothing. For two years I have been the willing fool of a little man."

"How will ya make a better showin' for yourself? What has changed?"

"I have met you."

Hugh received for a response a slap to the side of his head, sufficient to send him stumbling backwards.

"Knocked dead, lad. Now tell me what ya shall do."

"I don't know! I must obtain better information – or employ better what I know. A man must be of the financial means to prosecute, as you wrote in your letter. I knew that, perhaps I could have attempted... something with that knowledge. What else do I know that I do not employ?"

"You must think hard and ask for help."

"I do ask! I asked Benjamin! He might have reminded me of the costs involved in prosecuting, but he would never speak of it. If he had I might have done something long ago!"

Silence until Hugh came forward to attempt another blow. Brent caught his wrist. "Benjamin Sallow?"

As Hugh struggled to wrest free, Brent tucked a stray hair behind an ear, and brought him closer. "Sallow, in whose estate you were lodged during your illness?"

"Yes, of course. Should I not have asked advice of a trusted friend?"

"He was more than a friend to be trusted with this. He's the man lately left." Brent then took him into a vice-like grip, in which Hugh was obliged to remain else cut off his airway. "I shall teach thee next Cornish-Hugg wrestling, shall I?"

"Christ, Richard, I cannot breathe!"

"We stand in Sallow's rental property. Ya pay him for it?" At Hugh's silence he said, "Aye, he set y'up here for 'is enjoyment."

"That is a gross mischaracterisation!"

Brent hugged him closer. "Set y'up, then traded ya for a new wife, the bloody berk."

Hugh at last pulled free, falling to his knees before regaining his footing. "He was a fool, I told him so! I am not a side-dish to his entrée."

"And secret meetings now and again were the most he could offer?"

"Yes of course. What else could I expect?"

"Do not be daft; expect a man who will marry ya."

"*Marry?*" shouted Hugh. "You fool! Will you game me like a common strumpet with promises of marriage?"

In a quick rage, Brent seized his shoulders and slammed him against an interior wall, sending an old portrait crashing to the floor. Then he dragged Hugh into the next room and threw him onto the bed. "*Never call me a fool again, Hugh! Never!*"

Hugh turned, sitting up to push aside the bedcurtain – his persecutor pushed him down once more.

"For I wish to make my heart known," said Brent, his jugular pulsing and his breath coming fast. "I will not suffer ya in the arms of another, after my own. And I shall be true. That is marriage by my reckonin'."

"You may have me with no such promise."

"I require *your* promise in return, ya bastard. Never to look at another man, for I, Hugh, am a prize worth retaining. Have I yer promise?"

Look at another man? Hugh scarcely knew there *was* another man apart from Brent, yet he could scarcely summon a response. "You seem almost serious when you speak of marriage. If you are made much of by my father, it is on account of Alice. He will flatter you. He will keep on until you are got, but if you reject my sister --."

"*Got!?* Am I a donkey traded for a sack of flour? Do not laugh, Whistle, for here is what I say to tha: I shall grant your father's wish to attain me – he shall conquer me entirely! That I shall take his golden boy from him, and not his daughter, will require additional finesse. But I *shall* obtain his permission for your hand, which will defuse the power of the blackmail letter when it is presented. I am a well-connected man, and wily enough to make Sir Frederick Bart. swoon for all I can do for him. We *will* marry Hugh, and he shall give me his consent."

"You," Hugh hesitated, his head spinning at the madness

of the proposition, "you will insult him with your proposal! He will call you out, for all his effeminacy!"

As Hugh stood Brent dropped to one knee before him. "Could ya speak t'me so tenderly, and write t'me as ya have, and defend me as Marius, if ya do not love me? I have sowed my wild oats. I need a home, Hugh, and you are the one to make one for me. And I love you. It is not complicated."

Hugh strode past him, set to deny him in coarser terms. Ready to berate him for his stupidity, no matter the thrashing he would receive. Then he halted. His hands went into his hair. "What am I doing?" he said, rounding on Brent, who rose to his feet. "What am I *doing?* I almost said no and wished you away from me. I told myself I could not understand you. I wished to please my father, by denying you; but even by displeasing myself, I cannot please him. By all our actions we admit what we are and are hypocrites to deny. Yes, Richard, I will marry you. We have only the world to win to our favour."

Richard stepped forward. He took Hugh's hand and smiled. "You step to a strange shore, lad. It's what's required to win me."

"I know," said Hugh.

Brent touched his cheek. Then he said, "Get in bed. A demonstration, now, of good faith."

CHAPTER 10

When Kilmister arrived next morning, holding Brent's cleaned and dried shirt, the owner rose from bed, quick to apologise for his usage of the lavender robe. It lay unceremoniously in a corner, from which place he fetched it, folding it, and setting it on an end table, before downing a large goblet of water.

"Shall I attend you, Sir?"

"See to your Master, Jerry. Hugh, look sharp for your man."

Hugh stirred in bed, his hair standing on end like it had withstood several applications of a lightning bolt.

"Forgive the foul aroma of my breath, Jerry," said Brent, then nodded towards his companion. "He would have me drunk to have his way with. But a promise of marriage was made, and my hand has been accepted. Be the first to congratulate us."

"Oh Sir, best wishes on a most singular occasion! I like to know my Prince is made honest, and by so illustrious a man as the hero of London! I shall cherish my robe," he said, pressing it to his nose, "for the modest part it played in uniting you."

Then he turned toward the bed, uncertain where to start with the half-senseless tangle.

For as Hugh stirred larks were alighting upon his head, the bedclothes, and hanging from the bedcurtains. Into a riot of birdsong, the young man's eyes rolled back – two hundred larks took his nightshirt, then lifted him into the sky to observe the city – Blackfriars Bridge, the Tower, St. James's, the glorious, winding Thames. Then Hugh slipped through his shirt, fell through the clouds and back to earth...

Jerry tucked the nightshirt under his arm and pulled his charge up again, this time naked, from bed. Hugh kissed the valet's cheek, then his hand, as he sat to his shave. *O Jerry*, he thought. *If I had not deserved a Sharp use me so ill, can I justly claim a Kilmister as my right? The heart must ever accept, as its due, unusual good, decry unusual evil, though both are unusual; must ever see as great resilience, rather than human need, the ability to trust again. Let me take a little of the credit, at least, for finding you, for treating you correctly, and daring to take you close.*

After Brent retrieved his clothes from the drawing room, he sat on the edge of the bed and pulled Hugh from the hands of his attendant.

"I've business to attend to before our appointment at Star's. Did I oblige, at last?"

"Nay, from the first."

"Then I shall depart; exercise caution and do not approach your villain before we meet him. I'll have his name now."

"I had rather—"

"His name, Hugh, before I go."

"Somehow... my compassion for the wretch is strongly aroused. I cannot account for it. He only seeks his fortune, in a misguided way. Where does this sudden pity for my blackmailer come from? Pity which now outweighs my anger?"

"From spending free all night thy budget to fuck," said

Brent. "You are made stupid by it, so I shall protect you. His name."

"Jasper Sharp. My father's valet until May of last year."

"I might have known," said Brent. "And so, a trusted member of the house, who crucifies a puppy in love, must test my resolve against cold steel, and enliven my kidney."

When Sharp turned the corner, he was accompanied by a man near as tall as himself, perhaps twice his weight, and moving at two thick, meaty strides ahead of him. Hugh was put in mind of a yeoman farmer driving an ox, which, if considerably stupider, was brawnier and could affect far more physically than the ox-driver himself.

At the door of Star's Coffeehouse hands were left unshaken, and the stranger introduced only as 'Jack'. But he was, as far as could been seen, the only bull released from its pen to protect Sharp.

"Jack," said Sharp, after they continued inside and ordered their cups. "This is the benefactor pays my maintenance. He'll take two chaps over one, when he can get it, and so is much obliged to make yer acquaintance."

"Good of you both to meet on short notice," said Hugh, nodding to Jasper, "You favour establishments close to where you live, I know – this seemed the closest."

"Very considerate. Hugh is pleasant so ye will believe he bows easily to my upper hand. But soon as he can, rest assured, he will seek purchase to scramble over me, and is never, not on his best day, any better than he should be."

Both men assessed the bustling room, no doubt saw the back of Brent at a distant table though failed to distinguish him, nor see anything to concern. After the boy brought their cups Jasper withdrew the copy of the old letter. "Read it."

Over brews particularly smoky and thick, Hugh observed from the corner of his eye a rising and changing of position at the table in the corner. Then he opened the letter. After looking at the first line he averted his eyes, his heart coming fast. His words. This was unmistakably his. After attempting the second line he averted his eyes again. This was pain, this tardy announcement of a loving heart. James Bramble had never even received it.

"I don't wonder ye cannot read it, ye see it through the eyes of Sir Frederick. But for the payment, which is not yet lapsed, he need never see it, nor know those frolics and their consequences: what sent yer own brother running for the hills and the other, named in this letter, left to take all the blame. Yer father knows it all, in a shallow grave of his mind, ye might say. It is not even what ye did, *per se*, but how ye deceived him. Swearing on yer life, and honour, it weren't true."

Jack piped up: "You had yer fun, and still have your freedom. What the Devil is a few guineas, to keep the man happy?"

"I cannot pay," Hugh whispered.

"Never mind the lies," said Jasper lowering his tone. "I know ye can get the money from yer brother-in-law. Does yer father know he keeps ye in an apartment? I have a letter from the landlord on Charlotte Street, saying Benjamin Sallow is the owner of that place. It says, too, the landlord has yet to collect a penny by way of rent, though in the past the place has fetched a monthly payment of £7. He and his wife will testify ole Benjamin likes to call a couple times a week. I wonder what he gets for his trouble?" Turning to Jack: "No, I don't wonder. I have in my possession three letters between those two, what says what happens, all courtesy of an errand boy."

Three incriminating letters between himself and Benjamin? What few notes there had been were entirely innocent, nearly all carried by Benjamin's own Alfred, a grandfather. All had been burned. Sir Frederick appeared not to have confided anything of the Charlotte Street arrangement. It appeared Sharp wished more evidence and was gambling that a few poorly informed guesses would get him there.

Hugh said: "My errand boy is sweet, and trustworthy! I pay him too well ever to have him betray me like that. I'd lay my life on it!"

"A leopard don't change his spots, do he Jack?" Sharp said to his companion. "Ye *did* lay yer life on it, what will one day or other end in Tyburn. That messenger boy could tell ye wanted into his breeches and turned on ye."

That there was no messenger boy, and no incriminating correspondence gave him the first feeling of hope he had yet had – Sharp was overreaching.

Hugh faltered, looked desperately between the two, and attempted not to cry! "You horrid bastard!" he hissed, "how can you know so much? What else do you have against me?"

Sluicing a fair amount of coffee from the steaming surface, Jasper patted the arm of his friend. "Hugh's a bit of a dull-swift, amongst other things, but he always pays in the end." Turning to Hugh, "I may have something else, I may not. I think we can agree I don't need anything more."

And so, standing from the table, Hugh, at the top of his voice, shouted, "You chaps come direct from Hell! Sure, you are not human!" And he held his letter in the air. Though their intense conversation had, to this point, warranted a few sidelong glances from the other patrons, every face in the coffeehouse now turned, all conversations dead.

"Give the letter back, dog," sneered Jasper, taking a swipe at it.

"What is the world come to?" cried Hugh, "I only wanted a taste of coffee! No other means have I anymore, God knows, but by a little charity!" The two came around the table to take him from either side.

"The letter," said Jasper, in a lower tone, "give it back."

"Is that you, Entwistle?" said Brent, pushing his way through the crowd. "Pray lad what ails thee?"

"These two men, Brent," said Hugh, "An odious proposition I believe, though I confess I don't entirely make out the meaning." Snatching the letter, Brent stepped before his coffeehouse audience in a great Thespian circle, his brow furrowing as his eyes moved down the page.

"Good Heavens, what is this? 'Thy fond admirer, Monsieur Sharp, bids thee to his lodgings to Oblige himself in a Secret Pleasure he will teach to thee, as enjoyed by the Ancients...'"

"Give that letter over you lying son of a whore!" Jasper shouted.

"That's Richard of Runswick!" cried a man coming forward, with another in tow. "And I, for one, shall not suffer a Blackguard insulting the honour of this hero and defender of the Crown!"

"It is nothing," said Hugh, "Let us forget it. Only take the letter away, Brent, and destroy it. Scandalous nonsense."

Said Jasper, "You have but to read the letter! Will you believe a man who will not show the letter? He lured me and my friend here of a purpose..."

"There is enough of your jaw," said Brent. "Let us have the proprietor. Jenkins?"

Upon his arrival, Jenkins took the proffered letter and read through the first few lines with exclamations of great umbrage.

"The most shocking corruption of a young man I ever laid eyes on!"

Brent took the letter back and tucked it from view. "There now. Nobody has been harmed. Let us have an end to this."

"Not before a right pummelling these two Inverts hoping to game your friend, Brent!" said a pock-marked man with a dirty face. "I, for one, should like an impromptu display!"

"Search that one for the real letter," Jasper said, gesturing at Hugh, but whatever might have followed was subsumed to a crowd blocking his exit, many frosted or dripping from the snowy day, and ripening for a fight. "You have but to read the letter! The letters were switched!" shouted Jasper rounding upon the crowd, but reason would not win the day with masses so disinclined to listen.

"What I will not do, Mr Sharp," said Brent, "is insult the good people of this coffeehouse with more of that letter. We shall go our separate ways but know this: I shall take this letter to the magistrate forthwith should I hear you threaten or try to pursue my friend again. These are witnesses one and all, five of whom but this half hour my good friends, whom I trust will come forward should it come to that."

Jasper was too smart to remain in this volatile environment, shoving Jack out to the street, but at the door shouted, "Sir Frederick is at Anne's, Hugh. Yer dead to him!"

Departing the coffeeshop Hugh sought out a hackney coach for Brunswick Square, running through drifts of snow, which cascaded off rooves, driving up streets and byways, the grey bowl of sky threatening sleet. Sitting opposite each other he and Richard stared out opposing windows of the private coach; what was not white were halted vehicles in all directions. A stillness filled the carriage as they came to a stop. Began again. Stopped again.

Hugh had rather hoped to proceed quickly, and have it done with. Brent remained silent and discouraged talk, and now the copy of that letter from two and a half years ago lay before Hugh, drawing his eyes. He opened it. It was a nauseating memory of the drunken stupor which had produced it – things he knew he had written, things he hoped to God he had not. Names and places, celebrating his own craftiness, his carnal unions, even spewing hate about Anne. They were his words, unmistakably – soon his family would read every word.

"Christ, what have I done?"

Extending a hand for the letter, Brent read it through then tossed it aside.

"I regret what I've done today, Hugh."

"What you've done? Richard what do you think of my letter?"

"Very sad, but without power if we speak first to Sir Fredrick, if ever this damn carriage goes. We have one more blow to make at that son-of-a-bitch Sharp to secure you from prosecution. Commit to me now, that you are willing to destroy him."

"Can you doubt it?" said Hugh, though with hesitation at such a strong word, "I've wished him destroyed for two years."

"Then why do you ask, 'what have I done'?"

"He will retrieve the original letter and deliver it. Anne must be repulsed by it. And by me."

"If your sister can feel anything but pity for the poor soul who wrote that, she is not the lass I suppose her to be. She'll be shocked, she was not raised to know those things. Now why do you not think of me?"

"Think of you?"

Brent leant forward. "You are a child in this, Hugh. Those bastards got tossed from the coffeehouse on pretence of being *as we are*. Because we must have a fresh start in a life together and I could not see another way. But to help you, I debased myself."

"*Debased?* Do we have the luxury to think of debasement?"

"If you have not the luxury for that, then you do not deserve your liberty." When Hugh could only stare at him, he continued, "I get on in life because nobody thinks to touch me. A man cannot be touched, who tends his dignity."

"It was a foolish child wrote that letter; I don't deserve what Jasper's done to me!"

"I do not blame you for being a victim of that man. I blame the adults we are now, willing to debase ourselves to defeat him. I've been careless of my own trysts in the past; I've had blackmailers come at me. Ten times I've been thrown to the wolves, by slanderers and corrupt writers, with all the fodder in the world to call me an Invert, a Catamite, a Turk, a Jew and a Pathic. But have you heard that about me?"

"No."

"Nothing?"

"Grumblings, vaguely said. Rather it is said, but never takes root. Even Somersby cannot truly damn you; what he writes somehow lacks conviction."

"Aye. 'Tis no dumb luck tha, but the product of toil," said Brent, his eyes flashing. "Learnt by trial, and error, and pain. You owe me, for what I did today, and what I've yet to do to take that man down."

"I know I owe you."

"Then do not say, 'what have I done?'. You did what I require of you, as my mate and partner, *and it is not enough.*" He leant still closer. "You will face your father, for me. You will take his blows, for me. You will be thrown from his house, for me, if that is what it takes. For I am a purchase worth that cost."

Feeling he was already taking a right pummelling, Hugh had little stomach to imagine what his father would do to him. Where was Brent's pleasure at having made the real first strike against Jasper? There was more to do, but could not a moment be spared for the achievement?

"I shall do the things you ask. And more, when this damn carriage moves. You do not see it, but I am, I assure you, quite terrified of what my father will say when he knows. Knows, and knows I am willing to admit it."

"You feel fear. You are human."

"Because I will not know how to start. I wish to have done with this, only—"

"'Tis done already," said Brent, leaning back and crossing his leg. "You have but to tell him what has happened."

CHAPTER 11

"To what do we owe the honour?" said Duncan Sallow, meeting them in the vestibule of the home in Brunswick Square.

"Business with Sir Frederick," said Brent. "Is he to home?"

The footman soon returned, assuring them he would descend momentarily. In the presence of Richard, Duncan appeared in a state of reverence without knowing if he should be. His three years in England had been spent learning every rank, every address, every nuance of nobility, the name of every noteworthy family and their illustrious histories. Yet this person was far better loved than the Prime Minister and given more words in the papers than many an Earl or Duke. This left the conflicted American rather mute.

Sensing something was needed Richard said, "Your father-in-law is good enough to see us on short notice. The best men, Mr Sallow, are most at liberty to see one; the smallest and least productive must always defer, postpone, and stand upon ceremony."

"I wonder you never practiced in international trade," said Duncan, with a smile, "it is what my father said many times."

Brent inclined his head as Sir Frederick entered the room.

"Gentlemen! Do come up. I have had enough of my accounts for the day, tea shall be brought presently." The trio ascended, and upon Brent's asking after the family, the man showed him into an armchair in his make-shift study. "Her Ladyship is never unwell – you must meet Matilda. Ned, my younger son, makes considerable strides in his vocation – he's well into the second year of his apprenticeship with a bank in Exchange Alley. And Alice – well, I must say, there never was such a picture of health and fine spirits as my youngest daughter. She is calling upon a friend at the moment but will return by supper. I trust you will join us."

"I desire to speak to you about your son, Sir, then we shall see. A most singular young man – I have wished to say it to his father for some time."

"Here I am to hear it and could not be more pleased. If you distinguish Hugh, I wish to know why, for you are a Gentleman of much experience. Even before I was introduced, you held a fascination for me. You have the power, Richard, to *fascinate*. A boxer, a hero, a pirate; I was shocked, yet could not look away. Fortunately, I come to know the man you really are, now a common circumstance has brought us to greater intimacy. You both were cast to sea by that most unworthy Miss Coates. At first, I was discomposed; but you taught me, during our wonderful evening at Dolly's, such things may be laughed at. So I am, in your presence, improved. Claret, Richard, mellows and becomes palatable at sea; my fascination, with intimacy, mellows to admiration."

"You make much of me, Sir."

"England makes much of you because she cannot help it. A smuggler, a statesman, a self-promotor, a writer, a plaintiff, a defendant, eccentric, and strange!"

Brent threw a leg across his knee and laughed. "It is my life, let it divert whomever it may. You regret that a fine family like the Coateses could entertain a man like me, of dubious fame, when your son was on offer – once I knew him, I wondered at it myself."

"You are not a flatterer," said Sir Frederick, with a flourish of sobriety. "I know this, as only a man who is one can know it. I thank you. It has been my life's work to raise my children to be something beyond their contemporaries. There is Anne, whom I am told is the pattern of selflessness and kindness."

"Nobody will dispute it."

Sir Frederick inclined his head. "A lovely, still lake is Anne. And Alice… Hugh, how shall we describe her? A cool breeze on a summer day? But I leave it to the poets. A father, Richard, is ever apt to believe praise. Upon hearing it, he must be pleased. If he hears it many times, his vanity is brought to terrible heights! I have declined no less than four offers for Alice's hand, all before the age of seventeen. This has made me most protective and rather inclined to keep her with me into my old age. Oh, I am quite set upon it – who can ever be good enough for her?"

"Who indeed," said Brent. "And you may add to Hugh's accomplishments a promising boxer. Parries well enough to avoid a belly-full of drubbing. Tact and consideration in sport is, to me, more instructive of a true Gentleman than all the gallantries at Court."

Sir Frederick brought his fingertips together and considered. "Very well. But even a man inclined to such talk must announce when he is well-oiled and ask to what this all tends."

Brent leant forward. "Sir, you had occasion at Dolly's to pay me one of the great compliments of my life. It is an uncommon man, you said, who is an individual and true to himself; he holds a special place in your esteem. I, Sir, am that man."

"Yes, you are."

"Your son approached me at my performance in Kingston, an occasion I suspect inspired much uncertainty. He quickly gained my affection, by the esteem expressed for me and the professions of his heart. As you say, I am a man of much experience. In that experience, I have not known one like Hugh. I see you grow impatient my point, but there can be nothing more *to* the point than my praise of him. Sylvia was a match of half measures, for I mistakenly believed, for all my professed freedoms, it was what I must do, in the end, to make a home. I was wrong to think of her.

"What signifies half measures when one wishes to be happy? I have Hugh, and half measures are made whole. I desire a home, and a companion who will love me. I see you will rise — you wish to interrupt me; pray hear me out. For I demonstrate that spirit you admire and have never been shy. I have travelled, I have seen what is to be had by way of partners; I reject them all and ask for your son's hand. You are shocked — that must be when we surpass our expectations. But do not say my words offend you: they are the highest compliment I can pay. That is what I have to say."

Given leave to speak, Sir Frederick refused. For astonishment, and rage, had rendered him new. In look and manner, perhaps more revealed than changed, however Hugh could not, as he faced him, know him as his father at all. "Is this done with your consent, Hugh?" he whispered.

"Yes. I love him. He brings me joy. What is more, I respect the man he is, and the courage he shows."

Sir Frederick's eyes glazed. He fell to memories… then, hardly above a whisper, he spoke the word which was the deepest deception practiced upon him, for it was old and elaborately concealed: "Bramble?"

Hugh opened his mouth to respond, determined upon boldness, but found nothing at his command.

Brent said, "We will not offend you by remaining against your wishes. You appear seized of a choler."

"What signifies my condition? What signifies my response? I am presented with a *fait accompli*. The thing is done."

"What would you have us do?"

"Are my wishes sincerely sought, Hugh, or only as a balm for guilt?"

"Sincerely sought, for I have no guilt."

"And you Brent? Do you ask to know my response?"

"I do. The loss of your esteem for me is nothing to what your son loses. I destroy a house, your house. I seek the first brick to rebuild another, though I fear it is premature. No doubt far too premature."

"Yet I too am a man of the world," said Sir Frederick. "Here is a thing the first in fashion know and smile about. Richard of Runswick takes H Entwistle as his Second. It is tittered at in the best circles. It is the very Effeminacy of the Age."

Brent hummed. "That we have any words at all, and spoken civilly, I take as a blessing. But I must take my leave, for I cannot mistake your meaning and I do not wish to increase your distress."

"We are to go our separate ways?"

"What can we expect?" Hugh asked, glancing down at his hands at the fire in the man's eyes.

"What *would* you expect? Why do you not demonstrate this great joy you profess, though you cannot meet my eyes above a moment." Upon Hugh's defiantly raising his eyes his father smiled. "And if petulance is meant to represent joy, along with the other substitutions seeking acceptance, I shall say only this: let us proceed downstairs. To the back parlour. Up, the both of you. You may lead the way."

They proceeded downstairs and into the back parlour. Hugh took a seat in an armchair, Brent, after some pressing, sat in another, and when Sir Frederick joined them, he was followed by Anne and her husband, both looking rather perplexed. "Upon my word, I cannot think the occasion," breathed Anne, sitting lightly upon the sofa, and bringing beside her Duncan, who appeared merely curious.

"Your brother has something to announce," said Sir Frederick. "He has just told me, and I wish you both to hear it. It is a thing he is proud to say and stand by. Let us have it, Hugh, as we did upstairs."

Brent stood from his seat. "We do not sit like school-children, to be humiliated under the guise of grace."

"How shall I rephrase the request, Richard of Runswick? How comes your singular and fulfilling pride to require such delicacy of speech to procure it? Duncan, was there some-thing in my address which gave offense?"

"Nothing in the least." Then to Brent, "But I will take as an affront your refusal to sit if you choose to remain. I ask you do so, that we may determine rationally what has caused the upset."

"Sit," said Hugh, "For I am determined to say it now, and be damned the consequences." Brent sat, and Hugh, directing his eyes to his sister, took a breath. "Anne, I shall think no less of you if you cannot face me, or if you choose not to see me for a while. But, if by what I say, I thought you should be ripped from me forever, I must indeed lose courage. Your approbation and love have ever been my solace, in a life of turmoil you have not understood. Yet, if you can love me no more, I would not have the imitation of love affected. Be guided only by your feelings."

Now quite pale, Anne, with one hand to her mouth, said, "Tell me. I shall love you, as long as I have life in me to love. Tell me, now, whatever it is."

Willing himself to anger, that he could produce the sound, Hugh said: "Richard."

Looking quickly between them, she nodded and said, "Yes, Richard, have you something to tell me?"

"We are in love," interrupted Hugh. "This is, and has ever been, my Nature, though I have been unable to own it. And whatever the cost, whatever I must lose, and however it may be accomplished, we shall be married."

From his sister exploded one hysterical gasp of laughter,

and she said, "You are to be married?! You are not at Death's door? You are not tomorrow boarding a ship and leaving me forever?"

"No. If my obfuscations led you to that conclusion, I am sorry."

"But whom are you to marry? And Richard; you, too, shall marry at last? Shall you have a dual ceremony?"

The look of outrage from Duncan, and disgust from Sir Frederick, was enough to fire Hugh further: "Hate me whoever will, but do not disdain a young lady who must at first fail to take my meaning."

"Am I to understand," said Duncan to his father-in-law, the glitter of delight sparking his eyes, "That man, this guest in my home, went upstairs and asked for your son's hand in marriage?"

The silence lasted some moments.

"Asked for Hugh?" Anne said, looking wildly around the room. "*Hugh?* What can you mean? I…" she looked about her, tipping forward from her seat on the edge of the sofa, then back again. "Oh, I see. Brother. Brother, can you want this?" Grasping at her husband's arm she continued, "If you could but see him with the young ladies, Duncan, they are so taken with him. There were times I feared we would be brought a child," turning to Hugh. "Yes, I have wondered occasionally. I have thought you promiscuous. I am sorry but… But this? No. Do not say this has ever been your way, for I know otherwise. It is only your infatuation. A dare, and a fashion to be looked at. Yet very dangerous. You will imperil yourself and be thought strange and sinful. Hugh, can you be so wild?" At his silence she turned once more to her husband.

"Best plan the union in Newgate," said Duncan, "In a cell for Pathics before the marriage tour at Tyburn."

Brent stood. "That will do. Anne, I regret the pain and confusion this has caused you. But this is no whim. We are not ashamed but will remain here no longer. Excuse us."

However, Duncan understood an opportunity not only to impress Sir Frederick but to put into words the years of dislike he had felt towards his brother-in-law.

"I wonder you do not consider Alice, Hugh, as you consider Anne. Mild the insult of your disgrace, to the destruction of her hopes. The mind reels at such usage: that a brother would take that object *for himself,* which was hoped for her, is a feat of villainy never described in the annals of history! Could Shakespeare himself comprehend it!? You shall be presented at masquerades – fully concealed, of course, and for the general amusement. But who will want any child of this house? What of Ned and his reputation? And what of your father, who has, I have always said, done far too much for you. That tireless advocate, endlessly ambitious for you, the half of which you will never know. Is this how you repay him?"

"I'll thank you to keep a civil tongue," said Brent, "if we are to be detained a moment longer."

"Thank me to be civil? You with the gall to face the father of your Ganymede?"

Stepping forward Brent grabbed Duncan's collar. "Shut thy mouth, swab, else it swells shut. That is my loved one you speak of."

"Filthy Catamite, get off me!"

"Do not provoke him, Duncan!" shrieked Anne.

"Provoke me!" said Brent. "For this fair daisy shall lend thee a flick tha won' forget."

"Leave this house!" shouted Duncan, wresting free of the grip and ringing for the footman. "Leave, now you have made your ridiculous display! I shall pick up the pieces and see this family to success!"

Following Hugh to the door Brent turned to Anne, "I trust your heart will lead you right, but let me say this: the decision to tell you was one of necessity. Expect a visit from your father's former valet, the Mr Sharp I am told served your family for seven years. The dog discovered your brother's secret years ago and has been blackmailing Hugh for a letter he holds. We told Sharp today his fortunes have ended, so he will likely seek recompense now directly from your father. Give us some time, a week or so, and we will take him down. If you have occasion ever to read the letter he holds, remember the tormented soul who wrote it. You know Hugh's heart. That you are alone here in having one yourself, I do pity. When you deem it correct, write to us at The Farm. Good day."

Beyond Wimbledon, on a rambling, bleak common, The Farm stood, or rather crouched – simultaneously a rise and a tumble of blackening stones from the reign of Elizabeth. No road, not even a footpath, opened to welcome the traveller, the ancient, exhausted fields over which their horses galloped so overploughed they appeared to dissolve into themselves. Everything in Chessington existed to discourage, even to make one yearn for the forbidding and desolate moors of Yorkshire. This was a place for hermits – Brent's nearest neighbour was Chessington Hall, a manor nobody could locate without a guide, and whose owner, Mr Crisp, some believed may have departed this world entirely.

Still, this was a breath of new air. Looking about as his horse danced over scrub and kicked up dead dirt, Hugh tried to recall finding this place during his Rake. From here Brent's footman had carried him to a constable in Kingston after which he was delivered to Wimbledon – Hugh had no memory of any of it. And so, though The Farm and its environs appeared inhospitable, even repulsive, he blushed to follow his host up the steps, looking away in shame as the footman, John Sexton, nodded to him with a distinctly sour expression.

Hugh carried little by way of personal possessions; The Farm was best reached by a nimble man on horseback. Yet little did he wish of his old life. A course shirt of semi-worsted wool and buckskin breeches were discovered mouldering in the stables – Hugh slipped them on as his horse was rubbed down. And so newmade, he followed Brent around a rambling abode so ruined that one or two of its sixteen rooms had been sealed for their caved-in roofing. And yet...

As a warm sun stole over the parlour walls, of roughhewn stone and overlaid with tapestries, Hugh experienced a sinking into the place. Dying embers had left cold the large stone hearth, then a pair of hands withdrew the bellows from the dark wood mantle, igniting the heat which caressed the room up to the oak beams at its ceiling. Then down to the beer cellar, the apple cellar, where the pungent musk of two centuries sweetened the hops to syrup and made of the apples crisp confections. Outside to a pigeon house, of which only ancient droppings remained, and errant nesting drenched with melting snow. Yet it appealed as a place to cultivate and to raise – and with a roof in rather better repair than the library of the main house.

Into the fields beyond, into an expanse of high brush which had triumphed over the over-tilled land, The Farm brought Hugh, stepping in wide meandering circles, into its scrubby embrace. In a clearing appeared the famous boxing ring, nothing but four posts strung together with nautical rope and an earthen floor. Somehow more remarkable for its very unremarkable appearance.

Kicking aside loose rocks as they advanced, he said, "It will be work for twenty years to tame the beast that is your garden."

Stepping over logs and old, sodden hay Brent, who had owned the property just four years, said, "I had it from the former owners, that upon completing his work at Chatsworth, Capability Brown designed these fine slopes and shades to be the very mirror of what Nature intended. I merely continue his work."

When they came to a tangle of high weeds sufficiently reedy to have withstood winter, they crushed them into a dry bed. Brought suddenly close, Hugh met the eyes of his companion hoping for some acknowledgement of a life now unrecognizable to what it was just two days before. Brent touched him under the chin. "You are freer now, than at this time yesterday."

"But for you, I had never stepped so far into detestable honesty. There is a place in my breast, the very place, I think, the Greeks believed to contain the candle of life. The flame trembles with each breath I draw, and I ask myself: what is this new oxygen? Can the old flame understand how to live in it?"

"The flame will strengthen," said Brent. "It must. Quit the place in town. Today. Henceforward I want you here at The Farm."

Hugh stared a long moment. "To live with you?"

"Installed as my possession."

"Shocking gallantry."

"Have I not earned it?"

At Hugh's questioning look Brent leaned in on his elbow and put an arm around him. Hugh turned into his chest and said, "I am nothing at this moment you have not made me."

"Then send for your things; you shall not return. I want you in that other man's house no longer. Send word he may let it immediately – I wish never to hear his name again."

"I might retain the apartment another three months. I expect we shall be often in town."

"Beds may be found in London as needed. You were the plaything of a merry widower there; now you are mine."

"Your plaything?"

"Aye," he said. "And when I see fit, my wedded husband."

Wedded husband. Like a phrase shouted by natives from an unknown shore. "When I am away," continued Brent, "I shall know you wait for me, and pine for me, and shall run to me when I return. It is a need, Hugh…" He was silent a moment. "A deep-rooted need – one which has been with me for far longer than I knew."

"And, had no one more suitable come along, you would have accepted Miss Coates to achieve it."

For once, Brent appeared slightly abashed. "Aye, misguided wretch that I was. She was a pleasant lass; I wish her well. One can never…" He cleared his throat. "But will you not love to be mine, Whistle? You may write your articles, and keep my house, as we plan the future. You cannot suppose my ambition – every idea is achievable, if only I have my loyal lad at home to support me. Who gets a good tumble for his trouble, and the wide world I'll bring him."

Hugh turned his head towards the odd, the wonderful and yet horrible stone dwelling in the distance. Something of pity, and love, swelled for the place; it did appear to need him quite desperately. To have been waiting from him for some time.

"I shall want for nothing," said Hugh, trembling now the chill February ground was taking more hold of him than was Richard of Runswick.

"Then you win me body and mind. Only obey my commands, will you do that?"

"You shan't require so very much of me."

"I may do. You can manage it, without sinking to a courtier like your father."

Hugh grinned. It was the most profane bliss to surrender one's freedoms, and the reedy, dead grass of winter quickly became that fine jungle disposed to tumblers. Rolling with Brent, Hugh was soon over, below, and between, weeds in his hair, trembling and wet with cold to the bone, shouting, "I shall never bow and scrape! Or mellow like claret at sea!"

"You will, if I tell you to."

"Let me but worship you, as a divine his god! That is noble, that is not wrong!"

"Nay, that is devoted love!"

CHAPTER 12

About this time a new, criminal element was identified and pursued through the streets of London. Thanks to soaring sales of both the *Political Register* and the *Public Inquirer*, reporting on the House had exploded in countless papers across London. The House of Lords had closed its gallery in December, however the Commons remained open as Parliament struggled to tame the controversy. Freedom of the press was the darling cause of Wilkes, now a sitting magistrate in The City. With both political and popular power, he had awakened new fears in the government as the country awakened to his cause. Many in the House bitterly condemned the protesting of rabble the right to read what most, surely, could not. As such six City publishers were singled out and ordered to appear at the bar.

Two of the six made submissions which were deemed adequate. Two more, with inadequate defences, were reprimanded on their knees. The final two failed to appear before the bar and so were deemed Publishers-at-Large in The City. Not surprising Mr Flexney belonged to this final pair, choosing not to defend the tripping over benches and flatulence reported on in his *Public Inquirer*. As the House cast another net over London, hoping to haul in more of these miscreates of paper and ink, a cash reward was offered for the ever-increasing number of publishers said to have gone into hiding. Printer's Devils received bribes to tell what they knew. Paper suppliers were roughed up to know when so and so had last received a delivery. Then cascades of wily messenger boys, able to shimmy into hiding places which might allow for no more than a cat, descended into The City with official warrants from the speaker of the house.

And, had he been observed, the curious figure of Stephen Chandler may well have been taken for a messenger keen to make a citizen's arrest. At nine one evening the youth descended a hill in Holborn towards a solitary man just departed from a neighbourhood tavern. Through the dark night, into an alleyway still darker, he padded with light foot-falls across an intervening lane and tackled the solitary man into an adjacent byway.

A struggle ensued, clothing tore.

Then the young man screamed for a constable.

The same week Jerry Kilmister made the miserable journey to Chessington in a moving carriage. Hugh had requested the man hire the smallest carriage on offer, hoping to increase the chance of its actually reaching The Farm. The carriage was to contain Jerry and all of Jerry's possessions, though this would require leaving Hugh's escritoire and various other of his possessions for a later time. This served a two-fold purpose, as Hugh could not in good faith give up his link to the metropolis. Lacking some place in London, how could he possibly continue to contribute to the *Inquirer*? At least one night a week would be required in the city, where he might retire to write after a day learning the new gossip in Covent Garden. Flexney remained in hiding, but Hugh trusted he must soon re-emerge to resume business given the public support for a free press. After much consideration the Charlotte Street apartment would remain in his possession. A small lie, and Brent need never know.

And so, through the muck and horror of muddy fields, after stuck wheels and a thrown horseshoe, and coming very nearly to grief, the valet was at last reunited with his Master. Kilmister was predictably horrified by the condition of The Farm, once or twice obliged to produce his bottle of smelling salts though complimenting where he could. Then, with a wide smile, he handed Hugh a copy of the *Morning Herald* and told every detail of the other service he had been asked to organise – the hiring of a waif-like young man to attack Sharp. Jerry had discovered just such a one at Marathon Moll's in The Mint.

"Known as Sook Stockings in that establishment," breathed Jerry, "Sukey to his friends, but for your purposes Stephen Chandler. Lovely lad with a passion for the theatre."

All had gone to plan. After runners from Bow Street brought Mr Sharp into the rotation office, and the magistrate bound him over for trial, Brent had insinuated himself into the case, presenting the names of five witnesses to Sharp's illegal proposition in Star's Coffeehouse. The newspapers began to stir like leaves in autumn. The knowledge of Brent's involvement, however slight, promised heightened interest in the sordid case of Stephen Chandler versus Jasper Sharp: a charge of sexual assault, on the heels of a thwarted proposition of a similar nature.

Hugh sat down with the *Morning Herald*, a translation into print of his recent imaginings, save for the new caricature of Richard. In honour of the new court case, Brent had been sketched sailing a pirate ship into Newgate prison, offender in tow, a sword held starboard and, for a little variety, sporting a long, wooden leg set jauntily atop the bow.

Still, there could be only cautious pleasure in this final strike at Sharp. There was certainly more publicity than one might wish, yet it was Brent's name which had so easily persuaded the patrons in Star's. A public name was required in the background of the case, as the word of a Stephen Chandler might not suffice. And so, Hugh tried to put from his thoughts Richard's loathing of the entire affair.

Despite his complaints, they had agreed this was their best line of attack.

Over tea Jerry asked after the state of his family. Hugh was happy to say a letter had arrived from Anne, assuring him of her continued love but begging him to speak to a priest and to pray each night for guidance.

"But it is time I spoke to Benjamin. After he returned from his marriage tour he wrote and asked how I was and wanted to know about this friendship with Richard. Like a coward I never responded. Now of course he has heard it all from his brother."

And indeed, it had been a silence of far too long, with too much left unsaid. As Brent was still in London, he need never know of a visit to Wimbledon and Hugh sighed considering another lie of omission necessary to maintain peace at The Farm. A note was sent, an invitation returned, and Hugh set off at an easy trot. He was received warmly by the new mistress of the house and overcome entirely by the attentions of her stepdaughter, over-ripened by neglect.

"I must seek your counsel, madam," said Hugh to the new Mrs Sallow, as he held Paulina's head to his shoulder, "on how to make a house into a home. I am living with a friend in Chessington and we are in desperate need of assistance. Lovely as Sallow House was before, it did require a woman's touch."

Euphemia accepted the praise graciously and appeared a truly kind and lovely woman. Not surprisingly, Benjamin had done well for himself and Hugh promised, perhaps rashly, to see Paulina more often now he was living closer. At last Benjamin arrived and, with some formality, bid him into his study and onto the sofa. He, however, remained on his feet, striding to a window, and looking out with a great exhale.

"Say you are pleased to see me," said Hugh, "You know what passed at Anne's." The rather tired nod sufficed to say he knew, and was, despite his shock and disappointment, still fond of his friend.

After a moment Benjamin turned and said, "You could scarcely have made a more misguided decision. Or was it Brent?"

"I would pay Jasper no longer," said Hugh, sitting forward and looking Benjamin in the eye. "He was going to my father with the letter, so I told him on my own terms."

This had an effect, a rather remarkable effect. Benjamin came forward and, after hesitating, rested his hand upon Hugh's shoulder. "That was not the version told to me. I confess this does change my opinion."

"The bastard's in Newgate as we speak. With charges I hope will far out-weigh what he has to say about me. He tried to bring you into it; do not worry, it came to nothing. He had nothing, and I protected you. Neither you, nor your family, have anything to fear."

Benjamin shrugged, then suddenly looked quite helpless. "What can I say but thank you? From my heart. I was only too happy to hate Brent for provoking you to it. But look what you've accomplished. I am sorry I never did that for you. I did sincerely wish to; I didn't know how."

Unable to stop himself Hugh pulled Benjamin into an embrace, and for a moment felt that deep stillness he had nearly forgotten existed in the world. With his mouth to Hugh's ear Benjamin said, "I cannot, even now, comprehend how quickly I lost you. My daughter asks about you constantly. Do come more often to see her. And to see me. I fear I am losing even your friendship."

"You will never lose my friendship, or my love. Not now. Not when I am wed."

This was too much, and Benjamin recoiled less at the betrayal than at the utter absurdity of it. "Hugh, for all I love you, I do question your sanity. How can you continue under such an absurd notion? Live with the man you will, and sleep with him, and no doubt love him: you will *not* be wed to him, any more than you could have been to me. What are you thinking?"

"I am thinking what can be done when one is determined upon a thing. I have taken charge of my life. I always knew what my family would think of me should they learn of it – the only difference is they know it now too."

"Listen to me Hugh: for God's sake keep this quiet. Whatever you need to do. And Brent, too, *must* keep this quiet. If you can possibly…" Benjamin laughed. "I nearly said if you can possibly control him. But by every account he is the most impulsive, rash being imaginable!"

"That he is thought to be is why he so often succeeds. Do not underestimate him, or me. We are merely two friends living together, where is the harm? Brent is too much a hero of John Bull. Yes, Ben, a hero."

"Not a hero to everyone, I assure you. He is out for himself; he makes no effort to hide it, and this is not a quality widely admired. Turning in his smuggling associates was a gamble to avoid being hung or transported to the Colonies. Convincing French Viscounts to get themselves thrashed at The Farm ensured publicity before his book was published. He has remarkable fortune, I admit…"

"Fortune?"

Benjamin gave a most unbecoming sneer and said, "Yes, Hugh, fortune, not sorcery. And should rumours of his *amour* get about, not even a sorcerer could… Oh would the bastard had been transported six years ago with all his smuggling confederates!" Seeing Hugh's anger, he reached forward and shook him. "And had I been more a victim of my own passions, as he is, had I succeeded less in conquering them, would you still belong to me?"

"I can't know that."

"And I say boldly now: if you are ever ill-used, or even fancy yourself ill-used, have a change of heart, or merely seek comfort, I shall require nothing more than a line from you. I will come directly, we shall be together, whatever I must do to achieve it!"

"I will not hear——"

"But you *have* heard me now. I will accept but a hundredth part of what I had just a few months ago, that tenderness that I, a goddamned blundering fool, dismissed!" His voice cracked and Hugh was sickened to see tears standing in his eyes. "I would accept one night a year, just one, then allow you return to his house all the others!" Hugh rose to depart. "Do not leave. Pray do not go. I do not expect you to oblige me now. Or anytime soon."

They could do nothing but regard one another for some time. At last Hugh said, "I know how I must appear to you; I have said things today perhaps just as crazy as what you are offering. But even when I disagree, I know whatever you tell me you believe to be in my interest. Thank you. For all you have ever done for me. For letting me recover in your house..."

"I *need* to do those things for you, I wish to. It is what I take most pride in. And you *shall* retain the apartment on Charlotte Street, Hugh. For as long as you wish."

"You have every right to——"

"My right as the owner is to decide. I will not visit you there, of course... but neither will I let it to anyone else. Promise me, at least, you will drop in occasionally. Bed down whenever you have a need to be in London. There will be times, no doubt many times."

Hugh nodded. "Thank you, Ben. You do mean so much t——"

Holding a hand up to prevent any more talk, and remaining a few paces distant Benjamin said, "Just let me know you again slowly. That is all I ask. Slowly, as we did before."

Working up improvements to The Farm was the natural consequence of visiting the continually improving Sallow House. At first, Hugh's coal sketchings of the grounds and interiors were mere renderings of a general impression wished for each room: brightness, solitude, comfort. By the morning of Brent's return from London, he was attempting architectural accuracy, specifying the changes he believed must first be made to achieve the desired effects. The garden, as he continued to repair his relationship with Benjamin, he hoped would serve as their common project. And he hoped one day, as improvements were made, they might all somehow meet amicably.

When Brent stepped across the flagstones of the vestibule, he was carrying an opened letter from Frederick Entwistle.

"You read it?" said Hugh, looking at the broken seal.

"It was addressed to me."

Brent,

Much has changed. You wonder I should write to you, whom I must despise more than anyone for what you are doing to my son. Who knows, but it was Hugh seduced you to his way, I find I do not much know him. Still I have not disowned him, for my business interest, the work of nearly twenty-two years, are, shall we say, entrenched. What is more, there remains an affection for him. (Hugh, I know you are reading this over his shoulder — you will be pleased by this. That business back home with James Bramble I see as deception of no little skill. My policy is to retain one of your talents on my side, whenever possible. That is what I say to you.)

You must think it the height of comedy, Brent, to know of my hopes of attaching you to my daughter, who, nevertheless, will go quickly. Respect my ambition, at least. A man never receives what he will not ask for. So, what signifies you have, in her stead, my son, who is my first investment and upon whom so much relied and continues to rely. I ask fifteen thousand for him. This will, among other things, fund the dowry of the sister he used so ill. Is this the betrayal of all a father, and man of honour, should be? Indeed no, for he has done worse. I trust you are not fool enough to suppose approval of your union by this request, for though my disgust must be balanced against sound business prac-tice, yet I was given no choice in the matter, and so cannot bestow, or deny, consent.

But I am remiss if I do not advise caution, a word which seems never to have entered your vocabulary. Without it neither of you will be long for this world.

Sir Frederick Entwistle, Bart.
Brunswick Square

"Do not pay."

"Don't pay?" said Brent. "What did I do this morning before departing London? The draft on my account has been made and is gladly given. You are to be made honest and provide for your sister. We are known first by our actions, and this payment is not only made, it is received. Your father speaks of disgust and golden valour in business. But his is tinsel of gold. He glints in the sun upon one thing, then is blown away to glint just as brightly upon the next."

Seeing any further protest would be fruitless Hugh leant back, set his feet upon the table, and stuck his hands behind his head. "I am well bought at fifteen, I think. Though I shall be disowned I do not fret. I take as recompense The Farm, which I was told would be my domain to make a suitable home for you. It is, of course, mine now, to do with as I please."

Brent waved a hand then saw Hugh was quite serious.

"I shall be disowned, Richard. Once my younger siblings are married and settled. Ned will take Deerhurst Hall... it may even go to Duncan Sallow. Whatever, it shall not be mine. I ask at least full rein of The Farm. It's only fair."

This lip twitching, Brent nodded. "I suppose."

"As a man of honour? The Farm is mine?"

Brent grinned malevolently. "Sure as I purchased you, The Farm will be yours to do with as you like."

"Very well. After supper I shall lead you around the grounds on a tour of my grand ambitions."

"No," said Brent, crossing the room. "After supper we go to bed. I wish to discover what fifteen thousand pounds buys on today's market, where pleasure is dear. I'll warrant the sum affords, of that commodity, a man's due portion."

CHAPTER 13

25th March 1771 The Public Inquirer no. 387

The **Startling** Account of a **Dastardly Proposition,** then **Attack Upon** an **Innocent Youth!** – with an appearance by **Richard of Runswick**

by **Marius**

Readers: image to yourself an Overflowing courtroom, Richard Brent in attendance, and the feeling of a new Play, perhaps by Mr Foote, about to be performed!

Magistrate: "Plaintiff bringing charges of attempted sodomy, step to the bench and present your evidence."

Plaintiff: "Stephen Chandler Your Honour, against Jasper Sharp Esq. the defendant."

Noise and tittering from the gallery. In appearance, Mr Chandler is that species particularly prone to ridicule. He is a slight youth, with a slouch, a feathery voice, and a bandy leg.

Magistrate: "It is my understanding this attack came on the heels of another incident, which is said to inform the nature of this case."

Plaintiff: "Yes Sir, Your Honour."

Magistrate: "Bring forward this supporting witness to lay the groundwork, if you wish."

Plaintiff: "Thank you, Your Honour."

Witness 1 steps forward, a tall, fair man, of about twenty-one, with a swift blue eye and something of dignity in his person though, it must be admitted, in a suit rather the worse for wear.

Witness 1: "Mr E Your Honour, to testify on behalf of Stephen Chandler."

Magistrate: "Who is the accused in relation to yourself, and how does your experience relate to his case?"

Witness 1: "Albeit in episodes, the accused served seven years as *valet de chambre* in my father's house. After his third, and final, break in employment, which was this May, I was summoned with an invitation to his home, a request that I, in my naiveite, thought reasonable to accept."

Magistrate: "Have you this invitation to present to the Court?"

Witness 1: "Yes Your Honour, and my apologies to yourself, and to the gallery, for the content:

'Loveliest Hugh,

Thy fond admirer, Monsieur Sharp, bids thee to his lodgings to Oblige himself in a Secret Pleasure he will teach to thee, as enjoyed by the Ancients. You are returned from the Continent a Fine Young Gentleman. But knowing how you were always fond of wagering and hearing how Voluptuous have been these Indulgences, both at home and abroad, a Pecuniary Enticement *(Golden Guineas)* is, I believe, welltimed. Released now from the watchful eye of your father, and having observed you each year progress toward Luscious Manhood, I have bespoken for you a School Uniform in Blue. In it you shall be in the Style of a Young Scholar, and what you used to wear at the Age of Twelve, though made to your current dimensions, for our amusement. That I may Increase my Offering, from Two Golden Guineas to Four, I may invite other Fine Gentlemen of my acquaintance, all Merry as the day is long, who I daresay will be happy to share the expense.

Call tomorrow at Eleven precisely: Costume, Libation, and Rare Play await. I shall expect thee Promptly upon the hour!

With *Anxious* Affection, to be your most *Intimate* J Sharp Esq.'"

Defendant: "Lies lies, Defamer and Blasphemer! Yer Honour I protest!"

This is the first we hear from the defendant Jasper Sharp, tall, wiry and, to this observer, a trinity of rage, fear, and indignation.

Magistrate: "Order before the Magistrate, you will have

439

your time to speak. Mr E, have you any witnesses to this proposition?"

Witness 1: "About thirty-five, five of whom are present in the gallery, should they be required."

Magistrate: "And why would you agree to meet this man with such a dubious enticement?"

Witness 1: "What he said about my gambling was entirely correct, Your Honour. I needed ready cash. I continue to be in a bad way, as you can see by my modest vestments. But I was not so stupid as to proceed to his lodgings, as he asked, without better understanding what he meant. I insisted upon coffee at Star's to question him further as to his intentions. Owing to this he met me in quite a foul humour. He was upset, very nearly deranged, that I would not begin upon liquor forthwith, and come to see this costume he had commissioned for me."

Magistrate: "And had you really no idea what his intention might be?"

Witness 1: "I must have done, were he not so long a member of the household. But I am, I am told, an amusing companion, and could always make him laugh. I believed a bit of Costume and Libation would inspire great gaiety before his friends, and it is well known he is no great success entertaining anyone himself. The money would be payment for the service, or perhaps just a loan I might repay. But then at Star's he said something quite impertinent and scandalous to me, and I jumped up from the table. My friend Richard Brent, thank the Lord, happened to be there.

He saw my confusion as Mr Sharp began, with great impatience, to lure me back. Richard came over, perused the letter, understood entirely, and with great decorum and tact put a stop to the Mischief. As it is my honour to know this noble Gentleman, celebrated author, undefeated boxer, and Hero in service to the Crown, I assign him full credit for saving me, and for subduing the good patrons of that place who were out for blood on my account."

Magistrate: "Is that all, Mr E?"

Witness 1: "Yes, Your Honour."

Esteemed Readers, at his cue to re-approach the bench, Mr Chandler limped forward to much laughter from the gallery. And yet… at the thought of this whisper-thin David persecuted by that Goliath of a defendant, some sighs of sympathy were heard. Chandler presented himself to the room, bowed, then turned to face the court.

Magistrate: "Mr Chandler, is it your testimony Mr E tells the truth?"

Plaintiff: "I can only take his word, as you must do yourself, that he does not fabricate the story. And indeed, could not, as there were so many witnesses upon that occasion."

At his lilting, gossamer voice, there were more sustained guffaws at this effeminate Character, at which Mr Chandler straightened, or, straight as he could, Poor Rickety Soul, and looked about like a newly hatched sparrow.

Magistrate: "Let us hear your own account, Mr Chandler."

Plaintiff: "Yes, Your Honour, but where to begin? At
the fog of my intoxication that night? Or the Fair
Actress I pursued who cut me so cruelly? Or the very
Weaknesses which, from birth, have been my Bain? For
I am known as a Very Fine Fellow. Indeed, so fine I am
no less than three times a week taken for one of the
fair sex."

Some laughter, Readers, but perhaps less than before.

Plaintiff: "Aye, I can laugh with you, fellow citizens,
even as I relate what was said to me that night. For you
see I was making my greatest attempt yet to impress
my young lady. For the occasion I had dressed as a
dashing military hero, a Bold and Manish Gallant. I
pled hard, for the hundredth time, for my Angel's Kiss,
a lovely actress from Drury Lane. But, to my pleas, she
laughed and declared I must have worn her petticoats
better than she did, and unless I sought to employ
them myself, had no occasion ever to take them off in
my presence."

*The laughter at this, of which there was much, was of a rather different
cast, and a cry of 'cruel whore!', was heard, denoting, presumably, the
actress. The Magistrate insisted Chandler refrain from bawdy allusions
that had no impact upon the proceedings.*

Plaintiff: "I apologise Your Honour. But my Lament,
Prologue to the History of that unfortunate night,
informs the motivation for my drunkenness. For, nearly
penniless, I was obliged to gin of the coarsest quality,
for I had for months spent my every farthing paying
the debts of my fair lady." *Boos and moans, cries of 'buck
up poor sod', and 'there's a woman for ye!' brought him to stand
a bit taller, turn and bow.* "Who says the English are but a

cruel people enthralled to blood sport? How my heart swells within my breast…"

Magistrate: "You are dismissed, Mr Chandler, if you cannot proceed to your testimony against the defendant."

Quickly, then, Readers, his voice trembling: "And so, stupefied with liquor, in an attempt to outrun my distress I began walking the streets, and had just turned up a dark alley, when I was struck with such force I could not see what was up nor down, and with such malicious intent that half my clothes were torn from me! Your Honour I knew not what should become of me!"

Defendant: "This is a lie, as I live and breathe!"

Magistrate: "You are in contempt of court Mr Sharp and will have your opportunity to defend yourself shortly. Proceed, Mr Chandler."

Plaintiff: "Much as I would like to oblige Your Honour, Sir, I must here call up the constable who was so good as to hear my cries."

Magistrate: "The constable may step forward."

Witness 2: "Please Your Honour, on the night in question I was called to pull this wisp of a thing from under the tall, wiry man seated yonder, who claimed he was himself attacked and thrown to the ground. Upon observing their comparative sizes, this did not seem likely. This was observed along with vestments amiss or lacking entirely from Mr Chandler. I did at first, by his effeminate screams, suppose him to be a street nymph or the like. But soon understanding what was afoot I remanded Mr Sharp into custody."

Magistrate: "Is it not likely the defendant also took the plaintiff to be a young lady?"

Witness 2: "As already stated, and I can confirm, Mr Chandler had in his possession only manly-cut vestments: a cocked hat, military frockcoat, and a sword, though it were only an illusion to look like one. Nothing in it of woman's attire, what was left of it after the attack. It appeared the work of a maniac beast to strip anyone so entirely, and the intent must have been apparent to anyone."

Magistrate: "The entire story is quite strange yet coming on the heels of this other incident in Star's Coffeeshop, it seems unlikely to have been anything else. Are the two accusers known to one another?"

Witness 2: "By all accounts they are not."

Magistrate: "Is there any reason to believe this is a plot against Mr Sharp?"

Witness 2: "The first report was not, in fact, made by Mr E at all, but by Mr Brent, known to this gallery as Richard of Runswick, who wished only to have a record of it should another, bolder attempt be made upon Mr E."

Magistrate: "Does this end the testimony of the prosecution?"

Assured this was all, Mr Sharp was beckoned forward.

Defendant: "Yer Honour, it's only owing to my respect for yerself, and yer position, that I could restrain myself from protesting this gross mischaracterization of the facts."

Magistrate: "I do not recall this restraint, Mr Sharp."

Defendant: "Because it *was* restrained, Yer Honour! I admit I lost my composure once or twice, yet it was not a thousandth part what I had done had I the liberty to do it. Which of these bald-faced liars would you have me address first, Yer Honour?"

Magistrate: "Let us have the testimony regarding the night with Mr Chandler."

Defendant: "It has long been my habit to take my pipe and can at a neighbourhood establishment seven to nine each night like clockwork. You may ask the publican himself, who is here today on my behalf. I can only think that after a pint I was less the robust man than I appear. That womanly wretch what calls himself Mr Chandler came at me like a cannonball, clothes already in shreds, and flung me down till we was rolling in the mud and muck of the alley. Yer Honour, you must believe me, this was the case. For God's sake, I am a married man, and have no proclivity at all to that base and degenerate practice."

Magistrate: "What might have been the motivations of Mr Chandler, in hurtling himself at you and tearing his own clothes?"

Defendant: "To be a wretched, nasty Invert as they all

are, Yer Honour. You have but to look at him, and hear him, to know what he is!"

Magistrate: "The court sees what he is; indeed, he knows it himself. Yet I have known decent and respectable Gentleman, married as you and me, not unlike him to some degree. We cannot all be Richard of Runswick. But if you cannot suggest any motivation beyond mischief, no attempted theft or the like…"

Defendant: "Indeed, Yer Honour, there may have been. I daresay I did have a guinea in my pocket go missing, and a handkerchief."

Magistrate: "And was this made known to the constable?"

Defendant: "No, Yer Honour."

Magistrate: "Then the idea originates with me?"

Defendant: "Yes… no… well yes Yer Honour, but I had no occasion to tell the constable of it, for I knew this was all the Dark Villainy of that deplorable Pathic, Mr E, seated yonder!"

Magistrate: "Refrain from vulgarity when you speak to me, Mr Sharp. So, it is your claim that Mr E requested Mr Chandler attack you, in revenge for having shown the coffeehouse the letter you wrote?"

Defendant: "I never wrote that letter!"

Magistrate: "You never wrote the letter you yourself were demanding to have returned before witnesses?

The letter which has been deemed sufficiently like your own hand?"

Defendant: "Lies and trickery! I have no doubt that letter was written by the defendant himself, who can duplicate my hand having lived in the same house for years. I have another letter to present the Court, Yer Honour, a genuine letter, in his handwriting incontrovertibly, which opens to you a whole new prospect. Oh, the years of debauched Sin I was suffered to witness in his house! What his own father now seeks to conceal, only to have... rather before the fact... but then to suffer himself..."

Magistrate: "Mr Sharp, if you wish to address the incident in the coffeehouse, do so now, lest this testimony become too confused to allow. You may present your letter if it supports your version of the incident. How came Mr E to meet you that day, if it was not by your own request?"

Defendant: "Yer Honour he... I suppose he wished to see me after his return from France."

Magistrate: "And he had enjoyed a good relationship with you while you were in the service of his father?"

Defendant: "Indeed no, for I knew what he was, as I just said, for all his sneaking about and deceiving."

Magistrate: "Then why should he wish to see you upon his return?"

After a long moment, Illustrious Readers:

Defendant: "To get back from me that letter I hold, in which he confessed to all the debauchery of his Turkish Practice. And telling of the other youth he infected with it."

The magistrate, looking with some distaste at the defendant, extended his hand: "Let us have this letter… in wretched condition indeed. I see a date of September 1768."

Upon looking it over, his complexion deepening to scarlet, he presented it to Mr E, the first witness: "Is this your own composition?"

Witness 1: "Yes Sir. I wrote it more than two years ago on the date you see."

This letter, Delicate Readers, is said to be a most profane, salacious piece of trash. Marius was unable to secure a copy.

Magistrate: "I take it, Mr Sharp, this letter was being used to blackmail the writer, and this is why he came to see you?"

Defendant: "No Yer Honour, I would never have done that. However, I am at this time short on funds, and coming across this old letter in my possession, I thought…"

Then the testimony dried to nothing, Readers. It was quite strange!

Magistrate: "And you Mr E, have you an explanation why, at this late date, he might begin seeking to black-mail you with a letter more than two years old?"

Witness 1: "As he implies, Your Honour, he searched it

out from my belongings while I was on my Tour, and took it upon his departure from my father's house…"

Defendant: "I never said I stole it!"

With a jaunty smile, Readers, which caused a slight stir of mirth in the gallery, Witness 1 continued: "Then it fell innocently into his hands. I am, Your Honour, an aspiring writer, member of many writing groups and contributor to newspapers. I take my inspiration from those celebrated epistolary novels of Mr Richardson, and, I confess, that notorious novel of Mr John Cleland, *Fanny Hill.* Consequently, I wrote many letters on titillating subjects to see what I was capable of, thinking to compile them into a work. The one discovered by Mr Sharp is one of many, though perhaps the only one by which one might attempt to extort money. In it, like in *Fanny Hill,* I describe a scenario in which that particular practice is referenced."

Defendant: "You base liar, and will you deny the existence of James Bramble, the boy you seduced, is clearly the object of that letter?"

Witness 1: "I don't deny it was his name, he was my close friend at that time, just as I don't deny my sister's name was also used, whom I love dearly, as well as my own name. I have it on good authority, Your Honour, the best writing comes of taking on the role as does a player upon the stage and writing in that Character."

Defendant: "Yer Honour, you cannot believe such a shallow deception!"

Witness 1: "Had Your Honour better believe a self-confessed thief, blackmailer, and attempted rapist? This letter was handpicked from innumerable letters as what appealed most to *Mr Sharp*, for he told himself the author of that letter must be accepting of his offer of Frolic. I ask Your Honour to consider, if my letter was indeed intended for my old friend Bramble, why is it not in his possession? For, as you see, it was never sent. It remained with me, as did all the other writings which never saw the light of day. Until they were stolen from me."

Magistrate: "I have heard enough of this affair to render a judgment. There can be no doubt the evidence favours the Plaintiff, and the sordid letter, though lending support, only muddies the simple fact of an attack with intent to commit sodomy on Mr Chandler, took place as witnessed by a constable. Defendant is bound over for sentencing."

Afterwards the trio were escorted into an alehouse where pints were bought for all and congratulations bestowed. Scarcely able to believe the ordeal with Jasper was at an end, Hugh could not quite celebrate as he worked to steer the conversation away from Sharp: the reprehensible Pathic who would stand next week in the pillory. His complexion somewhat jaundiced, Brent appeared in a muted humour as Hugh at last succeeded in pushing another topic to the fore – the latest on the plight of the persecuted publishers.

"I believe," cried a reveller, "it should be Wilkes and Brent together, that is all we need to clean up the city. And I do mean *The City!*" He roared with laughter. "How do ya like that, for a joke? Haul your bones in from Chessington, Brent, and we shall elect you to something so you may sit beside Wilkes in Guildhall. Let all good men move into The City and to the Devil with the rest of the corrupt metropolis." And he laughed riotously and looked about for toasts.

The crowd waited for a response. However, Brent, having consumed two drinks in as many minutes, was maintaining the rather stiff face of a man impatient for libation to take effect. Another man seized him and begged the privilege of buying him a third. Brent accepted, then said to the noisy reveller, "Gape at me will ya – Wilkes and Guildhall: what do you speak of? Half the tale is left untold and nobody's laughin'."

"The case at City Court," said another in a pacifying tone, "Edward Twine Carpenter, the Printer's Devil, against Wheble the publisher."

"What of it?"

Hesitating, the pacifier continued, "Carpenter made a citizen's arrest and brought Wheble before Wilkes to claim his reward. Wilkes dismissed the case telling as how The City has from time out of mind operated under its own charter and laws, and the warrant from the speaker of the house had no power here."

"Was tha the amusin' part then?"

Both the pacifier and the reveller reddened.

Brent downed his third drink as Stephen Chandler lisped, "A more amusing example, I think, is that of a messenger making a citizen's arrest on a publisher named Miller. Miller was working *in tandem* with Wilkes and so remained outside his home in The City waiting to be arrested. When he was, a constable came forward, releasing Miller and arresting the messenger, charging him with assault on the person of Miller and false arrest. The messenger held up the official warrant and asked bystanders for assistance – but nobody arrived! There is a standing offer now for all publishers-at-large in The City – submit to being arrested so Wilkes can officially release them and make nincompoops of everybody in the House."

Brent's more civil reaction to the story of Miller inspired a muttered comment about Chandler and wonder that Brent should go around with such a prancing mammy-sick.

"Friend, what was tha?" said Brent, his eyes flashing.

"Who gives a bloody hell about Richard Brent? is what I say," said another, quite red in the face and stepping forward. "Not a barrel of laughs from what I can see and for five years nothing but him and his adventures in the papers. My own father stashed a bit of contraband in Penzance and never had his portrait in *The Gazette*. That is where it started with Brent – aye, and my father never betrayed his comrades for a pardon when it got hot on the high seas."

"Let me buy that man a drink," said Brent, with a grin, "Now, what else have ya to say about the pirate of the *London Herald*?"

This seemed a flicker of the tactic Brent had always employed to win people to his side, yet no charm graced the words. They rang hollow and he appeared unwilling to continue in the same vein.

"I'll say it, then," continued the red-faced man, seeing no resistance from Brent and sensing a place had opened for him, "I'll say it, if nobody else will: Miss Coates. I hear a boxing injury has left the boxer without the wherewithal to engage a young woman as she should be engaged, if you take my meaning. A rumour started by Somersby, no doubt, and I were at first loathe to believe that is why she absconded – yet you goin' about with these young men, one of which very nearly all woman… is it Sharp should be in the pillory next week, I wonder?"

The atmosphere in the alehouse turned so quickly many failed to comprehend it before the trouble started. The trio had arrived victorious revellers, yet in the stir aroused by these words, and Richard without his well-known charm, Hugh was pushed aside, and Chandler was lent a shove hard enough to send him to the floor. Brent needed no more provocation – he punched three men and had overturned a full table to get at a fourth before Hugh succeeded in dragging him out of the establishment. A hackney coach was summoned, but not before insults were hurled, primary at Chandler though with broader insinuations as to what the three intended to do with each other inside the coach. Hugh commanded the coachman to proceed wherever he wished until ordered otherwise, while Brent stared furiously at his trembling hands. Sukey looked between them as he worked to regain his breath, trying to understand how it had gone so wrong so quickly.

At last Hugh said, "Apologies for that. We never should have—"

"I've seen worse," said Sukey, dusting off his coat. "Give it not another thought."

Looking pointedly toward Brent Hugh continued, "And well done in court. I, for one, could not have asked more of you, and am grateful."

Brent dug in his pocket and handed Sukey five guineas.

"Leave off whoring in Moll's and get yourself onto the stage."

Going scarlet with joy, Sukey pocketed the money. "Yes… but now I must insist we return to Moll's to celebrate this victory with brandy and comfits and a bit of fiddle music. And should anything else strike your fancy, I shall consider it paid entirely in advance."

Brent laughed, as he only did when something was not to his taste, and said, "Indeed no. We are to be married and give up those delights."

Chandler narrowed his eyes: "The chapel is just upstairs. Marry, bed down for the night, and take me along if you've a mind."

"Not in that sense married. Married like anyone else, publishing banns in the newspaper and taking proper vows."

Hugh nodded at Chandler, who looked at them in perplexity.

"And pray, how can this be? You cannot be married in a

real sense. But really, Gentlemen, are you not a little happy to have won your case? Call me bold, call me saucy as a bechamel, but you both, lovely bucks though you are, look to have just swallowed sour lemons!"

"What comes of hollow victories, Sukey," said Brent.

"Hollow? Illustrious hero, playing a part in your victory today I shall remember as among the highest honours of my life! Divorcing your friend from rotten pullets such as black-mail! Mr Sharp indeed. Did I not break all his eggs with devastation and accuracy? Much as you do with all the big chaps you *touch* inside the boxing ring. I, however, am trained to deliver my blows in Brome, Gay, and Shakespeare, in that great ring of the Pathetic the Theatre!"

"Yes, and for God's sake," said Hugh, his voice rising as he turned toward Richard, "let us celebrate I am not myself going to prison. This has been my torment for two years. And you have all but won against Somersby for the property in York and North Carolina. And we have each other."

"Your father will hear of the manner in which we attacked Sharp; he will sneer at this betrayal of everything we are."

"So, we shall never rest, nor ever be content!" shouted Hugh. "It never ends with you! I shall lose my mind if I cannot savour the victories, without the cynicism. Have I not spared my father the torment of being blackmailed himself? Have I not served him well, even in banishment?"

After a prolonged silence Sukey sighed and said, "Seek no more to convince me of the marriage; I am convinced."

Though neither would address the other, each was betrayed into a chuckle at Chandler. As he stepped from the carriage in The Mint, he said, "The offer stands and may be redeemed whenever it suits."

Said Hugh, sliding across the seat, "I have had a change of heart, Sukey. May we come inside?"

The young man turned, looked at them both and nodded. "Yes certainly, now passions are aroused…"

To Brent's look of outrage Hugh jumped from the carriage, turned, and smiled. "Not for that I'm afraid. As I have been forbidden my apartment in London, I require a quiet, private room in which to write my account of the trial. I promised Flexney to drop it at the newspaper office before proceeding back to Chessington."

Back at The Farm they reconciled in bed, after which Hugh took Richard to his chest, and stroked his hair, and told him the things he liked to hear, the very things Hugh liked to say. After a long silence, Richard said, "Bloody Christ, I am tired."

"Let us sleep."

"No Hugh – I am tired."

And now he said it, it sounded in his voice, like a dying fire.

"You must learn to take a breath and be still," said Hugh. "It is only natural after so many years of turmoil – and wins, remember the wins…"

"Do you know why I wished so much to find a mate?"

"I think so."

"I don't know if you do. I had reached an impasse I could no longer consider crossing alone. There was nothing more for me. I know it is difficult to be an inmate in my home, Hugh. I am possessive, I fear I shall become more so. Now with you installed I have that tether, that anchor to allow me to strike out on new endeavours without feeling I shall go spinning off into the heavens. This is a new feeling… it is not freedom. I must call it liberty. The kind I knew you would bring me."

"But does liberty make you so very tired?"

"It does, for I am obliged now to pursue it. Liberty is a burden – a burden to oneself."

Brent was soon heavy in his arms and snoring, and Hugh

left to wonder what exactly he had meant, the conversation left somehow unfinished.

The following night Hugh was the first from bed and down the corridor towards the commotion. The flame of the candle he carried would not keep in the chill wind which swept across him as he advanced to the front of the house. John Sexton had left the main door ajar and was stalking through the weeds out front, returning to report three shapes on horseback galloping into the night. A large stone had entered the house through the drawing-room window and come to rest under an armchair in a wake of shattered glass. Hugh had no sooner taken in the scene, than he was struggling to contain Brent, who broke free and stormed outside in a hot rage. It was the work of much impassioned pleading to bring him back inside, lest someone be waiting in the dark. But such fears had soon passed. Nothing was to be seen or learned of the vandals who were now long departed.

With hands cupping the flames of fat candles they proceeded to the hefty rock. Hugh pulled from around it a layer of papers bound by coarse twine. It was an advance copy of the day's *Gazette*. Printed on the front page was a bizarre and misleading description of the Sharp trial, followed by caricatures of himself, Brent, and Stephen Chandler, joined in a circle, kicking up their heels in a lively dance, within a boxing ring. These were accurate depictions of their forms and faces, with fair assumptions as to those parts of their anatomies normally hidden from view. Beneath the drawing was a poem in the following rollicking stanzas:

The New Country Dance!

To all Gents, who've suffered Harm
Hark ye, Lads: Come to The Farm!
Be you betrayed, of late betrothed,
All shivering Youths will be well-clothed!

Escape the City, be Lithe, be Pretty
Take in Chessington, where its Rough and Gritty
A Pirate awaits, Cabins for all!
Disappointed in Love in a Marriage Hall!

What of Girls, you say, might not Young and Old
Proceed to The Farm, and into the Fold?
To be sure all Day, by the Oak Front Door
But Youths, through the Back, does Brent implore!

What better for Boys, these Farming Joys?
What better a Distance, conceals the Noise?
One's face to be pummelled by a Boxing hard
One's Backside treated to a thrusting Yard!

To this piece of impertinence Hugh said, his mouth going rapidly to chalk, "How do we take this? Do say we can laugh. Say this is what often happens, and you are grown used to it."

Brent held the page to read by candleflame, then took it about the room like a felled duck, laughing contemptuously, cursing Somersby. "I am grown used to fighting it, not used *to* it."

A violent trembling seized Hugh, quite sudden and unexpected. This was being in the public eye. This was not scribbled barbs in leaflets or titters at a masquerade. The circulation of the *Gazette* was many thousands.

"Everyone will see this. This is beyond humiliation. This might affect Ned's prospects in business, or the girl I am told he has begun courting. This could destroy Alice entirely."

"Somersby knows I will prevail in the lawsuit. Three years

and he shall be judged the loser. I offered to sell him back the land in Cornwall, but he would not shake hands with me. The bloody berk had but to agree it was a fight well fought, on both sides, and share a laugh – was a time I would have bought him a drink. Laughter, Hugh, might be the best, most brutal weapon in a man's arsenal – capable of diffusing tension, and restoring manhood, quicker, perhaps even better, than boxing."

"It was shown months ago those accusations against your father were baseless. Only with a very sloppy defence, and a very inept or corrupt court, could they succeed now. The whole affair was merely to torment you."

"Aye, and still he is angry to fail. He is a small man."

"He may be, but this could well destroy my family."

"Put your own pen to work, Hugh. Fight wit with wit. This piece in the *Gazette* is a good one."

"I cannot fight this! This is the kind of thing sticks to a person forever!"

Brent cast the newspaper aside and grabbed his coat. "Be wittier. That is all it takes to win," he said, then continued into the front to speak with John Sexton.

CHAPTER 14

Two hours elapsed in makeshift repairs to the drawing-room window. Fair employment for minds unable to decide on a counter blow against Somersby despite Hugh's having demanded of Brent every detail he knew of the man's life, every rumour, however old, ever spread about him. In a counterattack one hoped to discover some secret life, some rare debauchery, some skeleton in the closet. His Lordship, however, was by all accounts as dull as he was vicious and spiteful.

As dawn approached, the first rays of light showed flaws in the repair to the window. Together with the footman, Hugh left Brent to stew over a pot of coffee and stepped outside to mend it. A damp March chill joined with the yellow-grey light of morning to produce a deep uneasiness in him, a tightening in the gut, a constriction at his lungs. Then, as the sun broke the horizon, any thought of returning to bed, and to comfort, vanished. For the firelight of daybreak informed him the *Gazette* was circulating around London.

After securing a second tarp across the ruined window frame Hugh was descending the ladder when he heard a sound in the yard. Turning, he stared a long moment, unable, at first, to believe he had not returned to bed and was lost to dreams. American Indians – a tribe of four, falling out of a private coach which appeared to be lodged in a ditch in the distance. Hurrying over the exhausted earth, battling the weeds with tomahawks and what looked to be human scalps dangling from leather waistbelts. John Sexton gave a little cry of fright, but soon the shape of Julia Motley, for all her warpaint, became clearly distinguishable through her costume.

"What has happened!?" she panted, "have they come already?" crazed and on the warpath until she could be made to understand there had been no more than a rock through a window. Flinging herself into Hugh's arms, she may as well have struck him with her tomahawk – he was left speechless at the uncommon assault. News of an arson attack instigated by Somersby had arrived during a masquerade of much debauchery – rumour was hired men had been sent to burn The Farm to the ground.

After fifteen minutes, two Indians lay snoring in a tangle of limbs in the vestibule, Julia's own escort beside her on a sofa, senseless, in a cloud of cognac. Over a hastily produced pot of tea, she told them everything she had heard of the rumour then presented them with her own copy of that cursed edition of the *Gazette*. Glancing at Brent who, with little sleep, could hardly be made to care at the visitors, Hugh assured her again everyone was perfectly well and nothing but the window had suffered damage. "We shall hire men to repair the glass, and for protection if need be."

But despite the warpaint and feathers, Julia took on an air of grave apprehension. Their reputations, she assured them, were anything but safe, and reputations would be far more troublesome to repair than a broken window.

She turned to Brent. "The Three Graces, Richard. For a time. You must."

"I'll take a Soldier's Bottle of poison before I do it."

Julia nodded, as one does who has performed a duty from conscience without a hope of success. Then, with more earnestness, she took Hugh's hands.

"But for yourself, for your family, Hugh, you must. I shall organise it. Lord Allenby employed one, for a time, when the accusations became too hot. This story is set to explode; it is timed too well. Richard maintains public approval with charisma and force of character. But he did *not* charm in the alehouse after the Chandler trial. After that trial, of all his trials, he needed to retain public approval. It touched too closely upon a dangerous subject. You stopped in that alehouse to meet the public, but you offended John Bull, the single most important person in England. Richard sneered, refused to joke or jest, assaulted at least five of the patrons; one cannot have a bad performance. Public personas are elevated only so long as they amuse, and for the first time he appeared cold, arrogant, and profoundly unlikeable. The revellers in that tavern, there on his account, were shocked. Then they watched their idol push two young men, both supposedly suffering lost loves, one extremely effeminate, into a carriage and speed away. Those are the facts."

"Winning that trial signifies nothing?"

"Yes and no. Marius's account has sold well, but Somersby is telling anyone who will listen it cannot be believed as it was written by the very Mr E who was a witness in the trial. Not everyone believes this. Not everyone believes the rumour Stephen Chandler is here at The Farm in a ménage à trois. But people do know Hugh Entwistle is living with Richard Brent and there are many rumours about what is actually going on here."

Hugh looked at Brent, who had stirred from his lethargy and risen to his feet.

"The Three Graces, Richard," repeated Julia, "for Hugh, if not for yourself."

Advancing, Brent said, "Will ya betray me like that, Hugh?"

"Betray? I would never betray—"

"But are considering her proposal nonetheless." Stepping over Julia's companion, who had slid from the sofa to the Turkish rug, Brent descended to one knee. "Tell me why I should bear the insult. I saved thee; and paid thy father for thee; and own thee. That a my possession."

"There is no question, Brent, but I must. Do you think I wish to do it?"

With one hand Brent took the corner of Hugh's lapel, and with his other stroked his hair. "Put ya in the garret then, shall I? Till tha reconsider?"

"Richard!" cried Julia, "He is not a damsel in a tower!"

Hugh struggled to free himself, but Brent gripped him tighter and leaned in. "Tha have the look of a schoolboy who would have me get rough. Ya need me to subdue ya, lad."

Hugh wrested free and straightened his shirt. "Dalrymple, Julia, if she is available. Inquire for her first. I shall see her whenever she can admit me."

"Whistle…" said the other, but Hugh stuck a finger in his face.

"And you, Richard. I shall do something that has never been done for you. I shall turn the tables on his Lordship, I shall prove my love, and, above all, prove my wit. You will not lock me in a tower just yet."

And for once, Richard of Runswick appeared to back down. In Julia, Hugh observed a look approaching reverence for the man who could do it, and when she observed the boxer lower his head, she rose in a regal posture, straightened her feathered headdress, and said:

"Miss Dalrymple then, Sir? She is available, I believe."

"Thank you, Julia. For your concern, and your service. Richard wishes to thank you as well."

After a time, Brent turned toward them, and held out his palms.

"And so, make me accessory to the crime? Very well. Thank you Miss Motely, for your service."

"I have your approval to engage Clara Dalrymple?"

Brent glared at her a moment, then, running a hand through his hair said, "Yes, but for God's sake, do not make Hugh appear easy. Let your Three Graces have a smock race for him, at least. Let the Dalrymple horror win, at last, but let her feel some uncertainty. If ya have any pity for me at all, Julia, do that for me."

Arrangements were made for an interview with Miss Dalrymple at her residence in Prince's Court, an iron-gated square at the conjunction of Bird Cage Walk and St. James's Park. The women known as the Three Graces were united for no reason other than that all were beautiful, all had made uncommon achievements within the nobility, all ubiquitous on the fringes of accepted Society. The beautiful Miss Dalrymple was twenty-eight, insisting always she was four years younger, though this made her a girl of eleven when first the mistress of the Earl of Hardwick.

She received her visitors into a reception room in the style of a Botticelli painting, sky blue sofas and airy white drapes. The impression of peach marble was papered up to the ceiling, where wound about the cornices strings of pearls in bas-relief. As for the lady herself, Hugh observed all the attractions she had displayed eighteen months before on the arm of Lord Halifax, her swan's neck accentuated by an up-swept wig tinged with purple, the features of her face so symmetrical one could almost see the measurement lines of da Vinci's sketch-book ideal. But for a tendency to gossip, a habit said to have been tamed, she might have retained Halifax, or, indeed, her Earl. After her stunning attainment of Hardwick at fifteen, she had continued down the nobility, having been first passed to a Viscount, then to a series of Lords, and now potentially to a young man, though knighted, who would only be a Baronet.

But no one would suppose her losses with such a radiant smile and air of cultivated assurance.

"Gentlemen, you observe I keep a fine house, enjoy a situation of tasteful furnishings *à la mode*, and serve you tea on bone china. Yet you will discover, the door to my back parlour is locked, for the room is entirely empty. When I entertain, my china cupboard, too, is empty, for what you see of porcelainware is what I possess. I might obtain more however I choose for my indulgences items for display, and always neglect those places which might be shut from view."

"An admirable economy of living," said Hugh, "which bespeaks a knowledge of how best to employ your resources."

"I am glad you understand."

"And if I am happy enough to retain your company, when I require it, and furnish you a living, I suspect the cost of these services not to exceed what a lady of good economy would require."

Miss Dalrymple nodded, careful to avoid the countenance of his companion, whose gritted teeth could be heard above even the churnings of his sonorous stomach.

Hugh continued, "Perhaps we should ground a fine philosophy in the material world. What is meant by economy?"

"You may hazard your best estimate, Sir, for I know you will not come up short."

"£425 for a twelvemonth, not a ha'penny more," muttered Brent. "This house is two hundred, with servants and a stocked cupboard. Another two for vestments and entertainment. Twenty-five, various and sundry."

"£425 for all you see, Richard?"

"Yes, and I save you the trouble of countering with fourfifty, Miss Dalrymple, for the original offering was to be a flat four-hundred pounds."

"And you, Mr Entwistle, do you agree this offer is fair?"

"He may not," interrupted Brent, "but I am the one pays the tab, and four-twenty-five it shall be. I daresay you have done more for less."

Smiling pleasantly Miss Dalrymple said, "I daresay you are right. And so, you believe she is recompensed less, who is required to do less."

"We see eye to eye then. Very much obliged."

"But I do not see eye to eye. For whether your man wishes to enjoy, to its fullest, that which may be had, or whether he does not, has yet to be established. I assume nothing on that head, regardless his other proclivities. But whatever they are, £500 is the annual sum required. And I save *you* the trouble of countering, Sir, for it will not be a farthing less."

"He will see you only in company," said Brent, "never a day, and certainly never a night, here at your home with its locked, empty rooms. He, who is equipped to satisfy his lusts, does very well. So, your services are well-bought at four-twenty-five."

Taking up her teacup, Clara said, "There exists in finance, Sir, the idea of *foregone recompense*, and I wonder I must introduce such an elementary concept here. For it must, in some manner, have application to the bringing of tea at night from Denmark, or to other business in Runswick, where these estimates might do very well. I hang my shingle for an established set of services. That a purchaser neglects the sugar dish in a set of bone china, does not mean there is not another who would use it, and would be happy to pay for it. Whatever you think of me, I would not have attained my reputation if it was supposed I would, for one night, entertain any who is not my benefactor. I will not lose that reputation. I shall be faithful to Mr Entwistle, even as he is not faithful to me, else I could not ask even half five-hundred, which I *will* have, if we are to continue this interview a moment longer."

Hugh took the breath in the conversation to end this difficulty: "You will have the five-hundred, madam. Take this exchange as a test of your economic mind – you have passed the test. I do expect a faithful companion, and you have the added task to convince Society this is not a sham, and refrain from laughing, however much you might wish to."

Clara's brow furrowed. "If you believe the selling as solemn truth that which is absurd is in any way particular to you, Mr Entwistle, you are indeed a babe unborn."

Brent, too, looked askance at Hugh, and said, almost apologetically, "Aye, he is in some things. Very well, you do not come cheap – you shall have five hundred. But neither am I bought cheap, and so you must prove your worth to me. You know what Julia Motley can do to your reputation if you betray us. And what I shall do." Looking slightly uncomfortable, Clara nodded for Brent to continue. "But I respect a woman who makes shift in this world, and values herself. I had no great opinion of you when we arrived; what I offered was too low. However, I see you know what it is to love, as I love this one."

"Love?"

"One does not learn economy by overindulgence. If one is not overindulged, one is capable of valuing. And the ability to value, must be the ability to love."

Miss Dalrymple glared at him. "A woman has the ability to do many things yet might never do them. And for five hundred, I am promising not potential, but that which I am long proved to do."

Brent gave her a look which said this remained to be seen, but her manner softened considerably now financial matters had been settled. She waited for him to continue.

"How generally known in the *beau monde* are Whistle and Brent?"

"Whistle?" Letting a smile play over her lips, which appeared whetted for more intimate details, she trilled, "Charming indeed. Understand first there are some saying it is a ménage à trois; the silliest gossips always believe the wildest claim. Of those in the know, you are as well-known as the Marquess of Argyll and William Dempsey."

"What do you know of our history?"

"I had it originally that your man poisoned himself in the Wimbledon home of his brother-in-law, in despair at having such an illustrious rival as England's most renowned boxer. Then you, Richard, with a taste for such morsels, crept into his window at Sallow House, stole him away, and installed him in Chessington as a plaything. Do not look like that Gentlemen – you wished to know what has been said. That was the account first told me and it has been debunked."

"Yes of course," said Brent, with a sparkling grimace.

"What is generally known now," continued Dalrymple, "and I speak of course only of the *cream* of Society, is this: after Miss Coates eloped, Mr Entwistle, distraught at losing his first love, destitute, and possibly disowned for having failed to bring the dowry to his ruthless father, one night in a drunken stupor threw himself upon the mercy of his formal rival, who many have claimed called him out not long before the departure of the young lady. Mr Entwistle asked Richard Brent to keep their appointment, to run him through with cold steel, for he wished very much to die. But Good Richard, taking pity on the boy, did not prosecute the duel. Instead, he took him into The Farm, where they learned to comfort each other in their mutual loss. And so... continue to comfort each other."

Covering his face Hugh sank back on the sofa. Brent exclaimed: "How pleasant to know the invention of Swift did not die with him! See it is known tomorrow, Clara, that upon the same good authority it was in fact three hundred little people dragged Mr Entwistle into the house of their King. I want this known as fact by tomorrow evening – this is my first challenge to a woman of your skills."

"And what, in my version of your history, is to be so much disdained?"

"That is another way of asking how we came together, Clara, which we do not confide."

The lady still had too much of the gossip in her to like this very much, and said, "Understand, my considerable abilities are best employed when I am made privy to the facts. Once it is established I am with your friend, most of the tattle will go away, and Hugh may even remain at The Farm without much trouble, though a place in town closer to myself would be best. I suppose it is useless to ask what the true circumstance with your father's valet was, Hugh?"

"Is it."

"Very well. I trust with time I will be allowed more of your confidences. Rest assured the rumours of a romance between myself and Mr Entwistle shall begin tonight – I have whist at Lady MacDonald's at eight. Then on Wednesday, the Haymarket ball. That is where I suggest we make our first appearance together."

Hugh agreed. However, he had rather more planned than quelling the rumours about them.

The day of the visit to Prince's Court, adjacent to notices for *Pectoral Balsam of Honey Flu Remedy*, and a *Gentleman Practitioner of Physick and Surgery, with a discreet office in Black-Fryars*, the following announcement appeared in the *Gazette*:

At THE FARM, in Stoney-Lane, Chessington, Messrs HUGH ENTWISTLE Esq. and RICHARD BRENT (the famed boxer) PUBLISH, for the Public Digestion, the Announcement of their own BANNS, Academy of Improvement. This first of three Announcements, Records for the Public Register that PARTNERSHIP undertaken to commence BUSINESS, at the premises where continues Instruction and Demonstration of the Sweet Science of Bruising, though whose purpose shall not, in a like manner, be defined, nor expanded the membership, which, from this time and henceforward, shall be limited to TWO.

The paper lay open on the dining table until it was discovered. Hugh was reviewing an architect's renderings of his improvement to the library, when Kilmister's scream announced the discovery.

Brent left the glazier at the front window, and found Jerry attempting to embrace his master, holding the paper before his eyes with one hand and fanning himself with the other. Brent took the paper from him, read the announcement through, read it through again. Then he came forward and seized Hugh's face in one large, coarse hand.

"Do you approve?" said Hugh.

Brent threw the paper aside and walked a grand circle like a Spanish bullfighter, nearly colliding with a Chippendale sideboard just delivered. "This is elegant, Hugh." He gripped his hair, which strained at the roots. "More than elegant. It is fine." Coming forward he grabbed Hugh by the shoulders. "The banns of marriage! You did it just when it will be noticed and understood. To be published three Sundays consecutively?"

"Yes."

"Then I am a happy man. Vastly happy. It is not just a strike against Somersby, it is *the* strike – it will be seen, depend upon that. One may always strike at oneself, in the absence of a better target. It is done now. And now we have done it," Brent paused and glanced with some uncertainty at Hugh before continuing, "now we have done it we shall have done with London. The judgment in the Jacobite trial is due within the month, I shall have done with him and we shall have done with that city. We may leave that ridiculous world behind, for we have won…"

Then Hugh was swept into his arms, forbidden the world

outside, and taken sixteen hours into bed talking, laughing, dozing, eating, reading, drinking, sleeping and otherwise.

Perhaps it was elegant. Perhaps fine. Upon making his appearance with Miss Dalrymple at the Haymarket ball, Hugh observed the unusual number of eyes upon them. Clara urged them to circulate according to her direction, tarrying no place for long, and midway into this sparkling evening nobody had a thing to say save for her new appendage.

For *Hugh Entwistle was the young man ridiculed in that monstrously amusing caricature in the* Gazette. *And Mrs Simperingworth is saying there has been rather an odd announcement!* For only the well-informed Mrs Simperingworth had actually seen the advertisement on page four, for this was a room of committed front-page readers. As the *Gazette* was the favoured vehicle of Lord Somersby, most supposed it must be his doing. *But, if it is his, it is quite strange. She says there is subtlety to it. And its humble position beneath an advertisement for flu remedy rather beneath his Lordship's dignity.* Three couples left the assembly early to locate a copy of the paper.

His gleaming buckled shoes in fourth position, Hugh extended his arm; Clara drew aside the hem of her cream brocade gown in a curtsy. They touched hands in a minuet, he turned her in a lively gavotte, then, just as curiosity tipped above the brim sending the boldest across the ballroom to corner them, they stepped into the card room, out a side entrance, and absconded into the night.

Next day, swept into her reception room on the tide of rising scandal, Hugh sat beside Clara as she displayed the invitations flowing into Prince's Court. He selected the two best names and Clara wrote their acceptance.

The following exchange was typical of those first two occasions:

"And where is Richard this evening?"

Laughing, Hugh said to the stranger, "Thank you, Sir, I was in danger of thinking myself of too much consequence. That my claim to fame is my friend, I will readily own. But I do not know where he is. You may ask 'where are they' of some other of my friends, who are here tonight to answer for themselves."

"Sir, I ask after your business partner, whom you also live with, for I am curious about this new establishment advertised in the *Gazette*. What, pray, is Banns Academy? Nobody seems to agree. I hear it is nothing. Then I hear it is something, but it cannot be named."

"Banns Academy is our common endeavour."

"But to what end?"

"Of late, our personal and business affairs have become sufficiently intermingled as to warrant a partnership. The notice in the *Gazette* is to inform those who wish to know that the thing exists."

"But Sir, this does not help. What is to be taught at the Academy?"

"The lessons of life! Dr Johnson says: 'An Academy is an assembly of men, for the promotion of some art or endeavour'. Life is, you will not deny, the greatest endeavour there is, and requires no little art to prosecute it."

"But this new Academy is limited to two members, which it already has. Do you not seek to bring in new members?"

"No, we do not."

"Then I ask again: to what end this announcement?"

"To what end a death notice, lists of the bankrupt who cannot pay their debtors, or the *bons mots* of Lady Northumberland? To inform, declare, or, for those who desire such things, to divert."

And so, the man, still rather perplexed, was sent away well diverted.

Society was soon divided between those who believed his explanation and those who smirked in understanding – every-

one, however, understood there was a very fine line. Thereafter Hugh was taken into only those homes of note daring
enough to invite him. Those who did not admire his joke and
bravery beyond anything that season, refused to speak to him.
He was cut, doors were closed, and many left any assembly
into which he was admitted. But it was thought rather poor
sportsmanship to cut anyone willing to walk this tightrope, to
attack so audaciously Lord Somersby, though the weapon was
a thing they despised. For the production of wit, the most
splendid of all commodities in Society, must ever be
promoted. And one must be understood to comprehend it.

This led to a short-lived parlour game, played no longer
than May 1771, known as Brentwistle. A game of Brentwistle
was played after dinner over port and sweet wine, whenever
guests wished something other than charades or cards. With
Clara on his arm, patting his hand affectionately, and occasionally caressing his leg, Hugh was put through a series of
questions about who the boxer was to him and what, really,
was meant by the announcement in the *Gazette*. Dinner guests
were praised for their inventiveness in attempting to trip him
up. Yet Hugh was, on every occasion, able to explain it to the
satisfaction of both the innocents who believed him, and those
who believed not a word but admired his craft.

And so, it was asked, 'Who is Mr Entwistle, really? Beyond
his friendship with Brent?' With such attention, it seemed
likely he was more than a caricature with in the papers with
large blue eyes. To which at last he answered, "A brother," for
within the tide of invitations coming into Prince's Court a
note from his sister Alice had been plucked from the foam.

Brother,

> *You are a scandal. Everybody wishes to see you. My father hopes
> to benefit by it but will never stoop to asking you. Now I am used*

so ill by R Brent, will you see I am admitted with you into a fine assembly, as a condition of your presence there?

Yours ever,

Alice Entwistle

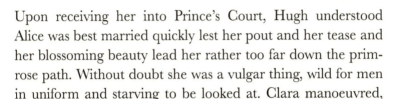

Upon receiving her into Prince's Court, Hugh understood Alice was best married quickly lest her pout and her tease and her blossoming beauty lead her rather too far down the primrose path. Without doubt she was a vulgar thing, wild for men in uniform and starving to be looked at. Clara manoeuvred, and that night a reply was received: Why yes. One spot could be opened to admit the sister of the curiosity.

Alice was introduced to Edmund Barnewall, son of the Earl of Limerick, who quickly fell, not only for her sweet figure, but for the spirit with which she defended her brother. She *did not care how foul the attacks of Lord Somersby!* she cried to a room of superiors both in age and station. She *had never seen a lovelier bum than her brother's in the* Gazette *caricature!* She stepped over a Baron of good fortune when Barnewall vowed: if she did not cease receiving addresses from the Baron, he would fight a duel to win her away. In just two weeks, though with horrified resistance from his family in Ireland, Alice was engaged to this man of an ancient estate, and fifty-thousand pounds. Sir Frederick was said to be uncommonly pleased at the connection, and the acceptance, by the love-struck suitor, of only seven thousand pounds for the hand of his pixie.

Lady Newcastle, at last, did the unthinkable. She invited Hugh and Clara to an assembly to be attended by Lord Somersby and his wife. At the mention of Entwistle and Dalrymple, many guests declined to come. Many more, however, horrified at the idea of missing a spectacle, begged an invitation.

Lord Somersby's very late arrival that evening was expected. As the attendees awaited his entrance, a Mr Dickinson, vehement supporter of the Drury Lane Ladies, a group formed to banish vice from the metropolis, sought to employ this delay and become himself what was talked of next day in the newspapers.

Said Mr Dickinson once every eye in the room was upon him: "Sir, I fail to see the hullabaloo about you. I own it honestly."

"I am happy to hear it," said Hugh. "Honesty must ever be our aim."

"There is no doubt, but you are announcing with these advertisements your intention to marry another man. And regardless your admiration of Brent, he is a man!"

"I seek by those notices, and, I hope, by all my actions, to defend my honour."

"Your honour? What honour is left a man who wishes to marry one of his own sex!?"

"Sir, I was accused publicly, with a bawdy poem and a caricature of my backside, of going off to live in sin and frolic with two other men. That was a lie, and so I will defend myself. You must allow a man fight on the same ground as a charge is made. If sexual orgy is to be the charge, I must announce, at least, my belief in committed marital union."

"You are sneaking, Mr Entwistle, and being slippery. I cannot oppose the right to defend oneself upon the same ground as a charge is made."

"Then I am sorry for it, if you feel the need to."

"Listen to me. Men are to be married to women, that is that."

"May a solitary man find an unattached woman, go about with her, and enjoy her company?"

"Certainly, he may, and so he should."

"Then I fail to understand you. Who is my friend Clara Dalrymple, if not the image of what you describe?"

"That is not what I am saying, and you know it."

"You wish to see me on the arm of a woman, and not a man."

"Yes."

"That is what you are seeing."

"Sir, I am going to say something I believe others do not dare, and I mean no actual offense to the woman. She is generally understood to be a courtesan and I daresay will admit as much. And so, your going about with her is merely a front."

"Did you say the same to the Earl of Hardwick or Lord Halifax? I can see your opinion of these men is put in the *Public Inquirer* tomorrow. You do wish to be in the papers tomorrow, after this exchange with me?"

Clara, who had been mingling at a demure distance, found this an opportune time to re-join her suitor. She slipped her arm about Hugh's waist, and whispered something into his ear. Then she smiled at Mr Dickinson and waited for him to continue.

Growing red in the face Dickinson said, "I do not, never, ever, criticise the Earl of Hardwick or his Lordship. I speak of *you* Sir. And you, young lady, your presence will not discourage me."

But her presence did appear to discourage him; he fell quite silent.

"You are shy, Sir," she said. "You wish to know what happens behind closed doors."

"No, I… that is rude and impertinent."

"Here is what I can tell you. I am with Mr Entwistle because he is a Gentleman. In every sense. I come to the relationship with a set of expectations. He fulfils those expectations…" she said with eyes glowing, "*Every one.* In my time I have entertained a boy of eighteen, and a mature man of seventy-two. I am now no more, no less, than I was with them, and all the others in between."

They heard no more from Mr Dickinson that evening and had to wait only twenty minutes more for the guest of honour, who threw his hat and coat at the butler and strode forward, his wife coming quickly at the train of his long frockcoat. In appearance, Somersby was something of a bulldog. One might have supposed those caricatures of his wife being the same to have been poetic license, but she was, in fact, something of a sister canine. From the leash allowed her she growled at Hugh, with eyes as well as eyeteeth, viciously.

"A pleasure," said Hugh, with an incline of the head. "The name is Entwistle. This is Clara Dalrymple."

"I know who you are," said his Lordship, "and Miss Dalrymple. One knows of many sorts, though is not usually obliged to mix with them."

"Obliged?" said Hugh. "Certainly, one of my station is obliged to meet with whoever will see me. But are you, Sir, obliged to debase yourself, if it is a debasement, if you do not wish it?"

"It is a debasement, but I have an end. I am told every waking moment, by covert sneers and sly looks, and even boldly to my face, that I cannot confront the one who makes a mockery of me and the morality I represent. Your silly articles as Marius were beneath my notice as a Gentleman…"

"Not all, Sir, you forget—"

"But now, in your endless attempts to defend your boxer, you have somehow made me a laughingstock by confessing to your own degeneracy. Well, I face you now, as everyone here sees, and wish to ask you something."

"What is that?"

"I ask what we are come to as a Society, when a Catamite, on the arm of a Whore, are taken for good company and celebrated."

"Many women are called whore by men who cannot

attain them," said Hugh, patting Clara's arm. Then again to
his Lordship: "Many men are despised for their nature, and
what they do behind closed doors."

"You fuck Richard of Runswick behind closed doors, or
he fucks you – no doubt it is both."

"Is that a question?"

"Do you admit it, Sir?"

"I do not argue with you."

"Do you admit it, Sir?"

"I do not need to."

"You cannot answer me because you are ashamed of
yourself. And so you should be. You and Brent should be hung
out an hour in the pillory, and pelted with mud and shit and
offal, like your brother vermin. Then strung up at Tyburn."

"I do not answer as you wish," said Hugh, "because I will
not destroy the good feelings of the other guests."

"And what does that mean?"

"It means I cannot win either way with you. I could say I
am not involved with Brent. You would not believe me, then
you would make an even bigger ass of yourself."

"And what if you admit it, buck?"

"Then it would be at the expense of the other guests. Not
because they must watch you gloat and bray; I understand you
do that at every assembly. The good people who have suffered
my company these four weeks play a game so they can meet
their own gaze in the mirror. The game keeps from one's
conscience the throwing into the street of a good and ethical
man. The truly moral, Somersby, wish to be lied to – and lied
to exceedingly well. Why? Because a good liar bestows permission to believe whatever one's heart says is correct, despite all
evidence to the contrary. That is the Society in which we live,
the Society you ride in, on a white horse, to defend. I look out
for myself, first and foremost. It is elegant, Sir, that by doing
so, I look out for so many others."

Hugh saw what would happen; his decision was not to

react. The fist wore a solitaire of a particularly large, finely set stone, which must have been that extra inducement to dislodge his left, front incisor, which cracked, flew down his throat then was coughed out in a spray of blood. Hugh crashed into a table of glass tumblers, rolled over a tragic loss of punch, Rhenish and sugar, but was on his feet again before Lord Somersby was entirely subdued. His Lordship made another swing, and missed, his wife contributed a few kicks to his shins then, secured by four of the other guests, both were hauled outside without a word more.

That his jaw was broken Hugh understood when he could not speak, began to swell, and grew faint. He sank back into a chair and Clara, kneeling at his side, took his hand.

He next opened his eyes in Prince's Court. He saw not only Clara, but Anne, Alice, Lady Highborough, and Ned, who came forward, poked Hugh's swollen cheek and said, "Pity. You were just getting tolerable to look at." Whatever rejoinder Hugh thought to make was lost in gauze and swelling, and his great surprise at seeing him. "They tell me Brent calls you Whistle. In Latin that's *nomen est omen*. Name is an omen. Your attendants say you are whistling all night through that gauze."

Lady Highborough shouted, "Ned, can you be so heartless!"

"He's laughing!" said Ned. "And I was only joking."

Brent, too, had been told what had passed. While Hugh slept, he had called in to see him for five minutes. After receiving the surgeon's assurance the jaw would likely set on its own, and the tooth could be replaced, he departed and was gone the remainder of the day.

Alice took it upon herself to read to Hugh from the newspaper, including the sole account of the exchange with Somersby. In it was described a minor confrontation at Lady Newcastle's between his Lordship and one of the boxer's *inti-*

mates, Hugh Entwistle, who had suffered a punch to the face which resulted in his Lordship's delivery to Bow Street. As nobody came forward to press charges he had been released next day. The rather dry retelling stated that both parties had declined an interview but ended in the hopeful supposition that there likely would be more in the continuing saga.

The hastiness of the account was also owing to a story which had overtaken nearly every paper in the metropolis – the release from The Tower of Oliver and Crosby, two City aldermen imprisoned for over a month for their support of City rights over the House warrant. For fear of the mob The House had not dared attack Wilkes for pardoning every publisher brought before him, however the persecution and arrest of these two lesser-known aldermen had resulted in popular support nearly equal to that for England's most prominent troublemaker.

Oliver and Crosby were released to a cheering throng after the House order for their arrest had lapsed, no further action forthcoming. Though something of a passive victory, this was seen as the greatest triumph thus far for the cause of freedom of the press. And for the first time in recent memory, John Wilkes was not the celebrated hero of the city. For some, the separation of Wilkes from a popular victory was unthinkable, a sign that the powers-that-be were downplaying his role in events. For others, it prompted a greater look at the event itself, and at passion no less intense even without the presence of the era's most celebrated rabble-rouser.

Nevertheless, John Wilkes, be it the man or only the idea of him, injected himself into the affair as London erupted into celebration. Forty-five horses paraded down the Strand with forty-five riders holding suspended forty-five different newspapers each trumpeting victory on the front page. A forty-five-piece orchestra lit up the gardens at Ranelagh and couples revived, in the gardens, on street corners, and outside the House of Commons, the Wilkes's Wriggle. Whatever might have been published of Hugh's confession to Somersby, and its implications for Brent, were drowned in the undertow attendant upon another great Wilkes wave.

"You will keep it quiet now," said Ned. "Promise me." Hugh nodded. "I don't know what happens out there at The Farm. I do not wish to know. The story is forgotten for bigger things, and if you do not persecute Lord Somersby any more there is an end to the ordeal. I have a girl now. She likes me and her family likes me. They blame *The New Country Dance* on Somersby's fight with Brent, and never even heard about your announcements in the paper. Don't do anything more, and ruin this for me."

Hugh nodded, coughed on a bit of gauze, and promised.

His bluster and wit had seen the promotion of Alice.

Silence, then, for Ned.

CHAPTER 15

Under Hugh's direction a level, if meagre, path now allowed a hackney coach approach to within a few feet of The Farm. Considering the still delicate condition of his jaw, Hugh had opted for a carriage return after two and a half weeks recuperating with Clara. In that time, within her guest room of Romanesque Arcadia, his jaw had mended, and he had become adept at maintaining the new ivory incisor inside his mouth. In the same time the Jacobite trial had concluded, after which, despite the favourable outcome, Brent had remained unusually subdued and incommunicative. He remained in this attitude in the carriage to Chessington, and as Hugh continued to experience pain while speaking, an hour passed in relative silence.

"I am come to a decision," said Brent. "You think I am angry at Somersby. You think I am angry at you, out so many nights with Clara."

'Aw uu?"

"Nay, that is in the past." After withdrawing the gauze, Hugh wiped his mouth and nodded for him to continue. "The land coming to me now is considerable. Land in York, and in Carolina not just land but a considerable operation. The tobacco plantation; my father's venture." Hugh felt compelled to catch his eye for whatever came next. At last Brent said, "You have worked up improvements to The Farm. It is improved; but it is not my home."

"What do you mean?"

"America, Hugh."

America. A minute passed in silence.

"I did tell you before of the plantation. Day in, day out, it is on my mind. A prime part of my estate, or so I am told. The revenue generated has been good, but I'm told management could be improved; I will not know until I see it. I must be there to assess it for myself."

Hugh looked out the window of the carriage. He had known something was coming. The wish to live far from London had been clear; The Farm had appeared to fulfil this desire. America was a shock; he told himself it should be a shock. Yet, somehow, it was not a surprise.

"Regardless, I shall remain no longer where I am. Yorkshire I may return to, in decades hence, I do not know. But I cannot, I will not, remain more here. I have had enough."

"When?"

"One week. I made inquiries last month, after you published the banns. For many years I have wished to know the limit. Publishing the banns, I am certain beyond doubt, was that limit. For now. And it is already forgotten. Our vows, when we take them, must come later, and I trust we shall know when that should be. I step away from it all, as I did from boxing, before I meet my James Figg. The seats for the journey have been arranged. Can you manage it?"

Hugh shrugged, said something non-committal, and when pressed, closed his eyes and said, "Allow me a day. Please."

Then Richard told him everything he knew of the land in North Carolina, the tobacco industry, all he had learned of life in America and Hugh understood this had been his plan for far longer than he had known him. At first, he experienced a fair amount of anger at the concealment, well beyond the small things he himself had been concealing. But, in the end, should he regret not knowing? For what would he, what could he, have done differently had he known?

And yet, as they took the turn to Chessington, and The Farm, down the drive Hugh had seen take form, to the house in repair, the stables, the garden, the emerging life, the tears rose in his eyes and he could not prevent the other passenger from seeing them.

Upon arrival, as they stepped inside the building, Brent muttered, "'Tis but a pile of rocks, lad." Hugh let out a piteous cry, lowering his head as Kilmister came into the vestibule, descending into his arms in a racking sob as had not consumed him for some time. Brent proceeded to the stables. No doubt looking much the worse for wear with the bandage about his head and a protruding ivory incisor, Hugh rolled into the cradle of arms as he heard that everything, *everything love*, would be just fine.

"Jerry," he turned and, grasping him, told him Brent's plan. "I cannot think of moving again. I am exhausted. I cannot live with him – Christ help me I cannot! I *must* have a home! Had he told me his next house was to be in America, I would never have known The Farm as that place where we could... where we *would*. And where next? After Carolina... down the Missouri into Indian territory?"

Cradling him close, Jerry kissed his eyes, his cheeks, then, just once, passionately upon his mouth.

Pulling away Hugh wiped his eyes. "If you love me Jerry, if you have any feeling for me, tell me how to delay. Richard has had months, years, to think this through; I have had less an hour. I am asked to contribute more as Marius. Flexney grows quite sour at the prospect of my living so far as Chessington and from the centre of things. He is right. If I cannot stop in the Bedford Coffeehouse, if I cannot be a part of London, I shall have nothing to contribute. I have a..."

"Tell Jerry, honey."

"God forgive me," he whispered. "I shall retain the apartment on Charlotte Street. Indefinitely. Benjamin knew I would need it, and I do very much long to be there again. Only to write my articles, you understand... obviously Benjamin expects me to see everything as he sees it and has always said it will be. And I am terrified he is right! I never wish to see him like that... ever again. Yet he has understood this profound need I have to retain a connection to the city... he will not let it again..."

"Quiet now. Hush."

Hugh nodded, waiting, hoping to be directed.

"You cannot leave," said Kilmister. "There is far too much to be done here. At the very least arrangements must be made for the properties here and in York. I daresay Richard has not thought of any of it and trusts to lawyers to do everything. A man, such as yourself, will be required to make decisions as they arise, which cannot wait two months for communications over and returned from the Atlantic Ocean."

Nodding, then rising and sitting up, Hugh said, "Yes. Yes of course. Let me have three months, before the chill of autumn arrives: I shall complete everything which needs completing and shall have had opportunity to say my goodbyes. With time and as they should be said."

And this is what he said later that day. Richard met his eyes, taken back, angry to have confirmed his reasons for having delayed the news. Because Hugh's response was a shock, as he knew it would be. But it was not a surprise.

"You are my property."

"I am the property too of those of my family who continue to receive me, and my friends. And I am the property of my conscious. I must be given time to break with them appropriately."

"Do you leave me Hugh?"

"Never. Never, Richard; I love you. You've given me my

freedom. If I give you grounding, as you say, and a sense of home, understand that is not a physical place, but something to take with you wherever you go. You may leave for America if you wish, and trust that you *have* the home; and in time I shall follow."

And this was, at last, the compromise.

The night before departure, holding Hugh in his arms, Richard said, "We search for something our entire lives, and name it liberty – whatever it is, I believe America is where we shall find it. What has come of the bluster of John Wilkes? The headlines, the continual noise? He is an elected official, and as such supports far more than he ever opposes. His victories only victories in reference to something far bigger than himself.

"What became of the Jacobites? Twenty-five years ago, they had their ideals to overthrow the government, install their rightful King, and their religion. Where are they now? Absorbed into the very system they sought to overthrow. One cannot find an exciseman now who is not Scotch. Most stalwart defenders of Catholicism yet come into every echelon of power in the Protestant state. Hated by the establishment, hated, too, by the supporters of Wilkes, all wishing Northmen back behind Hadrian's Wall. I cannot see this as anything but a herald of a land in decline. Naught but ugliness, pettiness, infighting, and people, and systems, too entrenched in the old ways ever to change. Decisions continue to be made by Lord North and his government which will lose America altogether. England does not deserve to keep her."

As Brent drifted to sleep Hugh looked about and thought: *The Farm shall be mine tomorrow. Thus far life in this place has been the colours of a prism, seen individually. Tomorrow: white light. For The Farm I claim as my choice. Else it is, like anything else, reclaimed by the scrub, the elements, the forest, or the bog.*

Yet simultaneously Hugh believed he would relinquish the place after three months and follow his leader to a new land.

The improvements to the property were his to see to fruition and he would simply understand when they were complete. After a few months to adjust to the idea of a new place, and to prepare for it properly, he could do it. Do it gladly, and with no regrets.

"The *Gazette*," muttered Brent, slinging a heavy arm around his companion, "asked what I thought of Lord Somersby's single night of incarceration. Was it enough, considering what he had done to my friend? And did I fear his retaliation after losing the suit?"

"What did Richard of Runswick say?"

"I said this: Richard departs for America. To a plantation, as has been his Lordship's wish for five years. Yet what his Lordship understands as transportation, is, for Richard Brent, freedom."

Next afternoon Brent departed for Plymouth.

The newspapers darkened the evening of Brent's departure. Some of the wild joy seemed to have departed England. The increasing staleness of the reporting on the antics of Wilkes, in favour of events in America. The understanding that creations such as *Joseph Andrews* and *Roderick Random*, *Tom Jones* and *Peregrine Pickle* were heroes now incontrovertibly from a previous era, never to rise again. Much of what Brent lamented, Hugh now felt in his spine, for he had lived just long enough to recognise a change.

Yet Hugh was not like Richard Brent. He did not feel all joy had left his country, all sense of future, all adventure. He felt the despair, certainly. Unease during a period of transition. Yet he did not relinquish hope.

Next day the tender green of Spring brightened as Hugh strode about the property, preparing for a morning gallop about Chessington before Benjamin's first visit to the place. The Farm was settling upon new ground, ground long turned, and overturned, by the Sweet Science of Bruising. Tears came suddenly and unexpectedly – movement catching his eye was not to be followed by heavy strides across the flagstones. Calling from the stables or from the back of the house was not cursing, was not the slamming of something which would not fit, but the hollow howl of the wind. Everything which was not Brent was easier – it was Jerry sliding the Chippendale sideboard snugly into a new space, the flapping in the wind of a tarpaulin strung over the collapsing roof in the back-parlour. No more that twine ever tightening in endless restlessness, threatening to bind Hugh at the wrists, or throttle him, though it had, so often, dragged him into the clouds.

He took his horse on a canter towards Chessington Hall, a place now easily discovered as the sun sparked brilliant upon the dew. After a few false starts, he had finally found the distant manor following a sound he had only heard in Italy – the rounded, resonant notes of a pianoforte. The stable hands of Chessington Hall had stood listening as a piece by Handel rolled into the air on the new instrument.

No doubt it was just the fine day, but Hugh fancied something was afoot in that place, something sweet and promising despite the two sour and reclusive bachelors who lived there. It was the property of Samuel Crisp, whose play *Virginia* London had so reviled it had sent him to seek solace out in the barren fields nearly two decades before. Hugh greeted the stable hands again, noting that there appeared to be more activity than on his previous visit. It seemed a young family friend, a Miss Fanny Burney, had arrived for the summer and her things were being unloaded. Miss Burney had departed London for the solitude, for it was her passion to write fictional stories in one of the private rooms obscurely called the Doctor's Conjuring Closet. With a mystified smile, Hugh stared a long while at the place then, recalling the time, departed for home.

Benjamin arrived on the horse he had taken to the boxing

performance in Kingston. He led the animal at a jaunty trot, and without the wig he occasionally neglected.

"So, here it is," he said, quite radiant to see Hugh and, at long last, this notorious estate. After his greeting, Benjamin remained at a distance of about six feet, studying his friend as he stepped about the house and grounds, unable to conceal a smile.

"Benjamin," Hugh said, as they stepped around the back kitchen, "I shall follow Brent to North Carolina in September. You understand my remaining behind was a business decision."

Benjamin nodded. "Yes, I know. You have made considerable improvements to the place. The layout of the garden of course bears a striking resemblance to the one at Sallow House; I helped design it. But I did not expect to see my house reflected in the changes you say you have made inside. Do you see it?" Hugh eyed one or two places but said nothing. "I have at long last cleared out that cottage you are so fond of. A sweet place – I paid it no mind until you mentioned it. Now it is tidy, with primroses up the walk, and a lovely interior. You must come to see it."

Hugh nodded, wishing there was something to refuse in the reasonable request.

"I understand things are mending with Anne?"

"She has never refused to see me——"

"Yes, I meant only that, with your father returned to Deerhurst, now he is out of her house, you will be able to see her more often in her home."

"I will, whenever your brother is abroad, which is usually. I shall see little Charles whenever I can, and her second child will be here before I depart."

"Children need very much to see their uncle. It is important."

"Benjamin…"

"Important enough for Anne to threaten separation from

my brother if you were not allowed to see them. You do know that." Hugh nodded. "You are uncle as well to my daughter. Do remember Paulina – a young woman soon, in need of guidance through those episodes of life here only for a moment before—"

"Are such vicious blows allowed outside a boxing ring?" said Hugh. "We have one, if you wish to step inside. Perhaps I will be that interesting uncle in America. Perhaps I shall host my nieces and nephews when they are grown and wish to travel. Or perhaps one day I shall return to England and bring home stories of my adventures for them, as I did from the Continent."

The visitor took his shoulder and said, "Is it true Brent intends to retain the land in York?"

"I almost regret inviting you today. He intends to keep it, as it is family land, and possibly return *in decades hence*. Those are his words, and—"

"Those are his words and he never, ever changes his mind. He might return next year, and you will have uprooted yourself for nothing at all."

"Certainly not! He has been considering the move for a very long time." Then Hugh said nothing more, as surely no good could come of it.

The guest pressed no further. They were soon in the parlour and he was working to repair his reputation with Jerry, who continued to see him as having done Hugh wrong and so had remained decidedly cool towards him. In a short time, there was some pleasant banter between them, however Hugh was uneasy for the remainder of the visit. Benjamin had left one weapon unused – the loss of Marius. One could write in America certainly, but it would not be the same. He was planning on four nights a week in Charlotte Street this summer, the better to see Anne, to attend meetings of the High Scribblers, but primarily to continue to produce for the *Public*

Inquirer – with his established name, writing about the society he knew.

North Carolina might have only Pilgrims and farmers and Indian attacks to write of.

Early the following week he happened upon Robert Snodgrass in Temple. And though they had gladly parted company so many months before, well rid of each other, Hugh warmed at the sight of his former guide through France and Italy.

"Allow me to buy you a coffee, Sir. Or," he said, sensing a change in the man, "whatever you wish." For Snodgrass was looking decidedly bedraggled. Only ten days returned to England, after a year chasing his lovesick charge who had refused to board the packet boat in Calais, then absconded back to Florence.

"Coffee, tea, or a stew in Babylon," said Snodgrass. "Makes no difference."

"Coffee, I think. My own place is just up there."

They continued to the Bucket of Brews to sit with Harding and Andrews, both slow to leave winter sloth, and ready for a diversion. For more than an hour they were regaled with stories from that year whose end, the very day of Hugh's return, had seen the introduction to their friend. And what, at this late date, was the state of Horatio?

"Master George is established with Signora Tosetti in Florence," said Snodgrass. "Lord George, now I've failed to retrieve his son and after months of abusing me by letter, goes himself to fetch him. God be with him; there never was a more devoted young man to his *inamourata*. They are joined as man and wife, and he will present his Lordship with a grand-daughter when he arrives."

"Dear Horatio. I must write him now he is happy."

"I failed you too, lad," said Snodgrass, hearing no talk of happiness, his intense, dark eyes preferring to drag his listeners into a peatbog. "The Continent weaned you of me as well. I place no blame at your door, Hugh, 'twas my own wretched failing."

Marvelling at the great change in the man, Hugh hazarded: "You admit that we do indeed have free will then." At the man's uneasy silence, Hugh said quickly to Andrews, "I was a right bastard to this man. Won every fight, defied every stricture imposed upon me, using the excuse of predestination. I was *destined* to misbehave, so I told him every day. How would you like to hear such impudence, when it was on your conscious to care for me?"

"If predestination was the philosophy subscribed to by Mr Snodgrass," said Andrews, "I should think it fair enough."

Warming his hands around his coffee Snodgrass hiccoughed, perhaps a first attempt at a thing the Scotchman had never before attempted: a laugh. "I take you to witness, Gentleman, as I sit in your fine company, and my chill bones are warmed, and my vision clears: I was Noah upon the waves, never wishing the waters to settle, nor ever see land. Now I touch ground in England, step from my Ark, and must decide where lies my destiny. 'Tis my future, look you. And 'tis a bit frightening."

"Does he not have a lovely way with words?" said Hugh to his companions. "Upon my soul they are fine cadences. Do you compose poetry, Sir?"

But Snodgrass was lost to reflections, then summoned the terrier to comfort.

Said Hugh, "Come Snodgrass. You failed to contain two silly young men while they travelled. We were not your divine charges; you were not destined to bring us to the Lord. Now you are experiencing a crisis of Faith; I should think entirely natural for a thoughtful man. You shall be reconciled at last, either to a new understanding of what you previously understood, or to something better. And I expect to see you in this coffeehouse more often."

Hugh glanced at the other men for encouragement. Andrews was a welcoming heart, but Harding, a dubious and doubting soul, shrugged, seeming to resent the expectation. He said, "You were used to dabble in poetry, Entwistle. Some diverting lines, before those Parliamentary transcripts, though I cannot recall any." Chuckling, "Reckon the sting you got from *The New Country Dance* silenced your glee for all such." Then after a pause, "No I mistake, was there a piece after the New Dance? I thought I heard something, but never saw it. Did you Andrews?"

"I must have missed that gem. Was it very diverting?"

"Not particularly," said Hugh, and supposed it as good a time as any to take his leave. He made an appointment to see Snodgrass in a couple days, pleased at the idea of helping him on in some course of life.

Then Hugh exited into the streets of London, that bubbling font of what was new, of old attempting to pass as new, of buried treasures long submerged, and, once dislodged, all attendant sludge and refuse. As his heels clicked along the cobblestones, he quickened his pace, turning once or twice with a feeling rather like he was being pursued. Pursued perhaps by this idea of Snodgrass, and a new life. Pursued by his imagination, as he passed a street vendor selling nosegays, an invalid passing in a chair, a drunk curled in a doorway. His hand itched to take up the pen, perhaps stop in Covent Garden to hear of that public figure whose latest travails might unite his errant ideas into a new sonnet.

But he opted first for Blackfriars Bridge, to recall the *Ode to Transport* and his meeting with Mr Chambers. Hugh took a moment to reflect on the encounter, and wonder at this raw, fiery new talent that had come into the world. Gilbert Chambers was one of the successes of the previous year. Over the winter he had solicited subscriptions, then brought out a slim volume to great acclaim and made a small fortune. He was a new favourite of the Queen, and even Horace Walpole had made complimentary noises – one of the most promising talents of his generation.

The voice of a new generation had first spoken here, as Hugh saw it. The moment Chambers had unfolded his poem to him.

After a few minutes, Hugh stood, straightened his coat, and rubbed his hands together.

A young man was standing at the bridge, observing him. Under the clear, blue sky. Tall, thoughtful, under a tri-cornered hat. He held something in his hand. And scratched his forehead.

It was James Bramble.

CHAPTER 16

"Hugh."

His name, like a stone into a pond. Neither man moved, nothing, on this still, clear day, appeared to move. Hugh took a shuddering breath – he heard only the sound of flowing water beneath the bridge.

Then, coming forward too fast, throwing himself against the stranger, Hugh held them together. Bramble initially shrank away; even in his mania Hugh saw the young man had held doubts of a cordial reception. He held them no longer; Hugh's were tears which had never flowed in his presence, but which now flowed freely. The kiss upon James's forehead, long and unstudied, a messy smear of emotion.

"It was my fault!" Hugh sobbed, burying his face in Bramble's neck, feeling immediately the turning of the head into his shoulder, as they were used to do. Stepping back, he looked about the street and the bridge, at the prolonged looks which met them. After pressing the heels of his palms to his eyes, forcing himself back to his senses, Hugh stared hard attempting to comprehend who stood before him.

"You are here James? You are *here*. Christ forgive me, what happened to you?!"

But Bramble remained reluctant to speak. He took Hugh's hand, putting into it a folded piece of paper. Sealed with wax, with the direction of The Farm. He said, "The *Gazette* quoted Richard Brent as saying he was leaving for America. When I understood you were staying on, I wrote this. I thought to send it to you, then I feared you would not receive it – perhaps you were no longer in Chessington. A Printer's Devil at the *Inquirer* told me you always submit a piece about ten on Tuesdays, as you did today. When you departed, I was about to approach when you met that other man in the street and went into the coffeehouse."

Scarcely hearing him Hugh said, "You cannot think how I have missed you. How I have longed to do everything differently. There are times, James, I nearly… I did write to you, only you never received it…" He left off. "Do tell me where you have been."

But Bramble frowned, instead urging him to the thoughts he had put in writing. Hugh looked down at what he held – a letter from James. The letter Hugh had looked for day, after day, after day on the vestibule table of Beaufort Buildings. The letter that had never come.

At last obliged to turn his wide, wild eyes from his companion, Hugh read:

To my former friend Hugh Entwistle:

They are Chains, if Man is weak
With a Voice, but will not speak
Chains, not of this World bestowed
But by his own Anchor slowed

They are Stains, upon the Heart
With a Will, but will not start
Stains, because they need not be
Left from Sight, where Men can't see

Still are Hands, these lifelong Fists
Freed, although the Heart resists
Hands, which flowered, first awake
Closed again, to heal the Ache

If a Child, betrays a Trust
Strikes in Rage, because he must
Child, never to Man shall grow
Till he seeks again his Foe

They are Men, who will lay bare,
Places, which have felt a Tear
Men, who dare a new Attempt
Risk a Cut, or cold Contempt
They are Chains, but need not be
I ask, they are cut free

I am sorry Hugh,

James Bramble

Shaking his head, more intent on looking in Bramble's eyes again than on what he had written, Hugh at last said, "This is good. Rather good, I... I cannot recall reading anything like it. I cannot respond..." After a long moment staring at each other, he said, "Yes, I can respond. Come to my apartment."

They set off toward the place, breath coming fast, nearly colliding into other pedestrians for their constant looking at one another until Hugh, unable to contain himself, pushed Bramble into a dark alley and kissed him more passionately that he ever had. This was not the panting of boyish lust in a stable loft – Hugh wept, filled with such alarming sadness, such regret it threatened to overtake him should they tarry too long. Then he pulled them apart and dragged them forward.

"Christ, forgive me," he said, wiping at his eyes. "Brent, forgive me. You know I am with Richard, James. I… I don't know my own feelings. Let this be forgivable. Still… I am determined not to make the same mistakes. I wrote you, I swear before God, before all that happened with Ned. I wrote and told you I loved you. I shall show you the letter."

"Don't speak of Ned, Hugh. I never wanted that; he never wanted me…"

"You fucking fool, I know that. You believed I never wrote you. You were desperate, what could you have done? It has been the trial of my life to know you never received that letter." He stopped them where they were, just before the turn to Charlotte Street, and put a finger in his face. "I love you. I shall say it now, as I did not before – I love you! I would have brought you to the city. Or tried. My intentions were honourable."

Bramble nodded, somewhat overwhelmed at passion which appeared undimmed despite nearly three years of separation. Hugh observed new lines about the young man's eyes; not a dimple, but a crease, at the mouth. Though he was perhaps more beautiful now, yet it would take time to see the alterations as anything but the product of pain.

Hugh took his friend up the stairs and into the apartment. He opened the sash windows then looked about the airing rooms, now nearly as foreign to himself as they were to James.

"This is the place," he said. They strode about until they came to the bed with its fall of dusty curtains and which, after a glance at each other, seemed to long for them. Hugh nearly forgot why they had come.

With a grin Bramble said, "You seem liberated."

"Liberated? Am I really?"

That singular creasing of James's features said this must be obvious to anybody. This old expression, not just from their summer together, but from his childhood days scrambling about the floor for treasures, led Hugh to approach him almost like a father, and take his hand.

"If I am liberated," he said, "you are a poet."

"Am I improved?"

"James, you know you are. You were always used to try. And they were good…"

"My poems were not good. But you would have me continue. Only after we were separated did I find I had something to say. This last, what I gave you, is my best thus far, perhaps not great—"

"James, if you are capable of this style of invention, I must see more. I will see you published."

"Really? Hugh, will you really?"

Turning at last to the escritoire, to a drawer which housed old documents, Hugh withdrew the yellowing letter. When it was brought forth, there was the first sign of uneasiness in his guest. Unlike Hugh, Bramble had not felt the surprise of the meeting, having watched, for however long, tracing him to Chessington, and learning of his life with Brent.

"Read it," said Hugh. "It was taken and used against me. That's why you never received it."

"I saw Marius's account of the trial of Stephen Chandler. Despite how it was presented I began to wonder if something of the kind had happened. Only I didn't know where to begin with you. I had only been in London a short time, and while Brent was still here it hardly seemed to matter."

Hugh determined to address this interpretation of Brent's having left without him at a later date and again directed him to the letter. Bramble sat on the bed, holding the paper in one hand, the other by his mouth, curled with the little finger touching the cleft above his lip. The words, thirty-three months delayed, could not be presented without a thought for the moment which had produced them. Now nearly twenty-two, Hugh was again nineteen, wretched for the comfort denied him the night he had written it – despite Brent, despite everything that had happened since.

As Bramble read, his mouth switched here and there, he laughed under his breath, and shook his head. When the tears fell, they were the production of the body, but not the heart.

Looking up at last, he set the letter aside, and quoted, "'You will grant, I hope, that youth and discretion are with respect to each other as two parallel lines, which, though infinitely produced, remain still equidistant, and will never coincide.'" And he was smiling.

"*What?*" said Hugh, his breath coming short – he should have known the passage. A misguided counsellor attempting to guide a young man in love, surely something by Smollett. Capable of coherent thought, no doubt he would have known it. But it hardly mattered. For he understood Bramble would take this path, and not the other. He would smile, and not look back, regret what might have been, or consider the pain Hugh was yet too frightened to ask him about.

"'And you will not deny,'" continued James, wiping his eyes, "'that the angle of remorse, is equal to that of precipitation.'"

Hugh had already brought him to his feet, drawing him into an embrace, laughing, pushing his nose into the nape of his neck, which yet retained a trace of that golden fuzz of childhood.

It was, *Dear Reader,* the road back to Bramble, all the time. What had they not endured, to reach each other again?

But no. This was the road to Benjamin. This youthful infatuation could not endure; Hugh had evolved and would realise it within the week. He would fall, and Benjamin would be there to catch him once more. For it was that wish for a home modelled in every detail upon Sallow House, that Hugh desired above all else. A secretive relationship, yes, yet that security of his longest confidant and the stability which would exist as long as he wished.

And yet no. This must be the beginning of his road to follow Richard. What was any of this to that culmination of all his experience: which had brought forth his voice, both with his father and as Marius. Everything must lead to a rejoining with that man. Forever moving forward, after Hugh had had time to say his goodbyes, to a new life in America.

And yet it was, just then, standing before him in the Charlotte Street apartment, James Bramble. Not just his first love, but the evolution of him; a poet potentially of some promise. So, Hugh kissed him, and embraced him, and vowed to never let him go.

For Hugh was Entwistle, a man of appetite. And in that fire, the confluence of Beauty and the Sublime, he brought them all down, Bramble, Benjamin, and Brent, into that old, that eternal, pleasure.

NOTE TO THE READER

Thank you for taking a journey into 18th Century England!

As a new author it is immensely important to hear from you, Dear Reader, either in a review on **Amazon** or **Goodreads**.

Connecting with readers is why I do this – this is the time for me to be quiet and for you to speak. Please let me know why you picked up 'Hugh' and what your experience has been!

ABOUT THE AUTHOR

A native of the American Southwest, David Lawrence has spent much of his life in Great Britain, France, and Finland. He now lives in the American Northwest – Helena, Montana – with his Finnish partner.

By day he loves hiking under the Big Sky of his beautiful adopted state.

By night, however, he prefers editing lost manuscripts and wandering the byways of 18th century London...

You can learn more about David Lawrence and his penned works by visiting his **website** and subscribing to his newsletter!

Made in the USA
Columbia, SC
01 March 2024

32526705R00305